JANET DAILEY

THE PROUD
~AND~
THE FREE

WARNER
VISION
BOOKS

A Time Warner Company

WARNER BOOKS EDITION

Copyright © 1994 by Janet Dailey
All rights reserved.

Cover design by Jackie Merri Meyer
Cover illustration by Lisa Falkenstern
Stepback art by Pino
Hand lettering by Carl Dellacroce

This Warner Books Edition is published by arrangement with Little, Brown & Company.

Warner Vision is a trademark of Warner Books, Inc.

Warner Books, Inc.
1271 Avenue of the Americas
New York, NY 10020

Ⓦ A Time Warner Company

Printed in the United States of America

First Warner Books Printing: August, 1995

10 9 8 7 6 5 4 3 2 1

Author's Note

While the main characters in this novel and their individual stories are fictional, the background against which they appear is fact. All incidents and events in this novel relating to the court battles of the Cherokee Nation, the harassment by the Georgia Guard, the Cherokees' valiant efforts to peacefully resist removal for eight long years, and the split within the Cherokee Nation between the supporters of the principal chief and the treaty advocates for removal are true. Unfortunately, so are the descriptions of the detention camps (which today we would label concentration camps), the long trail of tragedy and suffering, and the ruinous destruction that occurred in the Cherokee Nation during the Civil War.

The fictional characters in this novel—specifically those of Cherokee ancestry—represent the better-educated and more prosperous class that existed during that time. Their holdings, their life-styles, and their residences were typical of the Southern planters of that day—as evidenced by the homes of Chief Vann and Major Ridge in Georgia and the Murrell home in Oklahoma, all of which are open for public viewing today.

The Cherokee Nation had its own written constitution and laws, an elected government, and a judicial system. In addition, it had its own newspaper, *The Cherokee Phoenix,* printed in both English and Cherokee. They truly deserved to be called "one of the five civilized tribes."

It is in the context of fact that this novel is written, with the hope that through fiction we may all understand why the road they were forced to travel west was called by the Cherokee the Trail Where They Cried.

THE PROUD
~AND~
THE FREE

Part I

Build a fire under them. When it gets hot enough, they'll move.

—President-elect Andrew Jackson

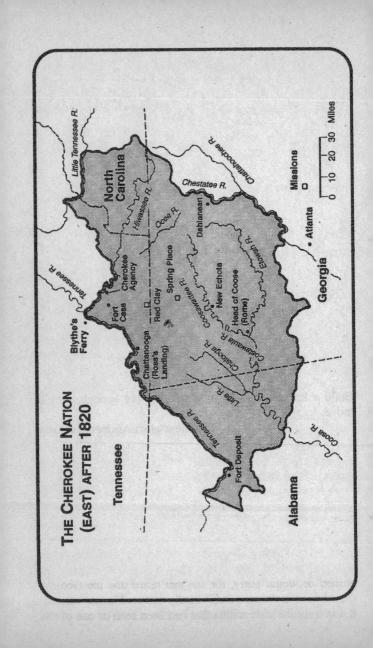

THE CHEROKEE NATION (EAST) AFTER 1820

1

The mud-splattered stagecoach rolled to a stop in front of the Chester Inn, where several people stood on the porch awaiting its arrival. Two were white men, each garbed in the plain suit and starched collar worn by missionaries. Two others were of Cherokee blood and wore an odd mixture of dress. Their leather moccasins rose nearly to the knees of their white-man's trousers, sashes belted the waists of their white-man's shirts, and brightly colored cloth wound turban-fashion about their heads.

A young woman of uncommon beauty and self-possession stood apart from the group. Clothed in a purple day dress and a matching silk bonnet trimmed with pink roses, the girl had lustrous black hair parted in the center and swept sleekly back from features that appeared to have been sculpted by an artist's hand. Her black slave hovered nearby.

Anxious to meet the new tutor, Temple Gordon glanced impatiently at the stagecoach driver. He moved, in her estimation, with irritating slowness as he climbed down from the seat and slogged through the mud to the coach door. She wished he would hurry, for she had heard that the Georgia Guard were in the area and it hardly mattered to her whether it was truly the state militia that had been seen or one of the numerous bands of marauders known locally as pony clubs. Temple knew the ill-trained and ill-disciplined Georgia Guard were essentially vigilantes with an exaggerated sense of self-importance and disdain for the rights of others.

She needed to collect the family's new tutor—Miss Eliza Hall—and be quickly on her way. She was not so much concerned for her own safety as she was for her mother. Victoria Gordon had remained at home alone with the children, and Temple was fearful of how they would react should the Guard arrive at Gordon Glen.

"Spring Place!" the driver yelled as he yanked open the stagecoach door.

A young missionary, thin of face and long of body, stepped out first. All arms and legs like some gangly colt, he turned to assist a female passenger, who was tall and plain. The woman bore no resemblance at all to the starched and primly groomed missionary wives who had taught Temple at the Brainerd mission school. Stray wisps of light brown curls poked out from beneath a bonnet that was slightly askew. Her brown traveling suit was rumpled and the angle of her chin was almost combative.

While Temple watched, the young woman negotiated the three muddy yards to the inn's steps and marched straight up to Charlie Blue Bird and Tom Morgan. "I am Eliza Hall from Massachusetts," she announced. "I am to be met at this place by Will Gordon."

Temple turned to her waiting servant, who was dressed in the livery of a footman. "I believe the woman in the brown dress is the new tutor, Miss Eliza Hall. Bring her to me, Ike."

"Yes'm, Miz Temple," he said with a quick bob of his head, moving to do her bidding.

The new tutor continued to stand before the pair of Cherokee men, bewilderment evident in her expression when neither responded. She took no notice of the servant's approach. When Ike reached her, he took off his hat.

"Beggin' your pardon, miss," Ike said, at last claiming her attention. "Be you Miz Hall from up No'th?"

It took the woman a full second to decipher his thickly drawled question. "I am, yes."

"Miz Temple, she be waiting fo' you over there." With a sweep of his doffed hat, Ike gestured to Temple, then indicated that the new tutor should precede him.

The woman cast a puzzled glance at the lanky young missionary with her. He too seemed a bit taken aback by the turn of events, but nodded for her to proceed, then followed himself as she walked over to Temple.

"That will be all for now, Ike." Temple dismissed her black servant with a flick of her gloved hand and studied the new tutor with undisguised curiosity. "You are Miss Eliza Hall from Massachusetts."

"I am." Eliza Hall raised her chin a little higher as she made her own thorough appraisal of Temple, whose eyes were as black as onyx, like her hair, and whose face was as fair and smooth as the finest ivory. Unprepared to find herself face to face with such blatant beauty, she stiffened, aware she was positively homely by comparison. Defensively, she searched for flaws in the young woman, and found them in the willfully proud tilt of her head and faintly autocratic manner. She was young as well—hardly more than sixteen. At the advanced age of twenty herself, Eliza Hall regarded sixteen as exceedingly young.

"I am Temple Gordon. My father sends his apologies. He was called away to an important meeting which has made it impossible for him to meet you himself."

"*Your* father is Will Gordon?" she asked, her surprise and shock showing.

"He is."

"I was told your family was Cherokee." As always, Eliza Hall spoke her mind, fully aware that few regarded candor as a virtue. But it was a trait she had never been able to control and had long since ceased to try, and right now she needed to clarify the incongruous images before her eyes.

"We are Cherokee," Temple asserted with a proud flare of temper that she quickly cloaked in a cool hauteur.

"Forgive me, but you do not look at all like an Indian." Eliza Hall stared anew at Temple and her elegant gown with its matching bonnet. She had clearly expected beaded buckskins, moccasins, and a long black braid.

Temple struggled to control her mounting indignation. She longed to turn her back on this woman and her ignorant attitude and walk off, but she was here in her father's stead. And Temple knew that her father would never be provoked into rudeness by such a remark.

"The blood in our veins is Cherokee, as are the feelings in our hearts," Temple stated, using the words her father would have chosen although her voice was more heated than his would have been.

"Miss Hall meant no offense by her remark, I assure you," the tall, pale missionary interposed in quick apology.

Temple turned her cool black eyes on him. "And you are?"

"Reverend Nathan Cole, newly assigned to the area by the American Board of Foreign Missions in Boston." He dipped his head in a faint, respectful bow. "Mr. Payton Fletcher asked that I accompany Miss Hall on her journey and see her safely into the care of her employer."

"Your task is complete, Reverend Cole. Thank you," Temple said, then directed her next remark to the tutor. "We have yet another hour's ride ahead of us. If you would point out your luggage, Miss Hall, I will have Ike load it into the carriage." With a brief wave of her hand, she indicated the open carriage and team of chestnut horses tied to a rail at the end of the porch.

Eliza identified her trunk and valise, then turned to take her leave of Reverend Cole, a trace of regret in her expression. "Your company has been most pleasant. I shall miss it."

"And I shall miss yours."

She was not so foolish as to read anything more into his words. She had once mistaken a man's words of kindness for romantic affection, and later suffered the abject humiliation of that mistake. It was an error she had vowed never to make again.

"I will write Mr. Fletcher and assure him that you saw me safely to my destination."

"I hope you will write me also, so that I may know all is well with you in your new surroundings. It would put my mind at ease." A hesitant smile broke across his thin, intense face, an awkwardness in it that matched the rest of him. "You know where I can be reached."

"Yes, and I promise I shall write you."

With her good-byes finally said and her baggage stowed, Eliza Hall climbed into the carriage and settled onto the black leather seat beside Temple Gordon. At a signal from Temple, Ike slapped the reins and the carriage lurched forward with a familiar rumble and rattle.

"You said your home is an hour's ride from here?"

"Yes. The rains last night have left the roads muddy, however. They may delay us," Temple replied tersely. Her thoughts again were with the reports of the Georgia Guard and precluded any idle chatter she might otherwise make with Eliza Hall.

Overhead, the sky had cleared and its pure blue color arced from mountain ridge to mountain ridge. The narrow road skirted the edge of a broad valley planted to corn, the green of the cornstalks contrasting with the red of the soil.

"I was told you live on a farm. How much land does your family own?" the tutor asked.

"None. The land belongs to all the Cherokee people. We have only the use of it. The buildings, the animals, the crops— these are the properties that are owned by an individual and may be sold." Temple turned her gaze on Eliza Hall, aware this was an alien concept to most whites. "That is our way, one not often understood by your people."

"It is different from ours," she admitted, then added, "You mentioned that your father had been called away. When do you expect him to return?"

"Within a few days, we hope. He is a member of the National Council, a legislative body similar to your House of Representatives," Temple explained. "They are meeting to discuss a bill recently passed by your Congress that advocates the removal of all Indian nations to lands in the West. Your president, Andrew Jackson, has issued an invitation calling for a Cherokee delegation to meet with him at his home in Tennessee next month."

"Removal?" Eliza repeated, her expression aghast.

"We will never move to lands in the West," Temple quickly stated in an emphatic voice. The very idea was unthinkable, not only to her, but to every Cherokee. In the collective memory of her people, this land had always been theirs. They had drunk from the waters of its rivers and hunted the game in its woods for generations. The bones of their dead were buried in its soil; their homes stood upon it. No amount of inducement would ever persuade them to give it up, and Temple said as much. "By law, your government must abide by the terms of the treaty it made with our people. It cannot force us to give up our land, and we will never sign it away."

"Will your father be one of the delegates who tells this to President Jackson?"

"He feels that we should not send anyone. We will not give up our land, and Jackson refuses to discuss any other subject."

A silence fell between them, and Temple turned her attention to the passing scenery. Ahead, the road curved through a wide meadow, green with a thick carpet of grass and speckled with wildflowers.

"Miz Temple." Ike shifted in his seat, angling his head back to her. "They be some riders ahead. They look like Georgians."

Temple's response was instant and sharp. "Drive on. Do not stop this carriage for any reason."

"But they be blockin' the road."

"Do as I say!"

"Yes'm."

The three riders pulled up and ranged their horses across the road. As the carriage drew closer to the spot, Ike shook his head. "They ain't room to go 'round, Miz Temple."

"Take the whip to the horses and go through them!"

"Yes'm."

With a shout to the team, Ike cracked the whip over their backs. The horses lunged into a gallop, jerking the carriage forward. Thrown back against the seat, Eliza grabbed at the sides for balance, while Temple remained perfectly poised and in place.

The three men swung out of the path of the onrushing carriage, one splitting off to the left and the other two going to the right. As the chestnut team charged into the gap, the three riders maneuvered their horses alongside and one man grabbed the reins from Ike, pulling back and forcing the carriage to a halt.

"You best be careful, boy," another rider drawled to Ike. "You nearly had yourself a runaway."

"Release my team at once!" Temple stood, her voice filled with fury. Eliza stared at her in astonishment. Still composed and confident, Temple allowed her temper to shine through eyes that Eliza felt certain could flash lightning.

"Well, well, well, what have we here?" the same man murmured as he walked his horse back to the carriage. "Looks like she's a real Cherokee princess, don't she?"

Undeterred by either his sarcasm or leering smile, Temple ordered again, "I said release my team."

"Now is that any way to talk when we just saved you?" the man chided in open mockery. "Don't sound very grateful to me."

"It sure don't," another man echoed.

"That sure is a mighty fancy carriage she's got, Cale," the third rider declared, addressing the man Temple confronted. "And a fine-lookin' team, too. Matched as purty as you please. My missus sure would look fine in a rig like this."

"Yeah. You oughta make her a present of it."

Eliza was certain they were about to be robbed.

"No, you will not take it!" Temple grabbed the whip from her black driver and brandished it threateningly.

An explosion ripped the air. Eliza nearly jumped out of her skin. She whirled toward the sound and saw two men on horseback emerge from the trees near the road. A telltale curl of smoke rose from the musket carried by one of them. From his bronze skin, high cheekbones, and straight black hair, Eliza judged him to be an Indian.

"You were told to release the team," the man said into the charged stillness. His tone was deceptively quiet, almost lazy in its inflection. But there was nothing indolent about the way he pointed the barrel of the musket in the general direction of the three men, a fact they noted with something less than pleasure.

"You're asking for trouble, Injun," the one called Cale muttered.

"And I think you are in no position to give it to me." He smiled and the smile was somehow deadly.

Fringed moccasins reached all the way up to his knees. A pair of close-fitting buckskin leggings hugged long, sinewy thighs. The dark blue of a hunter's shirt outlined the width of his muscled shoulders. But it was the dangerous-looking scar on his left cheek that gave weight to his words.

"What's that nigger doin' with a musket?" Cale demanded, waving a hand at the young colored man who accompanied the Indian rescuer. Belatedly, Eliza noticed that he was similarly armed. "You shouldn't give guns to coloreds."

"He carries it for me. But he tends to be careless. It might go off if you attempt to take it from him."

The colored man looked anything but careless or incompetent in his handling of the weapon.

"Come on, Cale." The heavyset rider released his hold on the reins and swung his horse away from the carriage team. "Let's get out of here."

The man wavered, his expression tightening in displeasure and his gaze stabbing at the Indian who sat calmly astride his horse. "I'll remember you, redskin," he warned and slapped his horses.

The trio rode off. Eliza stared after them, still dazed by the incident. "Those men, did they truly intend to take the carriage and leave us afoot?"

"They did indeed, Miss Hall, and we could have done nothing about it. Not now or later," Temple added somewhat cryptically before turning to face the buckskin-clad man who came riding up. There was something pleased and proud, and vaguely possessive, in the way she looked at him. "They would have succeeded if The Blade had not arrived when he did."

The Blade. Eliza frowned at the unusual name as Temple Gordon greeted him, breaking into a language that was obviously her native tongue. He echoed the sound, drawing Eliza's attention to him.

"Miss Hall, may I present The Blade Stuart," Temple began.

Eliza never heard the rest of the introduction. She was too stunned to find herself staring into a pair of blue eyes that appeared even more blue by the deep coppery shade of the man's skin.

"After your long journey, I regret that you were welcomed so rudely to our nation, Miss Hall." The sound of his voice jolted Eliza from her absorption.

Her glance darted briefly to the long and jagged scar on his cheek before his reference to the would-be robbers prompted Eliza to ask, "Who were those men?" She directed her question to Temple. "And why did you imply they could have stolen your carriage and team with impunity?"

But it was The Blade Stuart who answered. "They were Georgians, Miss Hall. They believe this part of the Cherokee Nation was given to them years ago by your federal government. When gold was discovered last year in our mountains an hour's ride to the east, Georgia passed a law seizing possession of all this land and forbidding any Cherokee to mine the gold or give testimony against a white man. Which leaves the Georgians free to come onto our lands, steal our property, and attack our people without fear of punishment."

"That cannot be true," Eliza protested, torn between outrage and disbelief.

"I assure you it is, Miss Hall," he stated, then looked at Temple. "In times such as these, you need to be wary when you venture from your home."

"And in times such as these, you are needed at home," Temple stated in sharp criticism.

"I am on my way there now."

"For how long this time?" Temple challenged. "A day? A week? A month? Before you succumb to your restless urges and leave again. Your father is no longer a young man. He needs your help. Your people need your help. It is time you assumed your rightful place as the son of Shawano Stuart."

The Blade was clearly amused by her lecture. "So you told me the last time I saw you."

"And you paid no attention to me. This time you must," Temple insisted.

"And if I do, will you show me the sweetness of your smile instead of the sharpness of your tongue?" His smile continued to make light of her words, but there was a darkening of interest in his eyes as he watched her.

Knowing she had won a small victory, Temple looked away. "I would at least view you with some respect."

"Perhaps it is not respect I want from you," he murmured, then smoothly switched the subject. "How is your mother?"

Temple started to protest the change, then checked the impulse. "She is still troubled by a cough. Otherwise, she is well."

"She will be anxious for you to return. Deu and I will ride a ways with you to ensure the Georgians do not decide to ambush you farther along the road." He backed his horse clear of the carriage.

"Your escort is appreciated, Mr. Stuart," Eliza declared, and she took her seat again.

As soon as Temple joined her, Ike slapped the reins and chirruped to the team, urging them forward. The Blade Stuart and the young black man with him cantered their horses to the front and ranged along the road ahead of the carriage.

"The Blade. That is an unusual name," Eliza remarked.

"It comes from his Cherokee name, which means 'the man who carries the mark of the blade.'"

"The scar on his cheek."

Temple nodded. "He received it in a fight when he was twelve." Her glance traveled to the man under discussion, and her expression softened. "He has been a disappointment to his father. And to others."

Eliza recalled Temple's earlier criticism of him and guessed, "You do not like him very well, do you?"

Temple gave her a startled look. "You are wrong, Miss Hall. If he would but remain here and assume the responsibilities that are his, I would marry him."

"What?"

"Our families have always wanted it."

"But is it what you want?"

"It is what I have always wanted," Temple stated with a determined set to her chin and a gleam in her eye that no proper young lady should have.

2

Thirty more minutes of travel brought the carriage and its occupants to a fork in the road. The Blade Stuart and his black companion took the rutted trail that branched to the right. Ike swung the chestnut team after them, and the federal road was left behind.

On either side of the rough track, the land had been tamed by the plow and planted to crops. Eliza saw fields of corn, indigo, and cotton, the green of young plants vivid against the red-colored soil. Here and there, pastures formed islands of solid green, thick grass providing forage for the cattle that grazed in them.

A mile from the federal road turnoff, The Blade Stuart reined his horse off the trail and pulled in long enough to make eye contact with Temple. Then, without so much as a nod of his head or a lift of a hand, he rode his horse into a stand of trees, the young black man trailing behind him. The carriage continued on, without any slackening of pace.

"Where is Mr. Stuart going?" Eliza inquired when he disappeared from view.

"The home of his father lies beyond that ridge. It will shorten his journey to ride across it."

"I see." Eliza faced the front again and inspected the

rutted lane ahead of them. "I hope we meet no more Georgians."

"Few venture onto this trail," Temple assured her.

"Let us pray that is the case today as well." Eliza clutched at the side of the carriage for balance as a front wheel dipped crazily into a deep hole hidden by a puddle of standing water. An instant later, the wheel rolled free with a bouncing jerk.

Ike pulled the team out of a trot into a walk. Directly ahead, a low-water crossing was flooded with runoff from the recent rains and dammed by a fallen limb of an ancient cottonwood tree and the detritus snared by it.

Two Negroes worked to clear the debris and let the water resume its normal flow. One stood in water up to his knees and tugged at the tangle of branches and brush, a single suspender holding his pants up, his dark skin glistening with sweat. The other wielded an ax and chopped at the thick cottonwood limb. The ringing *thwack* of the ax blade biting into the wood sounded above the rattle and rumble of the carriage.

A man on horseback had stationed himself on the opposite bank, where the towering arms of the cottonwood shaded him from the sun's burning rays. Eliza gathered from his watchful attitude that he was there to oversee the work. Slavery, she knew, was a common practice in the Southern states, but one she simply could not endorse.

"That is a shameful sight," Eliza stated, unable to hold her tongue any longer.

Temple gave an absent nod of agreement, her expression showing a similar displeasure. "Little progress has been made since first I passed here. Our field Negroes grow lazy in my father's absence. He will not be pleased."

"*Your* field Negroes?" Eliza repeated in surprise. "Those are your slaves?"

"Yes," Temple confirmed. "Did you think they belonged to someone else?"

"No. That is . . . I simply did not expect a Cherokee to countenance the owning of slaves."

"How else would we plant and harvest our crops?"

"Hire them as you would any worker and pay them a fair wage for their labor. This practice of slavery is an abomination. It should be abolished. Colored people are human beings; they are not livestock to be bought and sold."

Temple summarily dismissed the notion. "You are from the North. You know nothing of our blacks or you would not show such ignorance."

Eliza was about to argue her position when the full import of Temple's earlier remark registered. She sat up. "You said those were your field Negroes. That means we have reached the land you farm."

"We have, yes."

Eliza craned her neck, trying to catch an advance glimpse of her final destination. Several structures built of roughly hewn logs were visible through the heavily leafed trees just ahead. Two of them appeared to be little more than sheds.

A loud, raucous cry rent the air just as the carriage veered away from the buildings and started up a gently sloping knoll shaded by towering chestnut trees. Atop the knoll sat a three-story brick mansion fronted by a white-columned veranda and roofed balcony. Peacocks strolled the front lawn, which was landscaped with flowering shrubs and brick paths that radiated like spokes on a wheel from the imposing structure.

"What is this place?" The building had all the grandeur of some official's residence.

"Our home," Temple replied with unconscious pride. "Welcome to Gordon Glen, Miss Hall."

Eliza stared in amazement.

When she accompanied Temple inside a few minutes later, she discovered the interior was as grand in appearance as the exterior. A great hall, dominated by a handsomely carved walnut staircase, ran down the center of the first floor. At the opposite end was another entrance, a twin to the baroque door they had just entered, complete with a fan-shaped transom above it.

To the left, a set of double doors opened onto the front parlor. An intricately patterned rug of forest green and gold carpeted the room's wooden floor. Its colors complemented the green-velvet-covered mahogany settee that bore the distinctive design of a Phyfe-made piece. Yet the rug, the settee, the brass wall sconces, the Boston rockers—all the parlor's fine furnishings paled in significance before the room's massive fireplace. Carved out of walnut and crowned by a mantelpiece of chiseled marble, it rose the full height of the room.

From the staircase came a whisper of furtive movement. Two black children peered at Eliza from between the carved banisters.

Footsteps approached the great hall as a woman emerged from one of the main-floor rooms. A long apron covered the front of her gingham dress, and her black hair was twisted in a knot at the back of her head. Her face possessed the heavy bone structure associated with Indians.

"You are here, Miss Hall," the woman said when she saw the new tutor with Temple. A smile immediately lifted the corners of her mouth, but it didn't erase the hollowed look of tiredness around her dark eyes. Temple introduced the woman as her mother, Victoria Gordon.

"How do you do, Mrs. Gordon," Eliza murmured with respect, mindful of her position in the household.

"We are pleased you agreed to come here, Miss Hall," Victoria Gordon replied in somewhat stilted English, then looked past Temple and Eliza in a searching manner, a furrow of concern appearing on her brow. "Is Kipp not with you?"

"Kipp?" Eliza repeated.

"My oldest son," Victoria Gordon explained. "I told him Temple had left to fetch you. He was to be outside to greet you when you arrived."

"We saw no one," she replied.

Victoria Gordon nodded in acceptance. "He grew tired of

the wait, I think. He plays somewhere now." There was the tolerance of a mother's love in her voice.

Eliza had the impression that Kipp Gordon had known little discipline at his mother's hands. According to Payton Fletcher, the oldest Gordon boy was eleven—a difficult age, neither young man nor child. An age when a firm hand was required.

At the top of the stairs, twelve-year-old Phoebe shrank back from the carved railings and grabbed the arm of her nine-year-old brother, Shadrach, pulling him with her. Crouching low, she wrapped her arms around her bony legs and hooked her fingers around her bare toes to hold the position while she peered down at the strange white woman below.

"That be the teacher?" Shadrach whispered.

Phoebe nodded. The pincushion of ribbon-tied braids on her head bobbed with the motion. "She be from the North. Master Will sent fo' her."

"Master Kipp say them talkin' leaves be magic."

"Master Kipp be teasin' you 'gain." Phoebe didn't like Kipp. He was always filling Shadrach's head with stories and being mean to him. "Ain't no magic. An' they be books, not talkin' leaves. The Indians calls them that 'cause they dumb. Be you dumb?"

"No." But Shadrach didn't look too sure of that as he tucked his chin between his bent knees and gazed down at the white teacher.

"Deuteronomy Jones over at old Master Stuart's place, he reads an' writes jus' like white folks does. He be real smart." Phoebe rocked back and thought about that young black man from the neighboring plantation. She hadn't seen him in a long time, but she remembered he was sure enough a fine-looking man. He had a smile that was all big and wide, the kind that made her feel warm all over.

"I gwine to read an' write someday," Shadrach vowed.

Phoebe started to tell him that was never going to happen, but the dream took hold of her, too. She realized it would be a fine thing. She wouldn't be just a house nigger anymore. If she could read and write, maybe when Deu came back he would see that she was special too.

"Phoebe, is that you?" her mistress called sharply.

Phoebe sprang to her feet and quickly stepped in front of her brother to shield him from sight. "Yes'm, Miz Vi'toria. I be here." She scuffled her feet over the boards, making noise to cover the faint sounds Shadrach made as he crawled away.

"I told you to stay with little Johnny." Victoria Gordon came to the base of the staircase.

"I be comin' t' fetch you. He be fussin'. I be thinkin' he be hungry." Everything she said *could* be true. The baby was awake and acting cross. Course, her mammy claimed it was a tooth coming in that was giving him a fever and making him cranky.

Sighing, Victoria Gordon turned from the stairs and cast an apologetic glance at Eliza. "Temple will see to your needs." She started up the steps.

Halfway to the second floor, she was seized by a racking cough that slowed her pace. Temple watched with concern as her mother climbed the stairs. The look was gone when she turned to face the new tutor.

"Are you hungry, Miss Hall? I can have Black Cassie fix you something to eat."

"No, thank you." But Eliza took advantage of the offer to satisfy a curiosity whetted by glimpses of the other rooms on the main floor. "Is this the dining room?" She stepped closer to the archway on her right to see more of the room's interior. "I was told I would be taking my meals with the family."

"Of course," Temple replied as she came over to stand beside her. Sunlight streamed through the lace curtains on the four large windows and glistened brightly on the Sheraton-style mahogany table that stretched the length of the room. Twelve highly polished chairs were grouped around it. A fireplace of hand-carved walnut occupied the outside wall, its hearth closed off by a screen. A glass cabinet on the far wall housed an elaborate service of china and crystal. Opposite it stood a mahogany sideboard.

"In the evenings, we gather in the family parlor." Temple guided Eliza down the great hall to another room.

When Temple stepped aside, Eliza saw, to her amazement, a rosewood piano in the corner. A piano—here in the middle of the wilderness. She walked over to its velvet-covered stool and sat down, wondering when she would cease to be surprised by what she found here. She touched the smooth wood, then glanced back at Temple. "Do you play?"

"One of the missionary wives at Brainerd was teaching me, but—" She paused, then shrugged and smiled. "Father has become weary of listening to me play the same three melodies over and over. Do you play the piano? Perhaps you could teach me some new songs."

"I see no reason why music lessons cannot be scheduled in the afternoons." With difficulty, Eliza resisted the urge to raise the wooden cover and expose the keys. She stood and firmly clasped her hands together.

"The library is across the hall." Temple started toward the door, adding over her shoulder, "Father said you are to be allowed access to all of the books."

"How very kind of him."

The instant Eliza entered the library, she stopped and stared at the portrait above the fireplace mantelpiece. None of the library's other furnishings registered, not the large walnut desk, the elaborately carved sofa, or the vast collection of books on the shelves. All paled before the oil painting of a tall, stern-eyed man—dressed in a Scottish kilt.

"Who is that?"

"My grandfather Lachlan Gordon. He built this house," Temple replied.

"He wears a kilt." Eliza frowned, noticing for the first time the jeweled pin on the front of the man's plaid skirt. It was exactly like the amethyst brooch Temple wore.

"His father, William Gordon, came from Scotland. He was

the second son of a nobleman there. Shortly after he arrived in Savannah, he killed a man in a fight. The English were going to charge him with murder, so he fled here to the mountains among the Cherokees." Temple paused to gaze at the painting. "The kilt originally belonged to him. My grandfather Lachlan said he was tall and strong like an oak tree, with hair as red as the maple leaves in autumn. My father was named William Alexander after him."

"Then he remained in the mountains?"

"He could not go back. They would have arrested him for murder," Temple reminded her. "He married Dánagasta, a respected war woman of the Cherokees."

"A war woman?" Eliza questioned the term.

"A female warrior who has earned honors in war."

"You surely cannot mean she actually took part in a battle?"

"Why not? A woman can fight with a war club, musket, or bow and arrow as well as a man. In Dánagasta's time, it was not uncommon for a Cherokee woman to choose to become a warrior as well as the mother of warriors. When war was contemplated, war women sat in the holy area of the council and advised the war chiefs on the strategy to be used. My grandfather's mother was such a woman. Her English name was Jane Gordon." Temple again paused thoughtfully. "She and her husband, William Alexander Gordon, started this farm. When I was a small girl, their log cabin still stood, but it burned several years ago."

"I see." Eliza looked around again. "You say your grandfather built this house. It must have cost a fortune. How did he ever acquire such wealth out here in the wilderness?"

"He was a very clever man. He operated the trading post and gristmill his father had established. With the profits from those businesses, he brought in agriculturists to advise him, and purchased field Negroes to plant more lands to crops and orchards. A venture that proved most successful," Temple explained. "He fashioned this house after the fine homes he saw in Scotland and England."

"You mean the ones his father saw," Eliza corrected, certain Temple had misspoken.

"No, Lachlan Gordon saw them himself. He had heard so many stories from his father about Scotland that my grandfather wanted to see it for himself. He took my father with him, though he was only a young boy no older than my brother Kipp. They traveled all through England and Scotland and visited many of the grand estates there. They even met King George the Third."

Will Gordon, her employer, had met the late King of England? Eliza was startled by this revelation, then hastened to assure herself that she wasn't impressed by the royal title but rather by the historical significance of George the Third.

In retrospect, Eliza found it quite typical of the English to lionize a party of American Indians and fawn over them, according them the honors they would show visiting royalty. She had only to recall the legendary Powhatan Indian maiden Pocahontas and the fuss that was made over her when she went to England.

While Eliza inspected the rest of the library, Temple carefully scrutinized the new teacher. There was nothing particularly compelling about her strong features and small mouth. Her brown hair was curly and light in color like the wood of the hickory. Tall and thin, she held herself stiffly erect, the jut of her chin suggesting a willful personality. Temple had at first thought this Eliza Hall to be cold and stern without a woman's core of warmth and deep feeling until she had seen the delight that sprang into the teacher's hazel eyes when she spied the piano in the family parlor. At that moment, Temple had decided that she could, perhaps, like this new tutor.

Recognizing the signs of fatigue in the woman's slightly drawn look, Temple remarked, "You must be tired from your long journey. We have prepared a room for you on the third floor."

"Thank you." Eliza resisted the urge to run a smoothing hand over her rumpled and travel-stained dress.

Her quarters on the third floor were small and plainly furnished, but adequate for her needs. A single bed with iron posts and frame was tucked along a side wall, beneath a ceiling that sloped with the pitch of the roof. An oak washstand with a basin and pitcher stood beneath an east-facing window that gave the room some natural light and ventilation.

Eliza crossed the planked floor to the center of the room and surveyed the small touches that lessened the starkness. A patchwork quilt blanketed the bed, creating a cheerful splash of color next to the cream yellow walls. A rag rug in a rainbow of muted hues lay on the floor next to the bed. In a corner sat an ancient rocking chair, cushioned with a faded needlepoint pillow. A plain white curtain moved slightly at the window, stirred by a faint breeze that made a vain attempt to alleviate the room's collected heat.

"You have a wardrobe here for your clothes." Temple pointed to a crudely made piece Eliza had overlooked. Her trunk and valise sat next to it. "And there is a chamber pot in the corner commode for your convenience. Is there anything else you will require?"

"No, this is quite satisfactory," Eliza stated. "Later I will want to inspect the schoolhouse. I was told one had been built on the premises."

"Yes. It is the log building you can see from your window."

"Good, then I will have no difficulty finding it on my own."

"None at all. I will leave you to your unpacking," Temple said and retreated from the room.

Alone at last, Eliza untied the strings of her bonnet, swept it off, and tossed it onto the bed. Automatically, she pushed at the unruly curls that sprang free, then gave up any attempt to smooth her hair into order and crossed to the window to lift aside the curtain.

There, on the far edge of the lawn, stood a log building. As no other structure was visible from the window, Eliza surmised this was the schoolhouse. Peacocks strolled the bricked path that led to it.

More than once during her long journey from Massachusetts, Reverend Nathan Cole had assured her that "God, in His own way, prepares us for what lies ahead." But Eliza knew that God had not prepared her for this. She had believed she was venturing into the wilderness to live among savages and endure hardship and privation. Instead, she found herself confronted by a family residence that reminded her of a manor house.

She thought back to that day two months ago when she had entered the Springfield law office of Payton Fletcher accompanied by her mother, Nancy Chapman Hall. The New England countryside had been green with spring, and the challenge of the season had been upon her, making Eliza eager to throw off the gray, cheerless monotony of the past and begin a new life, one that offered a modicum of adventure and an opportunity to test her skills as a teacher. Payton Fletcher had advertised just such a post.

A portly man in his middle years and a member of a highly respected Massachusetts family, Fletcher had warmly welcomed Eliza and her mother to his private chamber that day. His round-cheeked countenance was almost jovial in its expression, and his gray eyes were kind yet thorough in their inspection of her.

During the first part of the interview, he questioned her at length about her qualifications, the academies she had attended, and the teaching she had done to support herself. To her great relief, he appeared to be unconcerned by her lack of extensive teaching experience. But that also prompted Eliza to wonder if there had been many applicants for the post.

It was then that Payton Fletcher finally provided more

information about the position—tutor to the children of a Cherokee Indian family.

Her mother's reaction was instant. "Indians? But they are attacking Georgia settlers, threatening the lives of innocent women and children—"

"I assure you, Mrs. Hall," Payton Fletcher interrupted calmly but firmly, "the newspaper headlines of recent months have been gross exaggerations. If any wrongdoing has occurred, it has been on the part of the Georgians, but that is another matter. As to Will Gordon and his family, let me put your fears to rest: they are far from savages. I have had the privilege of calling Will Gordon my friend for a number of years now, and can personally vouch for his noble character."

He explained that he had become acquainted with Will Gordon when they both had attended a private boarding school here in the East. The bonds of friendship then forged had only strengthened with the passage of time.

Payton Fletcher further stated that Will Gordon was a planter, farming one of the fertile valleys in the tribal lands near northern Georgia. A single-room log house had been constructed on the property to serve as a school for his children and those of his sister. In addition to a salary of four hundred dollars a year, meals and private sleeping quarters within the Gordon home would be provided to the tutor.

Eliza's imagination immediately took one of its usual melodramatic turns as she envisioned a room of brown-skinned children listening with rapt attention, a host of primitive minds waiting to be enlightened by her teaching. When Payton Fletcher offered the post, Eliza accepted on the spot, certain this was her call of destiny.

Now, she looked about the grounds through her bedroom window. "A prosperous farm," Payton Fletcher had said. The simple phrase hardly described the obvious wealth that surrounded her. She longed to sit down and compose a letter to her mother, describing it all while the details were still fresh in her mind. But common sense told her that was an impractical use of her time when she had other matters to attend to.

Letting the curtain fall, Eliza turned from the window and recoiled with a gasp of alarm as she realized that someone stood not four feet from her. Belatedly, she saw it was a boy of no more than eleven. He stared back at her, a sly gleam of mischief shining in his coal black eyes. Eliza pressed a hand to her chest to calm her rapidly beating heart.

"You startled me," she admitted, then suspected at once that had been his intent. "You must be Kipp," she guessed.

"And you are the new teacher from the North."

"I am." With her composure regained, she clasped her hands primly together. "You may call me Miss Hall."

Kipp Gordon merely smiled.

Trouble. With a teacher's sixth sense, Eliza recognized that here was a pupil destined to bedevil her at every turn. She vowed there and then to be more than a match for him.

☙ 3 ☙

The thickly leaved branches of the towering chestnut tree blocked the rays of the setting sun and cast a premature darkness on the small log schoolhouse. Eliza placed the copy of *Webster's Blue-Backed Speller* atop the stack of textbooks and primers on her desk, finished at last with her preparations for the next day's lessons.

All in all, Eliza felt she had accomplished a great deal in only three short days. The school hours were firmly established. The first class began at eight o'clock in the morning with the arrival of the four Murphy children, the Gordons' cousins: Charlie, age thirteen; Tom, twelve; Mary, ten; and Joe, nine. Lessons continued until the noon meal, then resumed at four in the afternoon, after the heat of the day had passed. The school day concluded with piano lessons for the three girls, Temple, her younger sister, Xandra, and Mary.

Eliza rose from her desk and circled the room, closing the four windows as she went. At the end of that first day, she had forgotten to shut them. The next morning, she had found a large ratlike creature nosing around her desk. Quite unintentionally, she had screamed, not frightened as much as startled. Kipp Gordon had charged into the schoolhouse just as the poor opossum scrambled across the puncheon floor to the open window. The sound of Kipp's ridiculing laughter still rang in her ears, a match to the scorn that had gleamed in his dark eyes. Trouble—he was definitely that.

With the contest of wills over for the day, Eliza cast a last look around the schoolroom, then walked out the door, closing it securely behind her. The three-story brick mansion crowned the knoll, its grandeur making it the focal point of the farm. Detached from it were two kitchens and a smokehouse. Brick paths from the mansion led to a stable of blooded horses, a blacksmith's forge, farm sheds, and a cluster of cabins for the thirty-some slaves owned by the Gordons.

Beyond the house grounds, milk cows grazed in a pasture next to the vegetable garden. Half-wild hogs foraged in the nearby woods. Stretched along the fertile valley were fields of corn, cotton, tobacco, wheat, oats, and indigo, in addition to fruit orchards. In the absence of Will Gordon, his brother-in-law, George Murphy, supervised the work of the Negroes in the fields.

However, the domestic side of the plantation's operation was solely the responsibility of Victoria Gordon. And that, Eliza had learned, included more than just the household. It ranged from the vegetable garden and the milk cows to the care and maintenance of the Negroes—a formidable task when one considered that more than thirty needed to be fed and clothed, their sick and injured tended. On her first morning, Eliza had witnessed the weekly doling-out of supplies by Victoria Gordon as a line of black women carrying wooden trays waited to receive their rations from the barrels of meal, tubs of pickled pork and corned beef, and rows of smoked hams and pork shoulders hanging from beams in the basement's locked storeroom.

Victoria Gordon rarely sat down except at mealtime. A thousand and one tasks demanded either her supervision or her participation, and Eliza began to appreciate the cause of the woman's harried and worn look.

Conscious of the lengthening shadows around her, Eliza

hurried along the brick path to the house. Ahead, the glass panes of the mansion's windows reflected the golden pink glow of the setting sun as the hush of evening settled over the plantation.

A pressing silence greeted her when she entered the great hall. Feeling its crush, Eliza paused by the staircase that marched majestically to the second floor. Tonight she wasn't anxious to climb the long flights of steps to her room. In truth, she felt lonely and a bit homesick. She missed her mother's company and the stimulating conversations they had always had in the evenings.

From overhead came the tread of soft footsteps approaching the staircase. Eliza looked up as the big-bosomed mammy called Black Cassie came into view.

"Good evening, Cassie." Eliza unconsciously shied from attaching the appellation of "Black" to the slave woman's name. It reminded Eliza of a milk cow called Brown Bessie her family had owned when she was a young girl. For all the darkness of their skins, Eliza could not regard these unfortunate Africans as animals.

Cassie came down the steps. "Was you be wantin' somethin', Miz 'Liza?"

"Nothing, thank you, Cassie."

The woman nodded and moved away. Eliza started to climb the stairs, then stopped when her glance strayed into the family parlor, with its rosewood piano. Not once since she had arrived had she played it for her own enjoyment, even though Victoria Gordon had given her permission to do so.

With a certain brusqueness of decision, Eliza entered the room and went straight to the piano. She sat down and adjusted the layers of her skirt and petticoats, then raised the hinged cover over the keys and located the pedals with her feet.

The instant her fingers touched the ivory keys, her manner changed. She played her favorite nocturne from memory, her fingers moving lightly over the keys, her body swaying gently with the soft, soothing song of evening.

As the last note faded, she began another melody, not allowing the mansion's silence to take hold. She went from one song to another with barely a pause in between, calling on her memory for selections by Bach, Beethoven, and Mozart, occasionally faltering when the notes of a particular measure escaped her.

When evening's shadows began to darken the parlor, Eliza paused long enough to light two candles and place them atop the rosewood piano to illuminate the ivory and black keys. Then she resumed her playing.

She finished what she considered to be a particularly inspired—although far from technically perfect—interpretation of a fugue by Bach, and held the last note, letting it fade on its own. In satisfaction, she drew her hands away from the keys and clasped them together in her lap, awash with the song's passion.

"Please play another," a man's voice requested. "Your music is very enjoyable."

Startled, Eliza looked up. A dark figure stood in the parlor doorway, one shoulder leaning against the walnut frame. The light from the two candles failed to reach that far, throwing him into silhouette. She could make out no detail about him, but the overall impression was one of height and power.

When he straightened to stand erect, he seemed to loom closer. For an instant, Eliza mistook him for The Blade. When she realized it wasn't him, she stood and picked up the brass candle holder, lifting it high above her head.

"Who are you? What are you doing here?" she demanded, sharp and wary.

The man stepped into the room, and into the light. He was dressed in trousers and the black frock coat of a planter. The wavering light from the candle flame reflected over the angled hollows and planes of his face and picked up the cinnamon lights in his brown hair.

"This is my house," he replied quite simply.

"Your house?" The answer was not what Eliza had

expected. It had never occurred to her he might be Will Gordon.

"And you must be the new tutor, Miss Eliza Hall."

"Yes." She lowered the candle, painfully conscious of her less-than-professional appearance and determined not to show it. "I was not told you had returned."

"I arrived home only moments ago."

As if to confirm this assertion, Temple rushed into the room, a cotton robe tied over her nightdress, her long hair unbound and tumbling in a thick black curtain about her shoulders and back. She stopped when she saw her father, her face alight with a child's pleasure.

"Father. You are here." Her voice was rich with delight.

"I am." The look he gave Temple was that of a doting father.

She moved to his side and turned her gaze on Eliza, amused to see the dozens of curls springing free of the teacher's prim bun, making her appear a bit of a madcap. This was the real Eliza Hall, full of spirit and verve despite the stiff and colorless image she tried to project.

"When you heard the piano music, did you think it was me?" Temple cast a teasing glance at her father.

"I knew it could not be you. The tune was not one I had heard before," he said with an answering smile.

Temple laughed. "Soon you will not be able to say that. Miss Hall is giving me lessons on the piano so that I may play it as grandly as she does."

"Let us hope." He raised an eyebrow in mock skepticism.

The tutor spoke up quickly. "Your daughter is an apt pupil."

Will Gordon recognized the combative stance of this tall, plain woman and resisted the urge to smile. Instead, he responded with a formal nod. "I am pleased to hear that, Miss Hall. Tell me, how was Payton Fletcher when you saw him last?"

"He seemed in good health," the tutor replied stiffly.

"Are his eyes still sharp and is his smile still wide?"

"Indeed." Eliza smiled at the accurate description of the Springfield lawyer. "He asked me to give you his warmest regards."

"It has been years since I last saw him. I must write him on the morrow." He looked down at Temple and forced a smile. "Now that Payton Fletcher has become a gentleman of the green bag, I may have more need of his counsel than I once thought."

There was a twinkle in his eyes when he used the backwoods term for a lawyer, but it couldn't cover the lines of strain and fatigue Temple saw in his face.

"You are tired from your long ride." She touched his arm in quick concern. "Have you eaten?"

"Your mother is preparing some food for me."

"I will see if it is ready." Temple knew as well as her father that his meal would be completely forgotten if her mother heard one of the children call out. It was something Temple could not understand, but it was nonetheless often the case.

As soon as Temple started for the door, the new tutor spoke up. "With your permission, Mr. Gordon, I will withdraw to my room and leave you alone to rest from your journey."

Without waiting for his reply, she followed Temple into the hall. Alone now in the family parlor, Will felt the silence of the room close around him. All feeling of ease was gone. Restless, he crossed to the parlor window and stared beyond the panes into the black of the night. In Cherokee lore, black was the color of the west, where legend claimed the land swallowed the sun. Will turned from the sight and moved to the piano. There he paused and struck one of the keys, listening to its clarion ring.

In his mind's eye, he again saw the new tutor, Eliza Hall, at the piano the way she had first appeared to him when he stood in the doorway, her fingers moving with fluid deftness over the keys, her body swaying with the rhythm, her expression rapt and glowing, her hair a halo of butternut curls about her face. For a brief moment he had been transported back to a less troubled time—to that fortnight he had spent in the Massachusetts home of Payton Fletcher and his family. Payton's mother had played the piano nearly every evening, accompanying Payton, who loved to sing.

That had been long ago. So very long ago.

Will sighed and glanced about the empty room, then moved toward the door. Tonight he didn't want to be alone with his thoughts. From the hall came the sound of a cough being smothered. Victoria, he thought, experiencing a stab of concern. When he reached the receiving hall, he saw her there, a wraith of the woman he had married eighteen years ago.

She smiled, but her smile held only a ghost of its former warmth. "Your supper is in the dining room."

"Those words have a beautiful sound to a hungry man," he told her, then walked with her to the dining room.

A trio of candles burned in the silver candelabra situated at the far end of the table. Will crossed to their light and sat down at his accustomed place at the head of the table. Temple entered the room carrying a pitcher.

"Would you like some cold cider with your meal, Father?" Temple asked.

"I would like that, yes." Will unfolded his napkin and laid it across his lap while Temple filled a goblet with cider, then placed the pitcher on the sideboard.

"Is there anything else you need?" Victoria stood by his chair.

Will looked up from his plate of cold pork and corn bread. The candlelight softened the hollowed look of her face, giving it the faint glow of youth. "Sit and keep me company."

Victoria shook her head. "I must see to little John. He is fretful tonight."

For one hot instant, Will wanted to demand a husband's share of her time. There was much he wanted to tell her about the meeting of the National Council, the stories from those in other parts of the Nation, the recent harassments by the

Georgia Guard, and the depredations of the pony clubs. But he knew the words would be wasted on his wife. Holding his tongue, he squared around to face the table and his plate of food.

"You should see to John then." With forced calm, he took the goblet of cider Temple set before him and lifted it to his mouth.

"Do you not want to hear the outcome of the National Council meeting, Mother?" Temple protested on his behalf when her mother turned to leave the room.

"Whatever decision they reached, I am confident it will be the best for our people." But Victoria's expression of confidence failed to conceal her underlying indifference.

Temple pulled out a chair and sat down. "Tell me about the meeting, Father. I want to know," she insisted, the glitter of suppressed anger in her eyes as her mother left the room.

Will studied his daughter, who was now more woman than child. As he had before, he suspected she sensed the emptiness of his marriage, the lack of closeness. In her own way, Temple tried to make up for Victoria's uninterest by stepping in and filling the void, as she was doing now.

It hadn't always been like this between Victoria and him. When they were first married, their lives together had been rich and full. When Temple was born, they had rejoiced together, and when their next baby died within hours of its birth, they had grieved together. But with the death of their next child their lives had begun to take different paths.

In all, four healthy children had been born to them. But they had buried five others. Victoria had seemed to die a little herself with the death of each, and she had withdrawn from him a little more each time, until they were two people living under the same roof, eating at the same table, but no longer sharing their lives or their marriage bed.

Victoria's entire world was centered on her children. Each living child had become that much more precious to her. She couldn't bear to be parted from them for even a day.

Will understood that. It was why he had hired the new tutor instead of sending the children away to boarding school. It was an expensive decision, and perhaps not a wise one, given the current state of affairs in the Nation.

Without thinking, Will found himself recounting the events of the meeting to Temple, censoring only those details that might unduly alarm her. He took a fatherly pride in the intelligent questions she asked, and he answered them all. When a silence finally settled over the table, his plate was clean and the hunger was gone from his belly.

"It is good to be home," he said in contentment.

"It is good to have you home." Temple gathered up his dishes and utensils and carried them to the sideboard, adding over her shoulder, "Have you heard The Blade has returned?"

Will smiled at the feigned nonchalance in her voice. "Does this please you?"

"It will if he stays." Temple threw him a quick smile that said she intended to make it her business that he did.

The sun sat high in the sky. With the heat of the day upon them, there were no classes in the little log schoolhouse. Temple stood in the shade of the back veranda and watched as the teacher set off across the lawn, a girl holding each hand, arms swinging, skirts swishing. The boys soon fell in behind them, forming a loose procession.

Temple had often observed Eliza Hall playing with the children in the afternoons. Each time, the teacher had given every appearance of being as carefree and happy as her young charges, a vast difference from the earnest woman who ruled the schoolhouse. Recalling the way the teacher's eyes sometimes shone with excitement for a subject, Temple realized that only around herself and her mother did Eliza Hall appear stiff and reserved.

Half an hour later, Temple rode from the stables on her spirited mare. Skirting the double row of Negro shacks, she turned onto a narrow field lane. The mare pranced and side-stepped the whole way, eager to run and impatient with the slow pace.

For a short distance the lane ran alongside the spring-fed creek that rambled through Gordon Glen. Through a break in the willow trees, Temple spied Eliza Hall crouched on the opposite bank, the children crowded around her peering at some object she was showing them. A pair of unlaced half-boots sat alone on the gravel bar that jutted into the stream, the white of a pair of stockings poking out of their tops. From the size, Temple knew the shoes belonged to the teacher. She wished she had ridden by earlier to see the proper Miss Hall wading in the creek.

Keeping to the shady side of the narrow track, Temple let the mare break into a slow canter. Ahead, a wheat field shimmered like golden silk in the sun. Tobacco grew in the next clearing, its long broad leaves tipped to catch and hold the sunlight. Farther on, the yellow tassels of cornstalks wagged in a south breeze. Riding closer, Temple saw slaves hoeing weeds, the women working alongside the men, their backs stooped by the steady swing of the hoe.

Her father sat astride his big blaze-faced gelding in the shade of a hickory tree. She rode over to join him, as always feeling a surge of pride that this man was her father.

"I thought you would be here." She halted her mare alongside his big gelding and surveyed the field before them, conscious of the closeness between them that didn't seem to need words. "The corn is getting tall."

"We should have a good crop."

"Are we going to have a Green Corn Dance this year?"

"No." Will Gordon caught the glimmer of disappointment in his daughter's expression and wished he could give her a different answer, but the cost of such a feast was more than he could afford this year on top of the expenses he had already incurred in building the schoolhouse, buying the necessary books and supplies, and paying for the teacher's travel fare and her salary. Still, he regretted that it was so. Of all his children, Temple was his favorite. The realization came as something of a surprise to him. He had always expected his strongest feelings would be for his son. But Temple reminded him of his father. She had that same proud spirit and sharp mind, the same boldness and energy, and a smile that could instantaneously win hearts. "Did you ride all the way out here to ask me about the Green Corn Dance?"

"No. I was restless." She reached forward to stroke the mare's sleek neck and smooth its wind-tangled mane.

Watching her, Will noticed the ripeness of her figure as the calico material of her dress stretched to outline the firm, round shape of her breasts. "Stay on Gordon Glen. Keep within its fences today." Before she could question his unusual edict, Will explained, "The Georgia Guard is in the area."

"How do you know that?"

Her sharply questioning glance held no fear, only surprise. That pleased him. "They were at the meeting of the National Council in New Echota."

"Did they cause trouble?"

"No. They stood around and watched, like those black crows strutting along the fence rail." Will indicated the black birds perched on a section of fence several yards away.

Temple laughed. "You are right, Father. They are like thieving crows." She rode her horse over to the fence and flushed the crows from their perch. "And like crows, we'll soon chase them from our land."

Will refrained from pointing out that the crows were already circling back. "Like crows they might be, but they are still men, Temple. Remember what I said."

"I will."

Off she rode, the mare lunging against the restraining bit. Will watched her, confident she wouldn't disobey his order. She understood the reason for it. Strong-willed she might be, but defiant she wasn't. When she rode out of sight, he directed his attention back to the field.

Conscious of the sun's rays heating her back, Temple turned in the saddle and glanced at the sun, shielding her eyes from its glare as she checked its location in the sky. With a sigh, she realized it was later than she had thought.

Reluctantly, she turned the mare for home and rode through the orchard toward the main road. The afternoon ride hadn't quieted her restlessness as she had thought it would. If anything, it was stronger.

When she reached the main road, the mare snorted and sidestepped, disturbed by something. A second later, she heard the muffled thud of hooves on hard ground. Recalling her father's warning about the Georgia Guard, Temple turned the mare off the road and hid in the thick woods bordering it. A hog darted out of her path, grunting an alarm that sent others scurrying deeper into the timbered brush.

A horse and buggy rambled into view, accompanied by two riders. With a warm rush of pleasure, Temple recognized The Blade and his black servant, Deuteronomy. She had always found much to admire about the tall, strongly built man, but today she was again impressed by how well The Blade sat his horse.

From the time she was her sister Xandra's age, Temple had wanted his blue eyes to look at her, to notice her. Even when he had teased her, which he had done unmercifully, Temple had still thought there was no one as wonderful as The Blade.

When he left three years ago to attend a college in the North, Temple had been proud of his achievements, though she had missed him keenly in that time. Once The Blade had rebelled against the confinement and strictures of college life and quit within the first year, she had mixed feelings at the prospect of his homecoming. The decision had been a blow to his father, Shawano Stuart, who had always shared Will Gordon's belief in the importance of education.

Temple could have forgiven The Blade for disappointing his father if he had returned to take his rightful place at his father's side. But he had come back for only a brief stay, then left again to drift to Tennessee, Kentucky, the Carolinas, and finally the mountain gold camps.

He was back now, but for how long? Would he ever stay

in one place long enough to fulfill his duties to his family and the Nation? Could he ever commit himself to a wife and children? To her?

Temple sighed in irritation and rode out of the woods to intercept the horse and buggy. Reining in beside it, she deliberately ignored The Blade and smiled at the man in the buggy. The darkness of Shawano Stuart's hair was thickly streaked with white. Age lines creased his broad face, but his blue eyes were as sharp and alert as a young man's.

"It has been a long time since I saw you last, Shawano Stuart. You look well," she greeted him in Cherokee. He understood English well enough, but the use of it came stiffly to his tongue.

"Young Temple, it is you," Shawano Stuart replied, gesturing eloquently with his hands in typical Cherokee fashion. "You have grown into a woman with the grace and beauty of a swan."

"She has the hiss of one, as well, Father," The Blade inserted dryly. "Perhaps that is why no one has come forward to make her his wife."

"How would you know, when you have made yourself a stranger to us?" Temple challenged.

Shawano chuckled at their barbed exchange. "There will be time enough for the two of you to sharpen your tongues and wits on each other later. We are on our way to see your father."

"When last I saw him, he was at the cornfield. Look for him there before you go to the house." She backed her horse away from the buggy.

"Where are you going?" The Blade frowned.

"To the orchard." With the breeze heavily scented with apples, it was the first place that came to her mind.

"The Georgia Guard has been seen in the area," he warned.

"Then you'd best ride with your father." Without waiting for a reply, Temple kicked her mount into a lope. She smiled in secret pleasure when she heard the echoing hoofbeats behind her.

She halted beneath a tree and dismounted to pluck a green apple from a low-hanging limb. The Blade swung out of his saddle and gathered up the reins. As she bit into the apple, everything seemed suddenly much sharper to her—the tartly sour taste of the apple, the fruity smell in the air . . . and the sound of his footsteps. She turned to face him, feeling very much alive.

"You should have accompanied your father. I am safe on Gordon Glen," she asserted, then looked at the apple and tossed it away. "I must remember to tell Mother the apples are still too green to pick." She began to walk, leading the mare.

The Blade hesitated, then fell in with her. She seemed almost a stranger to him, though there were still traces of the girl he remembered visible in the proud tilt of her head and the flashing challenge in her dark eyes. But the rest—the flat chest, the childlike eagerness, and the innocent beauty—they were gone. In their place was a disturbing ripeness.

"You should not put too much trust in the idea that you are safe from the Georgians on Gordon Glen," he told her, surprised by his own curtness. "They are not above accosting our people in their homes."

"I know," she replied without concern. "I have read accounts of such incidents in our newspaper. The *Cherokee Phoenix* has been filled with stories of homes being plundered, livestock stolen, crops burned, men flogged and beaten, women assaulted—violated—all with no recourse."

First published nearly two and a half years before, the national newspaper was a source of pride to the Cherokees. Its stories were printed both in English and the Cherokee syllabary devised nine years earlier by the Cherokee silversmith Sequoya, who sometimes went by his English name, George Guess. Estimates varied widely as to the number of

Cherokees able to read and write in their language. Some put the figure as high as ninety percent; others claimed it was closer to fifty percent. But all agreed that anyone who spoke Cherokee could learn to read and write in that language in only days with Sequoya's syllabary.

Regardless of which number was the true figure, the literacy rate among the Cherokees was still higher than that of the Georgians, who were, at best, only three generations removed from their beginnings as a British penal colony.

"You have only read of such incidents," The Blade said now. "In my travels, I have witnessed them. I can tell you firsthand that the Georgians take pleasure in subjecting our women to their abusive manner." The surge of anger that The Blade felt when he thought of some coarse Georgian putting his hands on Temple was obvious to her.

She halted and wheeled about to face him. "Then you should be working with others to stop it."

"There is little anyone can do."

"So you do nothing."

Rankled by the criticism in her voice, The Blade shot back, "What would you have me do?"

"The same thing our fathers do—meet, discuss, and search for a way to end it. But you cannot be bothered." She turned and started walking again. "When will you leave this time?"

"Maybe I have decided to stay for a while."

"Have you?"

"Do you care?"

"How typical of you," Temple retorted scornfully. "You avoid commitments and responsibility. You come and go with never a thought for anyone but yourself."

He caught hold of her wrist, bringing her to a halt. "If I did stay, then what?" He felt the rapid beat of her pulse beneath his fingers and dropped the reins to hook an arm around her waist and draw her closer. "Would the black swan stop hissing at me?"

"Perhaps." She breathed the word softly.

The Blade was conscious of the sensation of her firmly rounded breasts against him, and the closeness of her full lips. They parted slightly as her breathing quickened. He was only curious, he told himself when he bent his head to claim them.

Her lips were softer than he had expected, yet sharp with the taste of green apples. He wanted to tunnel into them and lick away the tart layer to find the sweet. He felt them give beneath his pressure, yet he was the one who felt consumed.

Perched on a half-rotten log, Eliza tugged at her stocking. It stuck to her damp foot, resisting her efforts to pull it on. By the time she won her battle with it, she felt as hot and sticky as she had before she had waded in the cool waters of the brook.

She pulled on her ankle-high walking shoes. When she bent to tighten their laces, a pin fell out of her hair. She immediately felt the sagging weight of her hair threaten to tumble free from its bun. Hastily, she scooped up the pin and tried to anchor it back in place.

The rumble of wheels and plodding hooves came from the lane next to the brook. Eliza frowned, certain it was much too early for the slaves to be coming back from the fields. But it wasn't the farm wagon she saw when she looked up; it was a horse and buggy accompanied by two riders.

One of them was Will Gordon. With a gasp of dismay, Eliza felt of her hair, discovering a hundred strands curling free. Why, oh why, had she ever let the children talk her into coming down to the brook to play with them? She was a mess.

"Father! Father!" Xandra ran out to greet him. Kipp and the other boys instantly abandoned the turtle they had found and dashed after her.

When Will Gordon glanced in her direction, Eliza knew there was no escape. Hurriedly, she bent over and worked at lacing her shoes, hoping against hope that if she didn't acknowledge him, he wouldn't find it necessary to speak to her.

She heard the chorus of young voices, all clamoring for his attention, but she was more concerned by the absence of hoofbeats. He had stopped. She refused to look up even though she could feel the blood rushing into her head, making her face feel hotter still.

She laced her shoes so tight her feet felt strangled. Aware that she had spent more time at the task than was necessary, Eliza reluctantly sat up and looked directly at Will Gordon. Young Xandra sat in front of him in the saddle.

"Do you not have lessons in the afternoon?"

Although the question was directed at his youngest daughter, Eliza knew it was meant for her. With a sinking sensation, she realized that Will Gordon undoubtedly thought she was neglecting her duties—or worse, purposely shirking them.

"When it is hot in the afternoons, Mr. Gordon, the school becomes quite stuffy. The children find it difficult to concentrate on their lessons."

"Do you know how a cricket makes that chirping sound, Father?" Xandra tipped her head back to look at him, her face alight with excitement, exhibiting little of her usual reserve. "It rubs its legs together and makes them squeak, like a saw cutting wood. Miss Hall said so. She knows lots of things," Xandra insisted, then paused, turning shy at the discovery that others were listening.

"When did she tell you this?"

"This afternoon," Mary Murphy volunteered. "Kipp caught a cricket and he was going to tear its legs off. Miss Hall said he mustn't because they was his musical instrument—like a piano."

"*Were,*" the teacher reproved. "They *were.*"

"They *were* his musical instrument," Mary repeated obediently.

Will cast a glance at Eliza Hall, prepared to concede that

the afternoon might not have been all play. She had definitely succeeded in gaining his youngest daughter's attention. Will had long ago resigned himself to the fact that Xandra lacked the intelligence her older brother and sister possessed. He was convinced Xandra sensed this too, and rather than draw attention to her slowness, she had become shy and withdrawn.

The buggy rolled forward a few inches, then stopped. "Shawano." Will turned to his guest. Out of deference to his old friend and neighbor, he spoke in Cherokee. "This is the tutor I hired, Miss Eliza Hall, from Massachusetts." He translated it into English for the teacher, adding, "Miss Hall, this is Shawano Stuart, a man who has been a good friend to my family for many years. He and his son will share supper with us this evening."

"It is a pleasure to meet you, Mr. Stuart."

"My son has spoken of you, Miss Eliza Hall," Shawano replied in stilted English, a familiar humor gleaming in the pale blue eyes that studied her. "He said your hair curled tight like the thin shavings of wood. My eyes tell me that this is so."

Observing the look of dismay that flashed briefly over the teacher's face, Will suppressed the urge to smile. "Miss Hall plays the piano. Perhaps we can prevail upon her to entertain us with her music this evening."

"I . . . would be delighted to play for you, Mr. Stuart," Eliza said, her heart sinking with dread. "Now I must ask you to excuse us. It is time for the children to resume their lessons."

Will lowered Xandra to the ground. "We will see you at supper, Miss Hall."

☆ 5 ☆

A cane thumped the dining room floor beside Will as the elderly Shawano Stuart, crippled by a long-ago war wound, maneuvered himself onto a chair. Instinctively, Will moved to assist him, but The Blade was already at his father's side, holding the chair steady and discreetly offering a supporting arm.

Looking at his friend's son, Will suddenly felt old. Tall and lean, but powerfully built, The Blade commanded attention with an ease that belonged to a man twice his age. But it was the boldness glittering in his blue eyes that Will envied. He had the look of a man who would dare things that most men wouldn't consider—though never recklessly or foolishly. Will sensed The Blade was not a man who acted without thinking, a feeling reinforced by The Blade's recent success in the gold fields near Dahlonega.

According to Shawano, twice The Blade had been arrested by the Guard for unlawfully—in Georgia's eyes—panning gold on Cherokee land claimed by the State of Georgia; twice The Blade had given the gold to his Negro servant, Deuteronomy, for safekeeping, certain it would never occur to the Georgians that he would entrust a small fortune to a slave.

There was no doubt in Will's mind that The Blade was

both intelligent and clever. He could almost forgive him for going against his father's wishes two years ago when he left the university in the North, abandoning his education.

It was the readiness of The Blade's smile, always there, lurking just below the surface, that Will interpreted as rashness.

Will took his seat at the head of the table and wondered what The Blade would do once he understood the seriousness of the current situation. There would be a need for men like The Blade if their nation was to weather these troubled times.

He and Shawano spoke often about the future of their children and their nation. Both agreed that the old days were gone; their new leaders must be able to read and write in English, possess an education equivalent to that of the men they would be dealing with in Washington. The old order was stepping aside, content to counsel the new.

Will glanced at Temple and caught the ardent look she exchanged with The Blade. Alerted by it, he studied both, noticing for the first time the possessive gleam in The Blade's eyes and the way Temple glowed with a woman's knowledge. Only this afternoon he had tried to remind himself that she was a woman grown. Now the evidence of it was before him.

"Tell me, Will." Shawano Stuart spoke, forcing Will to redirect his attention. "What was the outcome of the council's meeting? Was it decided to send a delegation to meet with the president at his home in Tennessee?"

Before Will could reply, Victoria interposed, "For the benefit of Miss Hall, we should converse in English. She does not understand our language."

"You are right. Forgive us." Will glanced at the teacher and switched to English. "The council agreed that nothing would be accomplished by meeting with President Jackson. The stated purpose of his invitation was to discuss a new treaty that would exchange our lands here for land west of the Mississippi River. We have no desire for a new treaty.

We want the federal government to abide by the terms of our existing treaty, and this the president will not discuss."

Shawano nodded agreement with the decision, then directed his bright gaze to Eliza, although she would have been just as glad if he had ignored her. "This land has belonged to the Cherokee people from time out of mind. Before there was a government in Washington City, we were here. Before the English with their redcoats, we were here. Before the Spanish in their iron shirts, we were here. We have always been here."

"If you have a treaty, I should think you cannot be forced to leave." Admittedly, being a woman Eliza had little experience with the workings of government or politics, yet she felt her statement was a logical assumption.

"If Jackson has his way, we will." Will Gordon carved a thick slice of smoked ham and lifted it onto Shawano Stuart's plate.

"Many times the thought has come to me that if I had known on the long-ago day when we fought beside Jackson at the Horseshoe that he would one day become our enemy, I would have killed him," Shawano declared.

"Why were you fighting with Andrew Jackson?" Eliza tried to cover her shock that anyone could talk so casually about killing the president.

"It was during your War of 1812 with the British. Many Creek Indians rose up against the American settlers in Alabama," Will explained. "Jackson was a young general in command of a militia from Tennessee. Many Cherokees volunteered to fight with him. Shawano and myself were among the ones who took part in the battle at Horseshoe Bend on the Tallapoosa River."

"You should know, Miss Hall," The Blade inserted, "it was the action taken by the Cherokee soldiers that ultimately won the battle. The main body of Creeks, over a thousand strong, had erected a breastwork of logs across the neck of a peninsula of land formed by a sharp bend in the Tallapoosa River. The Cherokees were ordered across the river to prevent the Creeks from escaping. Meanwhile, Jackson gathered his remaining force of some two thousand men to make a frontal assault on the ramparts. His artillery shelled the log breastwork for two hours, without success. My father and other Cherokees could see the canoes of the Creeks on the opposite bank. Finally, the Ridge and two others swam the river and brought back two canoes. With these canoes, and others they later obtained, they crossed and recrossed the river until the entire body of Cherokee soldiers were transported to the other side. Then they attacked the Creeks from the rear. The Creeks were forced to turn to defend themselves, enabling Jackson to storm the breastworks with his men.''

''It was during this battle that Shawano Stuart received the wound that crippled his leg,'' Temple explained.

''I see,'' Eliza murmured.

''When I returned home,'' Shawano said, picking up the story, ''I found my cattle stolen, my hogs butchered, and my corn shed destroyed for firewood by soldiers in the American army, the same army that I had fought beside. Still, I and many others believed that General Andrew Jackson was a friend of the Cherokee.'' Shawano smiled ruefully. ''After he was elected president, he stated in his inaugural speech to your Congress that he would initiate legislation that would call for the removal to the West of all Indian tribes 'for their own good.' Is it any wonder that we feel we have been betrayed by a man we once called friend, Miss Eliza Hall?''

''No. None at all.'' In fact, she could quite understand how they might feel bitter toward the president.

Will Gordon continued. ''Now this removal bill specifically states that the president is authorized to seek new treaties, but in no way does it authorize the violation of existing treaties. Our existing treaties with your country guarantee forever our territorial integrity and independence. By the letter of the treaty, the government in Washington must protect us from the actions now being taken by Georgia. Now Jackson refuses. Jeremiah Evarts, with the American Board of Foreign

Missions in Boston, has recommended to Chief John Ross that we take our case to the United States Supreme Court. The council has given John Ross the authority to hire attorneys for that purpose—although how we will pay their fees, I cannot say," he admitted. "Jackson's Secretary of War refuses to give our annuity payment to the Cherokee treasury. He insists it must be divided among the Cherokee population on a per capita basis."

"Why is that wrong?" It sounded logical to Eliza that the yearly monies from a treaty should go to the people.

"Would you travel two hundred miles to receive fifty cents?" Will asked. "That is approximately the amount per individual. This is unquestionably a deliberate attempt by Jackson to deprive us of the necessary finances to pursue our case in court. Our only choice is to pool our resources to raise what funds we can and appeal to outside sources for the rest."

Eliza stared at the china plate before her, the silver cutlery, the mounds of food on the table, the people seated around it dressed in finer clothes than she owned. She was confused. Everything she had heard since she had arrived at Gordon Glen—the depredations of the Georgia Guard, the confiscation of Cherokee gold mines, the law against testimony by a Cherokee in a Georgia court, and now the actions taken by the federal government in Washington—could not all be lies.

"I fail to understand this." She frowned. "Why are they trying to force you to leave?"

"It is simple, Miss Hall," The Blade replied. "The Georgians have seen the richness of our land—the gold, the fields of cotton and corn, the fertile valleys, the comfortable farms. They want it for themselves."

His smile took most of the sting from his words. But in Eliza's mind she heard the ironic question that could have easily followed his statement: why should an Indian have it? She experienced a faint twinge of guilt. Not long ago, when she still considered all Indians to be savages, it might have been her attitude, too.

"Ignorance is a terrible thing." She was speaking of herself when she said that.

"Maybe now you understand our confusion, Miss Eliza Hall," Shawano stated. "Long ago, the white men told the Cherokees to lay down their bows and arrows and take up the plow and hoe. They said we must learn the ways of the white man so we could live together in peace. This we did. Now they say we must join the western Cherokees in Arkansas and hunt deer again."

"How ridiculous," Eliza blurted, glancing at her employer, who was impeccably dressed in a frock coat, white shirt, and blue cravat. "Can you imagine Mr. Gordon in moccasins stalking a deer with a bow and arrow in a forest?" She tried, and failed miserably.

When The Blade began to chuckle heartily, Eliza was mortified. Then his father joined him. Soon everyone at the table was laughing, including Eliza, albeit self-consciously.

Even Victoria joined in the spirit of the moment. "My husband has not touched a bow of black locust wood since he was the age of Kipp. I fear he would no longer remember how to hold it, or notch his arrow."

Her comment produced another round of laughter.

The sound of merriment drifted through the dining room's open windows to the detached kitchen outside. Phoebe stopped scraping at the fat drippings burned onto the iron skillet and glanced at the tall, lank black man leaning in the doorway of the kitchen.

"What you reckon they be laughin' at, Deu?"

"Hard to say." He straightened slowly, then turned and wandered into the kitchen. "Master Stuart, he loves to laugh. And Master Blade, he's always smiling about something."

But Phoebe was convinced there wasn't anyone who had a finer smile than Deuteronomy Jones. He was smiling at her now, and his whole face shone with it. It made his eyes dark and soft like that velvet dress Miss Victoria sometimes wore.

Deuteronomy Jones wasn't just the proudest, smartest, handsomest Negro she had ever seen; he was the nicest, too. He didn't strut around like a big rooster, crowing about hisself all the time. And he never talked down to anybody.

"Master Will, he don't hardly never smile," Phoebe admitted. "His mouth do once in t'while, but his eyes, they all the time be so sad."

"He treats you good, doesn't he?" Deu studied her closely, not liking the things he was thinking. He had never seen whip marks on her, but masters had different ways of abusing their female slaves. Phoebe was too young for a man to take her. The thin dress she wore showed a body that was just maturing.

But she had the prettiest face of any woman he knew. Her big eyes were dark and shiny like the river at night with the moon full on it. Her cheeks were round as apples, and her mouth was about as perfect as a mouth could get.

Deu had been watching her for a long time now, waiting for her to grow up. Still, she belonged to Will Gordon. Likely as not, she would marry one of his field Negroes. Two or three of them were already old enough to have a wife. He couldn't sleep at night when he thought about her with one of them. It twisted him all up inside worse than that time he had the cholera.

"He treats me fine. Miz Vi'toria too. She be sickly, tho'. That cough she got, my mama say it ain't good. Course, this be the sickly season now. Reckon when the hot days goes away, she be better."

Catching the sound of footsteps on the brick path to the kitchen, Phoebe hurriedly turned back to the iron skillet and began scraping in earnest at the burned-on drippings. Deu crossed to the water bucket and lifted the drinking gourd as Black Cassie appeared in the doorway. She shot a dark look at Deu. He had the uneasy feeling she knew exactly why he was in the kitchen and it wasn't to fetch himself a drink. He drank down the water and wandered back outside.

"What you two be doin' in here while I's gone?"

Phoebe hunched even lower over the skillet, trying to avoid her mother's suspicious eyes. "Nothin', Mama. We jus' be talkin'."

"Was you shinin' up t' him?"

"No, Mama." She flushed.

"That man be trouble, girl. Don't you be messin' 'round wid him. Does ya hear me?"

"Yes'm." But she couldn't help wondering why he was trouble. Deu wasn't bad. She had never heard him talking about running away. He liked the Stuarts. He'd said so lots of times.

The sun hung heavy above the ridge top, setting the horizon aflame with its dull red light, when Deu drove the buggy up to the front entrance of the plantation. Stopping close to the veranda steps, he wrapped the reins around the standard and climbed down to assist his crippled master.

Shawano Stuart waved him aside and hauled himself into the buggy. He dragged his dead leg into position and propped his silver-headed cane against the seat beside him. Will Gordon came over to stand next to the buggy.

Shawano smiled at him. "It was good to speak with you again, old friend."

"You and your son are always welcome in my home, Shawano."

Shawano nodded and watched as The Blade mounted his horse and rode over to the young woman waiting on the white-columned veranda. "It is good you feel this way, Will Gordon," Shawano said, noting the way young Temple gazed at his son, her expression full of a woman's invitation. "I think you will see much of one of us in the days to follow."

Shawano was pleased by what he saw. It had long been his wish that his son would want the daughter of his friend Will Gordon to be his wife. In his heart of hearts, he believed a union between these two young people would make fine sons and daughters. Each was keen of mind and possessed of a proud, strong will. Wisely, Shawano had not voiced his desire.

"It would seem so," Will Gordon replied, casting a sharp look at The Blade. "She is still young, though."

"She is a woman. You have only to look to see this."

"Perhaps." Will Gordon released a troubled sigh. "Perhaps the eyes of a father always see the child in his daughter."

"Perhaps." Shawano smiled gently. "But that does not make it so."

"I know."

Shawano looked at his son and recalled the days when his loins had burned for a woman with the same fever. But those days were long ago. Time had shriveled more than just his lame leg. With a lift of his hand in farewell, Shawano gathered the buggy reins and slapped them smartly on the horse's rump. It trotted eagerly for home.

6

U p, down, up, down. Methodically, Phoebe lifted the dasher and plunged it back into the butter churn, pausing now and then to swat at a buzzing fly or wipe the sweat from her face. It was hot, with no whisper of a breeze, not even in the shade. Sweat rolled from her, making her dress cling to her skin like a tick on a dog.

Something rustled in the azalea bush near the detached kitchen. Phoebe stopped her churning, glad for an excuse to give her aching arms a rest. She spied her younger brother crouched next to the bush, careful to keep out of sight of the house.

"Ain't you done yet?" Shadrach whispered with an impatient frown.

Phoebe slid a cautious glance at the big house, then shook her head. "Hot as it be, I reckon it'll be a spell," she whispered back, careful not to look at him.

"Jus' leave it," he urged. "Ain't nobody gonna know. Miz Vi'toria be layin' down and Mama be cleanin' de parlor. Come on fo' we miss the whole mornin'."

She hesitated, knowing how much trouble she would be in if she did leave her work. But the temptation was too great. Watching the house, Phoebe left the butter churn and stole silently to the azalea bush to join her brother. Together, they ran across the prickly, dry grass, crouching low and dashing from bush to tree on a roundabout route to the schoolhouse. At its corner, they stopped. Phoebe struggled to quiet her breathing, conscious of the quivers of excitement that trembled through her, then followed Shadrach as he crept up to the open window.

Inside, the young mistress Xandra uncertainly mumbled the alphabet. "A . . . B . . . C . . . D . . . F . . . G—"

"She forgots the E." Shadrach hissed at Phoebe, then picked up a stick and started making marks in the red dirt. "It go this way. A . . . B . . . C . . . D. . . . E . . . F . . ." He paused and frowned intently. "What do a G look like?"

But Phoebe couldn't show him the mark for a G. She didn't have as many chances to slip off as her little brother did. With him being so young and puny, he never had much work to do. But she hardly got to listen at all before her mammy or Miz Vi'toria yelled for her. She wished she knew how to make the marks like Shadrach did and what letters they stood for. But the A, the B, and the C were the only ones she knew, and those only because her brother had showed them to her at night.

Shadrach poked his head above the windowsill to peer inside. Phoebe grabbed his arm and yanked him down. "What you doin'? If we's caught, we be whupped sure."

Impatiently, he pushed her hand off. "I does this all the time. Ain't never been catched yet. Now leave me go. I gots to fine out which a G is." More cautiously this time, he rose up to look in the window.

Whispers. Eliza heard the telltale sound coming from the back of the room. She turned away from young Tom Murphy, who was reading aloud from the hornbook, and covertly scanned the cluster of pupils in the rear, looking for the culprit. Not that she could entirely blame them for letting their attention stray. The heat was stifling. She had difficulty concentrating herself. Her mind kept conjuring up images of the cool brook.

With her linen handkerchief, she dabbed at the beads of perspiration pearling above her lip, and then glanced to the back window. A dark head appeared above the sill and a pair of dark eyes looked in. It was the young Negro boy Shadrach, and it wasn't the first time Eliza had noticed him lurking outside the schoolhouse. Curious, she wandered over to the window.

The boy bobbed from sight before she reached the open window. She paused to one side of it and looked out, half expecting to see him racing away. But he was still outside the window, squatting down and writing in the dirt with a stick. His sister Phoebe was beside him.

"This be a *G*," he whispered proudly and drew a crude likeness of the letter. Surprised, Eliza stepped closer and watched Phoebe's clumsy attempt to copy the letter.

The drum of hoofbeats broke across the morning's sweltering stillness. Eliza glanced at the road that wound past the schoolhouse. Below her, there was a wild scurry of movement. When she looked back, the two black children were racing for the main house as if the devil himself were after them. She watched them go and thoughtfully considered the incident she had just witnessed.

"Miss Hall."

Eliza turned from the window, conscious again of the oppressive heat. Temple stood before her. "May I be excused? A visitor has arrived. Father is in the fields and Mother is resting. I should be on hand to welcome him in their place."

Eliza guessed the visitor was The Blade. In the past month, he had made frequent visits to Gordon Glen. Instead of responding directly to Temple's request, Eliza clapped her hands to command the attention of all her pupils. "No more lessons this morning," she announced.

* * *

Holding her skirts well clear of the ground, Temple ran across the lawn, then slowed to a sedate walk as she approached the front of the house. She rounded the corner, conscious of the heavy thudding of her heart and aware that it wasn't caused by exertion. She stopped to watch The Blade dismount, admiring his tall, whipcord-lean body.

His servant noticed her first. He said something, and The Blade turned. As she went to greet him, Temple could feel his gaze travel over her, heating her skin with its invisible touch. She felt a tingling excitement, and an odd sense of power.

"Welcome to Gordon Glen."

"The daughter of the house greets me herself. I am a fortunate man," he declared in a voice all husky and warm.

His intent gaze challenged her to come even closer. Temple started to, then stopped and turned when she heard the front door open. Black Cassie stepped onto the veranda. Smoothly, Temple turned back to The Blade. "You will be staying for dinner, won't you?"

"Yes."

"Mr. Stuart will be sharing dinner with us, Black Cassie. Make sure a place is set for him at the table."

"Yes'm, Miz Temple." She continued to stand by the door.

"Shall we go inside?"

At his nod, Temple led the way into the house. Again, she felt the strain of his presence—of being with him and not being held by him. Not once during his recent visits had she been able to manage more than an unsatisfying minute or two alone with him. Either her mother was there, or her father, or her sister and brother, or the tutor, Miss Hall.

In the great hall, she paused and glanced impatiently at Black Cassie. The Negro woman bobbed her kerchief-wrapped head respectfully as she walked by them toward the stairs.

"I be lettin' Miz Vi'toria know she gots a visitor," she said.

"No," Temple ordered sharply, then tempered her voice. "Let her rest. I will entertain Mr. Stuart until she comes down. You may go about your work."

She waited to be certain Black Cassie didn't climb the stairs, then took The Blade's hand and led him into the main parlor. Once they were out of sight, his hand tightened its grip on her fingers. Her pulse raced at the commanding pressure. She didn't pretend to resist when he turned her around and pulled her to him, slipping an arm around her waist to hold her against his body. She smiled up at him, made faintly breathless by the contact, and confident, too. This was what she had wanted, but her pleasure was doubled by the knowledge that he had been impatient for this moment as well.

The glitter in his half-closed eyes was both possessive and accusing. "I think you have given me a love potion."

"If I did, then I have drunk it, too." She slid her hands over his shirtfront, glorying in the feel of his taut muscles underneath.

When his mouth came down to cover hers, Temple indeed felt that she was drunk on some magic potion that turned her bones to liquid. Nothing else explained the fire that burned deep in the pit of her stomach and made the blood race through her veins. She was sensitive to everything—the smell of him, the taste of him, the trembling of her flesh at the slightest touch of his hands.

Eliza made certain the school was tidy before she left it to venture into the morning's heat. She could hear the giggles of the two young girls as they trailed after the boys to the brook. But she chose not to accompany them today. Instead, she followed the brick path to the house.

As she approached the detached kitchen, she saw the slave girl Phoebe sitting in its shade, straddling a butter churn and vigorously pumping the dasher up and down, her head bowed as if she were trying to avoid Eliza's notice. A second later,

Eliza spied the black girl's younger brother slinking along the log wall. She altered her course and started toward the kitchen.

"Shadrach," she called to the boy, stopping him before he could make a quick dash away. "Come here. I want to speak to you and your sister."

With feet dragging, he came slowly back. Phoebe stopped her churning and glanced guiltily at her younger brother. Eliza could almost feel both of them cringe from her. Not visibly, perhaps, but in every other way. Why? They had no reason to be afraid of her.

"What were the two of you doing outside the school window this morning?"

"Nothin', ma'am," Phoebe mumbled.

Shadrach scuffed a bare toe in the dirt, digging a small furrow. "We jus' be listenin'. We didn't mean no harm."

"Did I see you writing in the dirt with a stick?"

"Yes'm."

"This is not the first time you sat outside the window and listened, is it?" Eliza knew the answer to that, and the knowledge of it was a wondrous, exciting thing.

"No'm," he admitted reluctantly.

"Why do you sit out there?"

He glanced at his sister, then chewed uncertainly at his lower lip and shrugged.

"You were trying to learn to read and write, weren't you?" Eliza stated, inwardly thrilled. Southern bigots might scoff and say these Negro children were nothing more than monkeys copying what they saw others do. But in her heart, Eliza knew better. Here were two young minds eager to learn. No, they were more than eager, she realized. These two *hungered* to learn. There was no discovery more exciting, more challenging, or more fulfilling to a teacher than this one.

"Is you gwine t' tell Master Will?" Phoebe hunched her

shoulders forward, drawing her body into a protective ball as if anticipating punishment.

Eliza hesitated, touched by her earnest plea. "We shall see."

"We wasn't doin' no harm," Shadrach insisted, striving for defiance although the quiver in his chin made it a pathetic attempt.

"I know." A daring thought began to form in her mind. But just how she could carry it out, Eliza didn't know.

A wave of coolness washed over Eliza when she entered the plantation house. She paused, appreciating the thickness of its walls that held in the cool of the previous night and blocked the heat of the day.

The house was silent. No voices came from its rooms. Frowning, she wondered where Temple had gone. She suspected that wherever she found The Blade she would also find Temple. He was too bold for Eliza to believe that young Temple was entirely safe alone with him. She really needed to take Temple in hand and teach her that primitive passions had to be suppressed, otherwise such feelings would hold sway and lead a girl to ruin. Busy hands, brisk walks in the open air, and cold-water baths usually banished those pernicious sensations. If those failed, a camphor compress was a certain remedy.

A faint soft sound like the whisper of clothing came from the main parlor. Thinking one of the house servants was there cleaning, Eliza went to the archway to inquire after Temple's whereabouts.

Short of the opening, she came to an abrupt stop, her eyes widening in shock at the sight of Temple and The Blade locked in an embrace that could only be described as passionate, their bodies pressed so tightly together that not even a feather could slip between them. It seemed to Eliza as if The Blade were devouring Temple's lips. She suddenly felt incredibly hot all over, so hot she was almost weak at the knees. When his hand glided up to cover Temple's breast, Eliza turned and fled blindly, too shaken to remain.

In the dimness of the great hall, she didn't see the large object in front of her until it was too late. She ran right into it. Before the impact could knock her backward, she was caught and held. Dazed, Eliza stared at the collar of a man's shirt before her eyes. When she looked up, she found herself gazing at Will Gordon's face, solidly boned and strong, his brown eyes dark with concern.

She was suddenly assaulted by a hundred different impressions—the sensation of his large hands digging into the flesh of her arms, the broad band of his chest before her, the heat of his body radiating around her, the warm, heavy smell of him, and the hard planes of his body pressing against hers.

"Are you all right, Miss Hall?" A brown eyebrow arched in sharp question.

Suffused with heat, Eliza hastily pulled away. "Yes. I . . . I regret . . . I failed to see you." She groped for the words, fighting this sense of embarrassment that was totally without cause.

"Father." Temple called to him from the parlor. Eliza turned guiltily, her cheeks hotter than before. For an instant, she could only stare at the black brilliance of Temple's eyes and the softly swollen look of her lips. She looked so . . . satisfied, so alive. Something twisted inside Eliza. Involuntarily, she pressed a hand against her stomach, trying to rid herself of the awful ache. "I thought I heard someone." Temple smiled, easily and naturally, then turned to include The Blade when he stepped into view. "The Blade is here."

Seeing them together, so boldly unconcerned, as if they had done nothing wrong, Eliza had to escape. When she saw Will Gordon's gaze narrow on his daughter, she felt she was somehow to blame for Temple's lapse. She hastily murmured an excuse and hurried to the staircase.

* * *

Shortly after the noon meal was over, The Blade rode off in the company of his Negro servant, Deu. Will watched them leave.

"Are you coming in?"

Roused by Temple's question, Will turned and followed her into the house. "Young Stuart has made a habit of stopping here lately."

"I know." She smiled, looking quite pleased with the knowledge. "But I don't think you should call him *young* Stuart. He is a man, Father."

That, Will did not doubt at all. He paused momentarily, watching as Temple swept into the dining room to help her mother lock the china and silver in the glass cabinets. Hearing Victoria's dry, hacking cough, Will tried to remember when she had been young and healthy, when their love had been new and strong. So much pain, grief, and guilt had come between them with the death of their babies, yet rather than bring them together, the tragedies had made Victoria turn from him.

He started down the hall. Eliza stood at the bottom of the staircase, one hand resting on the carved newel post. He nodded to her as he walked by.

"Mr. Gordon."

He stopped and looked backward over his shoulder. "Yes?"

"I should like to speak to you . . . privately." She had that stiff, no-nonsense look on her face that she usually wore around him.

His frown deepened as he considered her request and the possible reasons for it. "Shall we step into the library?"

Eliza preceded him into the room, her back ramrod-straight and her chin jutting at a determined angle. He wondered if she was unhappy here. Did she wish to leave? Or had she encountered difficulties with one of her pupils? Kipp. Will sighed, certain his son was the cause of the requested meeting.

"What did you want to talk to me about, Miss Hall?" He walked over to his desk.

Eliza glanced at the portrait above the fireplace, then at him. Squaring her shoulders, she drew herself up to her full height. "Phoebe and Shadrach . . . the children of your house servant Cassie . . . this morning, I found them outside the school window."

"Is that all?" Will frowned. "Do not concern yourself about it, Miss Hall. I will see that it doesn't happen again."

"No. You misunderstand," she said impatiently. "Both of them seem quite eager to learn. Shadrach has taught himself to write the letters of the alphabet. That is a remarkable accomplishment, one that should be rewarded, not punished."

"What are you suggesting?"

She raised her chin a fraction of an inch higher, the light of battle gleaming in her eyes. "I want to teach them."

"What? Why?" He was stunned into sharpness. "They are blacks. What good would it do—"

"I should think it would accomplish a great deal of good," she retorted. "They have shown an inclination to learn. Why not encourage it? Surely an education would increase their value. With a farm and a house this size, accounts must be kept. If these children can be trained to do such work, it would mean less for you and Mrs. Gordon."

She went on, but Will stopped listening, taken aback by the vehemence with which she argued their cause. She reminded him of a bantam hen coming to the spirited defense of her chicks.

"Well?" she demanded.

Belatedly, he realized a silence had preceded that single challenging word. She was waiting for an answer from him. "I will consider it, Miss Hall."

She hesitated, as if debating whether to take up the cudgel again. "Whatever you decide, Mr. Gordon, I do hope you will not find it necessary to reprimand them for this morning.

They were curious. They meant no harm. Of that, I am certain."

"Is there anything else?"

"No."

When she turned and walked from the room, Will half expected her to change her mind and come back to argue further. But she didn't.

7

*D*usk settled on the ridges and spread its purple glow into the valley that was Gordon Glen. Eliza wandered along the brick path that led from the log school to the mansion, her thoughts on the less-than-satisfactory meeting with her employer. He had agreed to nothing.

They were children. Surely Will Gordon would not be so cruel as to punish them over such a small thing. It would be her fault if he did. She wished now that she had said nothing to him. Perhaps she should appeal to him again, without being so argumentative this time.

When she glanced toward the house, she saw a large figure moving silently among the trees. His height, the wide spread of his shoulders, the way he carried himself—Eliza recognized Will Gordon instantly. Seizing the opportunity, she picked up her skirts and ran quickly across the lawn to intercept him.

"Mr. Gordon." When she saw him pause she slowed her own pace, covering the last few yards at a fast walk. Unconsciously, she lifted her head, trying to appear more like a schoolteacher and less like a nervous schoolgirl. "I want to speak to you."

"Again." He sounded amused, but his face was in shadow.

She couldn't see his expression to tell whether that hint of humor was kindly meant.

"Yes." She worried he might think she was belaboring the issue, but she couldn't turn away now. Conscious of his intimidating height and breadth, Eliza tried to remember all the things she should have said to him before. "Have you—" She stopped, the fact suddenly registering that his path led to the slaves' quarters. "Where are you going?"

"To speak to Ike and Black Cassie about this business with their children and the school."

Unwilling to make a positive interpretation of his ambiguous reply, Eliza hurriedly asserted, "I want you to understand the proposal to educate young Shadrach and Phoebe was solely my idea. The children never so much as hinted that it might be possible."

"I surmised that."

"Then ... what have you decided?" She hadn't intended to demand an answer, but she sensed that he was deliberately withholding it and that irritated her. "If I am to be teaching them, I need to know."

"I question how much you will be able to teach them. They are Negroes."

"How can you say such a thing? They are human beings," Eliza protested, immediately inflamed by such a biased attitude. "They have feelings and desires that go beyond mere creature needs of food and water and a dry place to sleep. Like all of us, they need affection and the stimulus of challenge in order to grow and achieve their potential. Such expressions of ignorance I would expect to hear from a white Southerner, but for it to come from the lips of a Cherokee is beyond my comprehension. I—"

"Miss Hall." He spoke sharply, halting her tirade. "I was about to say that my wife feels it will do no harm for you to try to teach them—providing—" he added forcefully at her murmur of delight, "—they continue to do the work expected of them."

Eliza was too relieved and elated by his favorable decision to regard that as a problem. "You are going now to tell them. May I come with you?" She wanted to see their faces when they learned they would be attending school instead of listening outside its windows.

He hesitated a moment, then agreed. "Very well."

"Thank you," Eliza declared fervently, again filled with the strong sense of mission that had brought her to Gordon Glen.

Phoebe sat on the cabin's stoop, her arms tightly wrapped around her legs and her chin buried in the crevice between her knees. She was miserable. She'd been miserable scared all day, certain each time she saw Miss Victoria that she would be punished for listening outside the school window.

Shadrach wandered over and scuffed his bare feet in the dirt. He flung himself onto the bottom step, then lay back and stared up at the night sky with its glitter of stars. When he clasped his hands together on his rib-thin stomach, Phoebe thought he was fixing to pray.

"Where you reckon them animals be?"

"What animals?" Phoebe frowned.

"I heard Miz Eliza say they be animals in them stars. I been lookin' an' lookin', but I ain't seen none." He frowned in puzzlement.

"You bes' not be lettin' Mama hear you say that name," Phoebe warned and hugged herself into a tighter ball, rocking slightly in an effort to ease her misery. Inside the cabin, she could hear their mama talking worriedly to their pa.

"Bad's gwine t' come from this, Ike. I knows it. I feels it in my bones." Black Cassie shook her head.

She had been shaking her head ever since Ike had walked in the door and she had told him what happened. "You don't know that for certain sure," Ike said again.

"They's gwine to think we's bad blacks. No tellin' what

Master Will gwine t' do when she tell him. An' that teacher gwine to tell him."

Ike nodded. Black Cassie worked in the big house. She knew more about what went on there than he did, working all day like he did in the smithy. "Master Will, he be a good man."

"He ain't gwine t' keep no bad blacks," she insisted. "What we gwine to do if'n he send Phoebe and Shadrach to the fields? Li'l Shad, he ain't gots the strength fo' that."

"I knows." Ike looked at his forearms bulging with hard muscles, just like the rest of him. He had never understood how a seed from his loins could have made such a spindly boy. But Shadrach was smart. Curious about everything. It didn't surprise Ike one bit that he had been sneaking around that school.

"Ike." Black Cassie turned to face him, her eyes big and wet with fear. "What we gwine t' do if'n Master Will sells them babies of ours down the river t' work on one o' them sugar plantations?"

All along he had known that was the fear behind all this fretting of hers. It had been years since she had talked about the other children she had borne. Her previous master had sold them, same as he had sold her to Master Will. She had been grieving for them when Ike met her. And he had wanted to give her more babies so she would stop crying about the ones she'd lost. Now here she was, fixing to cry about theirs.

"That ain't gwine t' happen." Reaching out, he caught her hand and slowly drew her around the table to stand beside him. He wrapped a powerfully muscled arm around her broad hips and pulled her to him. "That ain't gwine t' happen," he repeated, but he knew deep down inside that for all his strength, he would be powerless to stop it.

Farther up the row of cabins, a dog started barking. Phoebe paid no mind to its racket until the bark changed to a sharp yelp of pain. She peered down the row, suddenly conscious of the stillness that had fallen over the quarters. There wasn't even the tin clatter of dishes being cleaned after the evening meal. All along the stoops, other blacks stood silently, looking up the path to the big house.

"Someone be comin', I think," she said. Then, through the dull glow from the cookfires, Phoebe spied the master of the plantation coming toward their cabin. Sick with fear, she scrambled to her feet and ran to the door. "It's Master Will an' he be comin' here."

"I tole you." Black Cassie hurried to the doorway. "I tole you, Ike," she said again when he joined her. She stepped outside and caught Phoebe by the shoulders, pulling her close. "You's gwine t' git the whip taken after you fo' sure." Her mother spoke in a scolding fashion, but Phoebe felt the trembling of fear in her mama's hands and knew she was scared for them, as scared as Phoebe was.

"It be okay," Shadrach turned a beaming look at them. "Miz Eliza be wid him."

Eliza walked with Will Gordon down the row of slave cabins, smiling and nodding to the families of blacks gathered outside their crude hovels. Except for a rare "Evenin', Master Will," most were silent, responding with wary stares and closed-up expressions. She felt like an intruder, unwelcome and unwanted in their midst. Instinctively, she edged closer to Will Gordon.

The air was scented with the wood smoke from their cookfires. Most were banked for the evening, but the dying glow was reflected in the watchful eyes of the blacks.

As they approached the last cabin, Eliza saw young Shadrach obey the gesturing admonitions of his mother and climb the steps to stand beside his sister. He showed no fear.

"Evenin', Master Will." The deep-voiced greeting came from Ike, standing next to Cassie. Eliza was somewhat shocked to see he was without a shirt. One suspender diagonally crossed a gleaming black chest, a chest with the muscles of Samson. Eliza quickly averted her gaze, embarrassed by his nakedness.

"Ike, Black Cassie." Will Gordon stopped well short of the steps. "I have come about your children, Phoebe and young Shadrach. They were outside of school this morning, listening to the lessons. I understand this is not the first time."

"Ain't never gwine t' happen again, Master Will," Black Cassie declared. "I swears they won't go near that school again. Me an' Ike, we talked to them good and tole 'em they be bad. They be sorry fo' it. They truly be. Me an' Ike's told them if they ever catched near that school again, we's gwine t' whip 'em ourself."

"Miss Hall wants them to come to school and learn to read and write and do their numbers. She believes she can teach them." Will Gordon slid a brief, skeptical glance in Eliza's direction. Eliza was too busy watching the faces of her new pupils to notice. Shadrach opened his mouth in wonder, his dark eyes fairly dancing with excitement, but Phoebe just stared, as if unwilling to believe him.

"Hear that?" Shadrach turned excitedly to his sister, but Black Cassie quickly shushed him.

"Tomorrow morning Phoebe and Shadrach are to report to Miss Hall at the school to begin their lessons."

"They be there, Master Will," Ike promised solemnly, earning a sharp glare from his wife.

"I want it understood, however," Will Gordon warned, "Miss Victoria will expect them to do their work the same as before."

Heads bobbed in assent to his condition, all except Black Cassie's. She alone showed no liking for the turn of events. Eliza wondered at that. As a mother, she should have been pleased that her children were to be educated. Shadrach and Phoebe were certainly happy about it, and that was all that mattered to Eliza as she left the cabin with Will Gordon.

"We gwine t' learn 'bout readin' an' writin', Shad." Phoebe

was still afraid to believe it. At the same time, she could hardly wait to tell Deuteronomy Jones. Why, in no time at all she'd be smart just like him.

"I knows. Ain't it the mos' wonderful thing." Happiness fairly burst from him.

Mindless of their joy, Cassie turned on Ike. "Why'd you say they could go? Ain't no good gwine t' come from it. All that larnin' jus' gwine t' fill their heads wid foolish thoughts about bein' free. They be slaves. Ain't no place in this world fo' a black wid book-larnin'."

"Mebbe the world'll change, Cassie."

"Nothin' never gwine t' be no different. I wishes that Eliza woman never come here. She jus' bring misery on us and we gots enough o' that."

When Ike tried to put his arm around her, Cassie pulled away and stalked into the cabin. Ike stared after her, understanding the fear that gripped her but not agreeing with her. Master Will was a smart man, a good man, and Ike had heard him say more than once that the Cherokees needed to know the white man's books and laws if they were to stay free. Ike didn't know much beyond sharpening a plowshare, fixing a wheel, and shoeing a horse, but it made sense to him that if a white man's learning was good for the Cherokees, it would be good for blacks. Rising up against the master never got any slave his freedom. Maybe the Cherokee way was the right one.

When Eliza arrived at the schoolhouse the next morning, her two new pupils were outside waiting for her. Shy yet eager, they followed her inside and wandered about the single room, looking at everything while touching nothing. She let them explore on their own until she saw Shadrach intently studying the globe atop its pedestal in the corner.

"That is a globe of the world, Shadrach," she explained. "And this is approximately where Gordon Glen is located."

She pointed it out to him, then gave the globe a half turn. "And this is Africa, where you came from."

A bewildered frown creased his forehead. "How could that be? I be born right here on this plantation. I wasn't borned in no Africa."

"Perhaps not, but your parents or grandparents were brought here as slaves from Africa."

"How does you know that?"

"Because all the black people originally came here from Africa. In Africa, all the aborigines have black skin, like you."

"What's a aborigeez?"

"A native. Someone who lived in a land before the white men came . . . Like the Cherokees are natives of these mountains."

Kipp burst into the school and came to an abrupt stop when he saw Phoebe and Shadrach. "What are they doing here?" He scowled.

"Phoebe and Shadrach are my new pupils. They will be attending school with you from now on," Eliza explained, smiling at her new charges.

"Slaves don't belong here." He glared at them, haughty in his disdain. "They are too stupid to learn anything."

"That is how the Georgia Guard feels about the Cherokees," Eliza replied.

Saying nothing, Kipp included her in his baleful look. Eliza hadn't anticipated hostility from her other pupils. But there was little time to dwell on it as the rest of her students filed in to begin the morning session.

Thankfully as far as Eliza was concerned, none openly expressed Kipp's animus toward the two black children. In fact, the younger children, nine-year-old Joe Murphy and seven-year-old Xandra, seemed unconcerned by them. The rest, including Temple, were reserved and silent, but the opposition was there.

Eliza began the morning session with a prayer, reminding

her students of the Golden Rule and hoping that God would bring harmony back to her school. But no such miracle occurred. Later, when she divided her class according to the Lancastrian method and began assigning monitors, Kipp stood up.

"I will not be a monitor to those servants," he stated.

The silence in the room was crushing. Eliza sensed that all were waiting to see how she dealt with this challenge to her authority. "I have no intention of assigning you to be their monitor, Kipp. For that I will require someone who is intelligent. Perhaps someday that will be you, but not at the present."

An embarrassed rage mottled his face, and Eliza knew she had stung his vanity. Kipp believed he was the smartest. In truth, Eliza suspected that he was, but he already had too high an opinion of himself and deserved to be taken down a peg or two.

"That is not true."

"Do not embarrass yourself further by displaying your ignorance before everyone, Kipp. Please sit down." She carefully hid a smile when someone snickered.

Kipp scoured the room with a glowering look, seeking the child who had dared to laugh at him, but too many faces held suppressed smiles. Sullenly, he took his seat.

The following Sunday, the family attended the religious service held at the nearby Moravian church. Although a Presbyterian, Eliza had made it a practice to accompany the Gordons to their church.

When the services were over, the congregation gathered outside to socialize and exchange news. As usual, most conversations centered on recent harassments by the Georgia militia and rumors of proposed action to be taken. As a member of the National Council, Will Gordon was always at the center of these discussions. Everyone looked to him for answers.

Temple listened as her father explained to others that the

Baltimore lawyer William Wirt had offered his services to Chief John Ross to represent the Cherokee Nation before the Supreme Court of the United States.

When the congregation broke up to return to their respective homes, Temple walked with her father to their carriage. "What do you know of this William Wirt?" she inquired. "Is he the caliber of a Philadelphia lawyer?"

"Jeremiah Evarts of the American Board of Foreign Missions recommended him highly. Mr. Wirt held the post of attorney general of the United States for twelve years. Payton Fletcher has advised me that Wirt is considered to be a strict constitutionalist and Jackson has no use for that sort."

"I see." But Temple wasn't altogether sure she understood the significance of that. "When will Mr. Wirt go before the Supreme Court on behalf of the Cherokees?"

"When he finds a test case to bring before them. That shouldn't be difficult. Georgia has arrested many Cherokees for digging gold in our mountains. If any are jailed by the Georgia courts, Mr. Wirt can bring a claim of false imprisonment before the Supreme Court bench on the grounds that Georgia has no jurisdiction over our lands."

"But what does that solve?" Temple frowned.

"The issue of ownership. Georgia claims the land belongs to them. We say it is ours. If the Court rules against the State of Georgia, they are verifying the land belongs to us."

"And if Georgia doesn't own it, they cannot force us to leave."

"No."

She paused by the carriage's raised step and tilted her head back to view him from beneath the brim of her bonnet. "Then we have nothing to worry about, do we? This land was given to us by treaty, and the Supreme Court will have to rule in our favor."

"That is what we believe," Will said, then turned as Victoria approached, carrying their youngest.

Temple was relieved. The Blade was not as confident as

her father that the Cherokees would be fairly treated, and his doubts frightened her. She watched as her father helped her mother and then Miss Hall into the carriage. She took a seat opposite Victoria, who, after settling the baby on her lap, directed a wan smile at Eliza.

"How are the children progressing in school, Miss Hall?"

"Quite well, Mrs. Gordon."

"And your new pupils, Shadrach and Phoebe?"

"Extremely well," Eliza asserted, feeling defensive. "Shadrach has shown a particular aptitude for learning."

"Then you have had no difficulties with them?" Victoria said with mild surprise.

"None." But Temple saw Eliza glance toward Kipp.

Although her brother hadn't repeated his objection to the presence of Phoebe and Shadrach in the classroom, he had expressed his hostility toward them in other ways, taking malicious delight in any mistake they made and seeking every opportunity to torment them unmercifully outside of school. At times his abuse had bordered on cruelty. Yet Eliza did not bring his behavior to her employer's attention. The tutor's discretion pleased Temple. She hoped the Supreme Court judges would hold as wise a counsel as Miss Elizabeth Hall.

8

"You are a poor correspondent." Eliza turned a look of mild reproval on her unexpected visitor, the gangly minister Nathan Cole, who had accompanied her on her journey to this mountain frontier. "It has been weeks since your last letter."

In truth, Eliza had received one brief letter from him in answer to her rather lengthy epistle describing her new home at Gordon Glen. When her second letter met with no reply, she had refrained from writing a third.

"I apologize for that. I was away preaching in the mountains. When I learned I would soon be traveling this way . . ." He paused self-consciously. "I confess, I am a poor man with a pen. When I read your letters, it is as though you are in the room talking to me. Mine, I fear, are cold and stilted."

Eliza couldn't agree with him more, but she was too happy to see him to criticize. "Whatever your reason, I forgive you. You are here now and that is enough."

"I couldn't pass this way without calling to see how you were faring." He walked beside her, looking gawky and awkward, all arms and legs. Everything about him was exactly as Eliza remembered, from his thin face and straw-colored hair to his soulfully kind eyes. She found it difficult to believe that nearly three months had passed since last she had seen the young minister. Yet September was upon them, bringing milder days to Gordon Glen and ending summer's reign of heat. Eliza was grateful for that, and for the chance to have someone with whom she could talk freely.

As they strolled among the strutting peacocks on the lawn, she shared her recent triumph with Nathan Cole—her success in persuading the Gordons to let her teach the two slave children—and her trials, particularly her current situation with Kipp.

"His resentment of them borders on hatred," Eliza admitted. "I never expected to encounter such prejudice from . . . well, Indians."

"The attitude of the Cherokees is no different from many of the Southern whites'. They regard themselves as superior to the Africans. Although sometimes I think the Cherokees are slightly more arrogant."

"The entire practice of slavery is one I find intolerable. It should be regarded as a mortal sin."

"I know. In my heart, I cannot believe God intended for men to own other men. Yet when one reads the Scriptures, there are a number of passages that relate to slavery. Some of the missionaries hire slaves from their masters and then pay them a little extra so they can earn money to buy their freedom. The number is insignificant, though."

"But the gesture is a statement in itself." Eliza considered it a noble and laudable act, one that she quite admired. She had always believed one person could make a difference. It was that belief, more than any other, that had brought her to this place.

"I suppose it is."

The peacocks set up a noisy cry, ceasing their vain swagger to scramble about in alarm. Automatically, Eliza glanced toward the road leading to the plantation's manor house. A horse and rider cantered into view.

"They are more reliable than dogs in warning you of someone's approach," she said to Nathan, raising her voice to make herself heard above their racket.

"Such a terrible sound to come from such beautiful fowl." He smiled ruefully at their noise, then turned to gaze at the approaching rider. "More company?"

"The Blade Stuart. He comes regularly to court Temple." She tried to sound matter-of-fact about it, but the very subject of Temple and The Blade made her uncomfortable. Nathan Cole was a minister and she found it impossible to discuss her concern for Temple's virtue with him. She started walking again, angling away from the house so they wouldn't witness the meeting between Temple and The Blade, meetings that always seemed to be marked by the throb of passion just below the surface. "Tell me what you have been doing. You said you went into the mountains."

"Yes. There are many Cherokees who live in isolated cabins, venturing out one or two times a year." His glance swept their surroundings, taking in the bricked paths, the lawn, the ornamental shrubs, the numerous outbuildings of the plantation, and finally, the imposing brick mansion itself. "Not all Cherokees are as affluent as your Mr. Gordon. Many live in humble log cabins and farm a small patch of ground, raising only enough to feed their families. These are the ones we seek to reach now."

The living conditions he described were what she had expected to find when she arrived here, Eliza recalled. "And were you well received by them?"

"Yes." A musing smile curved his mouth, giving a roundness to his thin cheeks. "They have names for the missionaries from the different religions. The Presbyterians are called the Soft Talkers. The Baptists are known as the Baptizers. And the Methodists are called the Loud Talkers." Eliza laughed, finding the descriptions aptly matched the representatives that she'd met of the various sects. Encouraged by her reaction, Nathan Cole went on. "At one farm where I stopped, an old Cherokee by the name of Buffalo Killer asked me to tell him a story from the talking leaves—that's their phrase for a book. You should have seen him, Eliza . . . Miss Hall," he quickly corrected himself, a flush of red creeping up his neck at his inadvertent familiarity.

"You may call me Eliza."

"If you call me Nathan," he offered with a touching hesitancy.

"Very well, Nathan," she replied.

"Yes . . . uh . . . well, as I was saying, I wish you could have seen Buffalo Killer. He had snow white hair down to his shoulders, and he wore a red-and-yellow-striped turban on his head with a feather plume sticking out the back. His shirt was made of homespun and he wore buckskin breeches and beaded moccasins that came all the way up to his knees. He smoked a pipe continuously while I was there. Anyway, I told him the story of Christ and explained to him about the Bible and the teachings of Christ. When I finished, he was silent for a moment, then nodded very solemnly and said, 'The things you have told me are good. But my mind wonders—if the palefaces have known the message of the talking leaves for this many winters, why have *they* not become good?"

Considering the current situation between the Cherokees and the Georgians, Eliza regarded the question as a sadly accurate observation. "How did you answer him?"

"I had to admit there were many white men who failed to follow the teachings of Christ. I had the impression Buffalo Killer thought I should be carrying the Word of Christ to them."

"Sometimes I think a good thrashing is what these members of the so-called Georgia Guard truly deserve."

"Eliza." Nathan stared at her, surprised by the violence inherent in her remark.

"It's true," she asserted. "They are behaving like greedy little bullies trying to take something that doesn't belong to

them. I would not tolerate such behavior in my classroom."
She looked at him. "Does that shock you?"

He paused, then shook his head. "I agree disciplinary action
should be taken by the proper authorities."

"That is what the Cherokees are doing." Eliza went on to
tell him about the efforts being made by Chief Ross and the
National Council to bring their plight to the attention of the
Supreme Court. The recent murder conviction of a Cherokee
named George Corn Tassel had provided attorney William
Wirt with the test case he needed.

It troubled Nathan that Eliza was becoming embroiled in the
legal maneuverings going on. Such things were the province of
men. It was embarrassing and unbecoming that she should
take such an interest in them. He found it most uncomfortable
himself.

When Will Gordon returned from the fields shortly before the
evening meal, Eliza was obliged to introduce him to her
visitor. Will immediately insisted the young missionary stay
the night and continue his journey in the morning, an invitation
Victoria quickly seconded. After mildly protesting the incon-
venience to them, Nathan agreed.

When the meal was finished, they withdrew as usual to the
family parlor. Will Gordon poured a measure of brandy for
himself and another dinner guest, The Blade. Nathan
abstained.

Eliza sat at the rosewood piano as she did most evenings.
Instinctively, she began playing her favorite nocturne. One
song seemed to flow into another. Eliza was only vaguely
aware when Victoria Gordon excused herself to tuck the children into bed.

After several selections, she finally paused and glanced at
Nathan. He sat in a wing chair facing the piano. "Is there a
particular song you would like to hear?"

"No." He shook his head. "You play like an angel, Eliza."

"I have thought that myself," Will Gordon agreed, glancing up as his wife rejoined them.

"I have a request," The Blade inserted. "Do you know any music suitable for a quadrille, Miss Hall?"

Eliza hesitated a moment. "I believe so, yes."

"Temple says she has never danced it." He cast a challenging look at Temple. "This would be the perfect opportunity to teach her. You know the steps, do you not, Will?"

Briefly taken aback, Will Gordon frowned. "It has been years, but . . . Do you remember them, Victoria?" He turned to his wife.

"I think so." She laughed hesitantly. "I am not sure."

"Doesn't it require four couples to form the square?" Will frowned.

"Temple can learn it with two." Without waiting for them to agree, The Blade began moving furniture to clear a space in the center of the room. Everyone joined in to help except Eliza. She tentatively played the tune, trying to refresh her memory of the melody.

When all was in readiness, The Blade nodded to her, and Eliza struck the opening chord. She partially turned to watch, keeping the tempo slow as The Blade led Temple through the pattern.

The second time through, she played the song at its normal tempo and smiled briefly at Nathan when he came to stand beside the piano. Laughter accompanied the moments of confusion by the dancers. Eliza smiled along with them, never losing a note.

Soft as a murmuring breeze, the music drifted from the parlor into the night, its melody faint, too faint for Deuteronomy Jones to recognize. He waited on the hard wooden bench that ran along the outer wall of the detached kitchen, well within earshot of the house should his master call. Pale amber light streamed from the windows of the big house, laying a long trail on the ground and holding the darkness at bay. Deu was beyond its reach, sitting in the shadows.

The evening breeze, redolent with apples, whispered around him. It was harvesttime in the apple orchards of Gordon Glen. The sheds bulged with crates of red, ripe apples ready for shipment to southern ports. For now, the cider mill was silent, but come morning, it would be running again, crushing more apples and releasing the sweet smell of their pulp into the air; the kettles in the plantation's kitchens would be bubbling with more fruit being cooked into applesauce, apple butter, and preserves.

From the woods near the mill, Deu could hear the grunts of hogs greedily rooting through the discarded mash and skins. He huddled deeper in his coat, knowing how good a mug of hot cider would taste right now.

A dark figure hurried across the grass toward him, and inside himself everything tightened up. It was Phoebe, of the shy and dancing eyes. Forgetting the night's chill, Deu stood up, warmed by the gladness singing through him. When she stopped before him and gazed up with such timid eagerness, Deu wanted to look at her forever.

"I brung—I brought you some hot cider. I spilled some, tho', and it's prolly just warm now, but ... " Jerkily, she thrust the tin cup at him, along with an object in her other hand. "Here's an apple fritter, too. It's okay," she hurried to assure him. "Dat ... that reverend didn't eat his and I hid it away when I was clearin' the table. No one'll know I gives—gave it to you."

"I was wishing for some cider." When he took the items from her, Deu felt the coolness of her fingers, then noticed the way she quickly wrapped the old shawl more tightly around her shoulders once her hands were free. "Are you cold? Maybe you should drink this." He glanced at the thinness of her dress.

"No, it's for you," she insisted, then looked over her shoulder in the direction of the slave quarters, as if she should go back.

"Can you sit with me awhile?" Deu didn't want her to

leave, not yet. It didn't seem to matter how many times he told himself she was too young. Each time he was around her it was harder not to touch her.

"For a spell, mebbe." She tipped her head down, avoiding his eyes, but he saw her lips curve in a smile, and he knew she was glad he had invited her. Was she? Did she want to be with him? he wondered, conscious of the sudden leaping of his heart. She moved past him and sat down on the wooden bench. Deu gulped down a swallow of cider, barely tasting the tepid liquid, then sat next to her, careful not to sit too close. "You like de—the fritter?" she asked. "I made it m'self."

"I like it fine." Deu quickly took his first bite of it, his teeth crunching through the crisply fried batter that enclosed the spiced apple mix. After a couple of hurried chews, he washed it down with another drink of cider. "How have you been? I haven't talked to you in a while. Lately, every time I've been here your mama's had you busy at something."

"There's been lots of work to do, what with the apples and all."

"I get the feeling sometimes that your mama's glad of that. I don't think she likes me much." He finished the rest of the fritter and wiped his hand on the leg of his pants, still thinking about her mother.

"She likes you fine. It's just that . . . well . . . " She was reluctant to tell Deu that her mother blamed him for her interest in book-learning. "I guess you could say she's got a case of the grumps. She and Pa've been going round and round, and that's made her sharp with just about everybody."

"I'm glad I'm not the cause of it."

"Did you hear Master Will is letting me and Shadrach go to school in the mornings?" Phoebe saw his glance of surprise, and smiled proudly. "We's—we're learning how to read and write and do our numbers, and about geography and things like that. I can read real good, and I can write my name, too.

I'll show you." She picked up a twig from the ground and, bending forward, began to write her name in the red clay at their feet, printing the letters with painstaking care as she spelled them aloud. "*P* . . . *H* . . . *O* . . . *E* . . *B* . . . *E*. Phoebe." She straightened to study the drawn furrows faintly visible in the light from the house windows, then turned her head to look at Deu, almost bursting with pride at her accomplishment. "See?"

He leaned closer to look at her name. "That's very good, Phoebe." He nodded approvingly. She was almost certain that when he glanced at her, there was a new respect in his eyes. She wasn't a dumb nigger anymore; she was smart, like him. "Can you write *my* name?" he asked.

Phoebe faltered for an instant. "I don't know how to spell it. But I could, if I did."

"I'll help you." Deu crouched down on one knee and smoothed a long patch of dirt with his hand. "Come here."

She hesitated briefly, then knelt beside him, trembling and half sick with excitement. "The first letter is *D*," he told her. Phoebe desperately wanted to impress him with her knowledge and skill, but when she tried to draw it, her hand shook, making the first line squiggly. Hurriedly, she wiped away her mistake, conscious of Deu shifting his position and moving to kneel behind her right shoulder. She was about to start again when his hand closed around her fingers, tightening her grip on the stick.

"Your hands are as cold as a mountain stream in winter."

"I know," Phoebe whispered, but they didn't feel cold to her. His hand covering hers felt like a fire shooting up her arm and heating her skin. He was close, so close his body almost touched hers, his breath sweet with the smell of cider. She felt weak and all aflutter inside, afraid to move and afraid not to.

"It goes like this." Although she continued to hold the stick, he guided it. "*D* . . . *E* . . . *U* . . . *T* . . *E* . . . *R* . . . *O*

... *N* ... *O* ... *M* ... *Y.* Deuteronomy. *J* ... *O* ... *N* ... *E* ... *S.* Jones. Deuteronomy Jones." He leaned back, and Phoebe could feel him looking at her. "It's a long name."

"I'm glad," she said softly, surprised by her own boldness, and at the same time aware that his hand still loosely gripped hers. She liked the sensation and wanted it to go on and on. Slowly, she turned to look back at him, aching with the wish that he would feel the same way.

Deu stared at her rapt face. The longing in her beautiful dark eyes was more than he could stand. A tightness constricted his throat, making it impossible for him to swallow or breathe. The tightness spread, gripping the rest of his body, knotting him up inside until he thought he would die with wanting her. His gaze inadvertently shifted to her lips, soft and innocently inviting. The sight pulled him.

He didn't remember moving. He didn't remember anything until he felt the tentative pressure of her lips, warm and tantalizingly eager, against his own. He hadn't meant to kiss her, but now he couldn't stop himself. Hungrily, he tasted the ripe curves of her mouth as it melted against his like wild honey on the tongue.

Deu felt the touch of a hand sliding inside his coat. The contact seared through his shirt. He stiffened, discovering that his fingers held the stick alone. An instant later, he felt the press of her body against his—and the childishly small mounds of her breasts. Abruptly, he pulled away and shot to his feet, hot with shame and guilt.

"Deu?" Her questioning voice sounded small and faint. "What's ... what's wrong?"

"It's late ... and it's cold. You better get yourself home before your mama comes looking for you," he said curtly. The hurt in her eyes made him feel worse. "Don't look at me that way. Don't you understand, Phoebe? I shouldn't have done that."

She scrambled to her feet, catching at the trailing ends of her shawl as she moved toward him. "But I wanted you to."

"You shouldn't have." Deu was angry with her for saying that, angry because it made him want to kiss her again. "You're just a girl, Phoebe. Too young to be ... letting a man near you."

She stood before him, innocent and trusting, and so beautiful he wanted to groan with the ache he felt. "My mammy was only a year older than me when she had her first baby."

He did groan. "Phoebe ... don't."

"Didn't you like kissing me, Deu?"

The simple question unleashed a whole new torrent of feeling. "You know I did," he murmured thickly.

A wide smile split her face, revealing a set of teeth white as pearls. "So did I."

When she swayed toward him, he started to reach out— to check her movement or to take her in his arms, he wasn't sure which. Before he could find out, a deep-voiced summons came from the front veranda of the big house. "Deu. Deuteronomy!"

Recognizing the voice of Master Blade, Deu swung instantly toward the sound, a part of him relieved by the interruption. "Here, sir," he called in answer and cast one last glance at Phoebe before breaking into a run away from her.

When he reached the bottom of the side steps leading to the columned veranda, he saw The Blade at the top. "Fetch the horses. It is time to leave." Behind him, the front door opened and Temple stepped out, a shawl draped over her head, one end flung over her shoulder.

"Yes, sir." Deu backed up a couple of steps, then turned and headed off across the lawn to the stables.

The Blade watched him disappear into the night's shadows. Although aware of Temple's presence behind him, he resisted the impulse to turn and continued to stare into the darkness instead. Breathing in the crispness of the air, he felt that old restlessness return, the urge for action, something that would challenge both his brain and his muscle. More than once this past summer he had toyed with the idea of returning to the gold fields. It wasn't the gold that lured him. It was the game of danger, pitting his skills and cunning against the Georgians. He missed it.

His father wanted him to stay. He had openly encouraged him to see Temple. But The Blade wasn't sure he was ready to settle down to the tame life of a planter and the responsibility that came with it. As for marriage, a wife and a family, it sounded equally restricting.

Still . . . there was Temple. She aroused, stimulated, and challenged him as no other woman had. He wanted her more fully, more deeply, than any woman he had known in the past. After the monotony of a day spent supervising the work of the field slaves, it would be consolation to think of Temple in his bed at night. He smiled, conscious of the stirring in his loins at the mere thought.

"What are you looking at?" Temple's low-pitched voice came to him at almost the same instant that he breathed in her lavender scent. She was very near him.

Yet The Blade didn't turn. Instead, he lifted his glance to the diamondlike stars sprinkled over the dark cloth of night. "The sky. See it," he said, nodding faintly. "It has the blackness of your hair and the brightness of your eyes." Slowly, he swung to face her, feeling the heavy thudding of his heart.

"You have your father's eloquence." She smiled.

The Blade took half a step toward her, then paused. "And your father, where is he?" His glance flicked to the front door beyond her.

"With Mother. She started coughing again. I told him I would give his good-byes to you."

Even before he reached out to take her in his arms, Temple saw the desire in his eyes and anticipated his action. Too few times were they alone, away from spying eyes. She stepped into his embrace, impelled by her own needs more than the commanding pressure of his hands. Tilting her head back, she kissed him long and hungrily, thrilling to the caress of his hands on her spine and the demanding ardor of his lips. Straining to get closer, she pressed her body tightly against his hard frame and wound her arms around his neck, dragging her mouth across his cheek to nuzzle the lobe of his ear.

"I wish you didn't have to leave," she whispered.

"Are you afraid I won't come back?" he teased, then realized she never asked when he would be coming back—as if never doubting for a moment he would. It irritated him that she was so confident of the hold she had on him.

She drew her head back to look at him, her lips all swollen and soft from his kiss. "If you didn't, I would come after you," she declared.

"Would you?" The Blade stared, distracted by the sensation of her body thrust firmly against his hips.

"Yes." She wiggled slightly against him. He had the feeling that she knew precisely what she was doing. "Miss Hall says I have no shame."

"I am glad you do not." He smiled.

"So am I." She reached up and lightly traced the outline of his mouth with her fingers.

The Blade felt a groan rising in his throat and struggled to contain it as he caught hold of her hand, stopping its stimulating tease. He pulled her closer, intending to kiss her again, but from the lane came the steady clop of horses' hooves on the hard-packed ground. Deu was coming. He muttered a curse in Cherokee, and Temple laughed softly, then pulled away to rearrange her shawl to its former order.

"If you were a man, you would not find it so amusing."

"If I were a man, I hope you would not have this reaction," she said and laughed again, then walked to the front steps that led to the circular drive.

Starlight silhouetted a horse and rider followed by a second saddled horse emerging from the shadows of the trees. Without a word, The Blade walked past her and down the steps. He didn't wait for Deu to dismount. Instead, he took the reins to his horse and swung into the saddle, disdaining the aid of its stirrup.

"Give my respects to your father," Temple said once he was astride. "Tell him to come see us. We have missed his visits."

The Blade nodded, then touched a heel to the big chestnut gelding. It bounded forward, but he quickly checked it to a trot. Deu swung in behind him as they rode from the house along the circular lane. Halfway down the circular drive, The Blade caught a movement among the trees to his right. When he turned, a young Negro girl waved shyly at them.

In the parlor, Eliza looked on anxiously as Will Gordon gave his wife a sip of brandy. The pallor of the woman's face worried her. Her skin seemed almost translucent, blue veins showing through emphasizing her ghostly color. Victoria Gordon coughed again as the tumbler was taken from her lips, but it was an involuntary reaction to the strong liquor rather than the onslaught of another attack.

"Forgive me for being such a poor hostess, Reverend Cole," Victoria said, her voice hardly more than a whisper.

"Please do not concern yourself with me, Mrs. Gordon. After the hospitality you have shown today, no one could ask for better," Nathan assured her, his angular features gentled by a caring smile. "Rest is what you need now. And a poor guest I would be if I didn't allow you to take it."

"Rest she will get," Will Gordon declared firmly, setting the brandy glass aside. "I will take you upstairs."

"But I——" Her glance darted frantically around the room, taking in the dirty glasses and the ashtrays filled with charred pipe tobacco.

"Now," he stated. "Temple can see that Black Cassie clears this."

Eliza stood by and watched as Will Gordon carried his wife from the room as effortlessly as if she were their seven-year-old daughter. Instinctively, Eliza trailed after them and paused in the great hall.

"This cough of Mrs. Gordon's . . . " Nathan hesitated. "Has she recently recovered from a bout with pneumonia?"

"No. At least, not since I arrived at Gordon Glen," Eliza replied. "She merely has these coughing spells."

"An aunt of mine had attacks like that. It went on for years and years. Slowly, she seemed to . . . waste away." He glanced at Eliza. "She had consumption."

A breath caught in her throat. She looked up the stairs, wondering if Will Gordon knew the gravity of his wife's condition and if she should tell him. "Come. I will show you to your room."

Nathan was a step behind her when they started up the staircase. "Will you accompany the Gordons to the annual council meeting in October?"

"Yes."

"I have been assigned to the mission church at New Echota. I will be there too. I enjoyed our long talk this afternoon. Perhaps we will have the opportunity to do it again next month."

"I would like that," Eliza said, and meant it.

9

New Echota
October 1830

"Allow me to introduce our tutor from Massachusetts, Miss Eliza Hall." Will Gordon spoke in a voice reverent with respect, addressing his words to the unprepossessing man before her. "Miss Hall, this is the principal chief of the Cherokees, John Ross."

Face to face with the executive leader of the Cherokee Nation, Eliza struggled against a sense of disappointment. After all the talk she had heard about John Ross, she had expected someone with the physical stature and presence of Will Gordon, someone surrounded by an aura of quiet dignity and authority. Instead, she was confronted by a man of medium build and average height, with straight brown hair, a slightly florid complexion, and brown eyes. In short, there was nothing particularly striking about him at all.

"It is a pleasure, Miss Hall." He addressed her in English, prompting Eliza to recall that his command of the Cherokee language was reportedly poor. "I am told you play the piano as sweetly as the whippoorwill sings. Perhaps the next time I have the privilege of stopping by Gordon Glen, you would honor me with your music."

"I should be delighted, but . . . how did you know?" Eliza blurted in confusion.

"A certain young missionary by the name of Nathan Cole remarked on your ability," John Ross replied. "I believe you are acquainted with him."

"I am, yes." She nodded awkwardly.

Eliza was grateful that his attention reverted to her employer. John Ross exchanged a few more words with him, then moved on, wending his way slowly through the respectful throng that had gathered to see him. Everywhere, the Cherokee leader was treated with a deference that bordered on awe.

Eliza watched until he was swallowed by the crowd. She turned to Temple and discovered The Blade had joined them. She felt the stirrings of discomfort and unease that always gripped her whenever the three were together. She worried about Temple and his effect on her, and the heat that flowed between them, transmitted by a mere glance, made Eliza decidedly more uncomfortable.

After a brief exchange of greetings, The Blade asked, "What did you think of our chief, John Ross?"

"I think he is unquestionably a man of the people." Despite her initial reaction, Eliza refused to judge the man on his looks. She knew quite well there was no correlation between a person's appearance and his or her abilities. "It was good to find someone as humble as John Ross holding such a great office."

"Indeed." The Blade nodded his agreement, then asked curiously, "Is this your first visit to New Echota, Miss Hall?"

"It is, yes. To be frank, I had not realized so many people would gather here for the annual meeting of your National Council."

Whole families had spilled from the scarlet and gold foothills, coming from every corner of the Nation to fill the one-hundred-acre townsite. Tents surrounded the tidy capital city, springing up like mushrooms after a rain, and the wood smoke of campfires hung in the autumn air.

Despite the many serious issues to be addressed by the convening council, it was still a social time for the Cherokee people, with families reuniting after months, or sometimes years, of separation. It was a festive, pulsing scene that both fascinated and invigorated Eliza.

"Take a good look and remember," The Blade advised her. "This may be the last time the Cherokee will assemble like this in the capital of our nation."

"Don't say that," Temple flared.

Smoothly meeting her angry look, he replied, "I am only saying what others think but are afraid to voice."

"To even think it is an admission of defeat."

"Temple, the State of Georgia has issued a decree that makes it unlawful for us to meet on the soil of Georgia," The Blade reminded her, exhibiting the tolerant patience of an adult with a child.

"This is not Georgia. It is the heart of the Cherokee Nation," she retorted.

"So we say," he murmured dryly. "But how long do you think Georgia will permit us to defy her orders?"

"How can you talk that way?" she demanded impatiently.

"I am only describing the situation as it exists. If the Georgia Guard rode in right now, we would have no choice but to hold our council meeting at another site—one beyond their reach . . . to the north in Tennessee, or west in Alabama. You know I speak the truth."

"Perhaps." Temple shrugged with deliberate indifference. "But that will all change. The lawyers that Chief John Ross engaged are already appealing our case to the Supreme Court. When it rules in our favor, the federal government in Washington will have to enforce the terms of our treaty with them and protect us against the Georgians. Father says it is merely a matter of time."

"Time," The Blade repeated wryly. He would never possess such remarkable forbearance over the wrongs being committed against the Cherokees.

Temple touched Eliza's arm, claiming her attention. "Here comes your missionary friend, Mr. Cole."

Turning, Eliza caught sight of a widely smiling Nathan hurrying toward them with long, ungainly strides. "Eliza." He stopped and swept off his hat, holding it in front of him. "It is good to see you again."

"Hello, Nathan."

"I was wondering if you had arrived yet. Were you on your way somewhere?"

"Temple and I were going to the store. I have some shopping to do."

"Reverend Cole can escort you," Temple inserted. "I just spied Jane Rogers in the crowd. I have not seen her since our days at Brainerd."

Before Eliza could protest, Temple hurried off to see her friend. The Blade smiled and inclined his head to Eliza. "I will leave you in Reverend Cole's care."

"You are in luck," Nathan told her. "All four stores in town are open. Usually only one is, but with so many families in town for the annual meeting, it is a busy time."

"It is, indeed," Eliza agreed.

Together they set out from the tent city and headed for town, passing through the residential area marked by a half dozen white frame houses, most of them two-storied with spacious front porches. The town of New Echota itself was neatly laid out in a city form of one-acre lots, with a public common in the center of it. Near the common stood the Cherokee courthouse, where the laws of the Nation were enforced by its judges. Near that was the Cherokee council house, a large, two-story structure with brick chimneys and glass windows. It was here that the two legislative bodies of the Cherokee government—the National Committee and the National Council—held their annual sessions.

* * *

A few short days after the October session began, a white man came forward and identified himself as John Lowrey, an agent of the United States government assigned by Secretary of War Eaton. He requested permission to speak to the combined houses.

His address to the combined houses proposed that the United States enter into a new treaty with the Cherokees, offering the same old terms: in exchange for Cherokee land in the East, the United States would give them territory west of the Mississippi and pay for their transportation and the building of new homes and schools there.

He said only one thing that the Cherokees had not heard before, and that had an ominous ring.

"At whatever time the State of Georgia chooses to enter the land occupied by the Cherokee people for the purpose of surveying it, the president of the United States will *not* interfere."

A Cherokee delegation was immediately chosen to travel to Washington and protest the continued harassment of the Cherokee people. Will Gordon was one of the delegates selected to announce that the Cherokees would never again cede another foot of land.

By the end of November, the trees at Gordon Glen had lost their leaves. They stood stark and bare as the family gathered on the front veranda to see Will Gordon off on his long journey. Eliza hovered in the background, watching as he said good-bye to his children, affectionately embracing each of them in turn, then kissed his wife on the cheek.

Once astride his gray horse, he appeared to remember Eliza for the first time. "Miss Hall, I shall be meeting with Payton Fletcher while I am in Washington. Is there a message you would like him to take to your family?"

Eliza hesitated only a moment. "Ask him to inform my mother that I am well and in good spirits."

"I will."

"God's speed to you, Mr. Gordon, and good luck."

"We shall need it." With a saluting wave to all of them, he rode off to join the rest of the delegates.

⌐⌐ 10 ⌐⌐

*I*gnoring Phoebe's admonition to throw on a shawl, Temple opened the heavy baroque door, indifferent to the wall of January air that awaited her. With her father away in Washington, few visitors stopped by Gordon Glen, so the approach of a horse and rider at this hour of the evening heralded only one possibility—The Blade.

When the rider halted within the pool of light that spilled from the great hall, Temple was not disappointed. "What are you doing out in this cold?" she asked with a welcoming smile.

Puffs of steamy breath billowed from the nostrils of his horse, dissipating like thin smoke into the night. The Blade didn't immediately reply. He merely sat on his lathered horse and stared at the woman with moon-pale skin and night-black hair. "I saw your lights and hoped you might offer to share the warmth of your fire."

Shadrach ran out of the shadows to take the horse's reins. The Blade dismounted, passing the reins over.

Temple stepped back inside the house and swung the door open wider to admit him. The Blade followed her into the large entry hall and removed his coat, handing it to the waiting servant girl while Temple closed the door. When she turned to him, The Blade noticed the silence in the house.

"Where is your mother?" He glanced in the direction of the family parlor.

"Upstairs with little Johnny. He has been ill with the croup the last two days." Temple stepped away from the door. "We have a fire burning in the parlor." Leading the way, she entered the room and crossed directly to the fireplace, taking up the poker to stoke the smoldering logs into flame.

"It is quiet." The Blade walked over to stand beside her, holding out his hands to the fire's rising heat.

"Miss Hall has already retired for the night." Temple smiled absently. "We heard from my father today. Things seem to be going well. He was most encouraging in his letter."

"He was?" The Blade said, almost harshly.

"Yes." Her smile widened. "The Supreme Court has ordered the State of Georgia to appear before it and show cause why a writ of error shouldn't be issued against them in the case of George Corn Tassel. According to Father, that means the Supreme Court believes Georgia exceeded its jurisdiction when it convicted a Cherokee on land owned and governed by us." She beamed with triumph.

"You haven't heard, have you?" The tightness returned—the anger.

"Heard what?" She tipped her head to one side, still smiling at him.

"He is dead. They hanged George Corn Tassel."

"What?" Her dark eyes widened in disbelief, then narrowed in confusion. "I don't understand. Didn't they receive the order from the Supreme Court in time?"

"They received it—and ignored it. No, they did more than that." The Blade clenched his teeth in an attempt to control the rage that threatened to boil up inside him again. "When they received the citation from the Supreme Court, they advanced the date of his execution and promptly hanged him to show their contempt. Georgia claims that it is 'not accountable to the Supreme Court or any other tribunal,' and the interference by the Chief Justice was a violation of Georgia's rights?"

"But what of the rights of the Cherokees?" Temple demanded.

"When have the Americans ever been concerned with our rights?" he retorted cynically and turned away from the crackling fire. Pushed by bitter anger, The Blade crossed to the drink cart and picked up a crystal decanter of whiskey.

"There are many who care," Temple insisted. "Father wrote in his letter that David Crockett from Tennessee has allied himself with our cause. Crockett introduced the delegation to others who have also pledged their support in Congress. Henry Clay has shown himself to be a friend of the Cherokees. There is talk that he will defeat Jackson in the coming election and become the next president. He would enforce the existing treaties that Jackson turns his back on."

Flames leapt high behind her. The glass of whiskey sat untouched on the tray as The Blade studied the determination in her proud stance. By all that was sacred, she was the most beautiful woman he had ever seen. Abruptly, The Blade picked up the glass and stared at its contents, but whiskey wasn't nearly as intoxicating to him as she was.

"I do not find it so easy to place my life in someone else's hands." He wasn't thinking of Clay or Crockett when he spoke.

"But that is not what we are doing." Temple walked toward him, the woolen material of her long skirt and the layers of petticoats beneath it swishing softly with each stride. "We are reaching out to join hands with others so we can be stronger. We are seeking out more voices so that our cry for justice will be heard."

"You sound like your father." He eyed her briefly, then tossed down some of the whiskey, welcoming the burn in his throat.

"Is that wrong?" she challenged, drawing herself up to her full height.

"No."

Temple held his gaze for a long second, then partly turned, angling her body away from him, the bodice of her dress lifting and falling with quick yet deep breaths. "My father is strong and loyal . . . unselfish in his commitment to the cause of justice for our people. A more generous man you could not find if you traveled throughout the whole of the Nation. That summer when there was no rain and so many of the Cherokees in the mountains lost their crops, he opened our larder to them, gave them corn from our cribs for their live-stock, and the homespun from our looms. We had barely enough supplies left to last us through winter."

"I admire him too, Temple," he declared roughly. "My strength, my loyalty, my commitment run every bit as deep as his, but I am not like him. I never will be. If that is what you seek in a man—"

She turned on him. "Did I say it was?"

"No." The answer exploded from him, and The Blade sighed heavily, trying to expel the anger and tension that gripped him. He shoved the half-empty whiskey glass onto the tray and squared around to face her. "Temple, I don't want to argue with you . . . not tonight." Reaching out, he hooked her waist with his hand and pulled her to him. "I didn't come here for that."

At first Temple resisted, turning her head to elude his kiss and pushing against the muscled arms that bound her. She couldn't forget so quickly his callous and cynical remarks or the skepticism they contained, as if he considered the fight for their rights hopeless. Her father would cut out his own tongue rather than speak such treasonous words.

Soon she found it difficult to ignore the persistent nuzzling of his mouth as it lipped the sensitive skin of her neck, ear, and cheek, then teased the corner of her mouth.

"I need you," The Blade whispered against her skin, a beautiful rawness in the sound.

For an instant she held herself still, listening to the ache in his voice, an ache that was not solely desire, an ache that spoke of pain. The Blade had always seemed detached and hardened, mocking in his observations and smooth in his comments. She sometimes forgot the strong emotions she had discovered behind his aloof and charming exterior. She wondered where the pain had come from. And the anger and bitterness he had expressed tonight—that wasn't like him either. What was wrong? Why was he upset? She breathed in sharply, suddenly remembering.

"You knew him, didn't you? When you were there digging for gold, you met George Corn Ta—"

His mouth covered her lips, not letting her say more. But Temple didn't fight the driving possession of his kiss or the enveloping crush of his arms. She wanted to take away his pain and remove the specter of death that, for him, had a face as well as a name.

When at last he dragged his mouth from hers and buried his face in the side of her neck, hugging her close, she felt the sigh that trembled through him. Then the nuzzling started all over again as he kissed and nibbled at her, murmuring her name between each delicious bite. Temple trembled now, conscious of the play of his hands over her back. This time she deliberately sought his kiss, turning until she found his mouth. She tasted the whiskey on his tongue and felt drunk herself, wonderfully so.

Eliza approached the family parlor. She looked up and saw the entwined couple and halted in shock. "What are you doing?" The instant the question was out of her mouth, Eliza reddened.

The passion of the kiss was still in their expressions when they turned to her. "Did you want something, Miss Hall?" Temple asked.

"It is a bit late to be receiving guests." Eliza looked pointedly at The Blade.

"Yes," The Blade unexpectedly agreed. "It is time I left."

"But—" Temple turned to him.

He staved off her protest. "Miss Hall is right. It's time I return to the warmth of my own fire."

Temple appeared on the verge of arguing with him, then changed her mind. "I will have Phoebe fetch your coat."

"That isn't necessary," he said.

Temple watched him go, then crossed to the fireplace and added another log from the wood box. Eliza continued to stand inside the room. She said nothing until she heard the front door close behind The Blade. "How can you behave so wantonly, Temple? After the talks we have had about—"

"Silence!" Temple spun around, something almost regal in the blaze of her dark eyes. "Talk, talk, talk. You always lecture me on the feelings a woman should guard against. You do not realize a man can find comfort in a woman's arms, a comfort that heals the pain he feels and reminds him he is alive. And to feel alive is wonderful. For a woman as well. But you want to deny it. You want to deny the very feelings that make you a woman."

Stunned, Eliza couldn't say a word. Temple's voice carried such a ring of authority that she was hesitant to challenge it ... and more than a little subdued by the realization that she had suddenly become the student instead of the teacher.

Slowly, Temple turned to stare into the flames. "There is something else you should know. They executed George Corn Tassel. He is dead."

"What? How do you know?"

"The Blade brought word of it," she said, then went on to explain the circumstances, including Georgia's open defiance of the Supreme Court order and the claim of interference.

"Dear God. Your father," Eliza whispered. "What a terrible blow this will be to him."

"Yes."

The fire crackled in the background. Eliza tried to think of something encouraging to say. "All is not lost, Temple. You mustn't think it is. The attorneys are already preparing another case to take before the Supreme Court asking for an injunction that will prevent Georgia from extending her laws over the Cherokee Nation."

"I know." Temple nodded, unimpressed.

🢖 11 🢔

A cold rain drummed against the windows of the log school, its hard patter loud in the stillness of the classroom, now empty of its students. Eliza returned the last of the textbooks to its proper place on the shelf, then paused to gaze out the window at the gloomy gray and black world of heavy clouds and bare trees. Shivering from the damp chill in the room, she turned instinctively toward the fireplace, seeking the warmth of its blazing logs.

Nathan Cole sat before it, his shoulders hunched, his elbows resting on his knees, and his hands clasped together. He had arrived unexpectedly, shortly before noon, drenched to the skin and spattered with mud. It hadn't taken much persuasion on Eliza's part to convince him to stay the night rather than continue his journey to an outlying church in this storm.

"Weather like this makes me want to curl up in front of a fire with a good book," she declared, then smiled at her inadvertent pun. "By that, I didn't mean the Good Book."

"I beg your pardon. Did you say something?"

Eliza opened her mouth to repeat it, then observed his troubled expression and changed her mind. "I was remarking on the children and how much they seemed to enjoy your lesson today."

"Yes. Yes, they did." He nodded, his attention wandering from her again.

"Is something wrong, Nathan?"

"Wrong?" Again, there was that initially blank look, followed by a retreat into his thoughts. "No. Nothing."

"Nonsense. Something is bothering you. Now, what is it?" she demanded, unconsciously slipping into her crisp teacher's voice.

"I . . ." He rubbed his palms tightly together in a display of deep agitation. "I . . . can't burden you with my problems . . . my dilemma."

"Why not?" Eliza pulled a chair close to the fire and sat down. "I thought I was your friend."

"You are," he said forcefully, then sighed. "I am troubled by the new Georgian law. What do you think will come of it?"

"Nothing will come of it. It is a lot of humbug, if you ask me. Georgia cannot possibly believe it will get away with this bit of chicanery. The very idea of ordering a survey to be made of land that belongs to the Cherokees for the sole purpose of dividing it into lots—lots that will supposedly be given away to native Georgians in a lottery—is a ruse and nothing more. Georgia cannot give away land that doesn't belong to it." The mere thought made her angry. "Their true purpose is to raise a hue and cry from the people against the Cherokees by appealing to their greed. They will never go through with it." She looked at him askance. "Surely you don't think they will."

"I do not know. I wasn't thinking about that," Nathan admitted.

"Then what?" Eliza frowned.

"I was referring to the law that goes into effect the first of March, the one that requires all white men living in the Cherokee territory to obtain a license from the Georgia government. Before one is granted, an oath of allegiance must be sworn to Georgia." Again Nathan twisted his hands together in agitation. "I know you have no need to be concerned with it. The law doesn't apply to women. But it applies to me. And frankly, I am not sure what to do."

"About what?" She didn't see where the problem lay.

"The oath. Do I take it and 'render unto Caesar that which is Caesar's'? Morally, I believe the action Georgia is taking to force the Cherokees from the land is wrong. But I am a missionary. I am here to bring them the Word of God—not to become involved politically in their struggle."

Eliza stared at him in open consternation. "How can you consider taking the oath?" she protested. "You and the other missionaries are spiritual teachers to the Cherokees. All this time you have instructed them in the faith and urged them to keep it, no matter how difficult the times become or how harsh the oppression they face. If you swear allegiance to Georgia, are you not, in effect, surrendering and saying to the Cherokee people that their enemy is too strong, too powerful to fight, even for you?"

"I suppose it could look that way." Nathan released a sigh of despair and confusion. "Yet to defy Georgia's order means certain imprisonment. Of what help will we missionaries be to the Cherokees if we are locked away? Already the Moravians are moving out of Georgia and leaving their wives in charge of their missions." He combed long fingers through his hair, increasing its disarray, then clasped them together again in a tight, prayerful pose. He looked at Eliza, his eyes haunted by the dilemma that paralyzed him. "What would you do in my place?"

She hesitated, not out of indecision but from the stunning discovery of how much this place, this family, had come to mean to her. All of them . . . the beautiful Temple, who was like a younger sister; the arrogant Kipp, with his prejudices and sharp intelligence; the slow and shy Xandra, forever paling before her sister's beauty and her brother's intellect. And the baby, Johnny, whom she had watched take his first step; the slaves Phoebe and Shadrach, their eager faces drinking in every bit of knowledge she offered; fragile Victoria Gordon, a model of motherly devotion and sacrifice; and Will Gordon, the head of the family, a man she had grown to respect so deeply.

"I could not leave here," she said simply. "But our situations are not the same, Nathan. Surely the board in Boston has made some recommendations to you."

"They feel we should remain at our posts and see what happens. But it is only a recommendation. We are not bound by it."

"I think it is a wise suggestion. According to Mr. Gordon, the Supreme Court will be hearing the Cherokee case soon. If they grant an injunction, then you will not have to worry about this registration order. Georgia will not have the authority to enforce it."

"What if I am arrested before the Court hears the case, or what if the Court fails to issue an injunction? Do I take the oath or go to prison? I don't know what is right." He shook his head, agonizing over the decision. "My place is among the Cherokee people, not locked away in a cell. But if I take the oath, will I lose their trust and respect? It is my duty to serve their needs and give them the hope and faith that can be found in the Almighty God. How can I best do that?"

Eliza grew impatient with him. To her, the solution was clear. "If the Georgia Guard tries to arrest you, you should tell them that you consider yourself to be a Cherokee. It is what I would do," she declared.

"Eliza. You make it sound so simple." He smiled at her gently and sadly.

"It is. This entire situation is." She pushed herself to her feet and swung around to face the fire, trying to contain the anger she felt. "Everyone claims this is a dispute over who rightfully owns the land. But the Cherokees were here first, so how can there be any question? I am a woman, but even I can see that this whole thing is a conspiracy between the

State of Georgia and the Jackson administration. With tyranni-cal acts, common thievery, and whiskey peddlers, Georgia hopes to make life so miserable for the Cherokees that they will sign a new treaty and give up their lands. I would not blame the Cherokees if they took up arms against their oppres-sors."

"You don't know what you are saying. An armed resistance by the Indians would provide Georgia an excuse to send in troops. The situation would be worse."

"You are right." Frustrated and discouraged, she stared into the fire, watching the small tongues of flame dart over the glowing embers, slowly devouring the log, and listening to the relentless rain hammer at the school windows. She wondered if Georgia would eventually succeed in eroding away the determination of the Cherokee people. "Nathan, do you think Will Gordon and the other delegates will sign a treaty giving up their lands?" Even to her own ears, the question had a treasonous ring.

Snapping his head back, Nathan frowned at her in sharp disbelief. "No. It would mean their death."

His answer came so quickly, so filled with conviction, that Eliza was taken aback. "Their death? But why?"

"Because . . . it would be a violation of their Blood Law," he replied almost grudgingly.

"Blood Law? What's that?"

Again, Nathan appeared to be reluctant to respond. "It is a sacred law that calls for the death of any Cherokee who signs away any portion of the national lands without special permission from the council."

"I have never heard of this."

"I know of only one case where the law was applied, and that was back in 1807. A chieftain named Doublehead signed a treaty with the federal government agreeing to vast land cessions that included the Cumberland plateau and parts of what is now Kentucky. Bribery was involved. For this betrayal, a party of men was sent out to execute him."

"Did they?" Although she thought she knew the answer, something compelled Eliza to ask.

"Yes." When Nathan paused, she sensed that he did not altogether approve of such a severe penalty. "Two years ago, the National Council passed the Blood Law, making it officially a part of the Cherokee laws. Oddly enough—or perhaps appropriately—the Blood Law in its written form was framed by John Ridge, the son of Major Ridge, who was one of the men in the execution party. I have heard that Major Ridge himself proposed the legislation as a deterrent to those who might be tempted to treat for their own profit." Sitting back in his chair, Nathan released a heavy sigh. "It has been reported that both the Choctaws and the Chickasaws have negotiated a new treaty, exchanging their lands for territory in the West. I cannot imagine the Cherokees ever voluntarily agreeing to live there, considering their superstition about the West."

"What superstition?"

"When I was making my circuit through the backwoods last summer, visiting the mountain Cherokees, I talked to an old man who still clung to the pagan beliefs of his ancestors. He had no conception of heaven, or a hereafter. According to him, the lost souls of the dead wandered until they came to the 'darkening land' in the west. There they became extinct."

12

*T*emple overlapped the heavy drapes to shut out the morning sunlight, then turned and glanced at her mother, at last sleeping restfully in the big feather bed. Her lank black hair was loose about her face, accenting its thinness and pallor. Even though Black Cassie regularly bled her, her mother seemed to get weaker instead of better.

Maybe this time it would be different, Temple thought, and tiptoed to the door. She closed it quietly behind her and moved toward the staircase.

"Miz Temple. Miz Temple!" Black Cassie called anxiously to her from below, alarm in her voice.

"Quiet," Temple hissed, impatient with the Negro woman's thoughtlessness. "You will wake Mama."

"Miz Temple, you best come quick."

"What is it now?" she asked with undisguised irritation. Since she had been forced to take over the household duties because of her mother's illness, there seemed no end to the number of crises demanding her attention that occurred in the kitchen.

"They be riders comin', Miz Temple," Black Cassie declared, her voice filled with apprehension. "And they looks like they be Georgians."

"What?" Temple faltered in midstep halfway down the stairs.

"Hurry, Miz Temple," Black Cassie urged. "They be ridin' up the lane, bold as Satan. Somethin' bad's gwine to happen. I knows it."

Temple flew the rest of the way down the stairs and ran past Black Cassie to the dining room's front window. A blustery March wind chased dead leaves across the lawn, and her thoughts raced with them. The screeching of the peacocks at the as-yet-unseen intruders echoed the alarm she felt. They were alone, without a man to protect them. Her father was still in Washington and her uncle was away buying spring seed.

"Does ya see 'em?" Black Cassie hovered behind her.

"No."

Then Temple spotted them through the trees, a half dozen men on horseback, their hats pulled low and their collars turned up against the wind, all milling about the schoolhouse. Xandra, Kipp, her cousins—they were in there with Miss Hall.

Fighting down her fear, Temple swung from the window. "Where is Shadrach? That boy is never around when I need him."

"He be at school, Miz Temple."

Belatedly, Temple recalled that both Shadrach and Phoebe attended the morning classes. "Go to the stables as fast as you can and tell Ike to ride to Master Stuart's place."

"But he can'ts leave widout a pass."

"There isn't time for that. Go. Do as I tell you."

"No'm." Black Cassie stood where she was, shaking her head from side to side in defiant refusal. "If they stops my Ike on the road an' he ain't got a pass, they calls him a runaway."

"You will do as I say!" Temple lashed out in anger, striking the woman's cheek. She had never before hit a servant, but she had never before had cause. "The Georgians are at the schoolhouse. Do you hear?" Seeing the answering leap of fear in Cassie's eyes, Temple gave her a push toward the door. "Go. If Ike is stopped by anyone, he is to bring them here."

"Yes'm." The woman hurried off.

Temple turned back to the window and looked out one last time. A rider walked his horse along the side of the schoolhouse and stopped near a window. Grabbing up her long skirts, Temple ran to the front door and out of the house.

Hearing the *clump* of a heavy boot on the school steps, Eliza closed the primer in front of her and rose from her chair. An instant later, the door burst open and two men filled its frame, looming hulks in long winter coats.

"Who are you and what do you want?" Without thinking, Eliza snatched the pointer from her desktop, the only thing close to a weapon at hand. A third man climbed the steps behind the first two intruders, and three more riders sat on their horses outside the school.

The first man scoured the school's single room with a searching glance. "Where's yer husband?"

"I have no husband." The new law—Eliza belatedly recalled that the new law had gone into effect four days ago, on March 1, requiring all white men in the Cherokee territory to register or face four years' imprisonment.

His glance came back to her, sharp and accusing. "We heard this here plantation had a white teacher living on it. He ain't registered hisself with the proper authorities yet."

"*I* am the teacher," Eliza asserted. "As a female, I am not required to register with anyone."

"You're the teacher?" He gave her a long, sneering look, then turned and spat a stream of yellow tobacco juice on the puncheon floor. "I reckon you must be one o' them Injun-loving white women."

Eliza ignored that and moved out from behind her desk to

plant herself squarely between the ruffians and her young charges. "You have yet to identify yourselves and the nature of your business here."

"Is that a fact?" he jeered, then he puffed out his chest, swaggering a bit. "It so happens that we're with the Georgia Guard."

"Then you should be ashamed of yourselves, barging in here unannounced, spitting on the floor, and frightening the children," Eliza declared. "The Cherokees I have met are certainly not as uncouth as you and your men are."

His companion nudged the man with an elbow. "Lookey there. Ain't that a nigger holdin' a book?"

The first man's glance fell on Shadrach and turned cold with malice. "Hey, you. Come 'ere, boy."

"Stay where you are, Shadrach," Eliza ordered, not taking her eyes off the men.

There was a sudden flurry of movement outside the school as Temple came rushing up. She pushed her way past the man on the steps only to be snared by another before she could reach Eliza's side. She struggled, fighting wildly to free herself from his hold.

The man laughed and shifted his grip to hold her by the wrists. "Lookey here. I just caught me a real Injun princess. Yessirree, an' she's on the warpath, too."

"Let her go," Eliza protested. When he ignored her, Eliza brought her rod crashing down on his forearms. The man yelped in pain and jumped back, releasing Temple. She quickly retreated out of his reach.

The first man took a step toward Eliza. She raised her pointer, threatening to use it on him. He stopped, but his eyes turned colder and meaner. "You just struck a Georgia Guard."

"Only after he attacked the person of a young girl." With her free hand, Eliza pulled Temple closer to her.

He changed tactics. "What are them niggers doin' here?"

"They are my students."

"It's against the law to teach niggers in Georgia."

"Fortunately, this is not Georgia," Eliza retorted. "You happen to be in the Cherokee Nation."

"You got that wrong, ma'am. This here land belongs to Georgia."

"That, sir, is for the Supreme Court to decide." In all her twenty years, Eliza had never been confronted with a situation fraught with such peril. She had to use her wits. Neither she nor Temple were a match for the brute strength of these men.

"I still say there's a white teacher here," the second man complained, rubbing at a forearm that she had struck. "They got him hid somewheres."

"I told you, I have no husband. I am the teacher," Eliza insisted, conscious of Temple's fingers closing around her hand as if in support and reassurance.

"Search the school and the house, if you must," Temple challenged, all stiff and stormy-eyed. "But I warn you—if you lay a hand on a single person or damage one thing, we will have you arrested."

"Arrested?" The first man snorted in derision, then sent a sly grin in the direction of his companions. "Did ya hear her threaten us with arrest, boys?" The other two men nodded and grinned their unconcern. "You ain't got any rights around here, little princess. We can do anything we please an' you can't do nothing about it."

"I can," Eliza asserted. "I can testify against you. None of your spurious laws can silence my testimony. I am white, not Cherokee."

A dawning look of shock claimed the man's face as the truth of her words sank in. He tried, and failed, to assume his former belligerence. "You can't stop us from looking for that white teacher."

"I would not presume to interfere with your duty," Eliza replied smoothly, confident that she now had the whip hand. "But I will observe your every action."

Under Eliza's watchful eye, the men made a cursory search of the school and the grounds around it. "He could be hiding in the big house," one of the riders suggested.

The disgruntled leader flashed a baleful look at Eliza and shook his head. "By now he's probably hightailed it into the woods. We got other birds to flush."

Eliza didn't draw an easy breath until they rode out of sight. She hurried back inside the school and closed the door, then leaned weakly against it. With the danger passed, delayed reaction set in. Eliza wasn't certain if the loud pounding she heard was the hammering of her heart or the knocking of her knees.

Conscious of nine pairs of eyes staring at her in silent question, Eliza managed a somewhat tremulous smile of assurance. "They are gone."

Temple came forward, her eyes dark with concern. "Are you all right?"

"I am fine." Eliza pushed away from the door, determined to control her shaking limbs.

"You were extraordinarily brave." Temple looked at her with a new respect and admiration.

"I was extraordinarily scared," she admitted, then resorted to anger to cover the quaver in her voice. "Those brutes, they should be flogged for coming in here like that and terrorizing the children."

"I need to check on Mama." Temple started toward the door.

"Perhaps we should all go to the house," Eliza decided. "Come. Let us put everything away. Quickly now."

Twenty minutes later, they were all inside the thick walls of the red brick mansion, except for Phoebe and Shadrach, who were sent to the kitchen to prepare the noon meal. But Black Cassie was more concerned with assuring herself that they were unharmed and learning for herself all that had happened.

Phoebe let Shadrach do the talking, sensing the fear that

gripped her mammy and not understanding it. Yet it made her uneasy, the same as those white men had.

"—an' one of them men says t' Miz 'Liza—'What's that Nigra boy doin' wid a book?'" Shadrach tried to make his voice sound as deep as a man's. He lapsed into his mother's dialect, as he usually did when he talked to her. "'Come 'ere, boy,' he says, but Miz 'Liza say, 'Shadrach, you stay right there.' An' I did." Black Cassie started moaning low and shaking her head, her eyes all dark and worried. She barely listened when he told her about Miss Temple coming just then and how Miss Eliza took after that man with her pointer. "—an' then the man say it's against the law in Georgia t' be teachin' a Nigra."

She moaned louder. "I knowed it. I knowed somethin' bad were gwine t' happen."

"No, Mammy. It's all right." Shadrach frowned at the way she held herself and rocked, like she was in pain. "Miz 'Liza, she tole him this ain't be Georgia. This be Cherokee land."

Black Cassie wrapped an arm around each of them and pulled them tight against her. "They's gwine t' come in de night," she moaned. "That's what they gwine t' do. I seen it before. They's gwine t' come and drag you out an' whip you till there ain't one skinny breath left in you."

"But . . . why?" Shadrach pulled out of her smothering hold and stepped back, frowning in disbelief and the beginnings of fear.

"'Cause that larnin' you been so all fired t' git be for white folks. They ain't gwine t' let no black knows it. I tells Ike an' I tells him, 'Don't let those babies go t' that school. Bad's gwine t' happen.' Now, it's comin'.".

She sounded so certain that Phoebe started trembling, then nearly jumped out of her skin when she heard the thundering of horses' hooves coming up the lane to the big house.

"They's back." Cassie clutched Phoebe closer as Shadrach ran to the doorway. "Come away from there. We gots t' hide you."

"It ain't them, Mammy. It's Master Blade and Deu. Pa's with them," he said, then raced from the kitchen.

When The Blade rode up, Temple rushed out of the house. He was out of the saddle before his lathered horse came to a full stop. He caught her by the shoulders and held her firmly away from him.

"Are you all right?" he demanded.

"Yes—"

"The others?"

"Yes."

Only then did the pressure of his grip lessen. "How long have they been gone?"

"Twenty minutes, no more than that."

He turned his head and looked down the road, his jaw ridged and tight. Then he swung back to face her, the glitter in his blue eyes ominously cold and frightening. "What happened?"

Briefly, Temple explained it, then added, "Miss Hall says it's the new licensing law. They were looking for violators."

"Yes." He nodded slowly, twice. "I heard this morning three missionaries were arrested."

"You should have seen Miss Hall," Temple declared. "I have never seen her so irate—not even with Kipp. When one of them grabbed me—"

"He did *what*?" The words sprang from him in a snarl.

"He didn't hurt me," she assured him softly. "Miss Hall saw to that."

"If he had, I—" He clamped his jaw shut on the rest of the threat.

The scar stood out whitely against the bronze of his skin. Temple reached up to touch it, then let her fingers lightly caress his cheek. "Blade," she whispered, loving his fury, loving his strength—loving him.

His mouth came down on hers as he swept her into his arms, the rawness of his passion and his fears washing over her and spinning her into their turbulence and fire. The storm of feelings was what she wanted, what she needed, the lightning that tingled through her body, the thunder that rocked her to her very toes.

"Oh, Temple, the things I thought when Ike came," he murmured, then shuddered against her, struggling to regain control of his emotions. "Your uncle, how long will he be gone?" He drew back, cupping her face in his hands, a faint tremor in them.

"He should be back tomorrow or the next day." She closed her eyes, savoring the unexpected tenderness of his lightly caressing fingers.

"I will stay until he returns," he stated firmly, as if anticipating an argument from her.

"Yes."

"And when your father arrives . . ."

Temple opened her eyes and felt her breath catch at the look on his face—so serious, so possessive. "Yes?" she prompted him.

"I want you to be my wife." His expression flickered, subtly changing, the dimpling crease appearing in one cheek and a hint of mockery glinting in his eyes. "Aren't you going to say anything?"

"I do not recall being asked anything," she replied, deliberately matching his tone, feeling gloriously playful.

"It is what you wanted. Marriage has been in your mind from the beginning."

"But it has not been in yours."

"No," The Blade admitted. "A wife, a home, a family— I didn't want that yet. When I was in the mountains, I followed the vein of gold wherever it led me, digging, crushing, hauling off the leavings—all for the rich yellow dust and few nuggets I found that made it worth it. To have the thing you desire, you must accept what comes with it."

"And do you desire me?" She wanted the words. She wanted to hear him speak of his feelings for her.

"Desire? That doesn't describe it." He pulled her close again, burying his face in her hair. "To breathe and not inhale the fragrance of your hair, to listen and not hear your whispered words of love, to look and not see the midnight brightness of your eyes gazing back at me, to touch"—he paused to trail the tips of his fingers over her cheek and onto her neck—"and not feel the satin smoothness of your skin, and . . . to taste"—he brought his lips close to her mouth, brushing feather-light against her sensitive curves—"and not savor the wildness of your kiss, that would not be living, Temple."

"It is the same for me." Only with The Blade did she feel truly alive.

As her mouth moved against his, need whipped through him again, raw and urgent. Even as he satisfied it, it grew. In that moment he knew time would never lessen the feeling. That was the wondrous power of it—and the beauty of it.

When Phoebe and Shadrach failed to arrive for the start of school the next morning, Eliza rang the bell a second time. Unable to delay any longer, she began the morning lessons without them.

At the noon recess, the children ran out to play before the dinner meal was served. Eliza's thoughts turned again to Phoebe and Shadrach and their absence from morning classes. She found them in the kitchen with Black Cassie. The instant she appeared, Shadrach darted a look at her and bowed his head, concentrating all his attention on the potatoes he was peeling, his hunched shoulders conveying the impression of both guilt and dejection. When Eliza turned to Phoebe, she, too, was reluctant to meet her eyes.

"You were not at school this morning," she said. "I missed you."

"We's had to work," Phoebe mumbled.

"*We* had to work," Eliza corrected.

"Yes'm." She ducked her head and shot a quick, sideways glance at the buxom woman next to the hearth's cookfire.

Sensing something was wrong, Eliza wondered if they thought she was going to punish them for not attending classes this morning. Surely by now they had learned she wasn't given to corporal action. "You come early tomorrow and I will go over the lessons we had today," she promised, injecting extra warmth into her voice to assure them she wasn't angry.

Shadrach finally looked up, a hurt and resentful expression in his dark eyes. "We can't come no—anymore." Again he lowered his gaze, then mumbled, "Our mammy says so."

"But . . . why?" Stunned, Eliza turned to Black Cassie.

"They ain't gwine t' come t' that school o' yours no more."

"But they have learned so much," Eliza protested. "Shadrach is one of my brightest students. How can you deny them this opportunity to receive an education?"

"She thinks those white men will come back," Phoebe offered tentatively.

Astounded and mildly angry, Eliza stared at Cassie. "Surely you are not going to allow those bullies to frighten you into keeping your children out of school? This is not Georgia. There is nothing they can do."

"Oh, yes, there is. You don't know, Miz 'Liza, but I does," Cassie declared. "They ain't gwine t' allow no darky chillun t' be edjicated. They'll stop it, sure as night comes. But they ain't gwine t' hurt my babies, 'cause my babies ain't gwine t' that school no more. They knows their place, my babies does. An' they's gwine t' stay in it, too."

Eliza wanted to argue with her, but she was suddenly haunted by the image of the way those men had looked at Shadrach and Phoebe—the ugliness in their eyes. Had the children been in more danger yesterday than she had realized? The slave codes adopted by the Southern states, including Georgia, not only labeled the education of Negroes a crime, but also called for harsh punishment for any violators. Considering the way these bands of Georgian vigilantes had terrorized the Nation with their beatings and robbings, Eliza was forced to concede that Cassie had cause to fear for her children.

She could not, in good conscience, ask the woman to expose them to danger again.

"I understand," she said and quietly left the kitchen. She felt guilty and frustrated—frustrated because there was nothing she could do to change the situation.

She missed them, especially Shadrach's rapt face looking back at her. The first three days, Eliza kept watching the window, hoping he would be outside listening to the lessons as he once had. But he never appeared.

The haunting nightsong of a whippoorwill echoed plaintively through the darkness as Eliza retraced her steps to the log school to retrieve a shawl she had inadvertently left there. She sighed deeply, wondering if Shadrach and Phoebe felt as cheated as she did; they, out of the chance to learn, and she, out of the chance to teach them.

Glancing ahead, she noticed a faint glow lighting one of the windows. Had someone set fire to the school? Eliza experienced a stab of fear. The Georgians—was this how they intended to stop her from teaching slaves? She quickened her pace, then broke into a run. As she hurried up the steps, she heard a scuffling movement inside the school.

She flung open the door, demanding, "Who's there?"

When she crossed the threshold, someone scrambled out the side window. Eliza halted, stunned to discover the room was pitch-black. There was no light. But the intruder had been real, of that she was certain. She ran to the window just as the saucer-shaped moon came out from behind a cloud and revealed a small, dark figure racing madly for the big hickory tree and flinging himself behind its broad trunk.

She swung away from the window and looked about the shadowed room. In the dim light, Eliza saw something on the floor. She went to investigate and found a primer and a candle. The melted wax was still pliable and warm. Eliza picked up the book and smiled.

"Shadrach," she whispered and clutched the book to her

breast. "Dear little Shadrach. You want to learn, don't you? You will not be frightened off. Not to worry. I will help you, and no one shall ever know. It will be our secret. I promise."

She relit the candle and carried it to her desk. Blotting the tears from her eyes with one hand, she dipped the pen in the inkwell with the other and carefully wrote out the instructions for the next day's lesson, deliberately not addressing it to anyone and leaving it unsigned. She placed it atop the primer, set the candle near it, then retrieved her shawl and left the school.

As she passed by the hickory tree on her way to the house, something scraped against the bark. "You gave me a frightful scare, Mr. Moon," she said in a very loud voice. "I thought someone was in the school, but it was only you, wasn't it? I am glad I went in, though. I had forgotten to leave the instructions for tomorrow's lesson on my desk."

Eliza strolled past the tree, not even looking to see if Shadrach was still behind it. The next morning, the instructions, primer, and candle were sitting on her desk, *almost* exactly where she had left them. From then on, every day she left a different textbook on her desk, along with a set of directions and a new candle.

13

On a fine spring morning in late March, when the forsythia was a blaze of yellow and the blossoming dogwood spread a web of white lace in the woods, Will Gordon returned. Temple was on her way back to the big house after tending to the sick in the Negro quarters when she saw him riding up the lane.

Beside her, Shadrach paused to look down at his bare feet and the tender green blades of grass poking up between his toes, the weather now warm enough that the slaves no longer wore their winter shoes.

Temple pressed her woven basket containing bandages, herbs, and ointments into his hands. "Quick. Go tell everyone my father is back," she said, not taking her eyes off the approaching horse and rider.

Shadrach dashed toward the house with the news.

She veered off the brick path and cut across the lawn to welcome him home. Just short of the front entrance, he saw her and reined in his horse while he waited for her to reach him.

Suddenly the front door opened and Kipp and Xandra ran out, followed closely by Eliza and Victoria, with little John in her arms. Temple quickly reached them. Eliza stepped back, allowing them to rush forward and embrace him in affectionate welcome.

"I am glad you came home," Xandra declared, holding on to the leg of his trousers while Will shifted his youngest son to the crook of his other arm. "I missed you."

"I missed you, too." Will stroked the top of her head in a loving caress.

The news of his return from the federal capital spread rapidly through the countryside. By the noon hour, a dozen visitors were at the dining room table, including The Blade and his father, Shawano Stuart. All were eager to hear the results of the delegates' sojourn in Washington and to relate the latest happenings at home.

"The situation has grown worse while you were away, Will."

"Yes," another spoke up. "A dozen or more white men were arrested for violating the licensing law, including several of the missionaries—Samuel Worcester, Isaac Proctor, and Nathan Cole."

"A comic sight it was, too, Will," The Blade inserted dryly. "Men armed with muskets rode up to the missions, led by a wagon carrying a large drum. A boy not much older than your son Kipp banged away on it while another man marched behind it tootling away on a fife. They arrested the men—without warrants—let them say good-bye to their families, then marched them off to Lawrenceville."

"I was told they were released," Will said, an eyebrow arched in question.

"They were. The judge dismissed the charges against them. Since missionaries are also postmasters, he considered them to be federal employees, and therefore not subject to the Georgia licensing law," Eliza explained. "When Na—Mr. Cole stopped by afterward, he assured me he was treated well. He also said several prominent Georgians were very sympathetic and expressed strong disapproval of such actions."

"But even they want the Cherokees to remove," the man across from her asserted.

"You should hear the songs the Georgians sing, Father," Temple declared, then proceeded to give him a sampling of the latest air.

> " 'Go, nature's child.
> Your home's in the wild;
> Our venom cannot grip ye
> If once you'll roam,
> And make your home
> Beyond the Mississippi.' "

"Have you forgotten the other one they sing?" The Blade mocked.

> " 'All I ask in this creation
> Is a pretty little wife and a big plantation
> Way up yonder in the Cherokee Nation.' "

"No, I have not." For an instant, her dancing gaze met the challenge of his, then fell away.

"Is it true what they say, Will?" Shawano Stuart said in English, out of courtesy to Eliza. "The raiders have grown bolder?"

"I . . . have read some of the accounts published in the *Phoenix*," Will admitted.

"Then you know how they have ridden down some of our people and tried to trample them under the hooves of their horses," said one man. "They shot an old man who did not move swiftly enough to open a gate for them. Another hanged himself when he saw it. I think he was too saddened by all that has happened and could not bear to look upon more suffering by our people."

"No one is safe anymore," another insisted. "When they came here to your plantation—"

"What?" Will snapped, his head coming up, a frown creasing his face. "When was this?"

For an instant, there was silence in the room. Temple started to answer, but Eliza was quicker. "The Georgia Guard stopped by earlier this month. I saw no need to inform you about it since they caused no trouble and left almost immediately."

Temple smiled. "You would have been proud of the way she stood up to them, Father."

Conscious of his gaze on her, Eliza felt uncomfortable and awkward. She found it embarrassing when Temple went on to relate, in detail, the incident at the schoolhouse.

"You have my deepest gratitude, Miss Hall," Will said quietly when Temple finished.

"It is quite unwarranted, I assure you," Eliza replied briskly, trying to deny the blush that rosed her cheeks. "Your daughter has greatly exaggerated my role and downplayed her own."

"Somehow, I doubt that," Will countered, a hint of dryness in his voice. "But I can see that you have no wish to discuss this." With a turn of his head, he directed attention away from her, much to Eliza's relief.

Soon the conversation concentrated again on a general discussion of the current situation: the number of livestock that had been stolen—estimates ranged as high as five hundred head of cattle and horses—houses that had been burned to the ground, and the white squatters who had moved onto Cherokee property in anticipation of Georgia's planned survey and lottery.

To add to their grief, wagonloads of whiskey were being brought into the Nation by peddlers, in total disregard of the Cherokee laws prohibiting the sale of liquor. Georgia had already declared the laws to be unenforceable, effectively hamstringing the Nation's courts and its Light Horse police force with penalties for any who disagreed. Many Cherokees, despondent and demoralized by the current plight, had turned to drinking, sometimes becoming violent under its influence.

Gamblers, too, frequented the Nation in increasing numbers, cheating other Indians out of what the pony clubs didn't steal.

Despite this depressing news, Will Gordon insisted, "We must not give up hope. Instead, let us all follow the example set by our principal chief John Ross and our long-respected chieftain Major Ridge and spread the word that our nation—the Cherokees—must remain united in our stand against any new treaty calling for our removal." He insisted that they were not alone in their struggles, that they still had many friends in Washington and Congress. While Chicken Snake Jackson might be their enemy, it was widely believed that Henry Clay would defeat him in next year's election. And Henry Clay, as a friend of the Cherokees, would enforce the terms of the existing treaties.

Moved by his conviction, no one in his family could imagine disagreeing with him. No one did as they gathered in the main parlor at the meal's conclusion to trade further views on the situation and discuss potential strategies.

14

Gordon Glen
July 7, 1831

The guests numbered in the hundreds—neighbors, relatives, friends, some traveling considerable distances to be on hand for the joining in marriage of Will Gordon's daughter and Shawano Stuart's son, two of the most respected families in the Nation.

Eliza had made herself a new gown for the occasion, a serviceable one of floral-patterned linen, well suited to the South's warm climate, with gigot sleeves, collar, and fichu pelerine of white gauze. In a burst of extravagance, she had purchased a pink silk bonnet from the trader's store. With it and her black pumps, she felt extremely well dressed and slightly fashionable. Although why that mattered, she didn't know.

Yet she was nervous, and marveled that Temple was not. In fact, Temple looked quite serene as she calmly ate the food served to her by her mother and aunt. She seemed supremely confident, a characteristic Eliza had come to associate with the young woman. It was a trait she often envied for herself.

With the ceremonial meal finished, Temple rose and turned to her mother. Tears trembled on the rim of her lower lashes as Victoria Gordon smiled bravely and tried not to cry, as she had done at odd times for days now. They embraced, then

Victoria picked up an ear of corn and a blanket, her hands shaking visibly.

"It is time," someone said.

Eliza watched, waiting to see what to do next and privately wondering if it was the unusualness of the proceedings that made her feel so on edge. Temple had insisted that her wedding to The Blade be a combination of Cherokee traditional rites and Christian ceremony, with the former preceding the latter. On one hand, Eliza considered it a rare opportunity to witness native customs, but on the other, the pagan aspect made her uncomfortable.

As the other women, mainly family members—Eliza guessed they could be called attendants—walked to the door, Eliza accompanied them. Behind her, she could hear the delicate swish of Temple's silk gown of pale lavender as she followed them.

Once they were down the staircase, Eliza spied Nathan Cole waiting at the front door, his crossed hands holding the Bible. But the women didn't approach him. Instead, the attendants led the bride to the dining room arch. The Blade and his companions stood in the opposite doorway to the main parlor.

A woman handed The Blade a blanket and a ham of venison. Then Victoria tearfully gave Temple the blanket and corn she carried. With ritualistic slowness, Temple and The Blade walked toward each other, their eyes locked together. Eliza had the distinct feeling that no one else existed for them.

When the couple met in the center of the plantation's great hall, they exchanged the venison and corn, then placed their blankets together. John Ross, the principal chief of the Cherokees, who had been standing next to Nathan, came forward and announced, "The blankets are joined."

Victoria pressed a linen handkerchief to her mouth and began to sob softly into it, the tears now rolling freely down her sallow cheeks. Eliza moved closer to her, concerned that in Victoria's weakened condition, she might suffer another of her terrible coughing spells.

The bride and groom then moved to stand before Nathan. Eliza thought Nathan looked nervous—and proud—as he fumbled briefly before opening the book to the proper page. She smiled, remembering how happy he had been when Temple had requested he perform the wedding ceremony.

"Dearly beloved," he began, his voice cracking, "we are gathered here today in the sight of God to join this man and this woman in holy matrimony . . ."

As she listened to them exchange their vows, their voices ringing so clearly and confidently, rich with feeling, Eliza experienced a twinge of envy. She would never know a love like that. Just for an instant, she wanted to cry. Then she sternly reminded herself that her spinster status was by choice. She had her life's work, and her independence, something no married woman could claim.

"By the powers vested in me, I now pronounce you man and wife," Nathan declared.

Eliza didn't join the throng of family and friends that converged on the newly married pair. Instead, she joined Nathan.

"They make a handsome couple." He fairly beamed with pride.

"Indeed." She was obliged to agree.

"Now the feasting begins," Nathan said and smiled a warning. "It is likely to go on for hours."

"Heaven knows enough food has been prepared." Eliza watched as Will Gordon opened the door for the newlyweds.

As The Blade and Temple stepped outside to greet the mass of guests waiting for them to appear, each held an end of the blankets; The Blade carried the corn and Temple the venison.

"Shall we join them?" Nathan offered Eliza his arm. Together, they followed the couple onto the veranda. "This is symbolic, you know," he said in a quiet aside. "The joining of blankets represents a promise to live together, and the trading of venison and corn is an exchange of vows—the man pledging to provide food for her and the woman promising to prepare the meal. A silent but solemn commitment, I suppose you could call it."

The peacocks had long ago abandoned the lawn to the crush of guests now thronging around the newly married couple. The peal of their laughter and their happy shouts spread across the plantation. Caught by the joyous mood, Eliza paused at the top of the veranda steps and let it sweep over her.

When Nathan started down the steps, she pressed her hand more firmly on his arm, checking him. "Wait," she said, gazing at the scene. "Have you ever seen anything like this?"

From the veranda steps of the manor house, built on a natural rise, they could see everything—the swarm of people in their varied and colorful dress, the banquet tables heaped with food beneath the shade trees, and the chain of slaves, moving back and forth between the tables and kitchens. Over it all hung a canopy of blue sky, lit by the blazing bright ball of the sun.

"It seems we have some late arrivals to the wedding," Nathan remarked.

Following the direction of his gaze, Eliza noticed the riders coming up the road. Observing their dusty and slightly disheveled appearance, she wondered how far they had traveled to attend the wedding feast. As she caught sight of the wagon lumbering behind them, two things struck her—they were all men, and they carried muskets.

"The Guard." She dug her fingers into the sleeve of Nathan's coat. "It is the Georgia Guard," she said louder, her certainty growing.

Will Gordon stood before her, his narrowed gaze focused on the approaching band of riders.

"Why are they here? What do they want?" she murmured with both irritation and concern.

"Me." The answer came from Nathan.

Startled, Eliza turned to stare at him. There was a pallor to his face and a drawn, apprehensive look that hadn't been there before. Was he right? Lately the Guard seemed to take considerable delight in baiting and harassing the missionaries. On many occasions, their mockery had amounted to outright blasphemy. Once, after witnessing the baptism of several Cherokee converts in the river, members of the Guard had ridden their horses into the water and proceeded to baptize their steeds, repeating the holy words of the baptismal sacrament in open sacrilege.

Yes, Eliza suspected Nathan had cause to believe he would be the Guard's target. And she knew, too, that he had thus far refrained from swearing an oath of allegiance to Georgia. He was in violation of the law and subject to arrest. No longer did he have the protection of being considered a federal employee. By presidential order, he had been stripped of his position as postmaster.

Suddenly she was worried for him. "Nathan, you must leave . . . now."

He hesitated, as if tempted to agree, then his glance skittered over the milling throng, many of them as yet unaware of the Guard's presence. "I cannot," he murmured with a trace of despair.

Eliza regretted suggesting it. How could he flee from those who would persecute him and still urge these people to oppose peacefully any attempt to drive them from the lands that rightfully belonged to them? But Eliza knew from past conversations that there was another choice he would ultimately have to make—to take the oath or refuse. Freedom or imprisonment.

The small detachment of state militia cantered their horses into the crowd. The wedding guests scurried out of their way, the level of voices fading to a murmur. The air was no longer filled with festive sounds but was claimed instead by the clatter of hooves and the creaking of saddle leather. The mounted group reined to a halt and bunched loosely in front of the veranda, their bayonets glistening ominously in the bright sunlight.

"Good afternoon, gentlemen." Will Gordon stepped down, positioning himself between Nathan and the apparent leader of the Guard. "What can I do for you?" His expression remained blandly pleasant and unconcerned.

"Who are you?" Neither the man's tone nor his look could be described as friendly.

"Will Gordon. And you, sir?"

"Jacob Brooks, sergeant in the Georgia Guard." The man straightened, assuming a military erectness in the saddle as if to further assert his authority.

At that moment, The Blade moved to the base of the steps and paused before the mounted soldier. "Sergeant Brooks, we invite you and your men to dismount and join our wedding feast."

Eliza saw Temple flash an angry glance at her new husband. If he was aware of her disapproval, he gave no sign of it.

"A wedding, eh? And who performed this marriage?" the sergeant demanded, his glance already traveling to Nathan.

Nathan cleared his throat nervously. "I did."

"Seize him."

The suddenness—the casualness—of it caught Eliza by surprise. She stared in disbelief as three men dismounted and started up the steps.

"Reverend Cole is my guest," Will Gordon protested.

"He is the State of Georgia's guest now," the sergeant replied curtly.

When the three guardsmen surrounded Nathan and grabbed his arms, Eliza tried to stop them. "You cannot do this." When they pushed her out of the way, she turned on the sergeant. "Where is your warrant?"

"We have no need of one."

"Then what is the charge?" she demanded angrily. "Why are you arresting him?"

"We don't need a reason." He turned in his saddle, deliberately ignoring her. "Bring up the wagon."

Amidst the jingling rattle of harness and trace chains, a baggage wagon trundled forward. In shock and dismay, Eliza stared at the two men stumbling along behind it, frantically clutching at the neck chains that bound them to the back of the wagon. She recognized Samuel Worcester, Nathan's fellow missionary at New Echota.

As the guardsmen hauled Nathan to the wagon, Eliza ran down the steps. "No. You have no right!"

A pair of hands caught her from behind, crushing the full sleeves of her gown in an iron grip and stopping her headlong rush. "Miss Hall, no," Will Gordon muttered near her ear, urging caution.

But she continued to strain against his hold as she watched them wind a trace chain around Nathan's neck, then similarly attach it to a horse ridden by one of the Guard. Part of her knew she was powerless to prevent this, yet she refused to stand by and do nothing while they treated this kind, gentle man like a common felon.

The rider abruptly wheeled his horse around, causing a yank on the chain which sent Nathan to his knees. He managed to scramble to his feet in time to avoid being dragged when the rider put a heel to his horse and sent it lunging forward. He laughed at Nathan's frantic attempts to keep up. The rest of the Guard swung in behind them, cutting off her view.

Eliza sagged backward in defeat, now letting the hands support her. "Where will they take him?" she wondered aloud as the small cavalcade rode away from the house.

"To Camp Gilmer, outside of Lawrenceville, I expect," Will answered.

Eliza stared at the cloud of red dust kicked up by the

company of the state militia. "This is wrong." She balled her hands into fists. "All of it—everything—it is just so wrong!"

"Yes."

The wedding feast continued, but it never recaptured its earlier carefree and happy mood.

A purpling twilight bathed the shadows cast by the towering trees that graced the lawn of Seven Oaks. The main house was a large, two-story structure built of wood. Its exterior was weather-boarded and painted a crisp white. There were verandas front and back, and a balcony above the front porch supported by turned columns. And everywhere there were windows flanked by painted shutters.

At the back of the house, Phoebe counted two kitchens and decided the third building was a smokehouse. From the outside, Seven Oaks looked every bit as big as Gordon Glen. She leaned forward in the carriage seat, straining to see more of her new home.

She was excited and scared all at the same time. Her stomach was all fluttery and jumpy like a chicken with a fox outside the pen. She wasn't Master Will's property anymore. She was Miss Temple's dower Negro. She had on her best dress, made from store-bought cloth, and brass-toed shoes, while the rest of her few belongings were tied in a bundle at her feet.

She stole a glance at Deu, riding behind the carriage. She wished he would look at her. Maybe she wouldn't feel so scared inside if he would smile at her instead of acting like she wasn't even there.

The carriage rolled to a stop in front of the house. Phoebe picked up her bundle and clutched it tightly to her. Master Blade climbed out of the carriage, then turned and helped her mistress down. Phoebe scrambled after them, then hesitated, uncertain where to go or what to do next. She looked to Deu, hoping he would give her a sign, but he stood attentively before Master Blade, awaiting his own instructions.

"See that my wife's trunks are brought inside," The Blade said, arching a warm glance at Miss Temple. "Then you can show young Phoebe where she will stay. We won't need you anymore this evening."

"Phoebe is *my* servant. I shall dismiss her," Temple declared, her black eyes flashing fire as Phoebe had seen them do many times when she got cross about something.

The more she thought about it, Phoebe realized her new mistress had been almighty quiet during the carriage ride. She darted a quick look at Master Blade, wondering what he had said or done to get her all heated up like that.

She saw him smile at Temple, kind of amusedlike, and incline his head ever so slightly. "By all means, dismiss her."

Even though he had given in, it didn't appear to sit too well with Miss Temple. "That will be all, Phoebe. Go with . . . Deuteronomy."

"Yes'm." Phoebe bobbed a quick curtsy, but Temple had already spun away to walk to the front door.

Deu climbed the steps to the cabin ahead of her and pushed open the door. He had spent half of last night sweeping the dirt floor until there wasn't a piece of dust left, but it still didn't change what it was, a slave's shack with no windows, an open fireplace, a straw bed in the corner, and a crudely built table with stumps for seats in the middle of the single room. The only nice thing in the place was the rocking chair by the fireplace that old Master Stuart had given him when the seat busted. He had managed to fix it, although it still pinched your bottom if you sat in it wrong.

"Is this it?" Phoebe tried to peer around him to see inside.

"Yes." Deu hesitated a second longer, then walked inside. "It's dark. You'd better let me light the candle."

As the flame threw its wavering light over the room, deepening the shadows in the corners, Phoebe stepped inside, still clutching the bundle in front of her. He watched her look slowly all around the room, conscious of the spreading tightness in him.

"Phoebe . . ." But when he had to meet those big dark eyes of hers, the words wouldn't come out.

"Is something wrong, Deu?" She tipped her head to the side, studying him curiously.

"No . . . yes . . ." He stopped and started over. "Master Blade has given his permission for you to be my woman."

Her eyes widened into two big black pools of trusting innocence. "You asked him?"

"No." Deu looked away. "But he knew I had ideas in that direction. That's why he did it without waiting for me to ask. I know that you're too young—"

"But I'm a woman." In the candlelight, she seemed to float across the space to stand in front of him, her face all upturned and eager. "And I want to be your woman, Deu."

"You don't know what you're saying." He stared at her, hurting inside so much that he thought he would break apart from the pain.

"But I do." She smiled at him confidently, her face glowing. "Many's the night I've laid awake listening to the sounds of my mammy and pappy coupling in the next bed, pleasuring each other. I know all about it, Deu. I know why my pappy breathes so hard and why my mammy groans so soft and low. I've touched myself sometimes and . . . and the ache I felt was good," she admitted, briefly self-conscious. "And I want for you to touch me like that, Deu. I've wanted it for a long time." She moved closer to him. "Please."

Her words, her nearness were more than he could resist. He reached out and pulled her against him, shuddering uncontrollably. "I've wanted you for a long time, too, Phoebe," he declared. "I was just waiting for you to grow up."

"But I am grown." She removed the bundle of her belongings that kept their bodies from touching as fully as each wanted.

He wasn't sure about her being grown, but right now he

just wanted to hold her. "I wish I could have heard the words the preacher said today. I wish we could marry up proper. Say more and do more than just jump over a broom."

"Words or no words, broom or no broom, I'm going to be your woman for as long as I live."

She didn't understand and Deu didn't try to explain it to her. Being an educated slave, he knew there were other ways—proper ways—of making Phoebe his wife. Ways that gave it more dignity and meaning than the slave custom of jumping over a broom. Ways that expressed the feelings he had for her and made them something special and lasting.

He loved her. He loved the sweetness of her eager kisses and the innocence of her clinging arms, doubting she could possibly know the rough, raw needs she aroused in him as he struggled to contain them, afraid they would frighten her.

He pulled back and gazed at her face—at her glistening lips, wet from his kisses. "You're so young, Phoebe." His voice trembled like his fingers when he caressed the shiny roundness of her cheek. "A woman-child, that's what you are. A beautiful woman-child."

Hurt flashed in her eyes, then she stepped back, a determined set to her features as she unfastened her dress and pulled it over her head. Frozen, Deu stared at her naked, brown body and her young breasts that had ripened within these past months.

"Deu, please touch me," she whispered. But he couldn't. He couldn't move. The need in him was too great. He was certain he'd explode with it right there on the spot. "I want you to."

Reaching out, she took his hand and guided it to her breast. He felt the little shudder that quivered through her, but it was nothing compared to the quaking in his own body. His self-control was too fragile, his restraint too tenuous; he had to take it slow as he lovingly fondled her breasts, knowing it wasn't enough. He wanted to touch all of her and feel her body under his, all warm and open and giving.

She arched against his hands, inviting and encouraging him to explore and discover the firmness of her taut bottom and the thinness of her ribs. All the while, her eyes never left his face, their lids drooping sometimes in obvious pleasure or opening wide in wondrous surprise. When at last he dared to let his hand slide onto her mound, her knees buckled and she collapsed against him.

"Yes, there," she moaned, then lifted her head to gaze at him again, her own features slack with desire. "I want you, Deu."

He hesitated, longing to believe she knew what she was saying. Then he felt her hand at the crotch of his trousers gliding up to feel the outline of his erection. A groan came from his throat, destroying the last shred of his control. He carried her to the bed in the corner and laid her down on its straw mattress, then hastily stripped off his own clothes to join her.

As he moved to kiss her, he murmured thickly, "I'll try not to hurt you, Phoebe. I'll try." But he knew he would this time. Later she would find out how good it could really feel.

In the master bedroom of the main house, The Blade stood at the balcony doorway and listened to the sound of Temple's voice as she crisply instructed the servants in the placement of her trunks. Below, fireflies floated over the lawn, their winking glow appearing first one place, then another.

The door closed, accompanied by receding footsteps, leaving only the rustle of Temple's movements to mar the stillness of the room. Slowly, he turned from the balcony opening and the evening breeze that wandered through it. Temple had her back to him as she stood in front of the long mirror and unpinned the trailing white lace of her veil. Thoughtfully, he studied her reflection, noting the taut smoothness of her features and the anger that smoldered in her eyes.

"We are alone now." He watched her stiffen at the sound of his voice and caught the slashing glance she threw at his reflection. "Perhaps you would care to tell me why your eyes have been throwing knives at me all afternoon. I am fortunate to have only one scar."

She avoided his gaze as she swept the lace from her head. "How could you invite those . . . animals to our wedding feast?"

"What should I have done?" Idly, he moved away from the balcony doors. "Tell them they were not welcome and order them to leave? They would hardly have paid attention to that."

"No. But neither would it have appeared as if you *welcomed* them," she retorted, spinning to confront him. "Have you forgotten they are our enemies?"

"No, but I hoped I might distract them long enough for your Reverend Cole to slip away. I thought you would have guessed that."

"If I didn't, it is because you sounded much too sincere." She turned away, still angry, but The Blade could tell that her anger lacked its previous heat.

Moving to stand behind her, he slid his hands around her small, tightly corseted waist and bent to nibble at her neck. "I was sincere—sincere in not wanting our wedding feast spoiled."

"They *did* spoil it."

Taking her firmly by the shoulders, he turned her around to face him, then pulled her closer, a hand gliding to the small of her back to cradle her against his hips in subtle suggestion. He ignored the stiffness that was her one show of resistance. "Are you going to let them spoil our night as well?"

"No."

"Prove it," he challenged lazily.

She paused, peering at him through the top of her lashes, a knowing gleam in her eyes. "Maybe I have no wish to."

"You want to, all right." He smiled faintly, aware of her new pliancy in his arms.

An instant later she confirmed it, winding her hands around

his neck and meeting him halfway when he bent to kiss her. Her response seared through him, her lips devouring while her tongue enticed. The Blade was half convinced that he was the one being slowly seduced—not that he objected.

Again and again her lips claimed his mouth, sometimes softly, sometimes hungrily, sometimes yielding, sometimes demanding. Then, breathing heavily, she trailed her moist lips over his face, her teeth grazing over his jaw to stop near his ear.

"I love you." Her breath fanned his ear, warm and stirring.

"I must be mad," he declared thickly. "Because I love you, too."

"Do you?" She nibbled at him as her fingers worked to untie the silk cravat at his neck. "How much?"

After the cravat hung loose, her deft fingers shifted to the buttons of his tucked shirtfront and high-standing collar while her mouth continued its moist exploration of his jaw, ear, and neck.

"Too much." He caught hold of her hands, preventing them from undressing him further, aware that it would be too easy to let her take control of the moment. Something warned him not to give her that kind of power over him or she would lead him in a merry dance the rest of his life. It was a question of survival.

"Is something wrong, my love?" So innocent were her words, yet so knowing were her eyes.

His mouth quirked briefly in a dry smile. "The room has become uncomfortably warm, as if you didn't know." He shrugged out of his coat and his waistcoat and pulled the cravat from around his neck, tossing them all on a chair and leaving only the white cambric of his shirt and dove gray twill of his trousers to cover him. "Have you not grown warm as well, Mrs. Stuart?" he murmured, arching a brow in question.

"Indeed, sir, very warm." Gracefully, she turned her back

to him, presenting him with the row of buttons that fastened her lavender silk gown.

With deliberate slowness, The Blade unbuttoned her gown while he nibbled at her neck the way she had nibbled at his, then he expanded the area to the ridge of her shoulder, smiling at the shivers of pleasure that danced over her skin. When the gown was fully loosened, he slipped it from her shoulders and arms in a long caress, then let it fall to the floor.

Reaching around in front of her, he untied the ribbons that secured her bustle, spreading one hand against the top of her stomach and feeling her back arch into him like a cat's. Next he unfastened the strings of her petticoats. Then, picking up her chemise-clad body, he lifted her out of the layers of clothing. She turned in his arms, her mouth seeking his, for a moment distracting him from his task with the heat of her kiss. For an instant, he wanted to pursue it, but he forced himself not to until he had bared her flesh to his hands, determined to take his time and enjoy every second of the moment when she finally became his.

He lowered her feet to the floor once again and dragged the long skirt of her chemise up to her waist. With her help, he pulled it over her head, only to be confronted with another layer of undergarments, infinitely more stimulating ones.

"Something can definitely be said for the old ways of the Cherokees," he murmured impatiently as he gazed at the twin mounds of her breasts bulging from atop the corset that just barely covered her nipples, momentarily mesmerized by their agitated rise and fall. "A man had fewer clothes to contend with."

He glanced once at her lips, parted in anticipation of his touch, then watched her breasts as he freed the laces that cinched the corset together. When the front gaped open, revealing the full roundness of her breasts and their tantalizing peaks, he wasn't conscious of her hands tugging the hem of his shirt loose from the confining band of his trouser waist. Then he felt the coolness of her hands gliding up his stomach.

He pulled the shirt over his head, then carried Temple to the bed, setting her on the side of it. There, she slipped off her low-heeled white pumps and slowly rolled down her stockings for him. The Blade peeled off her drawers, conscious of the nearly unbearable pressure in his loins. At last she sat naked before him, his to touch, to take, and to love.

"Blade." The intense ache in her voice almost brought him to her side.

But he stepped back, his jaw clenched, and stripped off the rest of his clothes beneath her heated gaze. Her eyes were drawn to the bronzed contours of his chest, the masculine flatness of his belly, and the muscled tautness of his buttocks. Enthralled by the beauty of his body, Temple longed to touch his firm flesh, explore its hardness, and feel it against her own skin.

She had one very brief thought of Eliza Hall and her foolish sense of modesty, but when The Blade came to join her on the bed, her former teacher was the last thing on her mind. She went into his arms as naturally as if she had been there countless times before.

His kisses bathed her in pleasurable sensation as he nipped deliciously at her throat and ear while his fingers plucked the confining pins from her hair and combed it free. Her own hands, greedy for the feel of his body, stroked the tapering length of his back, the sinewed leanness of his shoulders, and the solidness of his flesh. As he laid her back on the bed, she was acutely aware of the responses he aroused in her.

His hands, lips, and tongue seemed to be everywhere, tracing every curve and hollow of her body, tasting her breasts and arousing her totally. Unable to remain still, she writhed against him, inviting him closer, urging him with her hands, her hips, and her body. She tried to return the caresses and excite him as wildly and as rawly as he did her. When his fingers slid between her thighs and explored the wetness of her opening, his touch intensified the throbbing ache she felt inside.

"Please," she moaned.

Maneuvering himself above her, The Blade moved between her thighs, then paused to look down on her, noting the cascading black silk of her hair, the kiss-bruised pout of her lips, and the stain of passion on her cheeks.

Steeling himself to keep control, he slid a hand under her bottom and positioned her to receive him. He found her easily, her body arching to accept him into her tight sheath. As he probed deeper, encountering her barrier, he felt her stiffen and try to strain away from him. He firmly held her hips in position and made one quick, sure thrust, cutting off her sharp cry with a kiss.

He remained buried inside her and forced his hips not to move as they wanted to, as his whole body desperately wanted them to. Instead, he concentrated his attention on her body, kissing her slowly and deeply, caressing the hardened points of her breasts, and waiting for the pain to subside and the tense resistance to leave.

Gradually, he felt her start to relax and respond tentatively to his manipulating hands. He began to move inside her, holding himself to gentle, undulating strokes. His patience was soon rewarded as her hips were no longer still beneath him. She met and matched his rhythm. Her hands glided over him, curling into his hair and splaying over his buttocks, urging and demanding in their exhortations. Again, moans of pleasure, like the throaty purrings of a cat, came from her lips.

The tempo increased with the mounting pressure that clamored for release. His driving thrusts became deeper and harder. He barely noticed the poised stillness that briefly had Temple straining against him, but he was aware of rippling tightness that seemed to draw him deeper inside her. For a split second he was shaken by the sensation that he was being swallowed whole. Then it didn't matter as a series of spiraling shudders swept him above and beyond.

Later, lying contentedly in his arms, Temple gazed at her

husband's face, admiring its lean, strong lines. Idly, she traced the white scar above his left cheekbone with her fingertips.

He took her hand and carried it to his mouth, pressing a kiss in its palm. "You have left your mark on me as well, Temple."

"Have I?"

"Such innocence from a woman who arouses me with her touch," he mocked, making her suddenly aware of the growing hardness against her leg. Then he was kissing her, blotting everything else from her mind except the sensation of his body loving hers.

The next time Eliza saw Temple, nearly a week after the wedding, she was struck by her radiance. Temple glowed with a maturity and a confidence that was new. She was a wife now, the mistress of her own household, a woman who had known a man's passion. It showed in her eyes, her face, and her bearing.

Eliza found it impossible to regard Temple as a former pupil. They were two women, conversing as adults. When Temple inquired about the latest news of Reverend Cole, Eliza was surprised to hear herself confiding her concerns.

In all, eleven whites, most of them missionaries, had been arrested by the Georgia Guard. They had been marched—chained like slaves and prodded by bayonets—some sixty miles over marsh and mountain to the jail at Camp Gilmer, where they were being held in poorly ventilated cells, without even the smallest of comforts. The commander of the Guard had refused them permission to conduct religious services for the other inmates, stating that they had been arrested to "curtail their activities, not to promote them." A judge was scheduled to hear their case at the end of the month.

On the twenty-third of July, the judge of the superior court for Gwinnette County indicted all the missionaries and released them on bond pending their September trial. Nathan was temporarily free but denied permission to return to Cherokee lands within the boundaries of Georgia. He wrote to Eliza from Alabama, expressing his fears that the coming trial was a mere formality. Georgia intended to convict them and sentence them to the fullest penalty: four years' hard labor in the penitentiary at Milledgeville.

"If I am in prison, how can I provide spiritual comfort to the Cherokees at a time when they need it so desperately?" he wrote. Reading between the lines, Eliza knew he regretted his decision to defy Georgia by refusing to swear allegiance to her.

She wrote back reminding him of the growing swell of sympathetic public opinion from as far away as Boston and Baltimore and as close as Georgia itself. If the worst happened and he were imprisoned, the injustice of it could only advance the Cherokee cause.

But as Nathan had predicted, the September trial was a travesty. The judge declared that it was "the duty of every Christian to submit to civil authority." This the missionaries had failed to do. On those grounds, he found them guilty and sentenced them to a term of four years of hard labor at the Milledgeville penitentiary.

Three days after he was scheduled to begin serving his term, Nathan arrived at Gordon Glen, thinner and paler from his ordeal. Haltingly, he explained that a pardon had been offered to all the prisoners on the condition that they either take the oath of allegiance to the State of Georgia or leave the state entirely. Nathan chose the former so he could return to the people who needed him.

"The others agreed to the conditions," he said at the dinner table. "All of them, that is, except Samuel Worcester and Elizur Butler. They refused to do either. The warden argued with them for hours, trying to persuade them to change their minds. All the while the prison guards kept opening and shutting the gate. I can still hear the grating of the hinges when it swung open, and that loud ominous clang when it shut." He paused, his expression haunted. "The last time I saw them, they were wearing prison clothes."

Vividly, Eliza pictured the scene he described. Her heart went out to those two brave missionaries who had chosen the martyrdom of imprisonment rather than bow to their oppressors. By the same token, she was disappointed in Nathan. She would have had much more respect for him if he had stood beside Samuel Worcester and Elizur Butler.

Later, when she and Nathan went for a walk by the creek alone, he seemed to sense her disapproval and tried to justify himself. But Eliza had heard it all before. "I know, 'render unto Caesar.'"

"It is that and more, Eliza," he insisted. "It is the whole issue of the separation of church and state. We have religious freedom because of that very precept. How can I disobey the civil laws?"

"But you were innocent." She didn't understand why he couldn't see that. "You violated no Cherokee law. And Georgia doesn't legally have jurisdiction here." When she saw his pained and tormented look, Eliza instantly regretted her sharp condemnation of him. "I am sorry, Nathan. I know you did what you thought was best, regardless of how others may perceive it—including myself. I admire you for that."

He took her hand and held it tightly in his. "Thank you, Eliza. If you had thought ill of me, I would have found that very difficult to bear."

There was something very appealing in his woebegone look. Eliza wished she had initially been more charitable. She felt guilty that she had even briefly harbored an unkind opinion.

The stand taken by the two missionaries accomplished two very important things for the Cherokee people, as Eliza had instinctively known it would. Their act of courage became a symbol for the rest of the Nation. That they would endure the injustice of false imprisonment had renewed the resolution of the Cherokees and provided them with a source of strength.

But Eliza hadn't guessed their imprisonment would give the Nation's attorneys another case to take to the Supreme Court of the United States, a case that gave the Court jurisdiction. Two white citizens were bringing suit against the State of Georgia to test the validity of Georgia laws over the Cherokee domain.

When Benjamin F. Currey, the new superintendent of Indian removal appointed by Jackson, arrived in the fall to pay any family who would voluntarily emigrate to the West, only a few accepted his offer. Adversity had united them. They would not be induced or driven from the land of the fathers.

Although the leaders considered it expedient to hold their annual October council meeting at a site in Alabama rather than risk a certain confrontation with the Georgia Guard by holding it in New Echota in defiance of the law, to meet at all was regarded as a moral victory.

The message that came from the October council was the same as all previous ones: the Cherokees were of one mind; they would not remove. A delegation was appointed to carry their messages once again to Washington City. This time, The Blade Stuart, the son of the highly respected chieftain Shawano Stuart, was to accompany his father-in-law, Will Gordon, John Ridge, and the other delegates to the federal capital.

When Temple learned of his appointment, she insisted on going with him. She had never seen any of the American cities others talked about. The Blade gave in to her demands and agreed to take her with him.

Temple immediately realized her wardrobe was inadequate for the trip. With Eliza, she pored over the latest periodicals in an attempt to determine the fashion in traveling clothes, day dresses, and evening attire. Eliza was concerned that Temple's preoccupation with fashionable dress exhibited an unbecoming vanity. But Temple's point was inarguable. She would represent Cherokee womanhood. Therefore, it was important that she look not only presentable but fashionable as well.

Styles were chosen, fabrics and colors were selected from the best store in Augusta. Thus armed, Temple set her Negro seamstress to work on her new clothes.

◅ 15 ▻

Washington City
December 1831

After checking their wraps at the cloakroom of a popular hostelry in Washington City, Temple and The Blade proceeded to the large reception hall decorated with mistletoe and pine garlands. When they paused inside the doorway, The Blade noticed the way heads turned to admire the woman at his side, stunning in an off-the-shoulder gown of white satin shot with gold threads.

"Do you see my father?" Temple asked.

The Blade spotted him on the fringes of a large group in a corner. "This way." He guided her toward Will Gordon, keeping a firm and possessive hand on her all the way.

Observing their approach, Will Gordon smiled a welcome. "I didn't see you arrive," he remarked as the man with him turned to view the newcomers. "Did you have difficulty hiring a hack?"

"Fortunately, no," The Blade replied.

"This stunning woman cannot be your daughter, Will," Payton Fletcher declared.

"Indeed it is," Will replied proudly. "Temple, I would like you to finally meet my old and dear friend from Massachusetts, Payton Fletcher. Payton, my daughter, Temple Gor—Stuart."

"I have long wished to meet you, Mr. Fletcher. My father has spoken of you often."

"My dear Temple, forgive me. I am speechless." With an elaborate show of gallantry, he kissed her hand. "Your father has often mentioned you as well, but I discounted much of what he said as a father's boasting. Now I see that he exaggerated not one whit."

"Nor did he exaggerate about your gift for words, Mr. Fletcher." A smile dimpled the outer corners of her mouth.

"Wit as well as beauty—I am in awe."

"And I believe you met my son-in-law, The Blade Stuart, earlier today," Will inserted.

"Yes, briefly. It is good to see you again, Mr. Stuart." A hearty smile once again ringed his face as Payton Fletcher shook hands with The Blade. "I don't need to tell you how lucky you are to be married to such a lovely woman. Your wife will be the talk—no, the toast of Washington City."

The Blade smiled in response, but none too warmly. He was well aware of the stir his wife was creating, and his feelings about it were mixed.

"Isn't that a delegate from the western Cherokees?" Will indicated a man entering the room.

"I believe it is," Payton Fletcher confirmed, then turned back to them, arching one eyebrow in grim resignation. "We aren't the only ones courting support."

"Unfortunately, it is our removal they seek so that they may gain more land in the West and a larger annuity," Will murmured.

Temple knew that twenty-three years earlier, in 1808, a band of some twelve hundred Cherokees, led by their chieftain, Tahlonteskee, had voluntarily migrated to lands west of the Mississippi River. A year before that, Tahlonteskee and Doublehead had accepted bribes from the federal government in return for ceding a large section of Cherokee land, a violation of the Blood Law. Doublehead had subsequently been executed for his role in the treaty, and Tahlonteskee, fearing the same fate, had chosen to leave his homeland with some of his people. Since then, they had called themselves the western band of the Cherokees.

"I doubt that they will have much success in acquiring more land," Payton said, then noticed someone in the crowd. "There's a young man here I want you to meet, Will." He raised a hand. "Jed. Jed! Over here." After gaining the man's attention, he said to Will, "Jed is my godson. He graduated from the military academy at West Point this past summer, and he has been assigned duty here in Washington."

His reference to the military instantly brought the Georgia Guard to Temple's mind. But the young, square-shouldered man in dress uniform who joined them bore no resemblance to those rough men. His hair was darkly golden, like tobacco leaves curing in the sheds. There was a freshly scrubbed look to his handsome, clean-shaven features, and his eyes were a clear, friendly blue.

"Will, may I present my godson, Lieutenant Jedediah Parmelee, late of Boston, Massachusetts, and now of Washington City. Jed, this is a very dear friend of mine, Mr. Will Gordon."

"How do you do, sir." With military precision, Jed Parmelee extended a hand to the man who towered over him by a good five inches, but he remembered nothing after that. His gaze was fixed on the incredibly beautiful woman next to Will Gordon.

He had thought such beauty existed only in paintings—or a man's imagination. The blackness of her hair, the creaminess of her skin, and her eyes—so darkly mysterious, yet so alive. They seemed almost boldly curious. An instant later he realized her gaze was aimed at him.

"And this ravishing young lady," he heard Payton say, "is his wife, Temple Stuart."

Wife. The word splintered through him, shattering his hopes, dreams, and desires before they could fully take shape.

"This is an honor, Mrs. Stuart." He bowed stiffly, not completely trusting himself to do more. He wondered which one was her husband. It had to be the one with the scar, the one staring at him as if he knew exactly what he was thinking—it had to be him. For one stormy moment, Jed wanted to challenge him to a duel. Pistols at ten paces.

But the reason and discipline that had been drilled into him at the academy led to cooler thinking. He smiled at her. "I was on my way to the refreshment table. May I bring you something, Mrs. Stuart?"

"The refreshment table?"

Her gaze roved over the crowded room as if seeking its location. Jed sensed her curiosity. "Perhaps you would prefer to peruse the fare for yourself. The table is on the far side of the room . . . where the guests are the thickest. I would be happy to escort you there," he offered.

"An excellent idea, Jed." Payton immediately voiced his approval. "I have a few things I want to discuss with Will and The Blade, and I am certain Temple would find them quite boring."

"I doubt that, Mr. Fletcher," she replied. "But my husband has already explained to me that you Americans are uncomfortable discussing political matters in front of a woman. Excuse me, gentlemen, while I accompany Lieutenant Parmelee to the refreshment table."

When she took his arm, her husband looked none too pleased, but he made no objection. Not that Jed took that much notice of him. He was still puzzling over Temple's remark about Americans.

"Where did you say you were from, Mrs. Stuart?" He found it difficult to keep his glance from straying to the low neckline of her gown.

"Our plantation is about an hour's ride from New Echota . . . in the Cherokee Nation," she added.

"The Cherokee Nation?" He frowned, then suddenly remembered his godfather talking about his Indian friend Will Gordon. "Then you are . . ."

"Cherokee? Yes, I am."

"I'm sorry . . ."

"That I am Cherokee?"

"No." He stopped. "You must forgive me for putting this so badly. I apologize if I offended you, Mrs. Stuart. It was not my intent."

"That is quite all right, Lieutenant." Her eyes smiled up at him, all dark and glowing. "Your reaction is typical of others I have encountered recently. I should have ignored it. Please accept my apologies for my poor manners and for deliberately embarrassing you."

"I deserved it." He couldn't help but admire her pride, although he still found it difficult to believe that this enchantingly beautiful woman was of Indian extraction. The black hair and eyes, yes, but her skin was as smooth and pale as his mother's best porcelain.

"Yes, you did."

Initially taken aback by her candor, Jed suddenly broke into a laugh. It felt good, the sound matching the gladness he felt inside. But it ended on a sigh of regret. "Your husband must be very happy."

"As I am," she replied smoothly and directed her attention away from him. "What is that dance?"

Jed turned, startled to discover that the lilting music playing softly in the background was real. Somehow it had seemed part of the moment. He glanced at the couples whirling gracefully about the floor. "A waltz."

"It is very beautiful."

In some circles, a waltz was considered quite scandalous. Yet what better excuse could a man have to hold a woman in his arms? He hesitated, his glance skimming her profile as she watched the dancing couples, obviously intrigued by their flowing movements. "The steps are quite simple and easily learned. I would be honored to teach them to you."

She turned, her eyes fully on him. "I would like to learn."

"In that case, I shall be the envy of every man here." Jed bowed to her.

He showed her the pattern of the steps, counting them out for her. By the time they had circled the dance floor once, she had mastered them and followed him effortlessly, lithe and supple as a willow in his arms, responsive to the slightest pressure of his hand.

"Are you quite certain I am doing this correctly?" she asked skeptically, her glance scanning the other couples. "People are staring."

"They are staring at you. You are the most beautiful woman here—the most beautiful woman in Washington . . . maybe even the country."

She laughed, and it was the warm, throaty laugh of a woman rather than the high-pitched titters and giggles of the girls he knew.

"You are as extravagant in your praise as Mr. Fletcher," she accused lightly.

"I speak the truth. I have never met a woman as beautiful as you."

His statement seemed to give her pause. She looked at him anew, more curious than wary, although she was cautious. "Your wife would not like to hear you say that. Are you married, Lieutenant Parmelee?"

"No." He didn't mention Cecilia. No formal announcement of his engagement to her had been made. He didn't want to think about Cecilia, not tonight.

In the hotel room of the Indian Queen, Phoebe removed the last pin from Temple's hair and ran her fingers through the length of it to separate the roped strands. Temple passed her the hairbrush and glanced sideways at The Blade. His cravat, coat, waistcoat, and boots had already been given over to his servant's care. With the frilled front and cuffs of his shirt unbuttoned, he lounged in the chair, his long, trousered legs stretched in front of him, his stockinged feet propped on an ottoman, his look hooded and faintly brooding.

"Surely you discussed something other than the preparations for the suit the missionaries are bringing against Georgia in the Supreme Court," she said, wondering why she had to prompt him to tell her what had been discussed.

"Many things but none of them new. It's always the same, over and over and over," he murmured, watching the brush as Phoebe repeatedly dragged the bristles through her mistress's hair, stroke following stroke. By his very stillness, Temple sensed the restlessness inside him. She smiled, knowing how that pent-up energy would find its release. "That will be all, Phoebe," she said.

When the girl withdrew from the room, Temple rose from her chair. "Did I mention that Lieutenant Parmelee has offered to show me around Washington some afternoon when you are busy with your meetings?"

Like a spring uncoiling, The Blade came out of his chair. "The man is enamored with you," he muttered.

"Are you jealous?"

His head came up. "Should I be?"

"No." She walked over to him and slid her hands up his shirtfront, feeling his stomach muscles contract beneath her touch. "With you for a husband, I have no need for a lover."

"Remember that." His arms wound around her as his mouth came down. Temple pressed closer, assuring him in the one certain way she knew that she belonged to him completely.

Through the rest of December and into the first weeks of January, Jed Parmelee wangled every bit of off-duty time he could get, trading with officers or persuading them to cover for him, anything that would permit him to see Temple Stuart for an hour, an afternoon, or an evening. At every social function she attended, he was there, sometimes able to speak to her for only a few minutes before someone more noteworthy claimed her. Once he had tea with her. Another afternoon he took her on a tour of Washington, describing the capture of the city by the British, the burning of the presidential mansion, and Dolly Madison's rescue of George Washington's portrait.

At first Jed tried to convince himself he sought her company out of courtesy. She was without friends in the city and her husband was away much of the time, attending meetings. His godfather would have wanted him to keep her entertained. But the truth was inescapable. He was in love with her. He had fallen in love with her the instant he had seen her. No matter how absurd or foolishly romantic it sounded, it had happened just that way.

But to what end? He was engaged; she was married. And he was a gentleman, a man of West Point. It became a point of honor and pride that he not act the lovesick swain, not let her know how deeply he had grown to care for her . . . even when she informed him of her imminent departure from the city.

"So soon? Congress is still in session, and the Supreme Court has yet to hear your case. Why leave now?" Then a possible reason came to him. "Has your husband or one of the other members of the delegation seen the president?"

"No." Her glance drifted around the large room that served the Indian Queen Hotel as lobby, bar, and office. "Mr. Jackson still refuses to grant them an interview, although he has received the deputation from the western Cherokees," she added somewhat bitterly. "However, we did hear from the president, through his Secretary of War, by letter. Jackson's position was clearly stated."

Temple recalled it vividly; the contents had become ingrained in her mind. Chicken Snake Jackson, as John Ridge called him, felt sorry for them, but he would not lift a hand to help them. Instead, Jackson advised the Cherokees to treat and remove west of the Mississippi and abandon the land that held the bones of their fathers.

Temple confided none of this to the young lieutenant. "My husband and John Ridge have decided to join Elias Boudinot, the editor of our nation's newspaper, on a fund-raising tour through the Northern states. My father and the other delegates will take care of the remaining business here," she explained.

"My husband tells me we will be stopping in your home city of Boston."

"I shall write to my parents and ask them to ensure that you are warmly welcomed."

More words were said, but, in this public place, not the words he might have said if they had been alone. Jed watched her walk up the stairs, followed by her colored maid. It was unlikely he would ever see her again. No, that wasn't true. He would see her all the time—in his sleep and in his dreams.

They traveled to Philadelphia by stage. The Blade, who had chafed at the endless and futile meetings in Washington, welcomed both the change of scene and the activity. After their frustrating stay in the American capital, the City of Brotherly Love seemed to greet them with open arms.

From Philadelphia, they journeyed to New York, a teeming, throbbing city with crowded streets and multitudes of people. Two successful rallies at Clinton Hall raised eight hundred dollars and placed six thousand signatures on a memorial to be forwarded to Congress deploring Georgia's actions against the Cherokees. They continued on to New Haven, Connecticut, achieving similar results.

In late February, they arrived in Boston. More rallies were held at the Old South Church, led by the sedate and aging Lyman Beecher and John Pickering, a student of Indian languages. At the close of the last rally, an older, well-dressed couple accompanied by a young woman approached Temple. The couple introduced themselves as Lieutenant Jedediah Parmelee's parents.

"He sends his regards, and hopes your visit to Boston is warm in spite of winter weather," his mother explained.

"Your son was very kind to me when we were in Washington," Temple replied, and heard a faint noise that sounded very much like a scornful snort coming from the young lady with them. Beneath the flared brim of her bonnet, the woman's hair was the pale yellow of young corn silk, and her eyes were a faded blue. Twin dots of natural pink gave color to her cheeks and reminded Temple of a china doll she once had. And like a doll, the woman showed no expression, although there was an aura of hostility about her that puzzled Temple.

"Forgive me," Mrs. Parmelee inserted. "I failed to introduce my son's fiancée, Miss Cecilia Jane Castle. Cecilia, Mrs. Stuart."

Temple glanced sharply at Mrs. Parmelee, aware the lieutenant had made no mention of a fiancée. She could only guess at his reasons. "It is a pleasure to meet you, Miss Castle."

"Mrs. Stuart." Cecilia inclined her head in acknowledgement but didn't smile. The bilious feeling in her throat wouldn't permit it. She despised this woman whose beauty everyone raved about. Some were calling her an Indian princess. She might give the appearance of royalty, with her velvet gowns and regal airs, but she was still an Indian. One look at those full lips and bewitching eyes and any decent woman could see she was a Jezebel.

Cecilia was thankful that Jedediah's parents were offering their words of parting. She barely gave them time to finish before she turned and walked briskly away.

Restless and bored with the conversation around him, The Blade stared out the window of the building that housed the Boston-based American Board of Foreign Missions. They had spent three months talking and what did they have to show for it? Enough funds to keep the newspaper in operation for several more months, perhaps a year. But what progress had they made toward improving the situation at home? None. Even more frustrating, he could discern no plan. They were in limbo, waiting for a decision from the Supreme Court.

"We must remain united"; that was the recurrent theme The Blade heard day after day. Noble words, but hardly a plan. The commissioner of the mission board counseled patience, faith in the Divine Creator, and prayer. Laudable, but hardly practical. The Blade had agreed to appeal to the courts and the public, but if that failed, what would they do?

No one save himself wanted to discuss that question except in the vaguest language. It was as if everyone—including Temple—were blind to the possibility. The few times he had attempted to express his concern and his desire for an alternative plan of action, Temple had turned him aside, saying, "It will never happen. We will not lose. We cannot lose."

Shifting his gaze from the skeletal tree limbs in the park at Pemberton Square, The Blade glanced at her.

"How long will it be before we receive word of the Supreme Court's verdict, Mr. Fletcher?" she asked.

"It's the first of March. I should imagine they will hand down their ruling anytime now." He rocked back on his heels, his thumbs hooked in the pockets of his waistcoat, the stance drawing attention to the protruding roundness of his stomach. He looked at The Blade, his gray eyes thoughtful and serious. "However, should the decision be made in our favor, you must know the existing laws do not give the president the power to enforce it."

"He cannot enforce a federal law?" The Blade narrowed his gaze in sharp question. "How can that be? What of his recent confrontation with South Carolina over the nullification issue? He threatened an invasion to ensure that no state overrules federal laws or secedes from the Union."

"But he will have to seek the authority from Congress before an invasion could be launched. The chief executive is not empowered to act on his own and order troops out."

Before The Blade could question him further on this new revelation, he was interrupted by the arrival of a gentleman known to John Ridge, Elias Boudinot. "The Supreme Court of the United States has ruled that the law by which Samuel Worcester and Dr. Elizur Butler were imprisoned is unconstitutional, and Georgia's entire Indian code along with it," Boudinot stated. "Marshall declared that the Cherokee Nation is a 'distinct community' occupying its own territory, and the laws of Georgia have no right to enter it! Justice Marshall declared the act of the State of Georgia to be void!''

The tension exploded in a burst of elation and congratulations. ''It's glorious,'' John Ridge declared exultantly.

''We did it! We won.'' Temple clasped The Blade's arm, hugging it in her excitement.

In the initial flurry of jubilation that enveloped the room, The Blade's silence went unnoticed. He smiled with the rest of them, and exchanged congratulatory handshakes.

The question was forever settled concerning the right of the Cherokees to their homeland. The controversy was between the government of the United States and Georgia.

The Blade wanted desperately to believe this signaled the end of their problems, but he feared it only marked the beginning of a new battle.

Within days, word filtered back to them of Jackson's response when he learned of the Supreme Court's verdict. He was said to have replied, ''John Marshall has made his decision; let him enforce it if he can.''

Soon newspapers were reporting that ''authentic sources'' in Washington confirmed the president was not going to enforce the ruling.

The delegates returned immediately to Washington City by stagecoach. This time, Jackson was quick to grant the delegation an audience. As they were ushered into his presence, The Blade could feel the tension in the group.

Lean of face and body, with still some of the roughness of the frontier about him despite his elegant attire, Jackson was a man of vigor and determination. The strong will that had prompted his opponents to give him the sobriquet King Andrew was very much in evidence. As a foe, he was formidable, The Blade recognized. Once Jackson set his feet on a path, nothing would turn him away from it.

Little time was wasted after the initial greetings were concluded. Jackson seemed to welcome it when John Ridge came directly to the point of the meeting. "What can the Cherokees expect?" he asked. "Will the power of the United States be used to execute the decision of the Supreme Court and put down the legislation of Georgia?"

"No. It will not." Jackson paused, letting the full weight of his answer resonate while his piercing gaze gauged the reaction of the delegates. "Go home and tell your people that their only hope for relief is to abandon their nation and remove to the West."

Visibly shaken, John Ridge could make no response. There was none to be made, no more to be said. The case had been won, but to no avail since Jackson refused to take the necessary measures to enforce it.

The Blade understood that they had won a victory but not the war. It was still being waged against them. As long as Jackson was siding with Georgia, there was no hope of retaining their land. In that moment The Blade wasn't certain the Cherokees could ever survive if they did not come to accept this reality.

They filed out of the room. None of them doubted they had heard the truth, and the reality of it was sobering.

As they started down the stairs from the second-floor offices, The Blade spied Temple anxiously pacing back and forth at the bottom. When she saw them, she stopped and went motionless for an instant. Then she ran to meet them.

"I could not wait at the hotel," she said. "What happened? What did he say?"

"Jackson will not enforce the decision," her father replied.

"No!" Temple drew back from him, her stunned glance sweeping the rest of them and seeing the confirmation written in their haunted expressions.

"You must not despair." Will Gordon drew her closer and put an arm around her shoulders. "Jackson occupies the presidency now, but the November elections will bring Henry Clay into office. He will see that the ruling is executed. We must be patient a little longer."

"Yes . . . yes, you are right," she agreed and tried to smile away her disappointment.

The Blade encountered John Ridge's despondent gaze and realized that Major Ridge's son was entertaining the same doubts he was. Both men knew their cause was lost. What The Blade had feared now loomed in his mind as the only viable alternative: to treat and remove.

The delegation remained in Washington, again making the circuit to reaffirm support for their cause. But, like the red clay banks of their home streams eroding away, their once staunch allies in Congress began to withdraw from them, expressing sympathy and giving pragmatic advice.

At an afternoon tea, Lieutenant Parmelee hovered attentively at Temple's side, relating some anecdote intended to entertain her. But Temple wasn't listening as she strained to overhear her husband's conversation with the congressional representative from Tennessee, the shrewd coonskin politician David Crockett.

"I understand you've been in touch with Justice John McLean," Crockett remarked, abandoning the backwoods dialect he often used in public to spin his frontier yarns. "What did he have to say?"

"He informed us that the Court does not have the power to force Jackson to implement its ruling."

"I also heard that he advised you to seek a new treaty, and offered to serve as one of the commissioners."

"He did. But our minds have not changed. We will not give up our land." The Blade mouthed the oft-repeated phrases, no longer feeling the conviction of his words.

"That's a noble sentiment, my friend, but it's also about as practical as grinnin' down a mean ole she-b'ar an' her cub," Crockett declared, a wry but sad smile edging his mouth.

"I know the war department has offered you some liberal treaty terms, giving you patents to land in Arkansas and allowing you to send a delegate to Congress, among other things. To be frank, I don't see where you have a choice. The wise course is to sit down and negotiate the best terms you can for your people."

His statement echoed the recommendations from virtually all their previous backers. The delegation had received a letter from the American Board of Foreign Missions in Boston—a group who had once championed their cause with all the zeal of the righteous—advising them to treat.

Of all the delegates, only The Blade's father-in-law, Will Gordon, continued to believe there was hope. He turned a deaf ear to the advice from their former allies and a blind eye to the steady erosion of their support. Only one other person aside from Will Gordon refused to accept the futility of the current stand against removal . . . Temple.

The Blade cast a brief glance in her direction, aware of the friction that now existed between them over this issue. To even hint that those around them might be right was to arouse her temper. After two heated arguments, he now avoided the subject entirely.

His glance fell on the golden-haired lieutenant. A part of him was glad that Parmelee had engaged her in conversation and prevented Temple from overhearing the discouraging advice from Crockett. But he also resented the attention the officer continued to lavish on his wife under the guise of friendship.

"I will inform the council of your recommendation, Mr. Crockett."

Temple caught her husband's noncommittal reply. At the same instant, Lieutenant Parmelee said something to momentarily distract her.

"I beg your pardon. What did you say, Lieutenant?"

"I wondered if you would like more tea."

"No, thank you."

"Is something wrong? Forgive me for being so forward, but you seem preoccupied."

"I was thinking of home." Which was close to the truth. "We will be leaving in a few days."

"Washington will seem very dull without you here to brighten it."

"That is hardly the impression I have received. Everyone I have met seems anxious for the Cherokees to leave." Behind the lightness of her reply, there was a tinge of bitterness.

"Not I. The thought of never seeing you again—" He broke off the sentence, his features stiffening into an expressionless mask as if trying to conceal the ardor that had been in both his voice and his eyes.

"Perhaps we shall meet again someday," she suggested gently.

"Perhaps," he agreed.

On the fifteenth of May, the delegation set out for home. When they returned, they found their families in high spirits, buoyed by the Supreme Court's decision yet puzzled by the continued imprisonment of the missionaries and the flood of surveyors from Georgia that had spread over Gordon Glen and Seven Oaks, marking trees and carving on posts, dividing the plantations into 160-acre parcels to be given away in a lottery in the fall.

With a heavy heart, Eliza listened to Will Gordon explain that nothing had changed. But he was convinced their vindication would follow the elections in November, elections that would vote a new administration into office, one more favorably disposed to the legal rights of the Cherokee Nation. Eliza believed as he did and wished that women had the right to vote so that she might cast a ballot against Jackson. She was tired of her passive role of moral support and longed for a more active one.

16

Gordon Glen
Christmas

A wet snow frosted the branches of the trees and covered the lawn of Gordon Glen with a soft blanket of white. In the dining room, flames danced over and under the logs in the fireplace, its mantel adorned with festive greenery. Platters of food crowded the table, leaving little room for the guests seated around it, members of the Gordon and Stuart families as well as Eliza and the visiting Nathan Cole.

With heads bowed, they listened to the grace offered by Nathan on this holy day. All except little Johnny, who fussed and fidgeted with a typical three-year-old's impatience at such things, mindless of his mother's quiet shushings.

When Nathan concluded the meal's prayer, Will Gordon picked up the carving knife and began to slice portions from the roast leg of lamb Black Cassie set before him. "This is indeed a bountiful feast you have prepared for us, Victoria," Will declared, glancing to the opposite end of his table at his wife.

Thinner and paler than a year ago, Victoria smiled back at him. "With reason. This is the first time you have been home to share it with us in several years. However, much of the credit for today's dinner belongs to Eliza. She supervised most of the meal preparations." Gratitude and a growing reliance mingled together in the look she gave Eliza.

"If the mutton is as succulent as it looks beneath the knife, it is an excellent job you have done, Miss Eliza Hall," Shawano Stuart proclaimed. "Mutton is my favorite. Did you know this?"

"No. For that, you must thank Mrs. Gordon. She chose the items for today's fare. I merely saw that her wishes were carried out."

With Victoria Gordon's health still precarious at best, Eliza had tried over the last several months to help in whatever capacity she could, gradually taking over many of the more arduous tasks. The additional rest seemed to have restored some of Victoria's strength. Eliza didn't mind the extra work, especially now. She shied away from that thought, not wanting the holiday spoiled by the shadows of gloom that Jackson's refusal to intervene had cast over the Nation.

"Miss Hall strung all the evergreen boughs, too," Xandra inserted brightly. "And she taught us the Christmas carol we will sing for you after dinner."

"You are stupid, Xandra." Kipp viewed his sister with superior contempt. "We aren't going to sing anything."

"Why?" Disappointment clouded her face.

"Because Charlie, Tom, and the others aren't here to sing their parts. That's why," he mocked.

"I forgot," she mumbled and looked down at her plate.

Eliza saw the pained look that flickered briefly in Will Gordon's face. A tense silence followed Xandra's unwitting introduction of the subject everyone had tried to avoid.

Temple sighed, and the sound carried a trace of anger. "I wish Uncle George and Aunt Sarah had stayed, at least until tomorrow. It is not the same without them around the table with us."

"It was their decision," Will Gordon reminded her.

"Do you think they reached Lookout Mountain before it began to snow?" Temple wondered.

"They should have," The Blade replied.

"Wet snows like this frequently cause avalanches in the mountains. What if they are stranded somewhere?"

"I am certain they are safe," Eliza offered into the silence that greeted Temple's comment.

"They never should have let those—people—have their house. Uncle George built it himself. It belonged to him and Aunt Sarah." Temple's voice trembled with barely controlled anger. "That lottery ticket the man had meant nothing. Georgia has no right to give away land and buildings that don't belong to it."

"Unfortunately, there is nothing we can do to stop them." Will forked a generous portion of the sliced lamb onto Shawano Stuart's plate.

"All this talk about lottery and giving away tracts of land to some holder of a pasteboard ticket. I never thought it would come to pass." Nathan stared at the platters of food on the table, but made no effort to dish any of it onto his plate. "I never believed Georgia would have the gall to commit such outright thievery."

"Now that Jackson has been elected to a second term, Georgia will grow even bolder," The Blade warned.

"You cannot be sure of that," Eliza protested. "Look at the stand Jackson took against South Carolina. He dispatched a warship and several cutters to Charleston, and threatened to send troops after Carolina attempted to overrule federal law and claim its own sovereignty. If he feels that strongly— to the extent that he would risk civil war—then he will not allow Georgia to defy the law."

"Jackson will not intervene, you can be certain of that, Miss Hall," The Blade chided her with a dry cynicism. "He has a double standard where Indians are concerned. South Carolina is wrong, but Georgia is right. He told us as much last spring."

"I have heard that Jackson fears if he sides against Georgia as well, she will join South Carolina and secede from the

Union," Nathan inserted. "Civil war would be a certainty in such an event."

"Jackson fears nothing," The Blade retorted. "William Wirt himself said that after Jackson's huge victory in the election, he could become president for life if he chose. The enemy is in power and our situation will only grow worse."

"We will survive," Will stated calmly.

"How?" The demand shot from The Blade. "What plan does Ross have?"

The tension became palpable. At the October council meeting, The Blade had joined with John Ridge and Elias Boudinot in advocating that a delegation be sent to Washington to negotiate a new treaty. Will and the vast majority had been upset by that plan. Emigration west was not an alternative in their eyes. But the split within the membership had occurred. No longer was the consensus unanimous.

"Now is not the time to discuss it," Will Gordon said sharply. "This is a day of peace. Let us observe it together."

"I agree," Shawano Stuart said, casting a reproachful look at his son, displeased with the dissension he had created.

When Phoebe entered the kitchen, she spied Shadrach at the sink, his sleeves rolled up to his elbows and his hands immersed in the water, scrubbing away at the pots and pans. She glanced surreptitiously over her shoulder to make sure her mammy wasn't in sight, then reached under her apron into the pocket of her dress and pulled out her kerchief, all folded in a small bundle to conceal its contents.

"Here. I brought this for you." She crossed to the sink and waited while her brother dried his wet hands on the front of his apron. "I know how much you like it."

When he took it from her and felt its contents, his eyes lit up. "Is it benne brittle?"

"Uh-huh." Phoebe watched as he carefully folded back the kerchief corners to reveal the thin chunks of hard candy inside. "Miss Temple made a big batch of it. I didn't think she'd miss this little bit." He snapped off a small piece of the brittle made with sesame seeds—or benne, as they called them—and popped it in his mouth. "Better not let Mammy hear you crunching on that," she cautioned. "She'll think you stole it from Miss Victoria."

"She didn't make any this year," he said, his left cheek bulging with the sweet.

"You better put that in your pocket just the same. If Mammy finds out, she'll start wailing about stealing and how much trouble you'll be in."

"She does it all the time." Shadrach buried the bundle in the bottom of his pocket. "You saw her today, taking a bite of everything. Just tasting, she calls it. She tasted the whole dinner."

"I know." Phoebe smiled, then studied her little brother, again amazed by how tall he'd grown. The last time she'd seen him, the top of his head had barely come to her shoulder. Now he could nearly look her in the eye. "You've shot up like a weed in a poke patch."

"You've been gone a long time. It hasn't been the same around here without you," he admitted self-consciously. "I can't talk to the others like I could talk to you. Mammy don't—"

"Doesn't," Phoebe inserted, correcting him the way Deu was always correcting her.

"—*doesn't* show it much, but I know she misses you a powerful lot."

"I've missed you too. All of you." Happy as she was with Deu and as much as she loved him, there were still times when she ached to be with her family. The longing was there in her brother's face as well.

Uncomfortable, he turned his head away. "Tell me what it was like when you went up North. Did you really see all those cities Deu said you did?"

"All of them and more. Lots of times, Master Blade, he'd give us a pass so we could go walking about when he and

Miss Temple were going to be away from the hotel a spell. I saw the big white house where the president of the United States lives. Nearly all the time, there was a whole stream of people going in to visit him. Course, we couldn't go inside. And when we were in Philadelphia, Deu took me to see Independence Hall. He said that was where America was born. And he showed me the big bell they got hanging in the steeple. He told me there's writing on it that says 'Proclaim liberty throughout all the land unto all the inhabitants thereof.' That comes from the Bible, Deu said. And New York—" She paused to shake her head, rolling her gaze to the ceiling. "That was the noisiest place I ever did see. And so many people, too. Deu wanted to take me around, but I knew we'd get lost. I told him he could go, but I wasn't setting one foot outside that hotel for him nor nobody. Boston was nice, though. Course, everybody was happy there," Phoebe recalled thoughtfully, then cast a rueful glance at her brother. "But the winters up North get brutal cold. Why, sometimes it was so bad, the hairs in my nose froze. And one time the stagecoach driver had icicles hanging off his beard. And snow, lordy, this isn't anything. Lots of times I saw it belly-deep up there and a fella told us that he'd seen it pile higher than the top of a window, nearly reaching the roof. And winter just hung on forever, too. I was so hungry for home when that plantation come in sight, I started crying. It was all something to see, Shadrach, but I wouldn't *never* want to live there."

"Was there any black folks like us up there?"

"No slaves. They don't own slaves up North. But we did see some free colored men."

"Were they educated?"

"I don't know." Phoebe shrugged, then darted a conspiratorial glance at him. "Deu's been teaching me, though. Master Blade lets him take books from the library. We've read about some knight named Ivanhoe and a wise Greek man—Plato, I think his name was."

"I've been learning, too," Shadrach admitted sotto voce,

a grin shining from his face. "Miz Eliza, she leaves books out for me, with the lessons all marked down. Sometimes she even leaves paper out for me and I write things for her and hide them under her pillow."

"She's doing that on the sly for you? That woman sure is filled with surprises." Phoebe shook her head in amazement.

"Yeah." He nodded. Then his expression flickered, like a shadow had fallen across it, and his smile faded, the line of his mouth becoming soberly drawn. "What do you think's going to happen to us, Phoebe?"

"What do you mean?" She frowned, puzzled by his question.

"All this trouble with the Georgians. What if one of them comes here and makes Master Will leave? I know Master George took his slaves with him when he left, but I heard him telling Master Will that he was gonna sell some so he could start him a new place in Tennessee. Maybe that'll happen to us."

"Maybe." But it was too frightening to think about.

Just then the door swung open and Black Cassie came bustling through. When she saw Phoebe and Shadrach standing together, she stopped. "Girl, what're you doin' standin' there? Ain't you got that hard sauce fixed yet fo' the suet puddin'?"

"I was just fixin' to do it," Phoebe lied.

"Humph." She snorted her disbelief. "The way you're movin', the snow'll be melted fo' you was through. I does it myself. You git yerself in there an' clear the dishes. And be quick about it. Miz Temple din't brings you over here t' stand around an' talk like you was white folk."

"Yes'm." Phoebe flashed a quick smile at Shadrach, then hurried from the kitchen.

From the window of the family parlor, Eliza gazed at the snow-covered landscape, so pristine and peaceful-looking, the crimson earth hidden beneath a smooth white blanket.

The limbs of the trees were dipped in snow, and the cedars bowed under the weight of it. After the uneasy tension between Will Gordon and the Stuarts at the dinner table, Eliza welcomed the tranquillity of the scene before her.

"I had forgotten how beautiful a snowfall can be," she mused aloud to Nathan as he added another log to the fire.

She turned from the window and wandered over to the fireplace, absently noticing Nathan's absorption in the crackling flames. They were alone, just the two of them. Will Gordon was in the library across the hall, going over the plantation accounts. Victoria was upstairs, taking a short nap with little Johnny. With snowy roads to traverse, the Stuarts had left shortly after the meal was finished. At least, that was the reason they had given, although Eliza suspected the current discord between Will Gordon and The Blade played a large part in the Stuarts' early departure from Gordon Glen.

A sadness pulled at the corners of her mouth, a sadness over everything. She tried not to think about how empty the school would be without the four Murphy children. Yet she couldn't entirely rid her mind of its melancholy thoughts.

"Here we are, standing in front of this cheery fire, our stomachs full from all that delicious food. But I can't help wondering about your two missionary friends still locked in their cells on Christmas. You must be thinking about them too," she said, guessing at the cause for his pensive silence. "How were Mr. Worcester and Dr. Butler when you visited them in prison last week?"

Nathan hesitated, as if searching for a reply that would avoid a direct answer.

"Is something wrong?" Eliza frowned. "Tell me."

"Nothing is wrong," he assured her, then hesitated again. "It's just that . . . they were both very troubled when I saw them. As you know, the attorney Wirt has brought another suit before the Supreme Court to force Georgia to obey its earlier mandate and release them."

"Yes, I know."

"The governor of Georgia has suggested a compromise. If they will drop the suit, he will pardon them."

"But they were wrongly imprisoned," Eliza protested. "Surely they cannot seriously consider this proposal. If they accept a pardon, think how it will look. The Cherokees will believe they have given up."

"Some may take that view," Nathan admitted. "But their incarceration has served its purpose. They won their case in court. If they persist, Georgia may align with the nullifiers, like South Carolina. The threat of a civil war has not completely been averted. This could precipitate one. They are missionaries, Eliza. The guilt they would feel if such a conflict should occur as a result of their actions . . . I don't think they could live with that on their conscience."

"I suppose not," she conceded.

"And it is a true compromise. Georgia is not demanding that they swear allegiance, only that they cease any further legal action against the state."

"What are they going to do?" Either way, Eliza could feel the weight of the potential repercussions.

"They haven't decided. They have written to Boston to see what the board of commissioners recommends. There hasn't been time to receive a reply yet."

"It takes two weeks for my mother's letters to reach me," she recalled idly.

In a sudden burst of obvious agitation, Nathan swung away from the blazing fire. "I shouldn't have discussed this with you." Then he turned a sharply reproving look on her. "You shouldn't concern yourself with such matters."

She had sat in on too many political conversations during the last two years to feel bound by convention, or to accept the foolish belief that, as a woman, she wasn't intelligent enough to understand the issues involved. But Nathan was already upset. Rather than add to his turmoil, Eliza chose to humor him instead. "But if you didn't talk to me about them, who would you confide in?"

His tension melted faster than the snow outside. A look of contrition and regret flashed over his long, thin face. "This is not the way I wanted us to spend our time together today."

"I know. I would suggest playing some duets on the piano, but with Victoria upstairs sleeping and Mr. Gordon working on his ledgers, it would be impolite. Shall we go for a walk?"

"No. Please, let's sit here by the fire." He motioned to the sofa that faced the fireplace.

"All right," she agreed readily and seated herself on one side of the sofa, angling her body toward him as he settled onto the opposite end. He seemed nervous, and she blamed it on their near disagreement of a moment ago.

"It occurred to me the other day that we have known each other more than two years now," he said with a forced casualness.

Eliza smiled, trying to put him at ease. "Sometimes it seems longer than that."

"For me, too." He brightened at her response, then faltered. "I think it would be fair to say we have gotten to know each other quite well."

"I agree." She had the impression she was being prepared for something. She wondered if he had been recalled and had come to tell her good-bye. "We have become friends."

"Exactly." He seized on that. "And friendship is very important. People need to care about each other."

"That is true. And I am fond of you, Nathan."

"I am fond of you . . . very fond." Awkwardly, he reached out to take her hand. Eliza suddenly had the strangest feeling—but it was too impossible to believe. "It would make very happy if you would consent to be my wife. I have already spoken to Mr. Gordon and informed him of my intentions—"

"I wish you hadn't, Nathan," she blurted, profoundly regretting the hurt and bewildered look that sprang into his eyes. "You are my dearest, dearest friend, but I must refuse your proposal."

"Why? I assure you there is no obstacle to our marriage. Mr. Gordon has agreed to release you from his employ."

"I don't wish to be released." Eliza could not leave Gordon Glen and abandon the family that had become as dear to her as her own. She would not desert them in this dark time as so many others were doing. "I am a teacher. This is my life."

"But you could continue to teach at the mission schools, the way other wives do."

"No. It . . . it wouldn't be the same." It wouldn't be Gordon Glen.

As she withdrew her hand from his, Nathan stared at her, his gaze narrowing in sharp suspicion. "Is there someone else? You should have told me—"

"No." She rushed to deny that. "I assure you there is no one in whom I am interested."

"Then . . . I fail to understand." There was a touching bewilderment in his expression. "You have a fondness for me. We get along very well, and you can continue to teach. As much as you care for children, I would think you would want children of your own to love. Why wouldn't you want to be my life's companion? Surely you don't want to grow old alone."

"Of course not." Yet she knew that was precisely what would happen. She faltered, recalling the lonely tone of her mother's last letter. That would be her own lot as well. Eliza bowed her head, for a moment finding it almost too frightening to face.

"Forgive me for saying this, Eliza, but . . . you are not a young woman—"

"Nor an attractive one," she inserted in near defiance, well aware of her drawbacks and well aware she might never receive another proposal of marriage.

"That is not true, Eliza." His long fingers curved under the point of her chin and gently lifted it, forcing her to look at him, his touch amazingly tender and sure considering his previous awkwardness. "You are a very handsome woman."

She almost believed him, but she had lived with her reflection in the mirror for too long and she was much too intelligent to be swayed by his compliment, no matter how flattering it was. Yet as his gaze wandered over her face, touching her hair and her eyes, her cheeks and her lips, so adoring in its inspection, she wavered for an instant and wished that Nathan wouldn't look so sincere.

Agitated by these stirrings of foolish vanity, Eliza turned her head from him, broke the contact with his fingers, and rose to her feet all in one motion. She took two quick steps away from the sofa, then stopped and hugged her arms around her middle.

"I have gone about this wrong, haven't I?" Nathan said from the sofa. "I spoke bluntly, I suppose because there has always been a frankness between us. It was very unromantic of me, wasn't it?"

"That doesn't matter, Nathan. Truly it doesn't," she insisted.

"It does. Friendship is not courtship. I should have realized that."

She closed her eyes and tried to picture herself being courted by Nathan, but she couldn't summon any image. More than that, she didn't want to. To marry him—to even encourage his suit—would be a mistake she would ultimately regret.

"It wouldn't matter, Nathan. My answer would not change. I have no plans ever to marry." She heard the flatness in her voice, devoid of all feeling.

"Eliza." He appealed for her to reconsider.

She swung back to face him. "I am sorry, Nathan. You must believe that I don't wish to hurt you. But in my heart I know it would be wrong to marry you. Will you please accept that and be my friend?"

His thin face was pale and tightly drawn. "It seems I have no choice."

In that instant, Eliza knew she had lost not only a potential suitor, but perhaps a friend also. They might never regain the close companionship they had once known. She wanted to cry at the unfairness of it. She hadn't wanted his marriage proposal. She hadn't sought it, or given him any sign that she looked at him in that light. Simply because she was a spinster teacher, did he think she was so desperate for a husband that she would seize on his proposal like a lifeline?

He stood up. His eyes avoided her completely. "Would you ask one of the servants to have my horse saddled?"

"You are leaving?"

"Yes. It is little more than an hour's ride to New Echota. If I leave now, I should arrive before darkness falls."

Out of politeness, she probably should have objected, but Eliza couldn't force a false protest. It was best that he leave. If he stayed, they would both be uncomfortable and the strain might destroy the last fragments of friendship. Eliza didn't want that to happen.

"I will fetch Shadrach." As she left the parlor, she knew she had never felt more wretched in her life.

Her glance strayed to the closed doors of the library. She wondered if she should inform Will Gordon of Nathan's imminent departure. No, she couldn't subject Nathan to that humiliation. Then she wondered, with a flash of raw anger, why he had told Will Gordon of his intentions in the first place. Now her rejection of him couldn't be kept private. She would have to inform her employer.

Will blotted the last entry in his journal, then read the crisply worded sentence again. The book contained a concise history of everything that had happened at Gordon Glen. In it, he recorded the dates various crops were planted, the number of acres, the dates of harvest, the amount of yield, how much was sold to whom and at what price, and how much was stored for use on the plantation. When he purchased a black, hired one, or sold one, when a child was born to one of them, when a black died—it was all there, along with weather data, insect damage, and repairs to or construction of buildings on the plantation. The births of his children and the deaths of those they had lost, the arrival of visitors and the purpose of their call—each was duly noted in the pages of the journal.

"The missionary Nathan Cole expressed his intention to marry the children's tutor, Eliza Hall." The stark words stared back at him in his own handwriting.

Abruptly, he rose from his desk and crossed to the fireplace. He vigorously stirred the fire with the iron poker, sending up a shower of sparks and crumbling the hot, glowing embers. He added another log from the wood box and listened to the flames roar anew, snapping and crackling loudly, consuming all other sound.

Sighing in vague dejection, Will gripped the mantel's edge in his right hand and stood staring at the greedy flames. Again he found himself wondering why the reverend's announcement had come as such a surprise to him. How many times had he observed them walking together? Her leaving was inevitable anyway. He knew that, and yet . . .

A trio of rapid knocks sounded at his door. "Yes?" He frowned in ill temper at the intrusion, but at the same time welcomed it.

A click of the latch preceded the opening of the door. Will half turned to see Eliza pause just inside the room. He stared at her face, her expression tense, tinged with a vague apprehension, but that wasn't what he saw when he looked at her. It was the strong beauty in the line of her features.

When had the change taken place? Why hadn't he noticed it before? Yet he wasn't entirely surprised by the transformation. Women were like flowers. Not all bloomed early in the spring. Some waited until summer, and others until late in the autumn. A few even dared to bloom in winter.

"May I speak with you, Mr. Gordon?"

"Of course. Come in." He turned crisply and walked back to his desk, pausing in front of it, his back to her. The words she had come to say were before him in the journal.

She took his former position in front of the fireplace. Her

hands were tightly clasped in front of her as she stared into the flames. "First of all, I think you should know that Reverend Cole has left. He decided to return to New Echota before nightfall." She paused. "He asked that I offer you his farewells and his gratitude for your hospitality."

Frowning, Will squared around to study her. "I thought—"

"No." She stopped him before he could say it, then added less stridently, "My answer was no."

He was vaguely conscious of a sense of relief washing through him as he slowly walked over to her. But when he halted behind her and gazed at the collection of shiny curls at her neck, he realized that nothing had really changed, except the fact that she wouldn't be marrying the missionary.

"I am sorry," he murmured.

"I am not," she retorted briskly. "I have always regarded Reverend Cole as a friend. I only regret that he thought he could be more, and that he spoke to you before he learned of my feelings."

"That isn't what I meant. You see, Miss Hall . . ." Will paused, finding it no easier to say the words than he had thought it would be. "My finances are such that I can no longer afford to pay your salary. When Reverend Cole asked me to release you from my employ so the two of you could marry, I thought he had provided me with a solution that would be satisfactory to both of us. Now I am afraid I must inform you that I shall have to let you go. I can offer you a month's wages and the fare for your transportation home to New England."

Eliza couldn't believe what she was hearing. She was being discharged. She had been aware, in a vague way, that the economic situation at Gordon Glen wasn't all it could be, but she had never thought it would affect her.

"Under the present circumstances, it is best that you leave anyway," he continued. "Today, tomorrow, there may be a knock at the door and you will find yourself without a place to sleep."

"So will you." She spun around.

"Yes," he acknowledged, his eyes warm and gentle on her, a trace of resignation in their depths. "But I cannot ask you to endure whatever suffering my family may know in the future. It would be wrong of me."

"This is wrong!" Eliza insisted. "I cannot leave. I *will not* leave!"

"Eliza." He shook his head, moved by her declaration.

"You need me," she argued. "You know you do. And I don't mean just to teach Xandra and Kipp. Victoria—Mrs. Gordon is not well. If she doesn't have the rest she needs, she will only get worse. And how will she do that if there is no one here to help her? The money doesn't matter. There is no need to pay me."

"I cannot do that." He was tempted to believe that she knew what she was saying.

"Then owe me the money. You cannot expect me to walk away when I know how much I am needed here," she reasoned. "Maybe you don't, but Victoria does—and Kipp, Xandra, and little Johnny, too. I have grown to care very much for this family. Don't . . . send me away," she said, her voice breaking on the last word.

She didn't beg. Request, argue, reason, yes. But she didn't beg. She had too much pride for that, Will realized. And pride was something Will understood as well as the strength and determination she showed him. Yet there was something in her expression that reminded him of a lost and frightened child in need of comfort and reassurance.

"I won't send you away," he promised at last, unable to admit that he needed her, much less admit to the tender feelings stirring awake inside him.

"Thank you," she said. "I promise you will not regret it."

"I hope neither of us will," he replied.

When she walked out of the library, Eliza was conscious that his gaze followed her until she was out of sight. She climbed the stairs to her third-floor room with a sedateness she didn't feel. Once inside, she sat down on the first available seat, her knees quaking too badly to support her. Everything was all ajumble inside.

She didn't want to admit to herself why she had refused Nathan and why she had been so determined to stay at Gordon Glen. Yet neither could she deny it. All the reasons she had given were true, but she had left out the main one. Unconsciously, she had compared Nathan to Will Gordon and found him wanting as a man. It wasn't merely respect and admiration she felt toward Will Gordon; sometime, somehow, an affection for him had taken root and grown without her awareness.

To her utter mortification, Eliza Hall, the avowed spinster, had come to care for a married man. How ridiculously romantic and tragic it sounded. But it hurt too much to laugh. She vowed there and then that no one must ever learn of her feelings. No one.

17

Seven Oaks

Deu stood attentively inside the parlor door, his hands clasped behind his back as he watched his master lounging in the chair. He didn't know what had happened at the Gordon plantation today, but something had. He had sensed the anger building in Master Blade during the entire ride home. Now it was visible.

Most folks wouldn't see it, though. The way The Blade smiled all the time and acted like nothing concerned him, few would believe he ever got really mad. But that was because he never got hot angry. He got cold angry. Those blue eyes of his would turn to ice, like now, and freeze a man with one look.

It took a lot to rile The Blade. Deu hadn't seen the likes of this in a long time. That time, he'd nearly killed a man. Mostly you could prod and prod, and he'd just shrug and turn away. But Deu wouldn't want to be the one to get on the wrong side of him now.

The Blade tipped the whiskey glass to his mouth and poured the last swallow down his throat, then reached for the crystal decanter on the side table, each movement slow and deliberate.

When he poured more whiskey into his glass, his father frowned in troubled disapproval. "Is that wise, my son? Three times you have filled the glass."

Smiling coolly, The Blade held his drink so the amber brown liquor inside caught the flickering light from the fireplace. "But this, Shawano, is forgetfulness. If you drink enough of it, you won't see what is happening around you. You won't care."

"Many of our people seek the stupor it will bring them, but they still must wake from it."

"True." The short breath The Blade released contained a silent, humorless laugh that twisted his mouth into a cold smile. "It never changes the view. It only clouds it for a time."

"What is it you see?"

Slowly, The Blade turned his gaze to his father, his head cocked at an angle that both challenged and defied. "The end." He smiled at Shawano's brief start of surprise. "One way or the other, it is coming. Can't you see it? Or are you blind, like John Ross and Will Gordon?" Deu frowned at the disrespect in The Blade's voice. He had never heard him speak to old Master Stuart like that.

"The whiskey works on you," Shawano observed sadly.

"I wish it did." The Blade glared at the glass, then set it down, its fresh contents untouched. He slowly rose to his feet, exhibiting in that movement the same taut control that had governed his thoughts for months. "Will Gordon's sister and her family will not be the only ones forced from their homes. They were just the beginning. Every time the lottery wheel spins, more will come to usurp our homes. And more and more and more."

"They will be stopped. When the Supreme Court hears the suit being brought before it, the judges will order Georgia to comply with its previous verdict."

"The judges can issue orders until the sun stands still in the sky and it will change nothing. They have no power to enforce them, and Jackson won't ask for it."

"Ross has gone with the delegation to Washington to meet with Jackson himself."

"Does Ross truly believe that he will be able to persuade Jackson to come to our aid when all the others who have gone before him have failed?" The Blade mocked derisively. "Jackson won't help us. I heard his words. I saw his face. He is committed to the removal of the Cherokee from this land. And it is like the grip of a mortally wounded man; he will not let go of his decision. Why should he? He has succeeded in obtaining new treaties with the Choctaws, Creeks, Chickasaws, and even the Seminoles, treaties that trade their lands for territory in the West. The Cherokees alone continue to defy him. We are a thorn he is determined to remove."

"We are not without friends in Congress," Shawano reminded him.

"They have no more power than the Court does, especially now that Jackson has swept the elections." The Blade picked up the whiskey glass again and walked over to the fire. He gazed at the flames for several long seconds, then bolted down a portion of the liquor. "I know of the dream Ross seeks to propose, to have the Cherokee Nation admitted into the Union as a state. Jackson will never allow that to happen. Ross is a fool if he thinks he will."

"John Ross is our chief." Shawano tightened his grip on the silver handle of his cane.

"But does that make his way the right way?"

"It pains me to hear such words coming from my own seed. When you aligned yourself with John Ridge and his followers at the October council and tried to have a delegation sent to Washington for the purpose of discussing treaty terms, I thought you would see your error when the great majority of the council voted against you. The stand of John Ross against treating is the stand of the Cherokee people."

"The Cherokee listen to Ross, but he will not tell them the whole truth. He refuses to allow the *Phoenix* to print anything that presents the benefits that might be gained from removal. I don't blame Elias Boudinot for resigning as editor of the newspaper. How can our people decide what is best if all dissension is silenced? Is it fair if they only hear one side?" The Blade demanded angrily. "Ross intimates that any who would advocate removal are betraying their country. I say that to deceive them into believing there is hope when there is none is an even greater betrayal."

"How can you say there is no hope?" Doubt flickered in Shawano's eyes for the first time. "The land is ours. Our rights to it have been acknowledged. We have but to endure."

"For how long?" The Blade challenged. "Daily our people are beaten, robbed, cheated, and humiliated. The Georgians are no longer content with taking our homes, our land, and our property. They take our pride and our dignity as well. John Ross says we must remain united and hold on to the land. But at what cost, Shawano? What price are we prepared to pay for that victory? The destruction of our people?"

"You believe we should give up our land and go west." Shawano spoke in a monotone, as if mulling the thought over in his mind.

"It is our only choice if the Nation is to survive. We must negotiate a treaty *now*, while we can still obtain the best terms possible."

"No," Temple whispered from the doorway, arriving in time to hear the last part of their exchange. "You are wrong."

After the briefest hesitation, The Blade swung around to confront her. "Why? Because I don't agree with your father? You have known that for some time."

"But I never guessed you were a traitor!" Her voice vibrated with loathing and contempt.

The Blade stiffened, the accusation ringing in his ears. Turning, he angrily hurled the whiskey glass into the fireplace; its shattering crash broke the taut silence. When he glanced at the doorway, Temple was gone.

"Many will say that," Shawano warned.

"Yes." The Blade acknowledged that truth, his voice coming from deep in his throat. "But what man wants to hear it from his wife?"

Shawano wisely didn't comment as The Blade turned and left the room, moving with long strides that quickened as he followed the sound of Temple's footsteps down the hall. He climbed the steps two at a time, entering their bedroom only seconds behind her.

The shock was gone. She stood before him, her dark eyes ablaze and her lips firmly set.

"What do you want?" she demanded, then immediately ordered, "Get out! I have nothing to say to traitors."

"How unfortunate, because there is much I want to say to you." Out of the corner of his eye, he caught a movement. A wide-eyed Phoebe stood next to the tall chifforobe, clutching Temple's pelisse to her bosom. Her glance ran apprehensively from one to the other. The Blade took a step backward and held the bedroom door open wide. "Leave us, Phoebe."

"Yes, go." Temple seconded the command.

Phoebe carefully laid the pelisse on a chair, then edged cautiously toward the door. He closed it on her heels.

"We are alone. That is what you wanted, isn't it?" Temple challenged his silence. "You are free to shout at me, to strike me and beat me—"

"I have never once touched a hand to you in anger in my life!" he exploded. "Although, by all the gods, you tempt me. You know I am no more a wife-beater than I am a traitor."

"I know no such thing, not anymore," she retorted, the accusation still in her eyes. "I never believed you would seek to sign away our lands. But I was wrong. How could you even consider giving away the land of our fathers?" Pain as well as anger was in her voice.

"Do you think I don't love it? Do you think I want to leave these hills and valleys that have been home to us for nearly all of our nation's memory?"

"It cannot mean much to you or you would not want to see us give it up."

"It doesn't mean as much to me as our people, Temple. That is what the Cherokee Nation is—people. It is not a piece

of land, however precious it might be to us. I can stand by
no longer and watch our people whipped and abused like
animals, degraded and humiliated in front of their families,
with little or no hope for relief. They are already demoralized
and despondent. How long before their spirit is broken as
well?" He tried to reason with her, but he could see she was
deaf to his arguments. Abruptly, he turned, his right hand
clenched in a fist. "This is your fault, Temple."

"Mine?" she protested incredulously.

"Yes, yours. I got involved in these politics because of
you, my father, your father. I wanted nothing to do with
the council or the negotiations. But the three of you subtly
pressured me into assuming responsibilities for the Nation's
affairs rather than continue in my solitary endeavors. Now
that I am involved, you are not liking it."

"You have always looked for the easy way to do anything."

"The *easy* way." He laughed at that, then came over to
stand directly in front of her. "The woman I love looks at
me with hatred and contempt and brands me a traitor. I am
viewed with suspicion and mistrust by nearly all our people.
Already, veiled threats have been made against me. If I wanted
the easy way, Temple, I would side with John Ross."

Her gaze wavered, then fell under the steadiness of his. He
smiled faintly, the anger gone from him as he sensed it was
also gone from her. She knew he had spoken the truth.

"Temple." He hooked a finger under her chin and lifted it
so he could see into her eyes. They peered back at him warily,
still a trace of hurt in them, and confusion. "You are free to
disagree and to argue with me all you like, but don't let this
come between us. I love you."

"I love you." A hint of tears glistened in the wells of her
eyes. "I just wish that—"

"Shhh." He lowered his head to claim her lips in a long
and tender kiss.

But he didn't take her in his arms. That decision was hers.
It had to be. Slowly, he straightened, watching and waiting,

needing confirmation that she was as determined as he not to let this drive them apart.

"Blade." The ache in her voice spoke of love as her hands slid up his coat and curved around his neck to force his head down.

No further urging was required. He gathered her to him, conscious of the tight wrap of her arms and the fierce hunger of her lips. He understood the fear that made her cling to him now, for he felt it too. They had come close to losing this. How much longer could they preserve their passion and love for one another when their support and loyalty lay in such different courses of action?

Part II

The soil that gave us birth . . . we cling to it because it is our first love; we cling to it because it will be our last. . . .
                    —**John Howard Payne, Cherokee memorial**

18

The *click-click* of knitting needles accompanied the sound of Eliza's voice as she read aloud from a newspaper. Temple listened without really hearing. She was too busy watching her mother. More than a month had passed since she had last seen Victoria, but in that short time her cheeks had become sunken and there was now a bruised darkness below her eyes. The increasing number of white strands in her once black hair made her seem older than she was. Temple noticed, too, how frequently her mother paused in her knitting, her fingers no longer moving with their former deftness or speed. Victoria used the pauses to observe twelve-year-old Xandra's knitting, but Temple suspected her interest in Xandra's progress was a ruse to cover her own weariness.

" 'Friends,' " Eliza continued, " 'the leafless season of our fate is come upon us. If you forget us, the fires will have consumed the fallen leaves, will kill the trees too, and to our winter there will succeed no spring!

" 'Our talk is over.' "

Our fate is upon us. Temple felt chilled by the ominous tone of the phrase. The flesh tingled along the back of her neck at the sound of portent.

"That was beautiful." Victoria's voice was choked with

emotion, her eyes, still bright despite her illness, brimmed with tears. "That is how I feel in my heart. My precious babies are buried here. I could never leave this land that holds them in its bosom. I would surely wither and die like the leaves he spoke about."

Her remark followed too closely on Temple's own sense of foreboding. She had to crush them both. "You certainly have no reason to be concerned about that, Mama. We will not give up our land."

"I know." Again, Victoria positioned her needles and curled the yarn around her finger in preparation for the next stitch, but she made only one, then paused to frown at the partially knitted stocking. "Yet I have this awful feeling . . . I keep remembering the night the sky was striped with fire. Then last year, when the sun was swallowed at noon and everything was so dark . . ."

"Despite what the shamans say, those were natural occurrences, Victoria. Remember, I explained them to you," Eliza chided, making light of them. "The first was a meteor shower. A spectacular one, I agree, but no more than shooting stars you can see any night. And then we experienced a total eclipse of the sun. It happens periodically. You shouldn't let yourself be influenced by the old superstitions."

But Temple knew her mother wasn't alone in her beliefs. Many of the less enlightened of their people had regarded the phenomena as signs of doom.

"Will you play some music for us, Eliza?" Xandra asked.

"I think that is just what we need," Eliza agreed. Like Temple, she feared the atmosphere had become altogether too cheerless.

With the newspaper laid aside, Eliza crossed over to the piano and began to play a well-known ballad. As the notes of the sentimental refrain filled the room, Temple heard the baroque door at the rear entrance open and close with a resounding slam. It was followed immediately by hard, swift footsteps striking the hall floor. Temple looked up from her knitting as her brother Kipp approached the parlor. The instant he saw her, he turned and strode into the room.

At nearly sixteen years of age, he was an inch short of six feet, but his hair and eyes were as black as ever, the latter now blazing with an anger he seemed to have been born with.

"Is *he* here?" He stopped in front of her chair.

Temple winced inwardly at the hatred Kipp managed to inject into what she was certain was a reference to her husband. "No." She didn't ask why he wanted to know—not with her mother present.

"Have you seen this?" He reached inside his coat and pulled out a large, carelessly folded sheet of paper, thrusting it at her.

Forcing herself to remain calm and composed, Temple laid her knitting aside and took the paper from him. It rustled noisily as she unfolded it, making her aware of the heavy silence in the room. She wondered if the song had ended or if Eliza had merely stopped playing.

"What is it, Temple?"

The vague apprehension in her mother's voice was nothing compared to the alarm Temple felt as she scanned the poster. It was a public notice of a council meeting to be held in New Echota on the third Monday of December for the purpose of agreeing to an acceptable treaty. Free blankets and subsistence money were to be distributed to all who attended.

"What is it, Temple?" Eliza rose from the piano bench.

"Nothing." She quickly folded the poster in half and ran her fingers along the crease, striving for nonchalance. "A notice about a runaway slave. Nothing that concerns us, Mama." She looked at Kipp, warning him not to deny it.

"But Kipp—"

"Kipp," Temple broke in quickly, "Kipp is an alarmist. I expect he thinks this runner stole the two milk cows you are missing. Isn't that right?"

For an instant, the muscles in his tightly clenched jaw stood out sharply. "It is possible."

"But hardly likely," she replied and turned away, releasing a long breath of relief when her father appeared in the doorway.

Will paused, his gaze slicing to the folded poster in her hand, then to her. With a slight movement of her head, she indicated that her mother was unaware of its contents.

"You all were sitting here when Kipp and I left," he chided lightly, walking the rest of the way into the family parlor.

"We have been visiting," Victoria explained and smiled at Temple. "We see each other so seldom we had a great deal to talk about."

"You promised you would rest this afternoon," he reminded her.

"I know—"

"That is my fault," Temple inserted. "I stayed longer than I planned, but now I must leave. Why don't you go upstairs and rest, Mama?"

"I will go with you." Eliza immediately went to Victoria's side.

Within minutes, Eliza had assisted Victoria from the room and Xandra had been sent to find her little brother, leaving Temple alone with her father and Kipp. She saw the question in her father's eyes, but it was Kipp who asked it.

"Did you know about this?"

"Of course not." She looked down at the poster in her hands. "The Blade tells me nothing unless I ask. And I didn't know about this to ask."

"Schermerhorn has to know that no one will attend." Will referred to the commissioner sent by Jackson to obtain a treaty with the Cherokees. "Not while John Ross is in Washington."

"Ridge and his traitors are behind this," Kipp accused. "All these lies of theirs that John Ross is not our chief because there have been no elections—no one believes them. They send delegates to Washington and sign provisional treaties. They seek to betray us all." He grabbed the poster from her and opened it up. "Do you believe this? They are trying to bribe people to come to their false council meeting with promises of blankets and money. Because they have sold themselves to Chicken Snake Jackson, they think others will. Then they dare to warn that any who fail to come will be counted as voting in favor of any action taken by the council."

"I saw that," Temple admitted, privately appalled and sickened that her husband had any part in this.

"They cannot truly believe it will give any credence to what they do," he jeered.

"I do not know what they think!" Temple was weary of his insinuations that she knew more of The Blade's activities and plans than she was telling.

"You had best warn them that they will pay with their lives for any deeds of treachery they perform."

Temple turned away to hide the whitening of her face. For the last two years, she had lived with these death threats against The Blade. Five—or was it six?—of his cohorts had been killed by those who took it upon themselves to invoke the Blood Law despite John Ross's constant appeals for restraint and peace.

When her father's hands settled onto her shoulders, Temple recognized the gentleness of his touch and relaxed. "I would not be greatly concerned about this council meeting, Temple. Both John Ridge and Stand Watie have accompanied John Ross to Washington. I doubt the treaty party will take any . . . questionable action with two of their most notable members absent," he said. "I am certain this is just another attempt to gain more supporters."

"Yes, it is the only thing it could be." Relieved by his logical explanation, she turned to face him, loving him all the more for allaying her fears. Her father had never once allowed his disagreement with The Blade's views to become personal, never once treated him with anything but respect, and never once made Temple feel that she was being pulled between them. She doubted if her marriage could have withstood the conflict if it had been otherwise.

At times she wondered if her father knew The Blade had

intervened on his behalf and used his influence with the governor of Georgia to ensure that her father remained in possession of Gordon Glen, when all around, prime properties, including John Ross's plantation, had been claimed by lottery winners. Such concessions were usually granted only to those Cherokees who advocated the signing of a treaty to remove. As a treaty advocate, The Blade had managed to obtain the exemption for her family home. She suspected her father knew that.

"It is late." She gathered up her knitting. "If I am to have supper on the table for my husband, I need to be leaving."

"How can you go back there?" Kipp demanded. "How can you stay with him?"

"Kipp, you will not speak that way to your sister!" The sharp reprimand exploded from Will in a rare show of anger.

"But she is living in a house of traitors," he protested in anger.

"And you live in my house. Which means you will respect my wishes. Is that clear?"

"Yes, sir." Kipp gave in grudgingly.

"Kipp." Temple wanted somehow to heal this breach, but he turned on his heel and walked stiffly from the room. "I am sorry, Father."

"You have no reason to apologize, Temple. Your brother needs to learn tolerance."

"I know." But it didn't make her feel any less guilty that she had been the cause of the harsh exchange.

"Kipp has to understand that however much he disagrees with the stand your husband has taken, The Blade loves our nation and its people every bit as much as we do. I cannot call a man who loves his country a traitor to it, regardless of what his other beliefs might be."

"He does love it," she asserted forcefully. "He is shunned like an outcast, called vile names, and threatened with violence. I have seen it. Like you, I think he is wrong, but I know, too, that he deeply believes he is acting for the good of our people. I cannot hate him . . . I cannot stop loving him for that.''

''I know.''

When Eliza descended the stairs to the great hall, a silence greeted her. She paused at the bottom to listen, slightly puzzled that Temple should leave without saying good-bye. It wasn't like her.

She crossed to the family parlor, but the chair Temple had previously occupied was empty, as were the others. Disappointed, she started to turn away, then she heard the soft plink of a piano key and turned back, ready to scold young Johnny for playing with the piano.

But it was Will who was seated at the rosewood piano. She stared, taking advantage of this unguarded moment to gaze at him, noting the way the dark material of his frock coat pulled across his wide shoulders, then tapered down his back. The afternoon light streaming through the window intensified the deep red cast in his hair and etched his finely chiseled profile in sharp relief. Just the fingers of his right hand were on the piano keys, lightly rubbing the ivory edges in a slow, circular motion. A tightness gripped Eliza as she imagined his hand caressing her that way. All those longings she had once told Temple were wrong to feel now consumed her until it hurt to breathe.

As if sensing a presence, he looked over his shoulder, his glance immediately locking with hers. After three years of practice, Eliza had mastered the skill of hiding her feelings. She calmly walked into the room.

''Temple has left?'' she asked, saying the first thing that came to mind.

''Yes.'' He turned sideways on the piano seat. ''She said to tell you good-bye.''

''I hadn't thought she would leave so soon.'' She stopped to stand next to the piano.

"She was upset."

"The poster," Eliza remembered. "What was it about?"

Briefly, Will told her about the special council meeting called for the stated purpose of agreeing on treaty terms. "It was done deliberately, knowing John Ross will be away in Washington." Her initial indignation quickly changed to pity for Temple, knowing how hurt she would be that The Blade was involved in such trickery. "Poor Temple."

"I told her not to attach too much importance to the meeting. Nothing will come of it," he said, then sighed heavily. "I only wish Kipp had not said some of the things he did. He has so much hate."

"Yes." Eliza was forced to agree. "Sometimes I think that instead of a heart, he was born with a fist tightly closed in anger." The instant the words were out, she regretted speaking so thoughtlessly about his son. "Forgive me. I should not have said that."

"No, you speak the truth. I only regret that Temple has to suffer the backlash of his anger. Her situation is difficult enough without Kipp adding more pressure to it."

"Temple can handle it. She is a strong woman."

"So are you, Eliza."

The simple compliment and the endearing warmth of his gaze combined were almost too much for her.

"Thank you." Conscious of her racing heartbeat, Eliza somehow succeeded in responding casually to him. "Unfortunately, I have neglected several of my duties while Temple was here. I must be about them."

With Victoria's declining health, Eliza had taken over the bulk of her chores. One of the blessings of running an extended household the size of Gordon Glen was that there was always something to be done. Occupied by work, she had little time to think about herself.

"Maybe tonight you will play the piano for me," Will said as she started to walk away. "Until I heard the music this afternoon, I had forgotten how long it's been since I sat and listened to you.''

''Perhaps.'' She wouldn't commit to it until she was certain she wouldn't be playing for him alone. That was a situation that was neither proper nor wise.

19

D ismounting, Temple passed the reins to the stableman holding the mare's bridle. As he led the horse away, she turned to the house, then paused, her glance unwillingly drawn to the motionless figure partially hidden by the chestnut tree on the far side of the lawn. The man was one of a half dozen that ringed the main house, keeping a sinister watch over its occupants.

Their faces were always hooded by the blankets they wore wrapped around them, making recognition nearly impossible. They never spoke or made any menacing gesture; they simply stared, letting their presence be a warning to those traitors within.

As if to assure her that he meant no harm to Will Gordon's daughter, the man nodded once to her. Temple hesitated, then nodded back, still chilled by the sight of him.

The mysterious figures had first appeared soon after John Ridge and the other delegates had returned from Washington with the provisional treaty they had signed. She tried to convince herself that she should be used to them by now, but it didn't help.

As she approached the front door, Phoebe opened it. As if reading the silent question in Temple's eyes, she said, "Master Blade hasn't returned yet."

Without replying, Temple handed Phoebe her riding crop and began stripping off her gloves. The Blade had left early that morning without saying where he was going or when he would be back. She hadn't asked. It was an unspoken agreement they had.

As she untied the ribbons that secured her riding hat, she heard the clump of Shawano's cane in the hall. She removed her bonnet and handed it to the waiting Phoebe, then turned to face the sound. She caught the flicker of disappointment in his expression when he saw her. She knew Shawano was as anxious as she was to see The Blade return safely from wherever he had gone. There was too much animosity in the air, too much talk about enacting the Blood Law, too many rumors of assassination for her not to be concerned. She needed distraction. That was half the reason she had decided to visit her family today—to distract her mind from worrying over him.

"Did you have a pleasant time with your family?" Shawano stopped and leaned heavily on his cane.

"Yes, I did."

"How is your mother?"

"She is better, I think." Temple hesitated, then asked, "Should I expect The Blade to be home for supper this evening?"

"Yes," he replied, not volunteering his son's whereabouts. Although not as active as The Blade, Shawano had come to share his son's views favoring a treaty. Thus he was also a participant in the conspiracy of silence.

She turned and started up the stairs. She completely forgot Phoebe was behind her until she reached the bedroom and the girl said, "Don't worry, Miss Temple." She swung around with a start. Phoebe smiled sympathetically. "He'll be all right. My Deu is with him. He'll look after Master Blade the same as I look after you."

Belatedly, Temple remembered that, as always, Deu had accompanied her husband. Phoebe's man was out there too, indirectly exposed to the same danger. Phoebe had to know that, or she wouldn't have bothered to try and reassure her about The Blade.

"They both will be all right, Phoebe." Temple smiled, briefly bridging the gap between mistress and slave to clasp the colored woman's hands. Releasing them, she turned away. "Now, help me change out of these clothes so we can have some hot food waiting for them."

"Yes'm."

An early mist swirled near the banks of the creek and rolled silently onto the narrow road, hovering close to the ground like thin white smoke. With the half shadows of twilight playing their usual tricks, there was an eeriness to the scene.

The Blade let his horse pick its own pace while he scanned the undergrowth ahead of them and the area where the road dipped down to ford the creek, now shrouded by the enveloping mist. Everything was still. He glanced at his horse. Its ears were pricked in the direction of the invisible ford, its entire attitude one of alertness.

Deu trotted his horse forward to draw alongside him. "I don't like this," he murmured low. "Something doesn't feel right."

"I know." Then The Blade remembered. "We came home this way the last time, didn't we?" He cursed himself for using the same route twice in a row.

When John Walker was shot and killed from ambush a year and a half ago, The Blade had stopped treating the talk of assassination as an idle threat. From then on, he never followed any path twice. He never rode the same horse. His caution had paid off in the past; he had twice avoided a band of men lying in wait for him.

But this time he had slipped up. In the immediate area, there were only two natural fords on this creek. Assassins could be waiting at both of them.

"Let me ride ahead and see what I can flush," Deu volunteered.

Although fully aware they weren't interested in his servant, The Blade hesitated, reluctant to put Deu in the path of trouble. Just then, a big black crow swooped toward a tree on the opposite side of the creek. Abruptly, it veered off, cawing a loud alarm.

"They're over there. Let's go!" Simultaneously, The Blade dug a heel into his mount, impelling the horse into a gallop straight at the creek.

Deu's horse matched his stride for stride. Together they charged the ford, water spraying and mist swirling all around them. Deu took the lead going up the sloped embankment on the other side. As The Blade followed, there was a rush of movement on all sides. A dark figure hurtled from a tree and landed on his back, hooking an arm around his throat.

The Blade grabbed at the man's wrist as something hot burned his side. Another figure leapt from the mist and seized the reins. His horse reared, squealing wildly in panic. The Blade succeeded in loosening his assailant's hold and pushed him off a second before his horse went down. The Blade tumbled from the saddle and rolled as he hit the ground. He sprang to his feet, his breath coming hard and fast, the blood pumping rapidly through his veins. A man came out of the mists, a knife flashing in his hand. Jumping backward, The Blade dodged its slashing upswing, then lunged, seizing the man's wrist and bringing it down across his knee, dislodging the knife from his grasp.

"Master Blade!" Deu shouted.

He turned as a black apparition parted the mists, man and horse melding together to form one shape. Grabbing Deu's arm, he heaved himself up, hooking a leg over the horse's rump as it bounded forward, running over the figure that loomed in its path.

For nearly a mile, they rode at a hard gallop, then they

pulled up and listened for any sound of pursuit. There was none. "They won't come after us," The Blade said, scanning the trail behind them. "They missed their chance. They will wait for another one."

"If we cut through that indigo field, the plantation is only a mile away. It might be best to get off the road."

As he considered Deu's suggestion, The Blade pressed a hand against the burning stitch in his side. The contact, instead of easing the discomfort, caused him to flinch in pain. He glanced at his hand. The wetness he had felt wasn't sweat. It was his own blood. He had been stabbed. He didn't think it was more than a flesh wound, but this wasn't the time or the place to worry about it.

"Let's cut through."

Temple was in the dining room when she heard the front door open and the clump of boots in the entry hall. A mixture of relief and elation rushed through her as she pushed the china plates into Phoebe's waiting hands and hurried from the room.

She paused in the opening to the large foyer, her gaze sweeping over The Blade. "You are home." She breathed out the words, somehow needing to say them to banish the last of her fears.

When he turned to face her, she took a step forward, then stopped, stunned by the cold look in his eyes and the hard set to his features. "Yes, I am," he replied, as if deriding her for stating the obvious.

Didn't he realize that she worried about him? Didn't he know what a torture it was for her to hear all the threats against him?

"Supper will be ready in an hour," she informed him stiffly.

"Tell my father I will join him shortly." He crossed to the stairs, Deu directly behind him.

After reading that poster with all of its traitorous implications, bearing the brunt of her brother's vengeful warnings, and defending her love for him to her father, Temple refused to be treated like a servant sent off to do his bidding. She watched him climb the steps at a slow, steady pace. Then, spurred by her rising temper, she went after him.

At the top of the stairs, he glanced back, catching sight of her behind Deu. There was a flash of irritation in his expression, accompanied by a tightening of his mouth, but he didn't pause. He continued to their bedroom without a break in stride. Furious at him for thinking, even for one moment, that by ignoring her she would go away, Temple followed him inside.

Halting, he half turned. "Did you want something?"

"I went to Gordon Glen today."

"Did you?" The indifference of his response was echoed by his actions as he began unbuttoning his coat.

"Yes. And I know about the meeting in New Echota," she challenged. "I saw the notice for it."

As the front of his coat swung open, Deu stepped up. "I'll help you with that, sir."

"No." The Blade briefly raised a hand, checking Deu when he started to remove his coat. "Not now."

"Do you really believe you will be able to induce the people to attend through bribery?"

"The money and blankets come from Schermerhorn, the treaty commissioner from Jackson. The treaty party had nothing to do with that."

"My father says your meeting will accomplish nothing. The people won't be taken in by your trickery. They won't come, not with John Ross away in Washington."

"Our trickery?" he retorted sharply. "What do you call Ross's methods? We brought to the council treaty terms that granted annuities to support schools to educate our children, provided liberal compensation to individuals for their homes and property, guaranteed our territory in the West, and paid the Nation more money for its land than anyone dreamed of."

"Yes, five million dollars—and our gold mines alone are worth that."

"What has John Ross offered? Only more of the same

suffering and humiliation we have endured for nearly five years now." Disgust and bitterness ridged his angry expression. "What proposals does he make to give us relief? He wants us to be allowed to become citizens of Georgia so that we can remain on our land, among the very whites who took it from us and look upon us with contempt because we are Cherokee. That would be even more degrading. No—John Ross does nothing but stall. He continues to hold on to the foolish belief that when Jackson's term as president ends next year, our situation will be improved by a new administration. But Jackson has already picked Van Buren to be his successor. And Van Buren too will side with Georgia against us. Yet Ross continues to fight to keep the land."

"But that is what we want," Temple insisted angrily. "Less than one-tenth of the Nation believes as you and your treaty group do. The rest of us want to remain on the land that has always belonged to our people. He obeys our will."

"Yes, he obeys!" The Blade shot back. "He is a follower, and what we need is a leader—someone who is not afraid to do what is best for his people!"

She didn't like the tone of that. It filled her with all sorts of dark suspicions. "Why did you call this meeting? What do you think you will accomplish?"

"Ask me no questions when you know you will have no liking for the answers!" When he swung away from her, she saw the dark stain on his coat.

"Master Blade, you're bleeding," Deu accused. "You never told me you were wounded back there."

He quickly clamped a hand to his right side and impatiently brushed Deu aside when he attempted to examine it. "It is nothing."

"Wounded?" Temple frowned. "What are you talking about? Deu, take his coat off." When The Blade tried to shrug him off again, Temple came to his assistance. She took one look at the blood-soaked shirt on his right side and felt sick with fear. Struggling to suppress her reaction, she immediately demanded, "How did this happen?"

"Some of your *friends* were waiting for us when we crossed the creek. They intended to make you a widow." His sarcasm cut deeply. "Maybe you will be luckier next time and they will succeed."

"You are cruel." Temple turned to hide the tears that sprang into her eyes.

"Temple." He caught at her arm, stopping her. "I . . . I should not have said that."

"Your wound, it needs to be cleaned and bandaged." She pulled loose and started for the door.

"Don't let my father know about this. I don't wish to upset him."

"But it does not matter that I am upset, does it?" she flung back at him. "I am only your wife."

His expression was sharp with regret. "If I could take back what I said to you, Temple, I would. I was angry and I hurt you. You didn't deserve it."

"No, I did not." She went to fetch water and her basket of salves and bandages, aware she would soon forgive him even though she wouldn't soon forget.

The wound was a minor one, as The Blade had said. He had lost some blood, but no muscles had been cut. The thickness of his heavy wool coat had prevented the knife from slicing as deeply as it might have. Yet the sight of his flesh ripped open confirmed all her worst fears. Her hands trembled ever so slightly as Temple bound the wound shut and tied the securing strips of cloth.

"You are shaking," he observed.

She turned away, fighting the weakness that made her want to cry. "I wish you would give up this treaty business."

"I can't."

She felt his arms encircle her. She turned into them and buried her face against his bare chest, weeping softly and helplessly, conscious of the soothing stroke of his hand. For now she tried to push from her mind the thought of this nefarious council meeting that would soon take him from her side again.

⤝ 20 ⤞

Temple examined the gleaming silver tray for any remaining traces of tarnish, careful not to touch it with her blackened fingers. She grimaced faintly at the sight of them. The only task she hated more than polishing silver was salting meat. In both cases, her hands suffered.

She carried the tray to the side table and set it among the other finished pieces, then returned to the worktable to check on the progress of her two house servants. Only a half dozen pieces remained to be polished. When they were done, everything in the entire house would be spotless.

She had managed to accomplish a great deal during The Blade and Shawano's week-long absence. Working herself to the point of exhaustion every day had enabled her to fall asleep alone in the empty bed, and to ignore the absence of the blanketed figures who had departed the same day The Blade and Shawano had left. Their absence was more unnerving than their sinister presence had been.

"Miss Temple. Miss Temple!" Phoebe rushed into the room, her brown face wreathed with excitement. "There's a rider coming. I saw him from the window upstairs."

"The Blade?"

"I couldn't tell for sure. He was riding through the woods

like he had Satan himself snapping at his heels. But I'm thinking it is," Phoebe declared. "You know how Master Blade and Deu sometimes come racing home like they can't wait to get here."

Temple looked at her tarnish-stained hands, then at the dirty apron she wore over her oldest dress. "Look at me," she wailed. "He will think I am a drudge. Quick, Phoebe, help me change."

Breaking into a run, she dashed to the back stairwell, plucking the white duster cap from her head and untying her apron as she raced up the steps to their bedroom. There, she flung both on the bed and hurried straight to the washbasin.

"Unfasten my dress," she ordered, immersing her hands and a chunk of lye soap in the water. "And fetch my blue calico."

"Yes'm."

Temple scrubbed her hands as clean as time would allow, then started to shrug out of her dress. Downstairs, the front door opened as Temple tugged in frustration at a stubborn sleeve.

"Temple? Temple!" There was a shout from below, but the voice wasn't The Blade's.

"Kipp." She stepped into the hall.

"Temple, where are you?" came his strident, angry demand. This time there was no mistaking her brother's voice.

She moved to the top of the stairs. "Up here, Kipp." When he appeared at the bottom of the steps, she was alarmed by the look on his face. "What is it? Has something happened?"

"Is he here?" Kipp paused on the second step.

"No, he hasn't come back yet."

Kipp bounded up the steps, his long legs stretching to span two and three at a time. "Get your things. I am taking you out of here."

When he grabbed her wrist, Temple planted her feet. "I am not going anywhere until you tell me what this is all about."

"You are my sister!" The fury that lurked in his every action and word now exploded. "I will not let you stay another minute in this house of traitors."

"Stop it!" She jerked free and faced him with fists clenched rigidly at her sides, every bit as angry as he was. "I will not hear any more of your hatred for my husband!"

"You don't understand, Temple." He glared. "The bastards have done it. They signed a treaty with Jackson's man last night in New Echota. They have sold our land."

"No." She backed away from him, numbly shaking her head, needing to deny it. "Not The Blade. He would never do that."

"You are a fool," Kipp snapped. "His name is there along with the other snakes'. Why do you think I came?"

"I don't believe you," she murmured, her voice threatening to break.

"Do you think I would lie about this?"

"I don't know." Temple turned to face the wall, her head pounding so viciously she couldn't think clearly.

"What proof do you want? Must you see the treaty with your own eyes? His name is there, I tell you—and the mark of his father. They have broken the Blood Law. You can't mean to stay with a Judas who has betrayed our people. They have done more than talk this time. The treaty has been signed." Kipp paused. "I speak the truth, Temple. If you don't believe me, ask him."

"I will!" Stung by his jeering taunt, she spun around. There, in front of her, stood The Blade, his face like stone and his eyes like blue steel.

"Ask him," Kipp challenged confidently. "Ask him if he signed a treaty selling our land."

She was afraid of what she saw in his face. "Is it true?" she whispered.

"Yes." Not even an eyelash flickered when he replied.

"You will die for that," Kipp declared.

"But you will live. I wonder where the justice is in that,"

The Blade mused, his tone hard and cynical. "Get out, Kipp, before I forget you are Temple's brother."

Kipp turned to her. "Are you coming with me?"

But Temple couldn't move. She could only stare at her husband—the man she loved—the man who had become a traitor to his people.

"You have your answer," The Blade said. "She is staying."

Kipp turned and ran down the stairs. When the door slammed below, The Blade swung back to face her, his probing gaze somehow breaking the grip of shock that had held her silent.

"How could you?" she accused, her voice still strangled. "It is true. They will kill you for this."

"Yes."

In his mind, it wasn't Temple he saw before him but the scene the previous night in Elias Boudinot's house when the committee of twenty had gathered by the wavering candle flames to smoke their pipes and review the document that outlined the terms of cession. Then came the moment to sign it, and the initial hesitation by all was followed by silence as each man stepped forward and picked up the quill pen. Major Ridge had been the last. Afterward, he had stared at his mark on the treaty papers and declared, "I have signed my death warrant."

They all had. By their act, they had broken the Blood Law. The penalty was death.

He stared at the whiteness of her face and the redness of her lips. Drawn by them, he slowly walked over to her and put his hands on her narrow waist. He ignored her attempt to push him away as he pulled her closer.

"Make love to me, Temple. Make love to a dead man."

He brought his mouth down to hers, swallowing her sob of protest. Then she didn't fight him anymore. Her fingers raked his hair and her body strained eagerly against him, all motion and urgency. He picked her up and carried her into the bedroom, taking no notice of Phoebe as she discreetly slipped out the door.

Within minutes, they both lay naked on the bed, their avid hands stroking and caressing, memorizing every curve and contour, their lips clinging and crushing, savoring the taste and texture of the other. The looming specter of death lent a desperation to their lovemaking, giving it a furious passion that lifted them above all their disagreements and, for a time, let them forget all but their love.

Later, the shadows and the pain came back. As Temple slowly fastened the blue calico gown, his favorite dress, she listened to the sounds of him dressing behind her. Her body was still warm from him, his smell still clung to her, her lips still tasted of him, but her mind recoiled from what he had done.

Turning, she looked at him. "You did it for nothing. Your treaty will never be upheld as valid."

He hesitated a fraction of a second, then pulled on his boot. "If all it does is force Ross to make another treaty, then my goal is accomplished." He stood up, his gaze absorbing her. "Will you stay?"

"For now." She wasn't sure which would be hardest— leaving him or remaining to witness his death.

🦇 21 🦇

Gordon Glen
June 1836

A curious honeybee dipped and darted close to her face as Eliza leaned on the fence rail and surveyed the huge garden. Row after tidy row stretched before her, planted with corn, cabbage, sweet potatoes, sugar beets, snaps, onions, squash, and more. On the far side, two slave children and their mother bent over their hoes, chopping out weeds and turning up chunks of clay-red earth.

"Is something wrong, Eliza?" Temple's questioning voice broke sharply across her silent reverie. "You seem preoccupied since dinner."

"I could say the same for you," Eliza countered as she straightened from the fence. "This treaty business has cast a shadow over all of us, I fear." She caught the flicker of pain in Temple's eyes. "I shouldn't have said that."

"Why not? It's the truth," Temple retorted with a proud, almost defiant tilt of her head. "The treaty is a sham Jackson is trying to force on us, but he will not succeed. Too many voices in Congress are protesting the outrage, strong voices belonging to men like Henry Clay, Daniel Webster, Davy Crockett, and John Quincy Adams. The false treaty will never be ratified. The sixteen thousand names on the memorial John Ross took to Washington prove that the treaty was not made with the consent of the majority."

Eliza was struck by the bitter antagonism that underlined Temple's denunciation. By condemning the treaty so vehemently, she was also condemning the actions of her husband. Yet she remained with him.

"You love him very much, don't you?"

"Yes." The hard, clipped answer was even more revealing. Temple turned from the fence. "Your garden is doing very well."

"The rain the other night certainly helped it." Eliza respected Temple's wish to change the subject, while finding the reference to "her" garden bittersweet. With Victoria practically incapacitated by the debilitating consumption, Eliza was the mistress of the plantation in all but name.

"You haven't mentioned Reverend Cole in a long time. Have you not heard from him?" When Temple began to stroll along the rutted track that led to the stables, Eliza turned and walked with her.

"I had a letter from him last month." It was the first correspondence she had received from Nathan in more than a year. "Just a short one, letting me know that he was leaving for the West." Like many of the missionaries, he believed that it was only a matter of time before the Cherokees joined the western band already there.

"A few years ago I was convinced you would marry him," Temple remarked idly.

"We are good friends. Nothing more."

Suddenly, Temple stopped and swayed unsteadily, lifting a hand and pressing it to her forehead. For an instant, Eliza thought she was going to faint. She quickly hooked an arm around her shoulders to brace her.

"Temple, what's wrong?"

"Nothing." Weakly, she tried to wave aside Eliza's concern.

But Temple was obviously ill. Eliza had treated too many of the plantation's sick not to recognize the signs. "Shadrach," she called to the young boy who trailed at a respectful distance behind. "Help me get Miss Temple to the house."

"No, please," Temple protested, but this time the hand that pushed at Eliza had some strength to it. "This will pass in a minute. I will be fine, I promise."

Eliza glanced at the tiny beads of perspiration that had gathered on Temple's upper lip. Her sickly pallor was receding and color began to return to her face.

"You barely touched the food on your plate at dinner," Eliza remembered.

"I couldn't." Temple avoided her eyes, keeping her own gaze downcast. "I am . . . with child."

Temple spoke so quietly that it was a full second before Eliza was certain she had heard correctly. She broke into a wide smile. "Temple, how wonderful!" she declared, then frowned as she studied Temple's faintly distressed look. "Isn't it?"

"I want it to be." Her hand glided over her stomach in a gesture that was both loving and protective. Then she looked at Eliza. "But how can it be when the father of my baby is a traitor?"

"He is your husband," Eliza reminded her gently.

In a burst of agitation, Temple pulled away from her. "Sometimes I wish—" She stopped abruptly and sighed. "I no longer know what I wish. Maybe I should have listened to Kipp and left him when he first started talking about a treaty."

"You don't mean that."

"Don't I?" Temple laughed bitterly, her glance rising to the blue sky overhead. "If I had known what was going to happen, I think I would have left. But I stayed. Maybe I thought I could convince him he was wrong. I don't know."

"Does he know . . . about the baby?"

Temple shook her head. "No one does, except you and Phoebe." She turned to her. "How can I let my baby be born in a house of traitors, Eliza? How can I let my baby bear that shame? And he will if I stay."

She understood how Temple could feel so torn. Either way there would be pain. Yet Eliza was reluctant to offer any advice.

An odd calmness settled over Temple. "I want this baby, Eliza." She began walking again. "It is all I will have of my husband to love. Next week, next month, next year, The Blade will be punished for his act of treachery. He knows that one day he will lie in his own blood. I could have endured it, but the baby—I don't want him to see it. And I think The Blade would not want it either."

"Then . . . you will leave him."

"I want my baby to be born here at Gordon Glen." There was something poignant in her expression as Temple gazed affectionately at the towering brick mansion, partially visible through a break in the trees. "It is a place where he can grow up proud and strong."

Conscious of the tears that pricked her eyes, Eliza struggled to shake off the grip of sadness. "Are you so certain the baby will be a boy?" she asked, striving to lighten the atmosphere.

"No." Temple became thoughtful. "It would probably be better if it was a girl. People would not be so quick to attach the stigma of traitor to her as they would to a boy."

"Temple," Eliza murmured in a surge of pity and pain.

"Don't. No matter how I might sound, I regret nothing I have done." She spoke with such assurance that Eliza couldn't help envying Temple's courage in the face of her difficulties. She wished she were half as brave. Then Temple looked back at the servant boy lagging several steps behind them. "Shadrach, run ahead to the stables and ask Ike to have my mare saddled and waiting for me."

"Yes'm, Miss Temple." Breaking into a trot, he dashed ahead of them, his callused bare feet slapping the crimson dirt with each stride.

* * *

After Temple left, Eliza started back to the house. Today the familiar path was crowded with memories, memories of more carefree days, the days before she recognized her growing affection for Will Gordon. Passing the creek, she recalled the hot summer afternoons when she had played there with the children, wading in the cool water and catching tadpoles.

She paused in front of the log schoolhouse. No one had set foot inside it for more than two years. With the new demands of the household duties and only Xandra and Kipp and little Johnny for pupils, Eliza had found it more practical to move the classroom into the house and instruct the children in their lessons there. A dozen times Eliza had intended to inspect the building for any damage, but there always seemed to be more pressing matters that demanded her attention. She had never managed to fit it in . . . until now.

When she started up the walk, Shadrach darted ahead of her and opened the door. She smiled briefly at him, distracted by the thought that the place was probably infested with mice and a dozen other equally horrifying creatures. But no frantic scurrying sounds greeted her as she stepped inside.

She halted in amazement, astounded by the sight she beheld. The school was spotless. The floor, the windows, the desk, the chairs—there wasn't a speck of dust anywhere. Logs and kindling were stacked in the grate in readiness for a fire. On her desk a glass of water held a spray of purple iris.

In a daze, Eliza walked over and lightly touched one of the petals. Catching a movement out of the corner of her eye, she turned to Shadrach. He glanced away from her to the desk as he self-consciously shifted his weight to one foot.

"I make sure there's always fresh ink in the inkwell, too, in case you ever want to write something."

"You did all this, Shadrach?"

"Yes'm." He nodded and looked wistfully about the single

room. "I thought maybe someday you'd want to teach in here again."

Tears filled her eyes, blurring her vision and knotting her throat with emotion. "I haven't had time to keep you up on your studies, have I?" Somehow, in her own personal turmoil, she had forgotten the way he craved knowledge.

"It's okay," he assured her. "I read every chance I get. A couple of times, I've taken a book from Master Will's library. They were kind of hard to understand, but I liked trying to figure out what they were saying."

"Sometimes that is the best way to learn, Shad. It's not the easiest, but . . . I am glad you kept at it. Don't stop learning as much as you can, no matter what happens, or how hard it gets."

"I won't," he promised just as fervently.

Blinking rapidly, she brushed the tears from her eyes and smiled. "Of all the students I will ever have, I think I shall always be proudest of you."

"Truly?" His eyes were big and shiny with delight.

"Truly." Eliza let her smile widen. "Do you know what I think?"

"What?" He was all ears.

"As hot as it is, I think we should declare the rest of the afternoon a holiday. Why don't we all go to the creek and play?"

"Can I go, too?"

"*May* I go," Eliza corrected, then added, a conspiratorial gleam in her eyes, "Of course you may go. You will have to watch young Johnny, won't you?"

"Yes'm, I sure enough will." Shadrach grinned back.

On his way home from the fields, Will Gordon heard the sounds of laughter and splashing coming from the creek, but it was the adult squeal of mirth that caught his attention. He rode over to investigate, already guessing what he would find.

Chased by sprays of water, a barefoot Eliza scampered for the safety of the bank, the long skirt of her dress gathered into a bunch in front, her hair a cap of curls barely held in place. Xandra and Shadrach waded after her, laughing and slapping more water at the teacher. Even little Johnny joined in the fun, though he lacked the accuracy of the other two.

"Three against one is hardly fair odds."

"Papa!" Xandra cried with gladness as Eliza spun around, conscious of the sudden, joyous leap of her heart at the sight of Will Gordon. But she had long ago mastered the art of concealing her true feelings in his presence. When he dismounted, the smile she gave him was genuine.

"I hope you have come to rescue me from these water imps of yours," Eliza declared lightly.

"No." He strolled to the water's edge where Eliza stood and swept a bemused eye over the two youngest of his brood. "I stopped to help you put them to rout."

With a swiftness that surprised all of them, he sprang at six-year-old Johnny with a whoop and a shout. Johnny shrieked and pretended fear and took off running. When Will splashed into the shallow stream after him, mindless of his boots, Eliza went after Xandra. Soon they had both children on the run, led by a laughing Shadrach.

In less than a minute, they had the children cornered against a tall bank. When Johnny made a dash for freedom, Will scooped him up. Johnny squealed with laughter and yelled to his sister, "Help! Xandra, help me!"

She went to his aid, and Eliza didn't interfere. Instead, she retreated and sought the dry footing of the opposite bank. Once there, she sat on a fallen log and watched the fun, smiling with pleasure at the scene. Between the demands on his time by his people and the duties of the plantation, it was a rare occurrence for Will Gordon to have time to spend with his children, let alone to be at play with them.

She watched as he laughed and tussled with the giggling

pair, getting almost as wet as they were. The years seemed to lift off this strong, handsome man who stood head and shoulders above most of his people. It was good to see him like this, happy and carefree, unburdened by the travails of his position.

Eliza said as much to him later, on their way back to the house, with Johnny and Xandra riding the gray horse Will led. "I am convinced the romp was as good for you as it was for the children," she told him. "We all need to put our troubles aside from time to time and enjoy the simple pleasures life offers. It is a balance we all need in our lives."

"The children give you that, don't they?" Will guessed, glancing at the tall woman in the water-splattered dress at his side, matching him stride for stride.

"They do." A warmth stole into her eyes and softened her expression. He wondered if she knew the deep affection she had just revealed.

"The children are very fond of you, Eliza." The formality between them had long since ceased. Will could no longer remember the last time he had addressed her as Miss Hall. He regarded her as one of the family, and treated her as such.

"And I of them," she replied easily.

As they neared the house, Will noticed a rider coming up the lane. "We have a visitor."

"Perhaps he brings good news from John Ross in Washington."

The rider brought news from Washington, but it wasn't good. On May 17, the United States Congress had ratified the false treaty. Six days later, President Jackson had signed it, proclaiming it law.

The unthinkable had happened.

That evening, after the children had gone to bed, Eliza sat in the family parlor, her knitting needles flying with the fury of her thoughts. "One vote," she fumed. "The treaty was ratified by only one vote. If only one member of Congress had cast his ballot against it, this terrible travesty would never have occurred.''

''I know.'' Will sat in the wing-backed chair, his shoulders slumped under the awful weight of the news.

Eliza heard the grimness in his voice and let her knitting needles fall silent. ''What will you do now?''

''We will resist it, of course,'' Will stated.

''How? I mean, will you fight, the way the Seminoles in Florida are doing?'' She had read accounts of the skirmishes between American soldiers and the Seminole Indians that had taken place in the swamps—the fighting and the killing. She dreaded the thought of Gordon Glen becoming a battleground.

''Fight with what?'' Will chided. ''We are farmers. We have no arms, other than the shotguns we use against predators.''

''But what is the alternative?'' Eliza wondered aloud, shaking her head in puzzlement and frowning.

''We have only one,'' Will announced. ''To redouble our efforts in Washington. The Phantom Treaty was ratified by one vote. If we can get a new measure introduced to repeal it, perhaps we can get it passed by the same margin. We have two years in which to accomplish that before the federal government enforces the terms of the treaty.''

''Two years is—'' Eliza was interrupted by the loud *thud* of a heavy object hitting the floor above them. Smiling, she laid her knitting aside. ''Something tells me Johnny fell out of bed again.''

''It has become almost a nightly occurrence,'' Will remarked.

''It has,'' she agreed and rose from her chair. ''I will go tuck him back in.''

Before she could take a step, a shouted cry came from the second floor. ''Master Will, Master Will, come quick. It be Miz Victoria.'' It was Sulie May, the servant girl who had taken Phoebe's place in the household and had been assigned to sit with the ever-ailing Victoria.

Will sprang from his chair as Eliza broke into a run. He reached the staircase a step ahead of her. Hampered by her long skirts, Eliza couldn't keep pace with him as he raced up the stairs.

When she reached the second-floor landing, Eliza could hear the muffled sound of Victoria's horrible racking cough coming from the master bedroom. She ran to the open door. There she hesitated for a fraction of a second, held motionless by the sight of Will Gordon supporting his wife as she was convulsed by the hacking spasms.

Swiftly, she crossed the room. "I will take over now," she ordered crisply. Victoria looked up, her dark eyes full of fear and a silent appeal for help. "I am here. You will be fine." Eliza fixed a reassuring smile on her face.

"The attacks, they keep coming one after the other." Sulie May hovered next to the bed, watching. "She don't have no time to rest 'fore another starts."

"You will find a bottle of laudanum in the top drawer of the bedstand, Will. Bring it to me."

An eternity seemed to pass before the coughing subsided sufficiently for Eliza to administer the drug. She gently wiped Victoria's face with a damp cloth and tried to keep her calm enough to allow the laudanum to take effect. But Victoria's own exhaustion hastened that.

Once Eliza was reasonably confident there would be no more attacks, she took the handkerchief from Victoria's limp fingers. She started to lay it aside, then noticed the splotches of blood on the white cloth. She looked at Will, more worried about his wife than before.

"What is it?"

She shook her head, warning him to keep silent, and handed him the kerchief. "I will get her a clean one."

A clatter of footsteps sounded in the outer hall. A second

later, Kipp charged into the room with Black Cassie directly behind him. He stopped and stared at his mother, his face stark with apprehension. In a stupor of exhaustion and laudanum, Victoria was motionless and pale as death.

"Mama—" He took a step toward the bed, his voice choked.

"She is resting, Kipp," Eliza said, regretting that she had ever believed that anger was the only emotion Kipp could feel.

When Kipp turned to his father, she noticed the furtive way Will balled the bloodstained handkerchief and held it at his side, hiding it from Kipp's view. "I got Black Cassie here as fast as I could," Kipp said as the buxom woman scurried past him to her mistress.

"You did fine, Kipp." Will laid a reassuring hand on his son's shoulder and slipped the soiled cloth into his own pocket with the other. "Your mother will be all right."

"I looks after Miz Vi'toria. You don't be worryin' 'bout that none, Master Will." Cassie took the clean handkerchief from Eliza and gently tucked it in Victoria's hand. "Does ya wants me t' cup her? I brings my things."

"No." Eliza spoke up quickly, not allowing Will an opportunity to answer. "Sleep is what she needs now."

"Yes," he agreed. "Tomorrow, move Miss Eliza's things to Temple's old room, Cassie." His glance locked with Eliza's. "I want you close by in case Victoria needs you in the night again."

"Of course." She nodded.

"Go back to your room now, Kipp," Will said. "There is nothing more you can do here."

Reluctantly, Kipp left. In the ensuing silence, broken only by the soft rustle of Black Cassie moving about, Will watched while Eliza tended to Victoria. Her calm efficiency and cool competence impressed him, especially after the righteous outrage she had displayed over the treaty's ratification only moments ago.

Leaving Victoria's bedside, Eliza approached him. "She is resting now," she said in an undertone. "Come." She indicated for him to follow her into the hall. Will did. Outside the bedroom door, Eliza stopped. "I will help Cassie move my things downstairs. If Victoria begins coughing again, you can give her some laudanum, but no more than ten drops," she cautioned.

"Ten drops," he repeated with a nod, then mused, "We have all come to depend on you a great deal, Eliza."

"I expect you have," she acknowledged, but she was uncomfortable with his words.

Will tried for a moment to imagine Gordon Glen without her; it was a bleak and cheerless place he saw. She had become more than just a teacher and housekeeper; she had become like a mother to his children, laughing with them, treating their cuts and scrapes, tucking them into bed at night.

But it wouldn't be only the children who would miss her if she ever left, Will realized. He would too. He had only to recall the lively conversations at the dinner table, the endless opinions Eliza had on almost any subject, the confiding talks they sometimes shared in the evenings about the children, or the letters she wrote him when he was away, letters filled with amusing anecdotes and information about the children or the plantation.

"I wonder if Reverend Cole really knew what he lost when you chose not to marry him, Eliza."

"That is the second time today someone has made reference to Reverend Cole. First Temple and now you. I cannot understand this sudden interest in him," Eliza declared.

"Perhaps both of us realized how very fortunate we are that you have remained here with us. I am glad you did, Eliza."

"Thank you, but your gratitude is quite unnecessary."

"It isn't gratitude I am offering." It was a simple statement, but there was nothing simple about the way he held her gaze.

Afraid of misinterpreting his words, Eliza remained silent.

When he turned and went back into the bedroom to stay with
Victoria, Eliza thought her heart would break into a million
pieces. But that was foolishness. Hearts didn't break, any
more than they soared. People imagined such things.

*T*emple shook out the blue calico dress and tried desperately to forget that it was The Blade's favorite. For the past two and a half weeks, she had postponed informing him about the baby—and her decision to leave. But she had seen very little of him during that time. What with the ratification of the false treaty by the American Congress and Ross's subsequent message that it was to be treated as though it didn't exist, The Blade had been away a great deal. When he was home, the time never seemed right to tell him.

Determined to delay no longer, she was packing her things now, before he returned, so that when he did, she would have to confront him. Behind her, Phoebe loudly blew her nose, the sound scraping her already raw nerves.

"Stop that sniffling, Phoebe," Temple snapped. "How many times must I tell you that we will not leave until they come back? You will get to see Deu before we go."

"I know," she said, her voice strangled with grief.

"It isn't as though you will never see him again. I told you he could visit you at Gordon Glen." Almost angrily, Temple folded the dress and jammed it into the open trunk.

"I know."

"Then stop this bawling! Do you have to make it harder than it already is?" She fought back her own tears as she grabbed up another dress.

Suddenly, Temple stiffened, sensing The Blade's presence even though she hadn't heard a sound. When she swung around, he stood motionless in the bedroom doorway, his lean features devoid of expression, his blue eyes colder than a winter sky. She couldn't remember the last time she had seen him smile. That side of him was gone, buried so deep she wasn't sure it would emerge again.

His glance flicked to the trunk. "You are leaving," he said flatly.

"Yes." Unconsciously, she held her breath, waiting for his response.

He started forward. She backed up a step, expecting him to rip the dress from her hand and empty the trunk. But he walked past her to the balcony doors. He stopped in front of them to stare at the treetops outside.

Finally she realized that he wasn't going to break the crushing silence. "I am going to have a child and I want it to be born at Gordon Glen." She deliberately linked the two statements together.

"When—" He stopped, then started over, his voice flattening out again. "When are you planning to leave?"

"As soon as possible." Her throat was so tight she could hardly get the words out. Beyond his initial surprise, The Blade acted as if he didn't even care that they were going to have a baby.

For several seconds he stood motionless. "I will have a wagon brought around for your things and send a couple of the field workers to load your trunks." He didn't look at her as he walked out of the room, and Temple didn't see him again before she left.

At Gordon Glen, Temple waited for The Blade to visit. If he wasn't going to acknowledge her pregnancy, she thought he would surely come to bring the news of the July arrival of federal troops commanded by General Wool and sent by Jackson as a show of force. But he didn't. Nor did he come to deride Ross's persistent attempts to obtain a new treaty that would cede only the Cherokee lands within the boundaries claimed by Georgia.

Nor did he bring a copy of the November general order number 74 posted by General Wool, which called for the original treaty to be enforced.

Her only news of The Blade came from Phoebe, who saw Deu frequently. Even that was scant and hardly satisfying. According to Deu, The Blade had become increasingly short-tempered and given to anger at the slightest provocation, a failing Temple had recently suffered herself. The family blamed her irritability on her "condition." She couldn't admit, not even to Eliza, how very much she missed The Blade and how much it hurt that he hadn't cared enough to come see her, knowing she carried his child.

In early January, two weeks before the baby was due, Shawano Stuart came to Gordon Glen to say good-bye. He was joining a train of emigrants composed solely of fellow treaty advocates which was scheduled to depart within days on the long trek to the lands given to them in the West. He was quick to assure Temple that The Blade would remain behind to handle some unfinished business, strongly hinting that the imminent birth of their child was part of it.

Before he left, Shawano gripped her hand in his gnarled fingers. "I am glad my grandchild will be born here in our beloved land that has nurtured the Cherokees for time out of mind. It is a good thing." Tears glazed his eyes.

"Yes." She wept softly, for herself and for him.

"Be well, my daughter." He squeezed her hand briefly, then released it and turned away, leaning heavily on his cane.

The Blade stood outside the store and watched as the trader led the three blooded horses around back. The money for them was in his pocket. With the sale of the horses, he had succeeded in disposing of the last of the livestock. Seven Oaks was now in the possession of its lottery-winning ticketholder, unless the new owner had already sold it to some land speculator. In any case, the plantation was no longer his problem. He no longer had any responsibilities for the crops, the workers, the maintenance. Once that had been precisely what he wanted—no home, no wife, no family. But what he found he now had was a gnawing emptiness.

He took the cigar from his pocket, the one the trader had thrown in as part of the sale price with such penurious generosity. He bit off the end, spitting it into the dirt street, and lit it. He rolled the cigar between his lips and squinted to peer through the curling smoke at the shabby remnants of New Echota. His people had once pointed to it with pride. The capital was in shambles, like the rest of the Nation, all the government buildings fallen into disrepair.

A few soldiers idled outside the army headquarters. Beyond, smoke from cookfires spiraled lazily toward the winter sky, marking the site of the small encampment of his countrymen who awaited the departure of the next train west, most of them destitute and dispirited. The still air carried the echo of a drunken hallooing.

Today the town looked almost deserted. Ten days ago the scene had been vastly different. For a moment it had been as if New Echota had recaptured its former glory. Its carefully laid-out streets had been jammed with coaches, carriages, and wagons, many of them drawn by caparisoned horses. Men in warm furs had sat astride some of the finest horseflesh in the Nation. Laughing women and children accompanied by entourages of black servants had filled the coaches and carriages. More Negroes had driven the wagons loaded with provisions, household furnishings, and furniture, while others had tended the large herd of livestock.

That morning The Blade had bidden his father good-bye and watched the large caravan of some six hundred Cherokee emigrants depart for the West. He could have been among them . . . he and Temple. The thought clawed at his heart, making it ache afresh. He clamped his teeth down on the cigar, aware that she still refused to regard removal as inevitable.

Van Buren would succeed to the presidency in March, but he was Jackson's man. Ross would have no more luck with him than he'd had with Jackson. The Phantom Treaty, Ross called it. House Representative John Quincy Adams had labeled it an "eternal disgrace upon the country."

Bitterly, The Blade wrenched his gaze from the scene and sent it slicing over his immediate surroundings. Where the hell was Deu? His business with the trader was finished. It was time they left.

There was a noise behind him. The Blade glanced back, still grimly clenching the cigar between his teeth. A turbaned Cherokee staggered from the store, a whiskey bottle clutched in his hands and a government-issued blanket around his shoulders. When he saw The Blade, he halted, reeled slightly, and stared at the old scar on The Blade's cheek. A look of utter loathing and contempt stole over his face. Coldly, The Blade held the man's eyes, aware that if he turned his back to him, he might end up with a knife in it.

The man slowly drew back his head, then spat at him. The Blade flinched as the spittle struck his cheek, but he made no attempt to wipe away the slimy liquid, feeling a mixture of fury and contempt for this poor misguided fool who turned to whiskey rather than face the truth. Or was it for himself for getting involved in the Nation's affairs? Which of them was really the fool?

When the man staggered away, The Blade dragged the back of his coat sleeve across his cheek, then yanked the cigar from his mouth and threw it into the street. Why did he stay here? Why hadn't he gone west with Shawano? But he knew the answer to that. Temple.

It had been months since he had seen her. At first, when the threats against his life had escalated to an alarming degree following the ratification of the treaty, he had stayed away out of fear for her. But the arrival of the federal troops had negated much of that. After that, he wasn't sure why he had stayed away. It had seemed best for her and the baby yet to be born, yet perhaps it had been pride that kept him away. Maybe he had wanted her to come to him and admit he was right. Or maybe he had hoped he could forget her. But time hadn't given him any immunity from the pain.

Did she remember that it was his connections, his influence, that had kept Gordon Glen out of the lottery? Did she know she had him to thank for the roof over her head? Did it matter?

"Master Blade!" Deu rounded the corner of the store, his dark eyes unusually bright.

"Where have you been?" The Blade snapped irritably, in no mood to hear any news Deu might have gleaned from the trader's black. He walked briskly to the hitching rack where their horses were tied. "I have been out here for ten minutes."

"Master Blade, wait." Deu grabbed his arm, then quickly released it when he felt the bunching of muscles. "Old Cato just told me the baby's come. You have a *son*, Master Blade."

Silence. Then he slowly turned. "A son! Are you sure?"

"Yes sir."

"Temple—"

"She's fine, sir. Just fine."

The Blade gave him a slapping shove toward the horses. "Let's go!" He sprang into the saddle and wheeled the horse from the rack before Deu got the reins to his untied. The Blade didn't wait for him, taking off out of town at a hard gallop.

Victoria lay on her side and gazed adoringly at the blanket-wrapped infant nestled in the crook of her arm. With the tip of her forefinger, she traced the curve of the tiny fist. "He is beautiful, isn't he?" she said, glancing at Eliza.

"Indeed he is." Eliza stood close to the bed, watchful for any signs that Victoria was overtiring.

"He is big for only three days old." She gently smoothed the bushy down of black hair on the baby's head. "It will be so good to have a baby in the house again," she declared, then struggled to swallow back a cough.

"Let me take him now." Eliza stepped forward and tunneled her hands under the sleeping infant, picking him up. "I think Mama would like to have him back for a while."

"Which mama?" Will inquired. "The boy has three of them. Four, if you count Xandra."

"At least no one can say he won't be well cared for." Eliza smiled as Will walked over to inspect the grandson she held in her arms.

"Father, you spoil him as much as they do," Temple accused from the doorway.

"Temple." Eliza turned in surprise. "You should not be out of bed."

"I can't stay there forever." She walked into the room, exhibiting only a slight gingerliness in her movements. "Especially, it seems, if I want to spend any time with my son. Every time I close my eyes, someone runs off with him."

"Your mother wanted to see him," Eliza explained as she transferred the baby into Temple's arms.

"I know."

"Miss Temple." Phoebe barged into the room, then paused, lowering her voice the instant she saw Temple holding the baby. "Master Blade's here."

"Here." Temple breathed the word.

"Yes'm. He's outside. He wants to see the baby."

"Well, of course he can." She beamed. "Tell him to come in."

"He . . ." Phoebe hesitated, regret flickering in her eyes. "He won't come in. He wants me to . . . bring the baby outside."

Temple stared at her, too frozen inside to speak. "Of course," she murmured at last and drew the blanket more tightly around her sleeping son. "It is cold out. Be sure to keep him covered." She gave the baby over to Phoebe.

As Phoebe left with the infant, Temple pulled her shawl up around her shoulders, then turned and went to the balcony doors.

"Temple, you aren't going outside?" Eliza protested.

She paused with one hand on the brass latch and said, without turning, "I want to see him." She opened the door and stepped out into the crisp January afternoon.

His horse snorted and impatiently stamped a foot as The Blade centered his entire attention on the mansion's baroque door, waiting for it to open. When Phoebe came out carrying a blanketed bundle in her arms, he unconsciously strained forward, every muscle tensing in anticipation.

"Here's your son, Master Blade." She held the small bundle up, offering it to him.

He stared down from his horse, gripped by a strange feeling of awe, then awkwardly took the bundle from her, conscious of the squirming wiggle of the baby hidden inside the folded cloth. It was so small he wasn't sure what to do with it, how to hold it. He felt clumsy as he finally positioned the length of it along his forearm and lifted the corner flap of the blanket.

A tightness choked his throat when he saw the little face inside and the blinking, bewildered eyes that stared back at him. Black hair, fine as silk, covered the top of his head and curled over his ears—perfect little ears. Then his son gurgled and flailed the air with tiny fists. A powerful emotion, too new to identify, swelled inside him, bringing tears to his eyes.

"Miss Temple named him Elijah William Stuart," Phoebe said.

"Elijah." The Blade caught one of the fists between his thumb and forefinger and smiled at the little fingers that tried to curl around his thumb but weren't quite long enough to encircle it. "Elijah."

"Master Blade," Deu murmured low to him, his tone telling him there was something or someone he should be aware of.

The Blade instantly sensed that he was being watched. Without hesitation, he looked straight up to the second-floor balcony. Temple looked back, her black hair cascading loose about her shoulders, a shawl hugged protectively around her shapeless white nightdress. She had never looked more beautiful to him. Motionless, an unsmiling statue, yet she seemed to reach out to him.

Then Eliza joined her at the railing, shattering the impression. He looked down at his son, the child she had given him, the living proof of the love they had known together. He caressed the fingers that held so tightly to his thumb.

"Did she teach you to hang on like that, Lije?" he murmured. "You have to learn to let go." His horse tossed its head and shifted restlessly beneath him. "Let go," he whispered hoarsely, and reluctantly lowered the baby to Phoebe's hands.

Immediately, he reined his horse away from the house and the black woman, and forced himself not to look back. He heard Deu ride up alongside him.

"That's a fine-looking boy," he said.

"I will never live to see him grow up."

Deu silently cried for him, a tear rolling slowly down his dark cheek. There wasn't anything else he could do to ease his master's painful loneliness.

From the balcony, Temple watched him ride away, her whole body aching at the sight. She felt Eliza's arm curve around her shoulder, but she found no comfort in it.

"He . . . he looked thinner." Temple remembered the way he had stared at her, mesmerizing her with his eyes. She choked back a sob, realizing again that she still loved him.

"Let's go inside, Temple," Eliza urged gently. "He has left."

Part III

... the opinion which is so generally entertained of its being impossible to civilize the Indians in our sense of the word. Here is a remarkable instance which seems to furnish a conclusive answer to skepticism on this point. A whole Indian nation abandons the pagan practices of their ancestors, adopts the Christian religion, uses books printed in their own language, submits to the government of their elders, builds houses and temples of worship, relies upon agriculture for their support, and produces men of great ability to rule over them, and to whom they give a willing obedience. Are not these the great principles of civilization? They are driven from their religious and social state then, not because they cannot be civilized, but because a pseudo set of civilized beings, who are too strong for them, want their possessions!

—George W. Featherstonhaugh

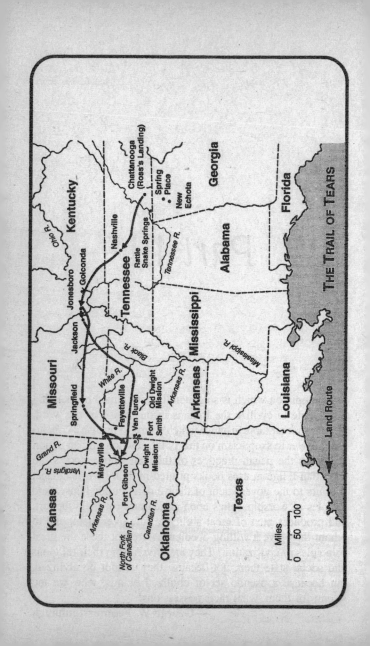

≫ 23 ≪

Hiwassee
May 10, 1838

*I*n full dress regalia, Lieutenant Jed Parmelee stood at parade rest, facing the sixty-odd Cherokee chieftains and headmen who had been summoned to the agency by General Winfield Scott, the new commanding officer of the federal troops. Jed was no longer the innocent and idealistic young officer fresh from West Point. He had spent the last four years in the Florida swamps campaigning against the Seminoles, losing many of his illusions—including the illusion of the glory of battle.

He had fought and lived while others around him had died. He had stopped asking why. Lieutenant Jed Parmelee was a professional soldier now, a combat veteran who fought because it was what he had been trained to do. He was loyal to the uniform he wore even if he wasn't always proud of it.

The subtropical sun had bronzed his fair skin and bleached the small mustache that grew on his upper lip. His sideburns and darkly golden hair had been streaked by the sun as well. And his eyes were old now with the hardness of experience, as old as some of the Indians' he now faced, old and sharply alert. He watched them, observing their stony faces and equally stony silence as they waited for General Scott to read his proclamation to them.

"Cherokees! The president of the United States has sent me with a powerful army to cause you, in obedience to the treaty of 1835, to join that part of your people who are already established in prosperity on the other side of the Mississippi." Scott spoke firmly but not unkindly as he addressed the gathering.

Jed glanced sideways at his commanding officer, taking in the man's plumed hat, lavish gold braid, and polished saber. The general's excessive fondness for military pageantry was well known. Old Fuss and Feathers, his men called him, but they also knew he wasn't to be taken lightly. A dominating presence at six feet four inches tall, the general from Virginia had directed the campaign against the Seminoles.

Last month Jed had arrived in Washington to begin his new assignment as an aide to General Winfield Scott. Cecilia had been overjoyed at his new post, and plans had once again been set in motion for their wedding, a wedding twice postponed—first by the orders sending him to Florida, then by battle wounds. By the time Cecilia and her mother had reached Washington, General Scott had been appointed to command the military operations aimed at enforcing the removal treaty with the Cherokee Nation. They would depart the city within days. The wedding had been postponed again.

"The full moon of May is already on the wane," Scott declared. "And before another shall have passed away, every Cherokee man, woman, and child must be in motion to join their brethren in the Far West."

The treaty had set forth the deadline of May 23, 1838. By that date, all Cherokees must be in motion westward. In the two days since their arrival at the military headquarters, Jed hadn't seen any indications that the Cherokees were preparing to leave. On the contrary, when he had ridden through the country, most of the Indians had been in the fields tending their crops, as if they believed they would be there in the fall to harvest them.

"The desire of every one of us is to execute our painful

duty in mercy," Scott stated. "Will you then, by resistance, compel us to resort to arms? God forbid! Or will you, by flight, seek to hide yourselves in mountains and forests, and thus oblige us to hunt you down?"

Silence. Jed scanned the crowd, trying to gauge their reaction and get some sense of what to expect. He briefly glimpsed a familiar face in their midst and sought to locate it again. There, the man in the back, taller than the others, with the gleam of red in his hair. It was Will Gordon.

Jed suddenly realized how hard he had tried not to think about her, tried not to remember she was here. But the thought that he might see her again had been there all along in the back of his mind. Temple. The image of her was strong and clear before him, the sultriness of her dark beauty as real to him as it had been the last time he had seen her.

"I am an old warrior," the fifty-six-year-old general offered in conclusion, "and have been present at many a scene of slaughter; but spare me, I beseech you, the horror of witnessing the destruction of the Cherokees."

With the general's warning plea ringing in his ears, Jed stiffened at the thought of what his orders might mean to Temple and her family. After the Cherokee leaders were dismissed to carry Scott's message back to their people, Jed took the opportunity to seek out Will Gordon. The man had changed little in the last six years. His face remained relatively unlined, though the haunting sadness that had always lurked in the somber brown of his eyes was perhaps more pronounced. Despite some graying of his hair at the temples, he looked like a man in his prime.

When Jed called him by name, Will Gordon turned and frowned. "Yes?"

Forcing himself to relax his military stance, Jed smiled. "I don't know if you remember me, but we met some years ago in Washington. Payton Fletcher is my godfather. I'm—"

Recognition flashed in his eyes. "Lieutenant . . . Parmelee, isn't it?"

"Yes. It is good to see you again, sir. I only wish we were meeting under other circumstances."

"We would both prefer that," Will Gordon agreed, a somberness returning to his expression.

"Your daughter . . . I hope she is well."

"Temple? Yes, she is in good health." He smiled faintly, a trace of pride shining through. "She presented me with a grandson last year."

"Congratulations." Jed fought down the wave of envy and jealousy that tried to surface. Already he regretted the impulse that had prompted him to seek out Will Gordon. "I know you want to be on your way."

"Yes, I have a long ride ahead of me."

"Please, give my regards to your family, and I hope the next time we meet, it will be on equally friendly terms." He hesitated, then warned, "General Scott stated the army's position quite plainly, sir. We have our orders. Any attempt at resistance would bring tragic consequences."

"How can we resist, Lieutenant? We have already surrendered our fowling pieces, and long ago we abandoned our bows and arrows and tomahawks. We have no weapons. We are at your mercy." The sadness in his eyes was heartbreaking. "But you must understand—this land is ours and we will never willingly surrender our homes. Would you?"

The gentle question haunted Jed for days.

⧉ 24 ⧉

Gordon Glen
May 26, 1838

*E*liza cast an inspecting glance over the table, then walked out of the dining room. Temple came down the stairs, carrying the meal she had taken up earlier to her mother. "Did she eat anything today?" Eliza asked.

Temple shook her head, her dark eyes mirroring Eliza's concern. "She drank all of the broth."

Eliza sighed, well aware it was barely enough to sustain Victoria. "Has your father come in yet?"

"I think he is in the library."

"I'll let him know dinner is ready. Will you tell the others to come to the table?" Taking her agreement for granted, she crossed to the library doors and knocked once, then paused by the door. Will stood at one of the windows, his back to the door, his hands clasped behind him in a pensive pose, seemingly unaware of her presence. Eliza stepped inside.

Outside, the sunlight beat down on the lawn, already parched by the scanty spring rains. Meteor showers, solar eclipse, unusually severe winters—Eliza hoped this wasn't the presage for a dry summer.

"Dinner is ready," she said. Will turned to face her, his expression still troubled and distracted. Eliza sensed immediately it wasn't the weather that worried him. "It's the waiting, isn't it?" she guessed. "The deadline has passed. Yet nothing has happened."

"You know me very well, don't you?"

She smiled and reminded him, "John Ross is still in Washington. Maybe he succeeded in renegotiating the treaty or getting it reversed and we have yet to receive word of it."

"Maybe. I know he continues the fight."

"And everyone is united behind him." Not quite everyone, Eliza thought to herself. Not The Blade. He had come to Gordon Glen a handful of times to see his son. Not once, to her knowledge, had a single word passed between Temple and him. Temple refused to talk about him. "The human spirit can endure a lot when it knows it isn't alone."

"No one knows that better than I."

"The family is in the dining room," she told him.

"We had better go then," he said.

When one-and-a-half-year-old Lije saw Will enter the dining room, he stood up in Xandra's lap and held out his arms to him, his fingers clutching and unclutching in a grasping plea. "Ganpa, Ganpa," he cried excitedly.

"There's my boy." Will walked over and scooped up the black-haired toddler. "Are you going to eat dinner with us today?"

"He insisted." Temple smiled indulgently at her son. "And Xandra volunteered to look after him."

"Lije is going to be a good boy for Aunt Xandra, isn't he?" Xandra crooned, tugging affectionately at his foot, the action stretching the bodice of her red blouse and revealing the voluptuous fullness of a woman's figure in the fifteen-year-old-girl.

"Goo' boy," Lije repeated earnestly, eliciting a chuckle from Will before he gave him back into Xandra's care.

The three-story brick mansion stood atop the slight knoll as if it had been born out of the clay-red earth that held its foundations. Jed reined in his horse to stare at the imposing structure, for a moment allowing himself to admire it.

"I'll be go to hell," muttered one of the soldiers near him. "This must belong to one of them rich Cherokee bastards."

Jed felt like cursing too, and had ever since Scott ordered him to the Third District to take part in the rounding up of the intransigent Cherokees and ensure his directives were followed through to the letter. This mass effort was being carried on throughout the entire Nation, squads of soldiers fanning out from every military outpost to seize and bring back all the Indians they found, wherever they found them.

He had already had a morning's worth of watching men being taken from their fields at the point of a bayonet, women and children dragged from their homes. The weeping, the wailing, the screaming, the pleading to be allowed to take some few of their possessions—it would live with him forever. That and the sight of the looting rabble that followed them.

Orders. With his jaw tightly clenched, Jed growled through his teeth, "Surround the house."

The gleam of fixed bayonets flashed in the sunlight as the squad rushed silently forward. Jed walked his horse after them and halted it short of the front veranda. When he thought of the civilized people inside that home, his stomach twisted in a sickening knot. No matter how humanely they might try to carry out this task, the cruelty of it was still there.

The sergeant moved close to the front door and looked expectantly at Jed, waiting for the command to enter. Swallowing at the bitterness in his throat, Jed nodded.

"Ned Rain Crow believes the troops are here to protect us from the Georgians." Kipp took the bowl of *connahinney* from Temple and spooned a large helping of the hominylike corn onto his plate.

"I—" Eliza looked up and saw someone outside the dining room window. "Who is that?" She frowned.

At the same instant she heard the front and rear doors in the great hall fly open, followed by the clatter of a dozen running feet. Will started to rise from his chair as soldiers burst into the dining room, their rifles at the ready, steel bayonets gleaming with threatening menace. Black Cassie screamed and dropped the bowl in her hand. It crashed to the floor, food and shards flying in all directions. Lije began to cry uncertainly.

"What is going on? What do you want?" Will towered before the soldiers, indifferently facing the sharp bayonet tips pointed at him.

An officer stepped into the room and halted abruptly. Temple stared, recognition jolting through her. Jed Parmelee, the young lieutenant she had met in Washington. Her father had mentioned he was in the Nation.

Now here he stood, stiffly erect, staring incredulously back, a slightly different Jed Parmelee from the one she remembered. The change was more than the pale golden mustache and long sideburns he now wore. The freshness of youth was gone from his face. He wasn't the gallant young officer anymore. He had the hardened visage of a soldier. But not quite, she thought, as she caught the flash of profound regret that flickered briefly in his eyes before he turned to her father.

"I am sorry, sir, but you and your family are obliged to come with us," he informed him briskly. "Please don't try to resist or flee, sir. We have the house surrounded. It would be futile."

"Where are you taking us?" Will placed a shielding hand on his youngest son, Johnny, drawing him closer.

"We have orders to bring all Cherokees to the fort in preparation for their departure to their new homes in the West." His crisp explanation was followed by a strident wail from Lije as he stretched out his chubby arms to Temple.

When she took a step toward him, a soldier bristled. Temple paused, her glance arching to Jed in anger and resentment. "May I go to my son?"

He hesitated briefly, then nodded, granting permission. She swept past the soldier and hurried to her sister's side, taking Lije from her and trying to hush his cries. Overhead came the muffled thud of footsteps, spreading through the second-floor rooms above.

"My wife is upstairs. She is too ill to travel," Will protested.

"I hope not, Mr. Gordon," Jed Parmelee replied. "We prefer not to separate families. However, if she is unable to accompany you, then she will have to remain here until suitable transportation and care can be arranged. I will allow one person to stay and look after her. The rest of you will have to come with me . . . now."

"You cannot mean that!" Eliza cried helplessly.

"I do, ma'am."

"We will need time to pack—" Will began.

"You had time, sir, and you chose not to take advantage of it. The general advised all of you to come to the staging areas with your families and belongings. He warned you not to wait until you were approached by soldiers." The words rushed from him, his voice vibrating with frustration and anger. "That day has come. It is out of your hands . . . and mine." He muttered the last, partially turned, then paused. "You have five minutes to gather what you can, but your children will have to remain here under guard. As for your wife, it would be unwise to leave her. If you have a wagon and team, I will order it brought around for her. But that, sir, is the best I can do."

"In that case, I have no choice but to accept," Will replied curtly.

"Is there anyone else in the house besides your wife?" he asked, still without facing them.

"My blacks."

"What of your husband, Mrs. Stuart?" He looked sideways at Temple. "Where is he?"

She tilted her head a little higher and hugged her whimpering son closer. "I don't know."

"Doesn't he live here with you?"

"No."

He held her gaze an instant longer, then turned completely away. "Five minutes, Sergeant, then I want all of them outside."

"Right, sir."

But the five minutes stretched to fifteen, prolonged partly by the time it took to calm a nearly hysterical Victoria and carry her downstairs, and partly by the time required by the soldiers to search every corner and cranny of the large house and roust the frightened servants from their hiding places.

The instant the family was herded outside, two slovenly white men snared Will and tried to convince him to sell them the house and its contents, his livestock, crops, equipment, and his field slaves, offering to pay him less than a pittance of what everything was worth. Even as Will rejected their offers, refusing to be cheated, the black smithy, Ike, came running from the stable area.

"Master Will, some white men's takin' yo' hosses. I tries t' stop 'em, but they knocks me down." Blood trickled from a cut on his forehead.

Hearing this, Eliza turned to the officer. "Aren't you going to do something?"

"No." Jed mounted his horse, well aware there was nothing he could do. Even if he managed to recover the horses from these thieves, there would be others, and he couldn't spare any men to stay behind and protect the Gordons' property.

Over and over again, he tried to convince himself that he wasn't to blame for what was happening, he was simply following orders. But as his men marched the Gordons and their house blacks away to join the rest of the captured Cherokees, Jed found it impossible to look Temple in the eye. Why did he have to be the one who had taken her prisoner?

⫷ 25 ⫸

*T*he Blade slowly walked his horse toward the stockade gates, its jagged walls built of split logs sharpened and set in the ground to form a high picket. From behind them, he could hear the bewildered murmur from the mass of humanity imprisoned inside. The sound was an echo of the voices he had heard at the previous three military outposts where he had searched for Temple and his son.

A week ago he had seen the military patrols scouring the countryside, driving the Cherokees from their homes, their fields, and their spinning wheels, and herding them like cattle to the outlying forts, prodding the recalcitrant with bayonets and curses, lashing the resisters with whips. He had immediately ridden to the nearest outpost, identified himself as a treaty proponent, and obtained a pass to search for his family.

At the stockade gate, the guard checked his pass and waved him inside. As he rode over to the commanding officer's headquarters, The Blade scanned the sixteen-foot-high pens that held the captured Cherokees.

Dismounting in front of the office, he handed the horse's reins to Deu. "Wait here for me."

He entered the building, his moccasined feet making almost no sound on the rough floor planks. The sergeant at the desk looked up in mild surprise as The Blade blocked the sunlight streaming in through the doorway.

"Are you here to give yourself up?" The sergeant's gaze traveled over him, taking in the moccasins, the buckskin leggings, and hunting shirt, then moving to the red turban around his black hair, finally stopping on the scar.

"I am looking for my wife and son." The Blade again took the pass from his pocket and gave it to the man. "They were taken about ten days ago. The name is Stuart."

"Names aren't much help around here. Most of them won't tell us who they are, and won't answer a roll call. Hell, we don't know who we have."

"What do you want, Lieutenant?" Temple stood before him, her dark gaze smoldering with resentment and distrust, her blue calico dress smudged with dirt, the hem tattered and water-stained from the river crossings. Jed tried not to remember how vastly different she had looked just two short weeks ago.

Perspiration trickled down Jed's neck and under the collar of his uniform as the sun broiled down mercilessly on the camp and its congestion of humanity. He looked down the long row of log pens, each sixteen feet square and every one crowded with captives, prisoners really. A few, like the Gordons', were partially and crudely roofed to provide them some shelter and shade from the summer sun. Conscious of the eyes staring back at him, Jed recognized his discomfort was not caused solely by the relentless heat.

"I have given your father permission to return home and load up the belongings that were left behind." Personally, Jed doubted there would be much left with all the pillaging and looting that had gone on and still continued. "He has taken the wagon and your Negro Ike. I expect it will be two or three days before he returns."

"And you are concerned he won't come back," she accused

with challenging bitterness. "You should not be. You have his entire family for hostages to ensure that he does."

"I know he will return," Jed asserted, stung by her tone yet unable to blame her for it. "I merely wanted to inform you of his departure and to inquire if there was anything I could do to help—anything within my power."

She smiled at his hastily added qualification, but the expression had a bite to it, like a sour lemon. Then it faded as her son toddled over to her side, chewing on a chunk of unleavened bread. When she looked at Jed again, all her previous hostility was gone, and her look now contained concern and silent appeal.

"Can you give us better food?"

The food issued to the camp's inhabitants was the standard military-prison fare of salt pork and flour, vastly different, Jed knew, from the Cherokees' customary diet of vegetables, beef, and fresh fruit.

"Nothing else has been stored in quantity—" he began reluctantly.

"Then let some of us forage in the woods for berries, pokeweed, wild onions . . . anything." Her request was neither an appeal nor a demand but fell somewhere between both.

Jed hesitated, aware of the risk that some might try to slip away. "I believe I can arrange that."

On his own responsibility, he allowed a half dozen women, including Temple, to leave the camp to forage. As a precaution, he assigned a detail of two guards to accompany them. At the last minute, he went along as well, staying close to Temple.

Hardly a breath of air stirred in the woods beyond the detention center, but it was free of the stench that permeated the camp. The trees provided a welcome shade from the unrelenting sun. Yet everywhere there was evidence of the damaging effects from the drought that plagued the entire countryside. The parched ground was baked hard; streams were dry; leaves withered on the bushes; the berries were scant and small.

Jed looked on as Temple reached for a dimpled raspberry hidden deep within the bush. He wondered how much longer the drought would last. Already reports were coming in of springs and water wells drying up and river levels dropping, making navigation of them questionable at best. One party of some eight hundred Cherokees had left the first of the month, traveling aboard a small flotilla composed of one steamboat and six flatboats. Another was scheduled to leave any day. If it didn't rain soon, transporting fifteen thousand Cherokees by the riverways to their new lands in the West would have to be halted.

Her fingers grasped the plump berry, one of the few on the bush, and tugged it loose from its stem. As she withdrew her hand, she scraped the top of it on a sharp thorn, gasping sharply when it scored her flesh. Blood instantly flowed from the cut. Jed saw her start to blot the wound on her dress and pulled a clean handkerchief from his pocket.

"Allow me." He took her hand and pressed the cloth on the cut, watching the red spread through the material. Yet he was more conscious of the warmth of the hand lying flat in his palm—and her nearness. When he slowly lifted his glance to her face, Jed found her staring at him.

"Now you have stained your handkerchief," she said.

"It doesn't matter." Gently, he wrapped it around her hand and tied it in a makeshift bandage, but he was unwilling to let the contact end so soon. "I have never forgotten those times we spent together in Washington. Remember, I taught you the waltz that first night we met." In his mind, he could still see her as she had appeared to him that night, dressed in a white gown shot with golden threads.

"Yes." She smiled faintly as if recalling the memory of it too, then sobered. "That was very long ago. Much has happened since then . . . much has changed."

Somehow Jed had the feeling she was thinking about her husband. He resented that, and knew he was wrong to. "Temple—sorry, Mrs. Stuart—if you would like, I could make inquiries at some of the other camps and see if your husband is being held at one of them."

Such a task wouldn't be easy. With few exceptions, most of the imprisoned Cherokees refused to give their names or line up for roll call. This stubbornness had made it difficult for the army to reunite members of families that had been captured separately and taken to different camps to await emigration.

Initially, Temple brightened at his offer, then the light died. "No."

Jed frowned. "What happened? Did he desert you?"

"I left him."

Her words pounded in his head, ringing with the implication that she was now free. For the first time he dared to hope there was a chance for him.

"Temple—" he began, then stopped, catching himself again familiarly using her given name. He laughed self-consciously. "I can't seem to think of you any other way. Temple." He repeated it with confidence, suddenly growing serious. "I want you to know how sorry I am about everything that has happened these last two weeks, and how much I regret my part in it. You have every right to—"

"I cannot blame you for what has happened," she inserted curtly. "If I sounded bitter earlier, it was directed at the . . . circumstances we find ourselves in now."

"But I put you here." He hated himself for reminding her of his role.

"The ones who signed the false treaty put us here. Your role was inconsequential compared to theirs." She turned. "If you don't mind, I would rather not talk about any of this."

She moved away, clutching the basket containing the small mound of berries. Jed instinctively reached out to stop her from walking away from him again as she had done all those years ago. "Temple—"

The instant he felt the firm yet pliant flesh of her upper arm, he forgot what he was going to say. It didn't seem to matter. Nothing did, except the feel of her flesh beneath his hand. Encouraged by her lack of resistance, he moved to stand behind her, grasping both arms and rubbing them in caressing strokes. All the love that he thought he had successfully banished came rushing back, stronger than ever.

"I didn't think it was possible for you to grow more beautiful, but you have," he declared huskily.

Once he had loved her, Temple remembered. Did he still? She ached to be held and loved. For two years, she had felt empty and alone. She had begun to believe her life would always be that way. Yet here were warmth, caring, and affection, the promise of desire and fulfillment—all the things she had missed. All she had to do was turn around. She was tempted, tempted by the pleasant memories of a happier time when she had smiled and laughed and danced with this man, a time when there had been hope for the future. She wanted to recapture that, cling to it and somehow ward off the ugly reality of the present. She wanted to, desperately, but she didn't turn and invite his embrace. Something held her back.

Yet she gave in to the pressure of his hands and allowed him to turn her. Her heart beat at a solid, steady rhythm as she stared at his mouth and the clipped, golden hairs of his small mustache above it. Tilting, it began to move closer. No, a little voice inside cried in protest, but she didn't pull away.

"Lieutenant Parmelee!" A voice intruded. Jed straightened, and quickly dropped his hands to his sides, a tautness claiming his features. One of the guards ran up and halted, coming to attention and saluting smartly. "One of the Indian women has disappeared, sir."

"What do you mean?" Jed snapped.

"She's gone." The soldier's Adam's apple bobbed. "I think she slipped away, sir."

Jed swore silently. "How long?"

"Not long, sir. One minute she was pulling up some roots by this tree, then . . . she wasn't there."

"Go find her," he ordered curtly. "In the meantime, we

will take the rest of the women back to camp. And, Private, inform the other guards that there will be no more foraging in the woods by the prisoners."

"Yes, sir."

Accompanied by one of the camp guards, The Blade walked slowly past the log enclosures, glancing at the occupants of each. Deu followed half a step behind, his gaze also fixed on the people penned like animals. After two weeks of visiting stockade after stockade, looking for the one that contained Temple and Elijah, the scene and the attendant smell of a thousand people or more concentrated in one small area had become all too familiar. The Blade had become inured to it, as well as to the hostile looks, the backs turned on him, and the low threats murmured in Cherokee from those who recognized him as a signer of the ignominious treaty.

But he also knew the very act that had made him an outcast among his own people had given him the freedom to look for his wife and son. The pass in his pocket protected him from the patrols that roamed the countryside and gave him access to the multitude of camps. Temple had to be in one of them.

As he moved on to the next pen, he caught a flash of blue directly ahead of him. The same shade of blue as the calico dress Temple used to wear. Instinctively, he swung his gaze to it and halted abruptly when he saw her walking toward him.

"There she is," he murmured to Deu and stared at her bedraggled appearance—the soiled and tattered gown, the untidy hair, and the cloth wrapped around the hand carrying the basket. She looked hot and tired, and thinner, judging by the looseness of the dress. God, how he loved her. The pain of it squeezed at him, nearly buckling his knees. He started toward her again, gaining strength with each step, paying no attention at all to the officer walking at her side.

When Temple appeared to stumble, Jed grasped her arm to

steady her. At almost the same instant he noticed the unnatural pallor in her cheeks and the round look of her eyes as she stared at some object ahead of them. Frowning, he glanced to the front. A Cherokee in buckskin leggings and a hunting shirt walked toward them, accompanied by one of the camp guards and a Negro. As the Indian came closer, Jed saw the brilliant blue color of his eyes and the thin white scar on his cheek. Her husband, the man he had volunteered to locate only moments ago.

"Hello, Temple." The Blade stopped in front of her, his greeting almost casual in its indifference.

"How did you know we were here?" Her voice was barely above a whisper.

"I didn't. One of your field darkies told Deu the soldiers had taken you and the others. I have been riding from camp to camp ever since."

"Is Phoebe with you, Miss Temple?" Deu inquired hopefully.

"Yes."

"Is she all right?"

"She's fine." Temple tried to smile at him, but her glance kept going back to her husband. "What are you going to do now?"

"Stay here . . . with you and my son."

Jed bristled protectively beside her. "That is not for you to decide, Mr. Stuart," he asserted, for the first time drawing her husband's glance to him. It probed every inch of his face.

"Parmelee, isn't it?" The Blade remembered.

"Yes."

"Why do you want to stay?" Temple asked.

"So we can travel west together." In his pocket was a letter he had carried with him for more than a year, intending to show it to Temple each time he saw her. Dictated by his father, it described the forested highlands, the clear, sparkling streams, and the fertile bottomlands of the new western territory.

She had to realize emigration was inevitable now. No longer could she cling to a past that was gone. She had to look to the future. Maybe she would finally see that it wasn't his fault their people were herded into pens like animals, deprived of their meanest possessions, abused and degraded. Maybe now she would put the blame where it truly belonged, on John Ross, who had given them false hope and urged them to ignore all other authority. Maybe now everyone would see that and stop regarding him and the rest of the treaty party as outlaws.

"Lije will be happy to see you," she said.

Was she? The Blade couldn't tell. Her expression was closed to him. He felt a riffle of irritation—frustration—and clamped his jaw on it. Patience he had never possessed in an abundant supply.

"Then you want him to stay?" Bewilderment and doubt were in the frown Jed directed at Temple.

"He can stay or go, as he pleases," Temple replied.

For one hot instant, The Blade wanted to take her in his arms and kiss away that coolness. The woman underneath was far from indifferent to him and he knew it. But no, he would wait. He knew that pride of hers. She wouldn't thank him for forcing her to admit she still loved him.

"I have two saddle horses and a pack mule tied at the rack. With your permission, Lieutenant, I will get my belongings."

"Granted" was the grudging and clipped reply.

Twenty minutes later, laden with saddle gear and pack and escorted by a guard, The Blade and Deu entered the log pen. Deu didn't have a chance to set anything down before Phoebe flung herself at him, wrapping her arms around his neck, kissing him and crying, murmuring his name over and over in a tear-strangled voice.

The Blade received no such welcome, nor had he expected it. He lowered the saddle and packs to the hard ground, his glance sweeping the enclosure, taking note of everything and everyone. Temple stood silently next to the center post that supported the crude roof covering half of the pen. In the far corner of the roof's patchy shade, her mother lay on a feather mattress, the only bedding he saw other than a couple of blankets. Xandra knelt beside her, the palmetto fan in her hand now motionless. The youngest Gordon child, Johnny, sat hunched against the log wall of the pen, staring back at him, hollow-eyed and pale. Closest to him was Kipp, his black eyes glaring their hatred of him. On his left, Black Cassie and Phoebe's brother, Shadrach, waited anxiously to greet Deu. Eliza moved to stand next to Temple. That small lump behind her was his son, curled fast asleep on the hard ground.

For an instant, The Blade was warmed by the sight of the boy lying there. Then the obvious lack of some of the most basic necessities asserted itself. From what he could see, they hadn't chosen wisely in their haste to gather belongings to bring with them. Except for the blankets, a bundle of clothes, and an iron kettle for cooking, it didn't appear that they had thought in terms of survival but of worth, sentiment, and comfort for Temple's invalid mother.

"Here are some cooking utensils and supplies—coffee, beans, hominy meal, cornmeal, some dried fruit, and jerky," he said to Temple, indicating the pack at his feet.

"We don't want it or need it." Kipp spat out the refusal. "My father has gone to get our own things. You can keep yours."

"Don't be foolish, Kipp," Eliza reproved sharply. "Your father won't be back for three days or more, and your mother needs something more nourishing than boiled salt pork."

"Maybe, but I'm not touching anything of his."

Eliza ignored Kipp's acrimony and smiled hesitantly at The Blade. "Thank you."

"I only wish there was more." He picked up his saddle and blanket roll and carried them over to an unsheltered corner of the pen.

The Blade could have told them that his father-in-law would

return virtually empty-handed. He had been to Gordon Glen and seen the empty stalls and pastures, the charred remains of the Negro quarters, and the sheds stripped of their stores and equipment. The main house had been thoroughly ransacked; the basement storeroom emptied of its food supply; chandeliers ripped from the ceilings and sconces from the walls. Furniture, clothing, dishes, books, all of it had been hauled away by looters. The only things he had found in the house had been a broken spinning wheel, some pieces of a chair, and feathers from a mattress covering a bedroom floor. Not even the small family cemetery had been spared, the graves unearthed by thieving rabble looking for any gold or silver trinkets that had been buried with the dead. No, he would leave the telling of the spoilation to Will Gordon.

Three days later, Will Gordon returned to the camp. All he brought back was a large basket of vegetables from the garden. The family thronged around him, but The Blade stayed in his small corner of the enclosure, keeping to himself as he had since he arrived.

After Will Gordon had related the destruction he had found, Temple walked over to him. "You knew, didn't you?"

"Yes."

"Why—"

The Blade didn't let her finish. "You wouldn't have believed me."

The following week, General Winfield Scott ordered the postponement of the removal deadline until autumn, due to the drought. The upper Tennessee River was no longer navigable. The third and last contingent of captive Cherokees to make the journey west had been forced to travel one hundred and sixty miles overland to Waterloo, in western Alabama, before they could board flatboats to begin the water trek. Five had died on the way to Alabama. The scarcity of water made the overland route equally impossible, especially with summer's fever season upon them.

The new September 1 deadline was both a blessing and a curse. The Cherokees were forced to remain in the crowded camps with inadequate sanitation, usually stagnant drinking water, and subsistence fare of salt pork and flour. The unhealthy conditions and heavy concentration of people bred disease and sickness. Epidemics of whooping cough, measles, bilious fever, and dysentery swept the camps, with disastrous results.

July came, and with it more scorching heat. Darkness brought little relief from the sweltering temperatures. The hard ground held the day's heat long after the sun went down.

Drenched in his own sweat, The Blade lay with his head on the baked leather of his saddle, listening to the low moans of the ill and the cranky wailings of feverish children, one ear tuned to the faint moans of pain coming from his own enclosure.

Thunder rumbled in the distance. He opened his eyes and stared at the bright stars overhead. Another groan, louder than the previous ones, came from the roofed half of the pen. Silently, The Blade rolled to his feet and picked his way through the fitfully sleeping figures scattered about. He crouched down next to the pallet that held young Johnny Gordon. He was curled up in pain, his arms wrapped around his stomach, his knees drawn up, the putrid smell of dysentery rising from him. His eyes were sunken into their sockets and his skin looked dry. When The Blade felt his forehead, it was burning to the touch. On the other side of the boy, Eliza squeezed excess water from a rag and proceeded to bathe the child's face.

"His fever is worse," he observed.

"I know." She nodded, then remarked idly, "I thought everyone was asleep."

"I sleep light."

"It is so hot I don't see how anyone can rest. I wish it

would rain." Pausing, she hunched a shoulder and wiped the perspiration from her mouth on the sleeve of her dress. Exhaustion marked her posture and her every gesture.

The Blade reached for the rag. "Let me do that and you lie down for a while."

"No." Ignoring his outstretched hand, she moistened the cloth in the tepid water and wrung it out again.

"You know you are tired. If you keep pushing yourself like this, you will be the one who is sick. Then what help will you be to the rest of them?"

"I will sleep later," Eliza insisted irritably, then sighed. "I am supposed to wake Will up in another hour or so anyway. He will sit with Johnny until morning. I can rest then."

Despite the darkness he could feel the curiosity of her boring gaze. "Why have you stayed all this time? You could be out west with your father instead of in this awful camp," Eliza said.

"Why do you stay?" he countered. "All you have to do is call one of the guards and tell him you are white, and you would walk out of those stockade gates a free woman within an hour."

"I . . . can't—for a lot of reasons, but mostly because they are like family to me."

"I love my wife and son, too."

"Mama," the boy moaned plaintively.

"Shhh, now." Eliza hurriedly began to bathe him again.

"Johnny?" In the far corner of the pen, Victoria Gordon pushed herself onto one elbow. "My baby, is he all right?"

"He is running a fever," Eliza admitted. "But not to worry, Victoria. I will stay with him. You—"

But he called out for his mother again. "He needs me. I have to go to him." As Victoria tried to crawl off the mattress, she started coughing.

The Blade moved quickly to her side, supporting her and lifting her back onto the mattress. "There is nothing you can do."

"No. He wants me." Although weakened by her debilitating cough, she tried to fight him. "I have to go to my baby."

A figure sprang from the darkness. "Take your hands off my mother," Kipp snarled. "Get away from her."

"Enough." Will stepped between them, throwing a warning look at his son.

The Blade suppressed an angry retort and returned to the small area of the enclosure that he had staked out for himself. Victoria Gordon continued to insist that her place was with her ailing child. No amount of persuasion from Will could convince her otherwise. Finally, Will carried his youngest son over to her and laid him on the mattress beside her.

She cradled him in her arms and crooned to him, stroking his hair and kissing his forehead, repeatedly thwarting Will's attempts to bathe him and give him water.

Shortly before dawn the next morning, Victoria screamed, "Johnny!" But he couldn't hear her. Young Johnny Gordon was dead.

He was buried in a makeshift graveyard outside the confines of the camp. Back in their pen, Victoria sobbed uncontrollably. When Will tried to comfort her, she turned from him and clutched at Xandra, wanting only the flesh of her flesh near her. Will moved away to stand by himself, his head bowed with the weight of a father's grief.

After a moment's hesitation, Eliza walked over to him and stood quietly at his side. As Temple watched, she heard the soft words Eliza spoke. "Remember that afternoon at the creek, Will? I still see him laughing and squealing with glee when you went splashing into the water after him."

A low, anguished groan came from her father an instant before he blindly reached out. Eliza's hand was there, closing around his to hold it tightly.

Three days after Johnny Gordon was buried, word reached camp that John Ross had finally returned from Washington.

All his attempts to get the treaty negated had come to naught. There was no more hope. They would be removed from the land of their fathers. All the suffering and hardship, all the abuse and humiliation they had known—and still knew—had been for nothing.

Yet not one angry voice was raised against John Ross. They had been driven from their homes at the point of a bayonet, herded into pens like cattle, and detained as prisoners in their own land. But no blame was attached to Ross for their troubles. They held Elias Boudinot, John Ridge, his father, Major Ridge, and the other members of the treaty party responsible for everything that had happened to them.

The Blade had thought once John Ross acknowledged defeat, he would be vindicated. It was his opinion that John Ross had been the one who betrayed the Cherokees by offering them hope when there was none. That wasn't the way Ross's followers saw it. If anything, they hated The Blade and all the other treaty advocates more than before.

Each day The Blade had with his son became more precious. And each day that Temple avoided his gaze became more agonizing.

⚛ 26 ⚛

Temple pushed her way through the crowd of women at the well who were waiting their turn to fill their containers. Sickness, despair, and July's enervating heat showed on all their faces as they stared disinterestedly at her. But not one of the women there was Xandra.

Temple swung around to scan the long, slow-moving line in front of the camp's storehouse. People waited to receive their week's ration of food. There were her father, brother, Eliza, and Shadrach, but not Xandra. Where was she? She had left more than an hour ago to fetch water for them and had yet to return. Was it possible Xandra had walked past without Temple noticing her? What other explanation could there be? The guards would never let her out of the compound and her gentle, pacific sister would never attempt anything so bold as an escape. Temple started back to the long row of pens.

Halfway there, she saw The Blade. He was carrying someone inside the enclosure. He was carrying Xandra. Temple broke into a run. Please, God, no, she prayed silently. Her mother was crazy with grief now over Johnny. She couldn't take it if anything happened to Xandra.

Temple entered the pen and paused long enough to glance

in her mother's direction. Victoria appeared to be resting. Ignoring the jabbered greeting from her son, Temple noticed only that Phoebe held him before she hurried to the near corner where The Blade had taken Xandra. Black Cassie was already there, trying to help him lay her sister on a blanket. But Xandra was fighting them, low moans coming from her. Was she delirious with a fever? But how could it have come on so quickly?

Temple sank to the ground beside them and shouldered Black Cassie out of the way. "Go sit with Mama," she ordered, then reached for her sister as The Blade pried at the arm wrapped around his neck.

"No," Xandra moaned, her head lolling back.

Temple stared in shock at her sister's disheveled appearance. Pieces of grass and leaves were tangled in the long, dirty strands of her hair. Tears left muddy streaks on her cheeks, and her half-closed eyes had a glazed look. Despite Xandra's clutching of The Blade, there was a limpness about her that Temple found frightening.

"What is wrong with her?" She put her arms around Xandra and tried to pull her away from The Blade. Xandra turned her head toward her. Temple unconsciously recoiled from the strong smell of whiskey and vomit on her breath. "She is drunk. How——" But she didn't need to ask that. Whiskey and cheap liquor were constantly smuggled into the camp. For too many of her people, alcohol had become the antidote for despair. "Oh, Xandra, why?" Temple murmured.

"It wasn't her fault," The Blade stated, his expression grim as Xandra appeared to recognize them. With a broken sob, she averted her face and buried it against The Blade's chest. When she did, the front of her dress gaped open.

"You have torn your dress, Xandra." Temple sighed in disappointment and disgust, wondering how her sister could be so careless when they had so few clothes.

"She didn't do it. They did."

"*They?*" Her glance shot to him. His bitter tone, the hardness in his voice, suddenly made her suspicious. "Who are *they*?"

"Two of your lieutenant's soldiers took her into the woods. Something about wild grapes—she wasn't very coherent when I found her." He paused briefly. "They gave her whiskey and got her drunk, then they took turns holding her down."

"You mean they—"

"Yes." An anger vibrated below the surface of his clipped response.

Not her little sister, not the gentle-hearted, unassuming Xandra who cringed from harsh words; she couldn't have been raped.

"Xandra, I am so sorry." She wanted to cry with her, but when she tried to take her sister into her arms and comfort her, Xandra cowered and pressed even closer to The Blade.

"I will take care of her," he said. Reluctantly, Temple sat back on her heels, vaguely hurt that her sister would turn to The Blade and not her. He held her like a child, gently and soothingly stroking her head. "You are safe now," he murmured. "You have no need to be afraid anymore. I won't let anything happen to you."

"They . . . hurt me," Xandra whimpered, slurring her words.

"I know." The Blade nodded. "But they are gone. I am here."

"Don't leave me."

"I won't," he promised.

Over and over he whispered words of assurance while Temple looked on, hating the helpless feeling but hating even more the men who had done this to her sister, hating with such force that she vibrated with it. When The Blade lowered Xandra onto the blanket that was his bed, Xandra immediately rolled onto her side, turning her back to Temple and hunching her shoulders as if trying to hide.

Her sister had always been the shy and quiet one, a little

slow to grasp things yet so anxious to please. Now she lay there motionless, her dress soiled and torn, her black hair in tangles, and her face smudged with dirt and tears like some battered doll.

Angrily, Temple rose to her feet, determined to make them pay for what they had done. She felt a hand on her arm and spun around to face The Blade. Yet she couldn't focus on him; she couldn't focus on anything except the blinding need for vengeance.

"Who are they? Which ones did this?" she demanded hoarsely.

"I don't know. She was alone when I found her."

She curled her hands into fists, digging her nails into her palms. "They should be hanged. I would like to kill them myself. I wish I had a gun, or a knife—anything!" Temple blazed. "I hate them!"

He seemed to study her curiously. "You are the Temple I married, fiery and alive," he mused absently. "Not the cold, passionless woman I have seen these last months."

"I wish you were the man I married instead of the traitor you have become!" she shot back, not noticing the way he recoiled as if she had physically struck him. She was too angry to care if she hurt him, too filled with hatred to remember the tender way he had treated Xandra. She whirled and ran out of the pen straight to the post commander's office to demand that the guards guilty of committing the vile act against her sister be punished.

A week later, Jed Parmelee made one of his infrequent visits to the camp. After being informed of the incident and the known facts surrounding it, he summoned both Temple and her father to the commander's office to advise them of the final disposition of the case.

Although he addressed his remarks to Will Gordon, Jed found it difficult to meet his level gaze, seeing in it the recent grief for his dead son and the anguish over his now damaged daughter. "The two soldiers involved in this regrettable incident have been confined in the guardhouse."

"For how long?" Temple demanded.

He hesitated a moment, then spoke briskly. "In view of their exemplary military record in the past, they will be serving a two-week sentence." When Temple breathed in sharply, Jed lowered his chin a fraction of an inch and added stiffly, "I am sorry, but that was the term handed down."

After what seemed a long silence, Will Gordon quietly said, "I understand."

"I do not."

Jed flinched inwardly at Temple's bitterly sharp response. "Would you mind waiting outside, Mr. Gordon? I would like to speak to your daughter alone for a few minutes."

"Of course."

As Will Gordon turned to leave the room, Jed glanced pointedly at the post commander, his senior in rank. "Sir, would you please leave the door open on your way out?" he requested, doubting the major would argue with an aide of their commanding general.

Temple left her chair and crossed to the small window, too upset and outraged by the lenient sentence to appreciate Jed's concern for her reputation.

A hot breeze chased a cloud of red dust across the compound, obscuring the ground in a swirling fog of powdery dirt. The sight of it made her conscious of the grit that clung to her skin and her clothes, and the matted filth of her hair. For weeks, they had had no soap for bathing and no water to spare. She hated being seen like this. It was humiliating and degrading—but not nearly as horrible as what Xandra had been through.

When the last footsteps receded from the room, she turned to face Jed, holding on tightly to the only three things she had left: her dignity, her pride, and her anger. "Two weeks. That is their punishment for what they did to my sister. You should see her," she protested thickly. "You should see the fear and the shame in her eyes."

"I am sorry."

"I don't want your pity. I want those men punished."

"You don't understand." He sighed. He stared at her for several seconds, a troubled frown knitting his brow together. "I ... couldn't tell your father this, but both men swore under oath that your sister was ... a willing participant. They claimed she agreed, if they would give her whiskey."

"That is a lie!"

"Temple, there was no evidence, no testimony to dispute their statements. Your sister refused to talk to the provost marshal or answer any of his questions."

"She refuses to talk to anyone," Temple admitted. Anyone, that is, except The Blade. Since that awful morning, Xandra had become his shadow. She wouldn't go anywhere or do anything without him. She even slept beside him at night. Yet she cringed every time one of the family approached her.

"I wish there was something I could do," Jed murmured.

"I know." She finally believed that.

He half turned from her. "I can't stand seeing you in this camp," he muttered savagely. "You don't belong here."

"None of us do." Her faint smile of sadness became twisted with the injustice of it. "We are imprisoned for the crime of loving our homeland. For that same crime, we are to be exiled."

He took a step toward her. "I wish you weren't going. I wish—" Then he stopped, checking whatever he was about to say. "Tell your father that Chief John Ross has met with General Scott. He has insisted on the closing of all grogshops in the vicinity of the camps and the suppression of any smuggling of liquor into them. The general has agreed. I know the action comes too late for your sister, but—"

"He will be glad that others will be spared. Bitterness and resentment are foreign to him."

"Ross has appointed a committee to make regular inspections of the camps and ascertain your people's needs, whether for food or clothing or medical help."

"Soap. We need soap," she said, then turned and walked from the room.

Moved by the poignancy of such a simple request, Jed stared after her. He tried to feel sorry for her, but he couldn't. All he could feel was admiration and the deepest respect. After all she had endured, her head was unbowed.

Ross obtained even greater concessions from General Winfield Scott. He requested and received permission for the Cherokees to organize and conduct their own emigration, taking it out of the army's hands. The council would arrange transportation, set up the detachments, and lead the emigrant trains to their new lands in the West. They accepted full responsibility for the conduct of their people in the interim.

In theory, the Cherokees were freed on their own recognizance pending the September 1 deadline for emigration. But they had nowhere to go. The camps were the only homes that remained to them, a source of food, shelter, and much-needed medical aid. But at least they were free to wander through the woods to gather herbs, wild berries, and nuts, and to privately bid farewell to their beloved mountains and valleys. And the daily rations now included the addition of coffee, sugar, and soap.

Another committee was set up to accept claims from individuals for property that had been abandoned. The list Will Gordon submitted for compensation was a lengthy one, billing the government for his fine brick home, all the elegant furnishings, the plantation's numerous buildings, and equipment, livestock, and carriages. It lay side by side with more humble ones requesting payment for a fiddle, a coffeepot, and six ducks.

September came, but not the expected rains. Again Scott postponed the deadline, this time until October.

27

Rattlesnake Springs, Tennessee
October 1838

The wood smoke from thousands of cookfires spread a blue veil over the landscape and scented the crisp morning air with its pungent odor. Beneath the haze, sprawling over ten square miles, were tents, wagons, horses, oxen, and the Cherokees, assembled at the departure point for the long trail west.

As he gazed at the vast camp bustling with activity, Will Gordon heard its underlying silence and understood. The last day of September, thunderheads had rolled out of the Smoky Mountains in the north and brought rain to the parched lands of Tennessee and Georgia, ending the summer-long drought. Again water chuckled in the streams, raised the river levels, and turned the wheels of the gristmills.

Honoring John Ross's word when he persuaded General Scott to lift the martial law and permit the Cherokees to organize and conduct their own emigration without army control, the people had gathered here at Rattlesnake Springs near the Indian agency, some thirteen thousand counting their Negroes. They came but without smiles, joyful hearts, or cheerful voices. That sense of silence came from heavy hearts and somber thoughts.

"Will?"

Recognizing Eliza's voice, he turned.

"It is time," she said.

"I know." For a minute he studied her, noting the familiar gold flecks in her hazel eyes and the attractive tumble of pale brown curls that framed her face. Love, gratitude, and need welled up inside him for this indomitable woman, emotions that added to the pain he already felt. Not wanting her to see it, he swung his gaze back to the encampment that stretched farther than he could see. He felt her eyes leave him to survey it as well.

"I have to agree with The Blade," Eliza announced quietly after the passage of several seconds. "A nation is made up of people, not land. It is their collective spirit that forms it, not boundaries. All these people are traveling as a nation with their laws, their constitution, their government, and their heritage intact. In its own way, that's a remarkable achievement, one they can all take pride in."

Nodding, Will acknowledged the truth of her statement. At the council grounds at Red Clay, all the records of the Nation had been safely packed and boxed to be taken west with them. More than just their constitution and laws, the documents included the succession of treaties the Nation had made in efforts to appease the appetites of their white neighbors, as well as correspondence with every president of the United States from George Washington to Martin Van Buren.

Yet it wasn't the pending transportation of the national records that made him frown but her initial statement. "I don't understand him."

"Who?"

"The Blade. He betrayed us all by signing that treaty. Yet in the detention camp, he didn't try to get favored treatment. We all know the supporters of the treaty received special dispensations from the federal government. But he hasn't asked for an increase in his travel and subsistence allowance. The group of seven or eight hundred that left on the eleventh with their carriages and horses, accompanied by their servants—he could have joined them and made the twelve-hundred-mile trek in relative comfort. They would have welcomed him. He could have been among friends instead of surrounded by those who regard him as a traitor and look upon him with loathing and contempt."

"His actions in the past were never dictated by a desire for personal gain. The things you have said prove that," Eliza reminded him. "And I think that is becoming obvious to a lot of others. Maybe I am wrong, or maybe I have become too used to it, but the hostility toward him doesn't seem as strong as it was in the beginning. Even Kipp seems a little more tolerant of him."

"I admit some of my respect for him has returned." Will stared at the vast camp. "Maybe in time I will forgive him, but I will never forget what he has done."

"I know." She nodded, the brightness of unshed tears in her eyes. "So does he. And which, I wonder, is worse?"

There was no answer for that, and Will knew it. Together they turned to face the line of wagons that stretched over the road into the heavy forest. Temple and the rest of the family were clustered beside the nearest wagon. Walking together, Eliza and Will rejoined them.

Four caravans had already started on the long overland trail, their departures staggered a few days apart. Theirs was the fifth to leave. Some forty wagons were loaded with fodder for the horses and oxen, blankets, cooking utensils, and provisions for the initial stages of their journey, with more to be purchased along the way as needed.

Only the very old and the very young, the ill and the infirm were allowed to ride in the wagons. Except for the ten mounted riders of the Cherokee Light Horse guard assigned to police the train, all the rest had to walk, carrying their few personal possessions in packs on their backs.

Will lifted Victoria into the wagon and tried not to notice her bony thinness and sallow complexion, or the deep melancholy and grief in her eyes. He made her as comfortable as he could and silently reminded himself that a physician would be making the trek with them. Should she need it, she would have good medical care.

"Try to rest," he urged.

When he started to leave, her talonlike fingers seized his arm. "Our dead babies, Will, I always wanted to be buried with them. Now we are leaving."

"I know." He patted her hand. The children—it was always the children. Once he would have resented that she hadn't considered being buried next to him. Now he accepted it. Will hesitated, then kissed her cheek and climbed out of the wagon.

Temple noticed his long face as she shifted a squirming Lije to her other hip. "Is Mama all right?"

"She is fine."

They both knew that wasn't true, but Temple accepted his answer and turned to face the long road and the line of wagons pointing the way. Here and there, people bade good-bye to friends or relatives who would soon follow.

It had come. The Blade lounged near the front wagon wheel, Xandra, as always, by his side. Temple could feel his gaze on her, but she couldn't look at him.

The pounding of a horse's hooves grew louder. Glancing over her shoulder, Temple saw the rider's plumed shako and blue uniform bearing an officer's epaulets. Almost certain it was Jed Parmelee, she turned. A smile broke below the rider's golden mustache as he reined his mount to a prancing walk. Lije clapped his hands excitedly at the snorting horse.

"Ho'se, Mama." Eyes as blue as the army uniform Jed wore beamed proudly at her.

"Yes, it is a horse, Lije," Jed agreed with a chuckle. "You would think by now they wouldn't be a novelty to him." He spoke casually, as though they had seen each other only yesterday instead of nearly a month ago.

"I hoped I would have a chance to tell you good-bye before we left," Temple said and grabbed Lije's hand when he reached to pat the horse's nose.

"Not good-bye. I will be riding with you—all the way to the Indian Territory. Strictly in the capacity of an observer, of course," Jed added with a wry smile.

Temple was spared an immediate reply as the horse swung its hindquarters around, forcing her to move out of its way. She wasn't sure whether or not she was glad he would be traveling with them. All she felt at the moment was confusion.

"It will be a long ride," she said finally.

The smile faded from his face as his expression turned sober. "And a longer walk."

The order came down the line to move on. Whips cracked over the backs of horse teams and yoked oxen as drivers shouted to them, curses mingling with commands. After the first groaning turn of the wheels, the wagons rumbled forward. Temple turned and started walking, carrying her young son in her arms.

Jed's horse impatiently pushed at the restraining bit, but Jed continued to check its forward movement. A horse carrying double entered his line of vision. It was Temple's husband and her sister. Briefly, Jed met the man's glance and saw the resentment in the grim blue eyes. But Jed didn't feel any guilt. While it was true Temple was married to Stuart, from all he had seen, their relationship wasn't that of a husband and wife. Maybe he was a fool to think he had a chance with her, but he had to find out.

He relaxed the pressure on the bit and the horse lunged forward, its hindquarters bunching and driving. At a canter, Jed rode up the line, the autumn-colored forest on his left a flashing blur of rich yellows, golds, and oranges.

The cavalcade of wagons and people stretched over a quarter of a mile. To Jed, it resembled the march of an army, the officers at the front leading the way, the wagons in the middle flanked by outriders, more riders bringing up the rear, and the infantry—in this case men, women, and children—trudging in small groups around and behind each wagon.

A few miles from Rattlesnake Springs, the caravan crossed

to the north side of the Hiwassee River by ferry, then traveled downstream to its mouth at the Tennessee River, following the well-worn route taken by the four previous detachments. From there, the trail would take them south of Pikesville to McMinnville and Nashville, then on to the Cumberland. But first they had to cross the Tennessee.

With Lije asleep on her back, strapped in place by a blanket, Temple stood at the ferry's rail next to Eliza and stared at the wide expanse of water before them. Their long journey had barely begun, yet already she was footsore, leg sore, and body sore. On the other side of the river loomed Walden's Ridge. As Temple looked at the escarpment of the Cumberland plateau waiting to be climbed, she could almost feel her leg muscles screaming in protest. Unconsciously, she leaned closer to Eliza.

"How many more will we have to climb?" she wondered aloud.

"It is probably best if we don't know." Eliza turned from the sight as if she found it too daunting as well. The most she had ever walked at any one time was perhaps two miles. Now she faced a journey of more than a thousand miles on foot.

When the ferry entered the current, it shuddered sickeningly, resisting the powerful tug that tried to sweep it downstream. Pulled taut, the heavy ropes groaned under the strain of holding the ferry on its angling course to the other side.

They reached the landing on the opposite bank and a fancily dressed white man accosted Will the instant he stepped ashore leading his horse. "They tell me you're the Gordon that had that big brick planation down in Georgia."

"I am." Will walked his horse up the dirt ramp, moving out of the way of the others behind him.

The man followed. "You owe me eighty dollars for seed and I want my money. Maybe you thought you could leave without paying me, but you were wrong."

"I paid for all my seed at the time I purchased it. You have made a mistake."

"You made the mistake thinking you could get by without paying me. Now I want my eighty dollars," the man demanded. "And don't tell me you don't have it 'cause I know the government paid you a handsome settlement for all your properties."

"I submitted a claim for the personal possessions and property we were forced to abandon, but I received no compensation before we left the agency. Few of us did," he stated crisply. "Your information is as false as your bill."

"I'm gonna get my eighty dollars one way or another," the man warned, then glared at Kipp when he walked up leading his horse. "Who's he?"

"My son."

"Since you say you can't pay me my money, I'm taking your horses." He snatched the reins from Will's hand.

Will argued with him, but it was useless. The Light Horse guard, members of the Cherokee police force, had no authority over whites, only their own people. They were powerless to intervene, and Jed Parmelee's orders strictly forbade his intervention. Observe and report, that was all he could do.

That night Jed entered the incident in his journal and questioned the validity of the man's claim. But it was only the first of several such entries he would be forced to make as white claimants plagued the caravan, seizing silver, horses, oxen, and sometimes even wagons as payment for alleged debts. This form of robbery was only one kind of highway piracy the Cherokees encountered. Jed soon learned there were others. Ferry rates were increased; landowners charged a toll for crossing their property; farmers and merchants inflated the prices on provisions purchased along the route, doubling, tripling, and sometimes quadrupling the costs.

The avarice sickened him, especially when every day Jed witnessed the travail of these proud people, the lines of weariness and despair etched deeper in their faces, their feet bleeding from the miles they walked. Regardless of his orders, Jed helped when and where he could, sometimes throwing a shoulder to the wheel of a stuck wagon or stopping to assist those who had fallen or gathering fat pine to burn in the wagoner's stone to make pitch for lubricating the wheels.

A third of the way up the steep incline Temple paused along the side of the trail to catch her breath. Lije, cranky and tired of the confinement of being strapped to his mother's back, wailed tearlessly in her ear and squirmed endlessly, his weight and his wiggling causing the cloth straps holding him to cut even deeper into her shoulders. She hadn't the strength to correct him, or the will—not when inside she felt the same urge to cry and the same longing to be free of the onerous grind of this trail.

A wagon lumbered past her pulled by two teams of horses, their heads bent low, straining against their collars, their hooves digging for each foot of ground while the teamster urged them on with angry curses and the crack of his whip. Temple watched dully, listening to the creaks and groans of the heavy wagon.

Eliza stopped beside her. "Are you all right, Temple?"

A cold wind stung her face when Temple turned her head to look at her friend. She almost smiled at the sight of Eliza's sun- and windburned face framed by the blanket draped over her head. With her brown hair and hazel-brown eyes, Eliza looked like a Cherokee. Temple nearly said so, but instead she replied, "I am fine."

"Let me carry Lije for you."

She started to agree, then noticed the bulge on Eliza's back and remembered the heavy pack she already carried. Temple immediately felt guilty that her only burden was her son.

"We will make it."

She lowered her head and started walking up the long slope.

The leather soles of her cloth half-boots were worn thin. With each step, she could feel the rocks, pebbles, and clods of dirt digging into her already tender feet. But it was no more uncomfortable than the rawly chafed skin of her inner thighs, so she plodded on.

As the trail sloped to a steeper angle, Temple leaned forward, trying to compensate for the wiggling burden on her back. Ahead she could see the aged and stooped figure of old Mrs. Hanks laboring up the trail, a broken branch for a staff. The old woman would never make it to the top without help. The thought had barely occurred to her when a rock rolled out from under her foot, and Temple slipped, one leg going out from under her. Then the other gave way and she fell forward, instinctively extending her arms to absorb the impact. For several seconds, she didn't move from her half-prone, half-kneeling position. The palms of her hands stung and her knee throbbed painfully.

"Temple."

At the sound of Eliza's voice, Lije started to cry in earnest. As much as Temple wanted to remain where she was until the pain and the tiredness went away, she gingerly pushed back, letting one knee support most of her weight.

"I—" She broke off the assurance when moccasined feet suddenly halted in front of her. In the next second, The Blade's hands were under her arms, lifting her to her feet.

"Are you hurt?"

"No." She stared at the rigid muscles in his jaw and the grim line of his mouth, then abruptly looked away, glancing behind him at his horse standing quietly. Xandra was astride it, expressionless and silent as always, and—as always— watching The Blade. As inseparable as they were, a stranger was bound to think Xandra was his wife. Jealousy was an ugly feeling. Temple hated it.

"Climb up behind Xandra and ride to the top of the ridge," The Blade ordered.

She felt a guiding pressure directing her toward the horse and realized that his hands still supported her. Instinctively, Temple resisted.

"No."

"She can ride my horse." Jed Parmelee swung out of the saddle and stepped to the ground.

"She will ride mine, Lieutenant. You are along to observe." The very smoothness of The Blade's reply carried a challenge.

"I am not riding either one," Temple inserted sharply. "Help Mrs. Hanks or that little boy with the bandaged foot. I can walk."

"Maybe you can, but you're not." The Blade didn't give her a chance to argue as he picked her up and heaved her onto the horse's hindquarters behind Xandra.

"I can walk," she said again, but she was talking to his back as he gathered up the trailing reins and led the horse up the slope.

If she wanted to walk, all she had to do was slide off, but the thought was a fleeting one. It felt good to let her legs dangle limply and just sit. Reaching around Xandra, Temple held on to the saddle horn and rested her cheek on her sister's shoulder, giving in to the waves of tiredness that washed over her. For once, she welcomed her sister's silence.

As they passed Mrs. Hanks, Temple felt a twinge of guilt that she was riding and the old woman was walking. Her conscience was eased a few minutes later when she looked back and saw Jed stop to help the woman.

But there were others. There were always others. Temple tried to shut her eyes to them as they plodded, stumbled, and struggled up the long incline. The Blade carried the hobbling boy with an injured foot and an old man hung on to the horse's tail, letting it pull him along. But the rest had to manage on their own as best they could.

At the top, the ground leveled off and the horse stopped. Reluctantly, Temple let go of the saddle horn. When her feet touched the ground, her legs threatened to give way. She briefly leaned against the animal's flanks, taking advantage of its solidness, then looked up at her sister.

"There is nothing wrong with you, Xandra," she accused. "Everyone else has to walk. You should too."

There was no response, but Temple hadn't expected one. She moved away. Later, when they reached the place where they were to camp that night, she saw Xandra walking. And when they pulled out the next morning, her sister was again on foot.

28

The Blade hunched his shoulders against the chilling drizzle and held the collar of his coat tightly closed. All day a cold and misty rain had fallen from the leaden clouds overhead. His coat had the musty smell of wet wool, and the penetrating dampness went all the way to the bone. His feet, encased in the mud-soaked leather of his moccasins, felt numb as he trudged alongside his horse. A mother and three small children were piled on its back, one of them a baby a few months younger than his son and ill with a fever.

The crowded wagon ahead of them bumped and bounced over the badly rutted trail. The Blade could hear the faint moans from its cargo of sick and infirm as they were tossed and jarred by the rough passage. The thousands of hooves and feet from the caravans that had traveled over this wagon road before them had chewed up the ground, gouging out jagged furrows and mounding up humps. The steady drizzle slowly turned the trail into a morass of red mud, further impeding their progress and adding to the hardship.

The sheeting mist obscured the road ahead of him. But, with the cavalcade strung out more than a mile, The Blade doubted he could have seen the lead wagons even without the rain. Still, he was certain the first of them had reached the night's campsite outside of the place previously called French Lick and now known as Nashville.

He peered off into the distance, recalling that Andrew Jackson lived nearby. After leaving the presidency, Jackson had returned to his plantation, the Hermitage, outside of Nashville. Ten years ago this very month, he had been elected president. In his inaugural address, Jackson had stated his resolve to remove all the Indian nations to the western lands. Never once had he wavered or compromised in achieving that goal. With the Cherokees now en route, he had finally succeeded.

The Blade wondered if Jackson had ever ridden out to watch their passing caravans. He doubted it. Recently there had been reports that Jackson was in poor health—growing deaf, losing the sight in his right eye, and suffering memory lapses. Supposedly, he was having financial problems, too. Perhaps there was justice after all, The Blade thought wryly. It was certain he would receive no sympathy from the Cherokees.

Beside him, Xandra stumbled over a rut, her foot slipping on the thin layer of slick mud. He tried to catch her as she pitched forward, but his reflexes were too slow, too numbed by the damp cold, and she fell.

"Are you all right?" He crouched next to her.

She nodded affirmatively and tried to push herself up, but her hands slipped in the mud.

"I'll help." When he hooked an arm around her middle to haul her upright, his hand moved over her stomach. Momentarily he froze, feeling its firm, protruding roundness—the distinctive roundness of a woman in the middle months of pregnancy. Carefully, he altered his hold and lifted Xandra to her feet. But she hung her head and refused to look at him, pulling the blanket even farther over her head to hood her face. "Are you with child, Xandra?" He fought to keep his voice level and calm, and not betray the anger inside him.

She nodded her head once, then whispered, "No one must know."

"Xandra." He closed his eyes briefly. "They have to know."

"No," she sobbed and pushed away from him to hurry up the trail.

By the time the last stragglers arrived at the selected campsite, the drizzle had turned to a slow rain that saturated the ground, leaving not a dry place to sleep nor a dry stick to be found. They gathered wood anyway, cut shavings for kindling from the dry heart, and built small fires beneath the shelter of canvas lean-tos to cook much-needed hot meals and drive out some of the numbing dampness.

The Blade poured more coffee into his tin mug, then set the pot on a flat stone next to the feebly burning fire. In the far corner beneath the sloping canvas roof, Xandra sat huddled in a tight ball beyond the reach of the small fire's glow and heat. She had avoided him ever since The Blade had discovered the secret she had tried to hide beneath the loose folds of her long dress and blanket.

He knew she was there, but it was the canvas flap of a nearby wagon that he watched, waiting for Eliza to emerge. She had gone inside several minutes ago carrying a tin plate of hot mush for Victoria.

Temple ducked under the dripping edge of the lean-to's roof. She glanced his way briefly, then moved to the fire and held out her hands to its rising warmth, shivering convulsively. He wanted to go to her and rub warmth back into her body, but she had made it plain to him, both at the detention camp and on the trail, that she didn't want his company or his affection.

Which made it all the harder for him to accept seeing her talk to that army lieutenant Jed Parmelee. She had to know the man was still in love with her. Temple was many things— willful, headstrong, volatile—but she wasn't blind. Why would she encourage him if it wasn't what she wanted? He was surprised Parmelee wasn't at their campfire tonight. But the night wasn't over yet.

A blanketed figure lifted aside the canvas flap and clambered down from the wagon. The Blade set his cup on the flat top of an upended cask and moved out from beneath the lean-to's shelter into the rain. Striding quickly through the sucking mud, he crossed to the wagon, passing Kipp as he returned with an armload of wet firewood. Eliza nearly ran into him in her haste to escape the cold raindrops.

She stopped abruptly when she found him in her path, and she tilted her head up, the blanket slipping back to reveal the tightly curling ringlets of her damp hair. "You startled me," she declared, adding a shaky laugh.

"Sorry." From the wagon came the sound of a racking cough. The Blade glanced toward the flap, then at the plate in Eliza's hand and the rain-diluted mush only half gone. "How is she?"

Eliza hesitated, her shoulders moving faintly in the suggestion of a shrug. "She was jolted around a lot today. And this cold, damp weather . . . it seems to aggravate her cough."

He checked the movement Eliza made toward the lean-to. "I need to speak to you privately for a moment."

"Of course." She paused, studying him curiously and losing much of her drawn and tired look in the process. "What about?"

"Xandra. She is with child." He needed the bluntness to take the edge off his anger.

"No." Eliza stared at him in shock, then turned toward the huddled figure tucked deep in the shadows of the lean-to, her expression ranging from sorrow to pity and covering all the shades in between.

"She is frightened and ashamed. She needs a woman. She needs you, Eliza."

He didn't have to say more. Eliza walked past him, slowly at first, then quickening her steps to dash across the mud.

When she reached the canvas shelter, she paused and shook the water from her blanket, then laid the plate on the stone next to the fire.

Over and over again the same phrase kept running through her mind: *Poor Xandra, poor, dear Xandra*. It wasn't fair. The girl had suffered enough. They all had. But pity wasn't what she needed, Eliza knew that. She walked slowly over to the girl and crouched down, catching her long skirt up and tucking it under her knees to keep it out of the mud. Xandra bowed her head even lower, the hooding blanket hiding most of her face. She was trembling. Whether from the cold or from fear, Eliza couldn't tell.

"Xandra, I know," she said gently. "The Blade told me." The blanket started to shake harder. "Will you look at me?" When she received no response, Eliza framed Xandra's blanketed head in her hands and forced it up. Tears streamed from Xandra's tightly closed eyes, her chin and lips quivering. "Look at me, please. It is going to be all right."

"No, it isn't," Xandra mumbled.

But Eliza wanted to cry with relief. Those were the first words Xandra had spoken to her since that awful incident had occurred. "Of course it will," she insisted. "No matter what you think, we still love you. We always will."

Xandra opened her eyes, though only to slits veiled with tears. She pressed her lips tightly together, her face contorting and twisting as violent, silent sobs racked her body. With tears now running from her own eyes, Eliza gathered Xandra into her arms and hugged her close, pressing her blanketed head to her shoulder.

"Everybody will know, won't they?" Xandra moaned softly and brokenly. "They will know. I am so ashamed."

"Shhh, now. It will be all right."

"They will look at me just like they look at The Blade. They will hate me, too."

"No, darling. No."

But Xandra wouldn't listen to her. Eliza let her cry for now and simply held her, rocking back and forth and feeling sorry, sorry for so many things. She felt a hand touch her shoulder and looked up.

"What's wrong?" Temple bent down.

Eliza hesitated, aware that she couldn't leave Temple's question unanswered, and aware that somehow she had to reassure Xandra. She chose her words carefully, trying to satisfy both. "Your sister is going to have a baby."

"She told you that?"

Eliza shook her head and nodded in The Blade's direction. "She thinks we will all hate her now, but I have told her she is being silly. Isn't that right?"

"Yes. Yes, it is," Temple murmured, stunned by her husband's choice of confidantes.

Temple straightened, then slowly turned. The Blade was drinking something and watching her, his rain-wet hair glistening blackly in the firelight. Angry and hurt, she walked over to him.

"Why?" Temple demanded, her voice choking on the thickness in her throat. "Why did you tell Eliza? I am Xandra's sister. Why didn't you tell me?"

"Because . . . I believed Eliza could give her the kind of understanding and support that Xandra needed."

"And you thought I couldn't?"

"Not as well as Eliza."

"How would you know?"

"I think I proved my choice was the right one. Your sister needs you, but it is Eliza who is with her. You are standing here talking to me. Why? Because your feelings were hurt. You don't care about anyone's feelings but your own."

"That is not true!"

"You never gave a damn about mine when you left. And you haven't since." He set the cup down and turned to leave her, all in one motion.

She wanted to shout at him that she did care about his feelings. She cared too much. That's why she was so hurt when he hadn't come to see her. And it was also why she went back to her sister and helped Eliza dry her eyes.

For three days, they remained at the Nashville encampment, resting from the arduous trek over the Cumberlands. They tended to their sick and injured, repaired their wagons, and purchased more provisions to carry them over the next leg. A cold rain fell two of those days. Not until the third were they able to dry out their clothes and blankets.

With winter approaching and less than a third of the trail traversed, the lack of adequate clothing became obvious. Seized in the summer and forced to march to the detention camps with only the clothes on their backs, the people had little to protect them from the cold but the blankets issued by the government. Some were without shoes, or, like Temple and Eliza with their cloth half-boots, they had holes in the soles and the material was rotting from the mud and streams they had waded through.

Overexertion and fatigue, constant exposure to the elements, lack of rest from trying to sleep on cold wet ground, and a summer spent in deplorable circumstances lowered their resistance. Many were already sick when they started out from Nashville following a northwest course to Kentucky.

Graves began to mark the route, graves of their dead and the dead of the caravans that had preceded them. Near Hopkinsville, a white flag hung limply over a wooden marker painted to look like marble, identifying the grave of White Path, one of their aged leaders. As their detachment passed it, Temple paused with her father to pray for the venerable old man—and for themselves.

The reports filtering back from the contingents ahead of them spoke of discouragement and despair. Many feared the claims for abandoned property they had submitted to the federally appointed commissioners prior to their departure would not be fairly settled, and that they would be cheated out of their just compensation by whites falsely dunning them.

But they had already come more than two hundred miles. There was no turning back. They trudged on, traveling on a road that was sometimes frozen solid and other times a mire of cold mud. And always, it seemed, with a bitter wind blowing in their faces.

⚞ 29 ⚟

The slow, rhythmic thud of the pickax reminded Eliza of the mournful sound of a bass drum beating out a funeral cadence. She watched silently as The Blade, Deu, and Shadrach chiseled a grave out of the frozen, snow-covered ground. Nearby lay the blanket-wrapped body waiting to be interred. Black Cassie knelt beside her dead husband, Ike, and rocked slowly back and forth, ignoring all of Phoebe's attempts to comfort her. Her low moans mingled with the keening sound of the wind.

Ike, Will's Negro smithy, was dead. It seemed impossible that a man so big and strong could fall victim to pneumonia. So many others had died, littering the trailsides with their graves, Eliza didn't know why she found this so hard to accept. She pulled the blanket higher, covering more of her nose and leaving only her eyes exposed to the frigid cold.

Maybe it wasn't his death but the icy fear she recoiled from—that terrifying sense of being trapped. Ten days ago they had arrived at this spot, only to find they couldn't go on. The Mississippi was frozen over, but the ice was too thin to support the weight of the wagons and too thick for ferries to plow through. Caravan after caravan was bottled up on this peninsula of land bounded by the Ohio and Mississippi rivers, bottled up with little to protect them from winter's brutal cold and raging snowstorms. Virtually everyone was sick, some more critically than others. To the dysentery, measles, whooping cough, and pleurisy of the detention camps last summer could be added frostbite, colds, consumption, pneumonia, and black tongue.

Across the ice-bound Mississippi from their encampment lay Cape Girardeau, Missouri. No one speculated when they might reach it. They were more than halfway to their final destination in the designated Indian Territory. The journey was supposed to have taken them ninety days. The ninety days were up and they still had four hundred miles to go once they crossed the Mississippi.

Eliza wondered if they would ever make it, if she would make it. God, what was she doing here? Then Will moved closer, huddling his blanket-cloaked body against hers and shielding her from some of the wind. That momentary panic faded. She knew the reason she was there, and the reason she wouldn't leave.

Jed Parmelee rode up to the gravesite. Eliza stared enviously at his heavy greatcoat, the wool muffler, and the thick gloves he wore. Dismounting, he let the reins trail on the snow and walked over to the grave. Without a word, he laid his hand on Shadrach's shoulder and took the shovel from him to scoop out the chunks of frozen earth. Shadrach watched, holding his rag-wrapped hands to his mouth and blowing on his fingers, trying to warm them. Then he turned and limped over to join his mother and sister, more rags covering his feet.

At last, the grave was dug. "It's time, Mammy," Shadrach murmured, gazing at her wet cheeks and tear-swollen eyes. "We have to bury him now." She broke into fresh sobs when he knelt beside Ike's body and began to tenderly lift back the overlapping folds of the blanket.

"What you doin'?" Cassie demanded through her weeping.

"Pa doesn't need this blanket anymore. We do."

"No!" She grabbed at his arm. "You cain't lay him in that cold ground wid nothin' to cover him."

"He can't feel the cold. You know he'd want us to have it so we'd be warm."

"Shad's right." Phoebe shivered uncontrollably from the freezing temperature despite the blanket around her shoulders and the extra pair of Deu's pants she wore under her thin summer dress. "He would tell us to take it, if he could."

Cassie cried as Shadrach unwrapped the blanket and exposed that long black body clad in a tattered shirt and homespun trousers held up by a pair of suspenders—his feet bare, his hands bare, and his face bare.

The whole family, except Victoria, looked on as Deu, The Blade, and Jed Parmelee lowered Ike's corpse into the grave. It was too cold to linger. They all in turn stepped forward to express their sorrow and regret to his woman and children. The bone-numbing weather made any physical gesture impossible. Then they all plodded back through the snow to the blessed heat of their fires, leaving Deu to shovel the clods of frozen dirt into the unmarked grave.

Jed stood next to the fire and pulled his muffler down to breathe in the warmed air. Out of habit, he held his gloved hands over the fire and stared at the flames, unconsciously working his mouth to ease its stiffness.

Summer's blazing heat was a distant memory—the heat and the sweat that used to flow from his pores. The lack of water had forced the postponement of the Cherokees' removal. If Scott had known how much these people would suffer trying to make the trek in the dead of winter, he would have postponed it again, Jed was sure.

The dead of winter—the turn of phrase was much too appropriate, he realized. The mortality rate was running close to twenty percent, and that didn't take into account the deaths of slaves, like Ike. When would it end? How many more would die before the caravan reached its destination?

He had never felt so utterly helpless. He had given away

every extra piece of warm clothing he owned—shirts, socks, flannel drawers, pants, boots, and uniforms—government-issue or not. If the army wanted to reprimand him for giving away government property, that was all right by him. But he couldn't stand by and do nothing to alleviate their suffering. He wasn't the only one. John Ross's brother Lewis, who headed one of the caravans encamped near Jonesboro, had gone north to St. Louis to try to purchase blankets and clothing with his own funds.

A paroxysm of coughing sounded behind him, breaking over the pleasant crackle of the fire. At first, Jed paid no attention to it, thinking it was The Blade. He had heard him cough several times at the gravesite and guessed he was nursing a cold. Then he realized the sound wasn't the same.

Frowning, he glanced over his shoulder as Temple's two-year-old son sucked in a long draft of air, then started to gag, finally expelling a clear, sticky mucus from his throat. The convulsive way he inhaled and the sound of it—Jed had heard it too many times in the camp.

"Has the doctor seen Lije?"

Temple shook her head and cradled her whimpering son in her arms, folding her own blanket around him. "It was only a little cough the other day."

It wasn't little anymore. "I'll find the doctor and bring him back."

Within an hour, Jed had returned with the caravan's cold, harried, and overworked physician. The doctor examined the child briefly, then helped himself to a cup of coffee and stood shivering next to the fire.

"Your son has whooping cough," he informed Temple. "There's not much I can do for him right now. If he starts vomiting when he coughs up that mucus, I recommend you feed him several times a day. It seems to help if he has plenty of sleep. I have some laudanum in my bag which I'll leave with you, but don't give him any more than four drops, and that no more than three times a day. If he gets worse, has trouble breathing, or anything like that, send someone to fetch me. Otherwise ... " He shrugged, raised the tin cup to his mouth, and sipped noisily at the hot coffee. "How is your mother? I might as well check on her while I'm here," he said and sighed heavily.

"I'll go with you," Eliza volunteered. "I was on my way to put these hot stones under her mattress."

"Bed warmer, eh? My mother put hot bricks in our bed at night when my brother and I were kids. Damned uncomfortable if you accidentally rolled onto one." As he walked by, The Blade coughed. The physician paused, frowning at him. "I don't like the sound of that, either. Does your chest hurt? Should I be examining you too?"

"No." The Blade waved him away.

"Suit yourself. God knows, I have more patients than I can take care of now." He walked off. "Don't let me forget to leave that laudanum with you before I go."

A north wind howled through the stand of trees as Eliza scuffed over the thin snow cover, looking for broken branches and dead limbs buried beneath it. Every day they had to range farther and farther from camp in search of firewood. She wondered how long it would be before the supply of deadfall was exhausted and they would have to resort to chopping down trees. At least there were trees. She hated to think what would happen if there was no fuel at all to burn.

Her toe struck something. She brushed aside the snow with her foot and picked up another large stick to add to her small bundle. Pausing, Eliza looked to see if Xandra and Kipp were faring any better. For an instant, she thought she was totally alone, surrounded only by dark trunks of barren trees. Then she caught a movement far to her left. Someone was leaning against a tree. Xandra. But Kipp was nowhere in sight.

Eliza glanced anxiously at the heavy gray clouds overhead. It was late, and there was a threat of snow in the air. Where was Kipp? Why hadn't she insisted they stay closer together?

Abandoning her search for more firewood, she struck out through the snow to link up with Xandra. She lowered her blanket and shouted, "Xandra! Where's Kipp? Have you seen him?" But Xandra didn't answer. Instead, she sank slowly to the ground. "Xandra?"

Eliza halted briefly in alarm, then broke into a run, the cold tearing at her lungs. By the time she reached the girl, she was out of breath, her lungs burning and her heart pounding. She half stumbled and half dropped to her knees beside Xandra, all curled up in a tight ball at the base of the tree.

"Xandra, what is it? What's wrong?" Forgetting her own blanket and the bundle of sticks, she cupped her hand under Xandra's chin and lifted it so she could see her face. There was hardly any color in it and it was all twisted in pain. Eliza breathed in sharply at the stark agony and terror in Xandra's dark eyes. Her mouth opened, but she appeared to be incapable of speech. Suddenly, Xandra doubled over again and released a gasping moan. Then Eliza noticed that she was holding her stomach.

"Dear God, no. Not the baby," she whispered. It was too soon. Much too soon. "We have got to get you back to camp. Come on, Xandra. Help me." Hooking one arm around her, Eliza tried to lift and push the girl to her feet. Then she saw the blood on the white snow underneath Xandra. "Kipp!" She screamed his name but she knew she didn't dare waste time waiting for him.

Holding Xandra under the arms and locking her hands together above the girl's breasts, Eliza started walking backward, dragging Xandra through the woods toward the wood smoke of the distant camp. Xandra's twisting and writhing in pain only made the task harder. Just when Eliza thought she couldn't haul her another step, that maybe she should leave Xandra and go for help, Kipp came running through the trees.

Anxious and restless, Eliza moved away from the campfire outside the doctor's tent. She shivered, but she didn't want to be warm. Will stood near the fire, staring into the flames, his expression blank. If she had only insisted Xandra stay close to her, Eliza thought, or if she had simply asked her how she felt *before* they went to gather firewood, she might have seen that something was wrong with Xandra, that she wasn't feeling well. Dear God, was it her fault? Eliza shut her eyes tightly, trying to squeeze out the pain and guilt, and instantly the image of that trail of blood in the snow flashed before her. She breathed in deeply to check the sob that rose in her throat.

Eliza turned and saw The Blade leaning against a corner of the wagon, forsaking the warmth of the fire as she had. She went over to him. Lately, people had paid little attention to him. They were more concerned with surviving than nourishing hatreds for past wrongs.

Now Xandra might not survive. There had been so much blood, Eliza remembered with a shudder. She glanced at the canvas flap. "The doctor has been with her a long time," she murmured.

"I know," The Blade said, then started coughing from the congestion in his lungs.

"Temple will be worried. Maybe one of us should go back and let her know there isn't any word yet."

"Send Parmelee. He wouldn't turn down the chance to comfort her." His statement implied bitterness and jealousy, yet his tone was flat, devoid of any emotion.

It hurt her to see The Blade and Temple like this, together yet so very far apart, especially when Eliza could remember so clearly the love that had existed between them, a love that had been expressed in every word, every gesture, every look they exchanged.

The doctor emerged. All eyes swung to him. For several seconds, he said nothing, but when he glanced away, the defeated look in his face said it all.

"I'm sorry." He sighed and crossed to the fire. "I lost her."

"The baby?" Will paused expectantly.

"A boy. He didn't have a chance."

"Oh, God." Eliza tried to swallow the sob. "Why couldn't I have found her sooner?"

"Even if she had been right here with me when it happened . . . " the doctor began. "I don't think I could have saved her, not under these conditions—maybe not under any."

Perhaps it was true, but Eliza knew she would always wonder. When Will slowly walked over to her, she wanted to run, certain she would find accusation in his gaze. But she didn't, just the pain of grief. He laid his rag-tied hand against her cheek and wiped away a tear with his thumb.

"I know how much you loved her, too," he said quietly.

She leaned against the comforting wall of his chest and cried.

They buried Xandra and her stillborn son the next morning.

☶ 30 ☶

His son, his servant, his daughter, and her child, all dead. Will sat on the ground near the fire, his blanket a tent around him. He was beyond thinking or feeling as he stared at the bright flames. Cold numbed his body and grief numbed his mind. He had reached the point where he couldn't cry anymore, on the inside or out.

He heard the crunch of approaching footsteps in the snow, but they didn't mean anything to him. When Temple crouched down beside him, his gaze never wavered from the fire. Faint wisps of steam rose from the plate of food she carried.

"Mama wouldn't eat tonight. She keeps asking for Xandra." She paused, waiting for him to speak, but he had nothing to say. "We aren't going to be able to keep it from her. She has already guessed that something is wrong. We have to tell her."

Wearily, he closed his eyes, wanting to shut out her prodding voice. Talking meant thinking, and thinking meant feeling. He preferred the numbness that had taken hold of him at the gravesite this morning.

From somewhere nearby came Eliza's quiet voice. "I will go."

"No." At first he didn't realize he had spoken the thought

aloud. It had come too quickly. With that first thought came more. He couldn't let Eliza tell Victoria about Xandra's death, not because of the guilt he knew she felt, but because it was his duty. Xandra was . . . had been their daughter. At almost the same moment he spoke, Will became aware of the radiating warmth from the fire and the coldness of the ground beneath him—and the dull pain inside. "I will tell her."

He pushed to his feet. The stiff, cramped muscles in his legs protested any movement, but he forced them to carry him to the wagon. It groaned and creaked, rocking slightly with his weight when he climbed inside. Nearly bent over double, he made his way along the narrow path to Victoria's side and lowered himself onto a keg next to her mattress.

"Temple said you refused to eat." He stared at the woman who was his wife, swaddled in blankets like some Egyptian mummy. Only her face was exposed, with its sunken hollows and underlying grayness. The smell of sickness was all around him. She looked tired, dull, and dispirited. Will dreaded telling her about Xandra. "Are you cold? I can have Black Cassie reheat the stones."

"Where is Xandra?" Her voice was thick and weak. Will looked away, avoiding the dark eyes that were trained on him, eyes already haunted by an endless string of sorrows. "She is dead, isn't she?"

"Yes. We buried her this morning." He braced himself for an outpouring of grief.

But all that came was a quavering sigh. "I knew," Victoria whispered. "She came to me last night in a dream. She had a little doll in her arms and she was crying because it was broken and she didn't know how to fix it." A terrible twisting pain gripped his chest, squeezing and constricting until he couldn't breathe. Victoria stared at the wagon's arching canvas roof, which was rustling softly in the wind. "I want to be buried with her, Will. Promise you will do that?"

He started to nod his head in silent acquiescence, then her

request struck him, along with the phrase *with her*, as if she thought her own death was imminent.

"Don't talk like that, Victoria," he murmured irritably. "You are not going to die."

"Promise me." She tried to sit up, a frantic look leaping into her eyes.

Almost immediately she started coughing, her body convulsing with the terrible, racking force of it. He held her, waiting for the spasm to pass, all the while regretting he hadn't simply agreed.

At last the coughing subsided, but it was as if it had drained every bit of her strength. She lay there, paler and more hollow-eyed than before. She looked at him, appealing silently as her lips formed the words *promise me*, although he could hear no sound from them.

"I promise."

She closed her eyes, her lips curving in a faint smile of contentment. He sat with her for a long time, then quietly left the wagon.

Victoria died quietly in her sleep that night. When Will said he wanted her to be buried in the same grave with Xandra, Temple instantly protested. "No. It isn't right."

"It is what your mother wanted, and I promised her I would."

"When? Last night?" She stared at him, stunned by the implication. "Then she knew . . . she knew she was going to die."

He shook his head, a vagueness in his expression. "I think she couldn't stand being separated from her children any longer. Not only Johnny and Xandra, but your other little brothers and sisters who died so very long ago."

"But why? I don't understand."

"You are a mother, Temple. You should know. The children come first. They always did with Victoria . . . always." His voice trailed off to a mere whisper of pain and regret.

Slowly, Temple realized what he was saying—that her mother loved her children more than she loved him, that she put their needs and considerations before his. He had been hurt by that, deeply hurt.

A brilliant blue sky and bright sun made the day look warm, but the air was frigidly cold. Temple huddled close to the fire, holding her croupy son on her lap. Keeping warm seemed to be their single occupation, the dominant thought that ruled every waking moment, taking precedence over even food and water. The cold had a way of numbing everything, including grief and hope, locking it inside with all the other misery. Three days ago they had buried her mother, then returned to the fire to mourn her.

The fire was all-important.

Temple tried to recall those languid summer afternoons at Gordon Glen when the sun blazed overhead and a hot breeze stirred the sticky air. But it no longer seemed real. There was only the cold, the never-ending cold and the collection of graves outside the camp and all along that awful trail they had traveled. Maybe they would all die. She hugged her ailing son closer. Lije squirmed and protested crankily, pushing his head back against her chest. Reluctantly, she relaxed her hold and murmured to him.

The crunching sound of hooves breaking through the snow's icy crust echoed loudly in the still air. Uninterestedly, Temple looked over as Jed Parmelee rode up, dismounted, and looped the reins over a wagon, then crossed to the fire. He squatted on his heels and held out his hands to the flames, his steamy breath rising from his mouth like thin white smoke. A wool muffler covered the point of his chin. His light blue glance went from her to the boy on her lap.

"How's Lije?"

"The same." No worse and no better, but Temple could find little comfort in that, not with three members of her family already dead, along with their blacksmith, Ike.

"Good. The doctor told me whooping cough runs its course in a couple of weeks. He'll be fine." As long as no new complications set in, like pneumonia; but Jed didn't tell her that. There had been enough tragedy in her life recently without raising the specter of another. "I rode out to the river. The ice seems to be breaking up. If it continues a few more days, the ferry should be able to make it across."

"Miss Temple!" Phoebe came hurrying across the snow to the fire. "Miss Temple, you better come."

"Why? What's wrong?" She rose to her feet.

"It's Master Blade. He's real sick. He won't let Deu fetch the doctor and he's got an awful rattle in his chest. I don't know what to do." The words tumbled from her in a puffy white rush. "You've got to help him, Miss Temple. He's in the tent. Deu's with him, but . . ."

When Jed saw the alarm and fear in Temple's eyes, he bit down hard on the jealousy that rose up in him. She cared. He had known all along that The Blade had wanted her to come back to him, but he thought Temple . . . but it didn't matter what he had thought. Her reaction was telling him something entirely different.

"Look after Lije for me." She handed the child over to Eliza, then turned to him. "Will you bring the doctor?"

"But Master Blade said—" Phoebe began.

"I don't care what he said!" Impatience, irritation, and concern were all mixed together in her sharp retort. "Bring the doctor."

"Right away," Jed promised, but she didn't wait for his assurance as she set off in the direction of The Blade's tent. He watched her go.

Nearby, Eliza whispered faintly, "She still loves him."

He shot her a savage glance. Eliza's face mirrored the thoughtful wonder that had been in her voice. A hint of a smile touched her lips. Jed turned from it and strode briskly to his horse. "I'll get the doctor." But he didn't want to, and knowing that didn't make him feel any better.

* * *

When Temple plunged inside the small tent, she was greeted by a thick, congested cough. She stared at the long figure swathed in blankets lying on the cold wet ground, his head and shoulders cradled in Deu's lap and arms.

Deu looked up. "You came. I wasn't sure you would."

"How is he?" Temple knelt down to examine The Blade for herself.

"He's bad. I tried to take care of him. I tried."

For an instant, Temple met the gaze of his black eyes. Deu loved The Blade as much as she did. She had always known The Blade never went anywhere without him. Yet she had never once suspected that the bond between them was any more than a master's regard for a faithful servant and a servant's loyalty to his master. It went deeper than that. Deu held him in his arms as he would a brother. Briefly, she was shocked by the discovery, then just as suddenly it didn't seem important.

"The doctor's on his way." When she felt The Blade's forehead, his skin was like fire to the touch.

He stirred, partially opening his eyes to look at her, their color a feverish blue. "Temple?" His voice was a mere rasp.

"I am here." She tried to smile, but she was too alarmed by his weakness and the awful sound of his breathing. Fresh in her mind was the image of him helping to dig Ike's grave, then digging Xandra's all by himself, and only three days ago helping to bury her mother. She didn't want him to die too.

His frown deepened, irritation flickering in his eyes. "Deu, I told you not to—" He started coughing again.

Shutting her ears to the sound, Temple refused to give in to the helpless feeling that assailed her. "Go heat some stones, Deu. We need to keep him warm. I will stay with him until the doctor comes."

Deu hesitated. "You have to keep him propped up, Miss Temple. It's too hard for him to breathe when he lays flat."

"I'll hold him." It was what she wanted, what she needed.

Too many months had passed since she had last had her arms around him.

As soon as his coughing subsided, she changed places with Deu and supported The Blade on her lap, cradling his head in the crook of her arm.

He made a protesting movement. "Lije . . ."

"Eliza is taking care of him."

Her answer seemed to satisfy him. Either that or he hadn't the strength to object further. Temple didn't know or care. Their son didn't need her as much as he did.

Pneumonia was the doctor's diagnosis. For two days and nights, Temple remained at The Blade's side, spooning warm broth down him, changing the smelly poultice on his chest, and holding him, only rarely allowing Deu to take over her vigil, and then never for long. She was afraid to sleep, afraid he would need her, afraid he would die if she didn't stay with him.

It didn't seem to matter that for three years she had known he was marked for death for what he had done. Now that he hovered so near it, she was terrified at the thought of losing him forever. Her fear made no sense to her, any more than her reasons for leaving him two and a half years ago did. All the well-thought-out logic of her actions now seemed flawed.

When Deu entered the tent near the end of the third day, she was numb with exhaustion and cold. Swaying unsteadily, Temple reached for the mug of warm broth in his hand.

"No. I'll feed it to him." Deu refused to give it to her, and she was too tired to insist. He lifted The Blade's pinning weight off her legs and Temple half fell and half crawled out of the way, her stiff, cramped muscles balking at the movement. "It'd be a good idea if you rested a little while," Deu suggested gently.

She nodded in agreement, yet she couldn't seem to make herself lie down. She sat with her legs partially curled beneath her and stared at The Blade's face, feeling lost without the sensation of his body pressing on her.

His eyelids fluttered as Deu held the mug to his lips. The Blade tried to avoid it, turning his head slightly and mumbling something. "Now you take a little sip of this broth, Master Blade," Deu crooned to him. "Phoebe fixed it specially for you. She'll be upset if you don't take a taste of it. Come on now, try a little bit."

Frowning deeply, The Blade pushed his head back, forcing the mug away from his mouth with his chin. "Temple. I thought . . . I thought Temple . . . was here," he murmured weakly.

"I am." She ignored the tingling protest of her limbs and crawled to his side, leaning forward so he could see her. "I am right here."

He focused his eyes on her with an obvious effort. "Don't leave . . . don't leave me again." His voice was little more than a faint moan, his lips barely moving to form the words.

"I won't. I will be here right beside you." The instant she made the promise, a strange calm took possession of her. She wasn't going to leave him, not while he was so ill, and not even after he recovered. She knew that as surely as she knew the sun would always rise in the east. If she could have taken back the months they had spent apart, she would have. She had hurt him by leaving him. She had hurt both of them.

At the time, she had been convinced it was best for their son that she left him. Now she remembered all the times she had watched The Blade with Lije in the recent months, playing some baby game with him or simply letting Lije crawl around on him. Wasn't it best that a child should know his father's love? Wasn't it better that he should grow up with that, even if he heard all the hateful things others might say about his father, whether true or not? Yes, The Blade was wrong in what he had done, but she was equally wrong in leaving him. She could see that now, and prayed that it wasn't too late.

"You drink that broth," she urged, hearing the tremor in her voice. "You have to get well. Please. Please get well." She lay across him, resting her head on his stomach and crying softly, letting his blanket muffle her quiet sobs.

After a time, Temple closed her eyes—just for a little while. But it was pitch-black inside the tent when she woke up. Instantly, she had the sense that something wasn't right. Levering herself onto her knees, Temple leaned forward to check on him. He was lying completely flat.

"No," she gasped in alarm and scrambled forward to pick him up. A pair of hands pulled her away, resisting her attempts to struggle free of their grip.

"Let him sleep, Miss Temple," Deu's voice whispered near her ear.

"But—"

"Shhh. Listen. He's breathing easier now. You can't hear that rattle in his lungs anymore."

She stopped fighting Deu's hold to listen. "He's getting better, isn't he?" She was almost afraid to believe it.

"In another week or two, he'll be walking around here as good as new. Go back to sleep now, or he'll be takin' care of you next." She began to weep softly in relief. Gently, Deu laid her down next to The Blade and tucked the blanket tightly around both of them. "Don't you worry about anything. I'll be right here all night."

The ferry, loaded with the first of the cavalcade's wagons, pulled away from the bank and plowed its way through the river's floating islands of ice. Jed Parmelee watched from the Mississippi's east bank. They were on the move once again.

In his journal that night, he meticulously recorded the resumption of the journey after a month's delay. Observe and report, those were his orders. But many of his observations went unreported, like when he watched Temple, aided by her husband's colored servant, lift The Blade onto his horse and tie him to the saddle. In the dark recesses of his mind, Jed had secretly hoped the man would die. He despised himself for wishing it, but it was true just the same. Just as it was true that The Blade was still a very sick man, and the winter journey was far from over.

Once the caravan had regrouped on the other side of the Mississippi, north of Cape Girardeau, it was learned that the game and winter fodder along the more direct southern route through Arkansas Territory had been severely depleted. They were forced to travel the more northerly route across Missouri.

A frigid wind out of the arctic north swept across the rolling prairie, blasting the beleaguered travelers and sending the temperature plummeting. Weary and ill-clad, weakened by the hardship and disease they had already suffered, the exiled band now faced the ravages of exposure.

There were times when Jed's legs were so numb with cold, he could barely stay in the saddle. He lingered long in front of each fire built by outriders in advance of the caravan, then rode on, passing the plodding, stumbling, laboring Cherokees, to reach the next.

Every day, he rode past more graves, some in the process of being hacked out of the frozen ground and others with the sod freshly turned. After each bitter night, there seemed to be another body to be buried in the morning. Yet every morning, there was The Blade tied on his horse and swaddled in blankets, often with Temple behind him, holding him on.

It was rare for the caravan to cover fifteen miles in a day. Ten miles was average, and anything in between was considered a good day's travel. For days it was the same— an ice blue sky, a bitter wind. Jed was never sure whether it was the wind's moans he heard or those of the sick, the dying, or the mourners. But the sound haunted the trail from Cape Girardeau through Jackson, Farmington, Potosi, Rolla, and Lebanon to Springfield, Missouri. There, the trail turned southwest and the rains started falling, sometimes changing to sleet, but always very cold.

Few offers of food or a night's dry shelter came from the

white inhabitants of the towns and isolated farmhouses along their route. Not that Jed entirely blamed them. By now, the Cherokees were a ragged, sorry-looking lot, riddled with contagious diseases and without funds to pay for a night's lodging or food.

And Missouri was the frontier, newly wrested from the grasp of the warring Plains Indians. The word *Indians* conjured up images of savages. Few could believe the Cherokees knew little of war. They were farmers—some, like the Gordons, owned large plantations, and others worked small plots of corn, cotton, or tobacco, eking out a living from the soil, as many of the Missouri farmers did.

Ignorance bred mistrust. And there wasn't anything Jed could do about it.

With her clothes and blanket completely saturated by the falling rain, Temple wrapped her arms tightly around The Blade and tried to absorb the shivers that continuously shook him. Every time she thought he was getting better, he would have a setback. She wasn't sure he could endure another night sleeping in wet clothes on wet ground.

A croupy cough punctuated the steady drum of the rain. Temple glanced at Eliza, plodding through the mud alongside the horse, a blanket draped over her head and body. That large hump on Eliza's back was their son. Lije, too, desperately needed dry clothes and a warm place to sleep. With this rain, there wasn't much chance of either.

Leading the horse, Deu glanced back at her. "They're making camp for the night just ahead, Miss Temple. I can see a couple tents."

When Temple looked for herself, she spied a curl of white smoke rising from the chimney of a farmhouse ahead of them. Near it stood a sturdy barn. Without hesitation, she slipped off the horse's back into the mud and hurried forward to take the reins from Deu. Clicking to the horse, she pulled it after her and left the trail, heading straight for the farmhouse.

"Temple, where are you going?" Eliza called.

"All of you, come with me," she shouted back and ignored the bewildered looks from her family. She hadn't the energy to expend in explanations. She was too cold, too tired, and too wet.

When she reached the front porch of the farmhouse, she dropped the reins and moved quickly to the saddle. She fumbled briefly in her initial attempt to untie the small bundle hanging off the left side. Then it was free. A dog bounded out from under the porch, barking furiously in warning, when she approached the steps. Forced to stop, Temple glared in frustration at the door, wondering if she dared approach it. The dog's barking grew more ferocious when her father and Eliza came up behind her.

"Temple, it's no use," her father began.

"You don't know that," she accused angrily.

Just then a man stepped out of the house and swore at the dog. The barking immediately dissolved into a whine of submission as the animal turned and wagged its tail at its master. The instant Temple took a step forward, the dog blocked her way again, a menacing growl rumbling from its throat.

"You're part of that bunch of Indians on the road, aren't you?" The man glowered at them from beneath thick, bushy eyebrows. Gray hair, peppered with black, framed a worn and deeply lined faced, weathered to a leathery brown from years of exposure to the elements. Temple tried not to look at the rifle cradled in his arms. "If you come lookin' fer a handout, you best just keep movin' on down the road 'cause you ain't gettin' one here. Now, go on. Get outta here before I sic my dog on you."

"Please . . . my husband and my son are sick. They need a place out of the rain to sleep tonight. Could you let them stay in your barn?" She tugged frantically at the wet knot tying the small bundle together. "I can pay you." At last she worked it loose and plunged her numb fingers inside, feeling of the bundle's meager contents and finally finding the silver pin. She pulled it out and clutched it tightly for an instant, then held out her hand, opening her palm to show it to him. "See."

The old man hesitated, the scowl turning to a suspicious frown as he moved to the top of the steps. The pin glistened wetly in her hand, the large amethyst in the hilt's crown gleaming a deep purple in the absence of sunlight, the pearls shining like snowdrops.

Eliza gasped when she saw what was in her hand. "No," she protested. "You can't give him that."

But it was too late. The man had already plucked it from her palm to examine it more closely. Temple shut her mind to the thought of losing the valuable heirloom that had been in her family for years. But she would willingly sacrifice it and more for a warm, dry shelter.

"How many of you are there?" His glance shot over them, as if he were counting noses.

"Ten," Temple acknowledged. "My father and brother, my ... cousin"—she hesitated at identifying Eliza— "myself, my son and husband, and our four blacks. Will you let us sleep in your barn tonight? We won't steal anything."

He turned the pin over in his hand. "I reckon it won't do any harm. You're all standing there shiverin' like a bunch of half-drowned pups anyways. Never could stand to see somethin' cold and wet," he declared gruffly. "You can sleep in m' barn." Temple felt her knees start to buckle with relief. Before she could thank him, he went on, "This here's a pretty bauble. My wife woulda liked it, but she's been dead now close to three years. I ain't got no use for such things. Reckon you might as well keep it." He grabbed Temple's hand and pressed the brooch back into her palm, then turned abruptly and walked back to the front door of the house. He paused there, glancing back at them. "I got me a milk cow with a calf on her in the barn. You can take some o' her milk fer your little one."

"Thank you."

He grumped a reply and went back inside the house.

An hour later, he stomped into the barn carrying a basket of fresh eggs in one hand and a bundle of quilts tucked under his other arm. "Don't need these." He set them down beside one of the stalls and left.

Temple ran after him, catching up with him a few feet outside the barn door. "Please, what's your name?"

He ducked his head slightly, rainwater running off the brim of his hat. "Cosgrove. Hiram Cosgrove."

"I am Mrs. Stuart." She offered him her rag-bound hand.

He shook it awkwardly, bobbing his head in a quick acknowledgement. "Mrs. Stuart."

"Thank you, Mr. Cosgrove. I wanted to be able to tell my son the name of the man who helped us. Thank you."

"Out here in the rain and the mud ain't a place to be thankin' somebody. You best git in where it's dry," he declared brusquely.

She lingered a second longer, then turned and ran back inside the barn.

Later that night, Temple lay beside The Blade, the two of them half buried in the hay and wrapped in one of Mr. Cosgrove's warm, dry quilts. Their own wet blankets and their clothes were draped over the stanchions to dry. She breathed in deeply, inhaling the hay's strong fragrance and trying to remember the last time she had felt this warm and comfortable. The Blade stirred and shuddered convulsively.

"Are you cold?" she whispered, and immediately turned to hold him, pressing her body to his length to let its heat warm him. "Does that feel better?"

"I don't think I want to feel better," he murmured, a rasp in his voice from days of coughing.

"Don't talk like that."

"Why?" He rolled onto his side to face her, the hay rustling noisily beneath him. "We both know that once I am well you won't be lying beside me anymore. Why would I want to get well when it means losing you again, Temple?"

"You are wrong." She reached up to stroke his face. "I will not leave. You have to get well because I want to be your wife again."

He caught hold of her hand and halted its idle caress, surprising her with the strength of his grip. "Don't say that if you don't mean it," he warned thickly.

"I mean it."

Nothing; he said nothing. Instead, he pressed the hollow of her hand to his mouth and held it there. She could feel the faint vibration of his body, a trembling that wasn't from the cold or a fever but came from strong feelings. Temple quivered a little herself, thrilling to the certainty of his love. Then he lowered her hand to breathe in deeply and sigh.

"I have missed you. By all that's holy, I have missed you," he murmured. "Maybe I should accept that you want to come back to me without questioning it, but I can't. Why, Temple? Why have you changed your mind?"

"Because your son needs you, but—more than that—I need you. I love you," she said quietly and moved closer to lay her head on his chest. She could hear the congested wheeze of his lungs and the steady rhythm of his heartbeat. "We have both made mistakes, though we didn't think they were at the time. When you signed that treaty, you thought you were doing what was best, but you were wrong, very wrong. And when I left you, I thought I was doing what was best for our child, but I was wrong, too. Much has changed in the last two years, but not the way I feel about you." Temple closed her eyes, conscious of the enveloping heat of his body and the aching tiredness of her own. Part of her wished it wasn't so. "Hold me."

She felt him kiss her hair before a cough forced him to turn his head. The spasm intensified the rasp in his low voice when he spoke again. "I don't have the strength to do anything else but hold you. I love you, Temple. I never wanted you to leave, but I couldn't ask you to stay."

"I know." The decision had to be hers, one made freely, without the coercion of his love. Otherwise she would have resented it. She understood that.

The rain pattered on the barn roof, but they were warm and dry in their soft bed of hay, snuggled closely together. They drifted off to sleep that way.

Fort Gibson, Indian Territory
Late February 1839

*T*he big bay horse snorted impatiently at the slow pace and strained against the bit, its neck tautly arched by the curbing reins. Jarred by its eager prancing gait, Jed nearly gave the animal its head and let it run off some of that freshness as he rode out of the fort along the military road that stretched between Fort Gibson and Fort Smith. But the sight of tents sprawled along the valley of the Arkansas River checked that impulse. It wasn't an army bivouac, but the final encampment of the caravan.

At Fayetteville, his detachment of exiles had branched west, making for Fort Gibson, although most of the caravans had continued south through the Ouachitas to Fort Smith. Two days ago they had reached journey's end.

He had slept twenty-four hours of those two days, in a warm bed with dry blankets and on an army mattress considerably softer than the cold, hard ground. He had wakened from a heavy sleep with stiff, sore muscles. A hot bath, a shave, a clean uniform, and a hot meal had alleviated a great many of his aches, but not all.

Still, looking at these people who had spent another night outside with only blankets and fires to warm them, who had eaten another meal of salt pork and mush, and who possessed little more than the clothes on their backs, Jed couldn't complain. At the officers' mess this morning, he had listened to the laughter and easy voices. Yet here in the camp, the absence of those sounds was deafening.

When the caravan arrived two days ago, he hadn't seen a single smile or heard one expression of relief that the costly and brutal trek was finally over. The survivors had merely scattered over the river valley in a desultory fashion and methodically pitched their tents.

His skittish bay horse shied at a bird that flew out of the marshy canebrake growing along the riverbank on his right. Jed checked the bay's sideways lunge and settled it back into its jolting prance, cursing the animal in a soft, soothing voice. He almost wished that he had ridden one of the caravan horses instead of borrowing one of the dragoons' mounts. But his horses were as footsore and weary as everyone else's.

He reined the bay off the road and walked it into the large and sprawling encampment. This would be his last time to observe and report. After two days of rest and recuperation for the Indians, he had expected to see some change. But the range of expressions he saw was the same as the day they had arrived: distraught, desperate, sullen, and bitter.

Maybe it wasn't so surprising. The hegira was over, but at what cost? Hundreds had died, in the detention camps and on the long trek. The Trail Where They Cried, that's what Jed had heard the Cherokees call it. He had the feeling he would always hear the moaning of their grief in the wind.

And what had they found when they got here? More of the same shoddy treatment they had endured on the trail. True, the land was good. The hardwood forests would provide game for their tables, lumber for their homes, and fuel for their fires. The rich soil of the river bottoms and valleys would grow their crops. But the rest of the promises in the treaty, the treaty they had never agreed to—in one short morning, Jed had seen and gleaned enough information to know just how well those were being kept. Maybe it didn't fit squarely under the heading of army business, but Jed intended to report those things as well.

Just ahead, he spotted a small gathering and rode over to investigate. At his approach, the group began to disperse, wandering off in twos and threes. A half dozen remained, solemnly shaking hands with a man clad in a heavy mackinaw with a wide-brimmed hat pulled low on his forehead, partially concealing the shock of sandy hair beneath it. Jed glanced at the book in the man's hand and reined his horse to a halt. Was it a Bible? From twenty feet away, Jed couldn't tell.

Despite the angular thinness of the man's face, one glance and Jed knew the man hadn't been on the trail. The warm clothes, the sturdy shoes, the ruddy color of his cheeks, and the well-fed horse tied to the wagon behind him marked him as either one of the mixed bloods already settled here, one of the white traders under government contract, or a missionary. Jed was curious to learn which. He waited until the man was alone, then walked his horse closer.

The man smiled, his glance flickering briefly to the lieutenant's bars on his shoulder. "Good afternoon, Lieutenant."

Jed caught a glimpse of the book's gold lettering. It was a Bible. "Afternoon, Reverend. It is Reverend, isn't it?"

"Yes. Reverend Nathan Cole from the Dwight Mission."

"Dwight Mission. That's about halfway between here and Fort Smith, isn't it?" Jed recalled, and observed the missionary's affirmative nod. "That's a long day's ride. You're ranging pretty far afield."

"Perhaps. But with so many caravans arriving from the East, I felt I should come where I could do the most good. From the tragic stories I have heard, these people are in need of spiritual sustenance now."

Jed laughed. "Forgive me, Reverend. I don't mean to make light of God or His power. But I don't think prayer is going to take the weevils out of the flour they have been issued, or make the meat taste less rancid, or put fat on the sick and scrawny cattle they have been given in place of the quality beef they were promised by the government. If you want to pray for someone, pray for the men who won the government contract to supply them with provisions and are now making a huge profit by issuing substandard goods. If you want to try and help these people, get them warm clothes, find homes for their orphans, and look after their sick. That will do more to restore their belief in a fair and just God than reading a few passages out of the Bible." He paused and smiled ruefully. "Seems like I'm the one who's preaching now. My apologies, Reverend Cole."

"It isn't necessary. Perhaps the sermon was deserved."

"But I'm not the one to be making it. I'll let you go on with your work. I have some good-byes to say." He wheeled the eager bay away from the missionary and pointed it toward a small semicircle of tents some distance away, the site of the Gordon camp.

When he rode up, Eliza stood next to the cookfire, a hand raised to shield her eyes against the glare of the sun. The ravages of the trail were evident in the stringy thinness of her arms and the dark hollows under her eyes. Looking at her dirty and matted hair, her ragged and soiled clothes, Jed was more conscious of his own cleanness than ever.

"Lieutenant Parmelee. Without your beard, I almost didn't recognize you," Eliza said when he reined in. "Step down and warm yourself by the fire. Although it isn't all that cold today. I can't help wondering why we could not have had some of this mild weather on the trail."

"I don't expect we will ever know the answer to that." He swung down from the saddle and scanned the camp. Except for the stout colored woman and her son, there was no one else in sight. "Where is everyone?"

"Will and Kipp went to apply for our rations," Eliza said, then hesitated. "Temple left this morning. They went to join The Blade's father. He emigrated here more than a year ago and built a home farther north along the Grand River."

"I'm surprised the rest of you didn't go with them."

"The Blade and his father are members of the treaty party. They signed it. To live with them, even for a short time—" Eliza searched for the words that would explain the deep resentment Will would have felt, with all the pain and suffering of the trail still fresh. Not to mention the violent hatred Kipp felt. Finally she settled for an inadequate "It would never have worked."

Jed tried to think of something else to say—anything— but the words wouldn't come. Temple was gone, and he'd had no chance to tell her good-bye.

"I . . . I wish I had known Temple was leaving. I would have liked to wish her well."

"I am sure Temple knew that."

"I am leaving myself in the morning, traveling by riverboat this time," Jed explained. "Before I left, I wanted to come by and . . . tell you all good-bye, I guess." He inwardly struggled to hold on to his purpose in coming. Without Temple here, he had no desire to linger.

"I will tell the others for you. I know Will will be sorry he wasn't here to wish you a safe journey home. You were a friend to us, Jed. Thank you."

"Good luck to you." Jed climbed back on his horse and turned it toward the fort.

All the way back, he kept telling himself it was just as well he hadn't seen Temple again. It was over. She had made her choice. In his pocket was a letter from Cecilia. Written just before Christmas, it had been waiting for him when he arrived. She had suggested a spring wedding. Why not? Jed thought, gripped now by a mood of sober resignation.

As Eliza laid Will's freshly laundered spare shirt atop the blanket on the ground inside the tent, she noticed a tear in the sleeve. Sighing, she picked up the shirt and examined the rip. She supposed she could patch it with some material from her petticoat. The poor undergarment was so tattered now it was hardly worth wearing.

"Miss Eliza," Shadrach called from outside the tent.

"Yes, what is it?" She didn't mean to sound so tired and irritable, and lonely. Temple had left only this morning. It was silly to be missing her already. Yet the camp seemed so quiet and empty without Temple, The Blade, and little Lije . . . and Deu and Phoebe, too.

"There's a rider coming this way," Shadrach said.

"I will be right out." Eliza refolded the shirt and put it back on the blanket, unable to summon any enthusiasm for the unknown visitor, certain it was probably someone looking for Will. With an effort, she pushed to her feet and crossed to the tent flap. When she lifted the canvas aside, she felt the soreness of her raw, chapped hands. Momentarily preoccupied with the throbbing pain in them, she stared blankly at the man on horseback.

"Hello." He leaned forward in the saddle. "Do you speak English?"

Frowning, Eliza nodded. That voice, it sounded as if it belonged to someone she had known long ago. Or was it only her imagination conjuring up something familiar?

The slanting rays of a setting sun shadowed the man's face. He dismounted to stand beside his horse. "I am Reverend Cole from the Dwight Mission."

"Nathan." She spoke his name in shock and took a single step forward. "Nathan?" She questioned her own eyes. Did that bulky coat hide a slim, gangly figure? Was there a thatch of sandy hair under that hat? "Is that you, Nathan Cole?"

"Yes." He moved hesitantly toward her. "I'm sorry. Do I know y—Eliza?" He frowned in disbelief.

"Yes." She swallowed back the hysterical laugh that tried to bubble out of her throat. She knew how she must look to him, her dirty hair all loose and matted instead of tightly pinned in its bun, her gown soiled and torn with a blanket draped around her shoulders instead of a shawl, her skin chapped and red instead of fair and smooth, not to mention the weight she had lost and the hollows under her eyes. "I know I don't resemble the Eliza you remember, but it really is me."

"How—" Nathan seized her arms and held her away from him, unable to believe his eyes. "What are you doing here? I thought you had gone home to New England. How did you get here?"

"I came with the Gordons." Eliza could feel the tears coming.

"Over the trail?" Nathan said incredulously.

"Yes."

"But . . . how? You're—"

"I claimed I was a cousin. Although actually no one even asked whether I was Cherokee or not," Eliza remembered, then noticed the look on his face. "I couldn't leave them, Nathan. I couldn't let them go through all that alone. They needed me. They . . . needed me." Her voice trailed off to a whisper as tears began to roll down her cheeks. When she swayed toward him, Nathan gathered her into his gentle embrace. She rested her cheek against the wool of his coat, letting it absorb her tears. "Little Johnny, the baby, he died while we were in the detention camp. Then on the trail, Xandra died . . . and Victoria. Shadrach's father, Ike, is dead as well."

She wept softly, crying for those they had buried, for the suffering they had all known, for the grandeur of Gordon Glen forever lost to them, for the log schoolhouse she had taught in, and the clothes and personal items she had been forced to leave behind. It was gone. It was all gone.

"I'm sorry," Nathan murmured when she finished.

"We lost virtually everything." Eliza breathed in deeply to check the flow of tears. Drawing back, she self-consciously wiped the tears from her cheeks. "I had forgotten how easy it always was to talk to you. I have missed that."

"I have . . . often thought about you."

"I haven't asked how you are," Eliza realized guiltily.

"I am fine." He dismissed the question with a quick shake of his head.

"Would you like some coffee? I can have Cassie put some on to boil. Although, I warn you, there is more chicory than coffee in it."

"No, I don't want any." He sounded impatient with her. "Eliza, I can't allow this deception of yours to continue. You can't live like this." He swept a hand at the tent, the primitive cookfire, and her own disheveled appearance. "I want you to come back to the mission with me. The women there can look after you and—"

"No."

"It isn't right, Eliza. I will be leaving for Tennessee in a week or two. You can travel with me."

"I am grateful for your concern, Nathan, but I am not leaving here, not after all I have gone through to get here."

"But what will you do?"

Just then Eliza saw Will and Kipp approaching the camp. "We have a visitor, Will," she called to him. Will hesitated in midstride, then continued toward them. Eliza noticed for the first time the faint stoop of his broad shoulders and the distinct sprinkling of gray in his hair. "You remember Nathan Cole, don't you?" she said as Will walked to them.

"Yes, of course, Reverend Cole." He reached out to shake hands with him, rags still tied around his own for gloves.

"Mr. Gordon," Nathan acknowledged. "It has been a long time."

"Yes," Will agreed, then glanced at Eliza, a deep, haunting sadness in his eyes. Finally, he looked back at Nathan. "Several years ago, you performed a marriage ceremony for my daughter. Would you be kind enough to perform the same service for Eliza and myself?" He ignored the surprised look on Nathan's face and glanced again at Eliza. "That is, of course, if it is agreeable to you?"

She didn't understand why he considered it necessary to ask. "It is."

There had never been any discussion of marriage between them, not even after Victoria had died. In the back of her mind, Eliza had known Will was free to marry her, but it hadn't seemed important, involved as they were in a daily struggle just to survive. It had always been something she would think about another day, when she was warm and the ordeal was over. Now that day had come—for both of them.

She completely forgot that she had ever told Nathan she was never going to marry. When he pronounced them man and wife, she didn't hear his voice break or notice the stiffness of his features. She was Mrs. Will Gordon now.

ᘓ 32 ᘔ

Cherokee Nation, Indian Territory
June 1839

The tension at the table was dreadful, belying the cheerful twittering of the birds. Out of the corner of her eye, Eliza watched as Black Cassie served Nathan a portion of fresh green beans from a clay bowl, a bowl Eliza had crudely fashioned and baked herself. The ladle Cassie used had been carved out of wood by Kipp, as were nearly all their utensils.

Certain that she had never endured a situation as awkward and uncomfortable as this, Eliza fixed her gaze on the table-top's rough planks. She had no cloth to cover it, and if she had, the numerous splinters of wood sticking up would have snagged it. Why had she suggested that they have their noon meal outside where the sunlight could expose the rustic simplicity of their existence? But it would have been worse if Nathan had seen the inside of the primitively furnished shack that was their home.

Self-consciously, she reached up and felt the back of her hair to make certain the mass of long curls was still securely bound by the childish blue ribbon. There hadn't been time to sweep it into a neat bun. When Nathan came riding up around midmorning, she had been unable to do more than pull the kerchief off her head, quickly run a brush through the tangle of thick curls, and tie it at the nape of her neck with the ribbon.

As for changing clothes, Eliza had nothing better than what she was wearing now. The top was one of Will's shirts that she had cut down, and she had pieced together the skirt with material from her old petticoats. With Cassie's help, she had made up some indigo dye and dyed them both blue. The apron was one that Temple had given her. Eliza tucked her feet farther under the chair so her long skirt would hide the leather moccasins she wore, the only covering she had for them.

When Cassie served from the last of the dishes, Eliza dismissed her with a nod. She took a bit of food from her plate, then laid her fork down and hid her hands under the table so Nathan wouldn't see the rough calluses on them. She pretended to be interested in what he was saying, but she kept thinking this was all a farce. She sat at the foot of the table, directing her Negro servant, and acting like she was mistress of some great plantation when nothing could have been farther from the truth.

Why was she trying so desperately to convince Nathan that everything was fine? Nothing was fine.

Will sat at the head of the rectangular table, as befitted the master of a plantation. Eliza watched as he methodically ate the food on his plate, taking a bite, chewing it slowly, and taking another bite. When Will had selected this plot of land located a few miles from the Stuarts, Eliza had thought they were putting the past behind them and starting over, just as Shawano Stuart had done with Temple and The Blade's help.

In some respects, they had accomplished a great deal in three months, but Eliza knew a lot more could have been done. They had a roof over their heads, something to sit on, and vegetables in the garden, but no fields were plowed, no crops planted, no livestock bought except for some chickens. And Will didn't care.

He had changed. That's what hurt. In the past he had rarely smiled. Now he never did. Once, having a visitor at the table would have meant lively conversation. Will would have asked endless questions about conditions elsewhere, the latest news, the current political or economic situation. Yet he had barely said ten words to Nathan since he had arrived.

In the beginning, she had blamed his lethargy and indifference on the trail, aware that it had drained them all, physically and emotionally. The memory of that terrible ordeal would always be there. She didn't expect him to forget it. She knew she couldn't.

Eliza had tried to be patient and understanding. Black Cassie and Shadrach had helped her dig up the soil for a garden, plant the seeds, and hoe the weeds. She hadn't asked Will to join them. Shadrach and Kipp had cut the wood, hewn it into planks, and built the crude table and chairs. Eliza had tried to make do and not press Will to improve their circumstances. She hadn't uttered one word of complaint when he sat for hours on end staring into space while she saw to it there was food on the table and clothes on their backs.

But she didn't know how much longer she could endure. She was his wife, and she was becoming the very thing she had sworn she would never be—a man's drudge with no freedom to call her own. What good was her education if she spent the rest of her life standing over a kettle of laundry, patching ragged clothes, and cooking meals—not just for him, but for his grown son and two black slaves?

"How is Temple?"

Belatedly, Eliza realized that Nathan had addressed the question to her. "Fine," she said quickly and wished he hadn't mentioned her, fearing it would set Kipp off on another of his vindictive diatribes against those who had signed the treaty forcing them to this place.

"On my way here, I passed their fields. They have a fine stand of corn growing," Nathan remarked.

"Why should that surprise you?" Kipp challenged. "The traitors claimed all the best land for themselves when they came here."

"Kipp," Eliza murmured in warning.

But he wouldn't listen. He never did. "It's true," he insisted bitterly. "They sold our land, then came here and took the best of this for themselves. They killed my mother, my baby brother, and my sister as surely as if they had plunged a knife in their hearts. They are the reason we lost everything, and why we are living like this today. They did this to us!" Kipp pushed his chair back and stormed away from the table.

Eliza glanced at Will, but he didn't call his son back and insist that he apologize for his rudeness. Awkwardly, she tried to cover for him. "Kipp blames the treaty party for everything. He has been consumed with hatred since we arrived here."

"I understand." Nathan smiled gently.

She didn't . . . not any of it.

As soon as Will finished his meal, he excused himself from the table and wandered off. Probably to sit somewhere and stare, Eliza thought as she watched him walk away. She felt the smoothness of Nathan's fingers slide onto her wrist and press lightly, offering comfort.

"Eliza." His voice, his face, held pity.

She wanted to cry. But she refused to give in to the threatening tears. There were already enough people in this family feeling sorry for themselves.

"Are you finished?" She forced a lightness into her question, not caring that it might sound brittle. "Let's go for a walk. Cassie can clear the table." She knew she was playing the role of the idle grande dame, trying to appear carefree and intent only on entertaining her visitor.

"I would like that."

"When you came to Gordon Glen, we used to go for walks all the time. Remember?" The instant the words were out of her mouth, Eliza realized that she, too, was guilty of clinging to a past that was gone.

"Yes, I remember." But he seemed vaguely troubled by the memory.

"How was your trip east? You have hardly mentioned it

at all." She thought to change the subject, but judging by the frown on his face, her choice wasn't the best one. "What's wrong?"

"Nothing."

"Yes, there is." Eliza wasn't fooled by his denial. "You might as well tell me."

"I didn't want to. I guess that's why I have avoided talking about the trip, in case I accidentally mentioned . . ."

"Mentioned what?"

"I went back to Red Clay with Dr. Butler to help him pack his belongings and bring his family here." Again he paused as if reluctant to continue.

"I know that much, Nathan."

"I was curious, I suppose, to see what things were like, so I took a tour through the area. I went to Gordon Glen." Tilting his head, he looked up to the sky, his Adam's apple jutting out like a large knot in his neck. "Dear God in heaven, I wasn't prepared for what I found."

"What?" Unconsciously, Eliza stiffened, bracing herself against his answer.

"It is so ironic, Eliza," he murmured. "I went there expecting to see . . . It doesn't matter." He shook off the thought. "Weeds had taken over the fields. The house . . . the house was empty. It was the same at farm after farm. Deserted. Abandoned. The Georgians took them and then—they left them. They were so determined, so ruthless about wresting the land from the Cherokees. Now they have it and it lies fallow. It's insanity."

Stunned, Eliza remembered the hot, dry summer they had spent penned in the camp and the chain of graves that marked the long trail they had walked. "Why?" she whispered.

"I was told some of them packed up and moved west to find out if this land was as rich and filled with plenty as the government assured the Cherokees it was."

"No." The protest was little more than a moan.

"Yes."

In her mind, she kept seeing Gordon Glen as he had described it—rundown and abandoned, the black eyes of the mansion's windows staring out over a lawn choked with weeds.

She recalled a line of Wordsworth's: "Dear God! the very houses seem asleep, / And all that mighty heart is lying still!"

"I shouldn't have said anything," Nathan said.

"It is so wrong . . . so unfair. But it's done. We cannot change that. I suppose that is the hardest part to accept." She discovered the tears in her eyes and blinked quickly to clear them. "It is futile to keep crying over what has been lost. We must go on."

"Then it is still 'we'?"

"Yes."

Several seconds went by in silence, then Nathan ended it. "I don't know what is the matter with me. I meant to give this to you earlier." He removed a square package from the side pocket of his black frock coat and handed it to her. "I bought it for you while I was east. A wedding gift. Not a very practical one, I'm afraid."

"A book." As soon as she touched it, she knew.

"Emerson's *Nature*. I am told it is quite good."

She ripped off the brown paper that concealed it. The instant her fingers came in contact with the finely grained leather cover, they began to lovingly caress it. "A book. It has been so long since I touched one." Eliza clasped it to the bodice of her apron and gazed at Nathan, her eyes blurring with tears. "It is the perfect gift, the most precious thing in the world. Thank you." Her voice wavered badly, choked by the welling emotion inside.

"I . . ." He glanced back at the shack. "I wish it were more. I wish—"

But she couldn't let him say it. "Will is going to be so happy when I show it to him. This will be the first volume in our new library."

Quickly, Nathan masked his look of skepticism that they

would ever have a house with a library. "Of course." He hesitated, then added, too casually, "I fear I have tarried here longer than I should. It's time I was on my way."

"I suppose it is." Eliza avoided his gaze, aware of the awkward tension that made both of them choose their words so carefully.

"If there is ever anything I can do, you have only to get word to the mission and . . ."

"Thank you. I will remember that."

When they returned to the clearing, Eliza sent Shadrach to fetch Nathan's horse. Neither Will nor Kipp were anywhere around. Nathan left without telling them good-bye.

Watching him ride away, Eliza recalled that long-ago day when he had proposed to her. She couldn't help thinking how different her life would be if she had married him. She would still be teaching instead of working from dawn to dusk trying to keep food on the table and clothes on her back. Tears burned her eyes, tears of resentment and frustration.

"Is that a book?" Shadrach stared at the bound volume clutched to her apron-covered bodice.

"Yes." Absently she stroked it, conscious of the smoothness of the leather and the roughness of her hands. "It has been so long since I held one. It seems like a lifetime ago. What has happened to us, Shadrach?" Eliza murmured.

"You are tired. Why don't you go rest?" he suggested gently.

For an instant she was tempted to give in to the weariness that claimed her body and soul, but she shook her head. "There is too much work to do. Where is Will? I wanted him to stop up that hole in the coop before raccoons get any more of our hens."

"I think he went down by the river."

"Go tell him—never mind, I will tell him myself. Here, put this in the house for me." She shoved the book into his hands and set off for the river, anger simmering just below the surface.

She found Will sitting on the bank, leaning against the trunk of a cottonwood, his arms listlessly resting on his upraised knees, his hands dangling while he stared indifferently at the murky, red-brown water. He barely looked at her when she walked up.

"Nathan left. He said to tell you good-bye." When she heard the kindly pitch of her voice, Eliza became irritated with herself, and tired of being patient and understanding. "You were supposed to repair the coop this afternoon. If all you plan to do instead is sit here, at least you could catch some fish for supper tonight."

"I forgot about the coop," he said. "Have Kipp—no, he left."

"He left? To go where?"

"To the council meeting at Takatokah."

"But—" Eliza frowned. "I thought—aren't you going?"

"No."

"Why? You've always attended the council sessions in the past."

"That was before."

The lethargy in his voice was more than she could stand. "But this is the first meeting here, the first time the western Cherokees have met with you in council since they emigrated here nearly thirty years ago. How can you miss an occasion like this?"

"It doesn't matter." He stared off into the distance.

"How can you say that? Of course it matters."

"There will be others to take my place." A hint of impatience crept into his voice at her persistent prodding.

"But how many of them will be like Kipp, filled with hate for the treaty party? You know as well as I do the hostility that abounds here, the enmity that has surfaced everywhere since we arrived. How long do you think John Ross can stand alone against the calls for vengeance? What has happened to you?"

"Eliza, I am tired."

"So am I! I am tired of watching you feel sorry for yourself day after day. Do you think you are the only one who has suffered? Thousands of others buried family members on that horrible trail, including John Ross. His wife died of pneumonia after she gave her blanket to a sick child. Oh, Will, why can't you see that the time for weeping is over?" Eliza demanded angrily. "Now is the time to begin again, to build a new home—"

"Build for whom?" Will finally looked at her, his brown eyes dark with pain. "Do I build for little Johnny? We buried him at the camp. Xandra's grave lies near the Mississippi. Victoria's dead, too. So tell me, for whom should I build again?"

"For us! For our baby!"

His stunned expression dissolved almost immediately into one of regret. "Eliza, no," he murmured.

Stunned by his reaction to the news, she turned and ran for the shack. All the way, she listened for the sound of his footsteps behind her, hoping against hope that he would come after her and tell her that he truly wanted this child. But there was nothing, nothing but the rustling of the tall grass in the wind and the *ka-leep, ka-leep* of a scissortail in the meadow.

The emotional pain was real and deep, but Eliza wouldn't let herself cry. To cry meant to admit that she was as weak as he was. She wasn't. She would never be. She was going to have this baby and see that it had a good home, with or without his help.

She approached the shack and saw Shadrach sitting on the rickety stoop reading the book Nathan had given her. With so much work to be done, his idleness infuriated her.

"What are you doing with that? I told you to put it away. I didn't give you permission to read it." She snatched it from his hands, blind to the startled and hurt look on his face. "Go find a stick or something and repair that coop. When you get that done, go hoe the weeds in the garden. I will not tolerate any more of this sitting around." She pushed by him and stormed into the shack. When she saw Cassie standing in front of the dishpan, she stopped abruptly. "Haven't you finished washing the dishes yet? Am I surrounded on all sides by sloth and laziness? Must I do everything myself?"

Eliza dropped the book on a chair and continued on to the crude wooden stand that served as both sink and worktable. "At the rate you are moving, it will be suppertime before you finish. Give me that."

Impatiently, she reached for the clay bowl Cassie was scouring, but the wet sides of the bowl slipped from her fingers. Eliza cried out in dismay as the homemade pottery crashed to the floor, breaking into pieces.

"My bowl." She fell to her knees.

"I'll picks 'em up fo' you, Miz 'Liza." Cassie stooped down to collect the broken pieces.

"I don't need your help," Eliza retorted. "I don't need anyone's help. Just . . . go away and leave me alone."

Outside the shack, Will heard every unusually harsh word Eliza had spoken. And each one struck him like the lash of a whip. He had never meant to hurt her. But he had. She was going to have a baby—his baby. He had buried so many.

Slowly, Will walked to the doorway, then paused. Black Cassie continued to hover beside Eliza. Will nodded for her to leave them. As Cassie's broad, bare feet carried her to the doorway, Eliza let the rest of the pieces lie untouched on the floor, her shoulders sagging in an attitude of defeat. For a few seconds, Will stared at her bowed head. What had he done to her? He took a step toward her.

Hearing it, Eliza immediately busied herself gathering up the rest of the broken pieces. "I dropped it," she said defensively. "It was the best bowl I made, too. Shadrach will have to dig some more clay and make another one."

Will hesitated a fraction of a second, then said, "Don't bother. On my way back from the council meeting, I will stop by the sutler's store and buy some dishes and whatever else we need."

When he mentioned the council meeting, she looked up sharply, but didn't remark on his sudden decision. "I thought we couldn't afford such things."

"He will give us credit. Make a list of the things we need so I can take it with me."

"I will."

As he turned away, he spotted the leather-bound book on the chair. "What is this?"

"A gift from Nathan."

"That was thoughtful of him."

"Yes, it was," she agreed briskly.

"You would have been better off if you had married him when he asked you, Eliza. You would have been spared a lot of hardship and suffering."

"Have I ever complained, Will Gordon?" she demanded.

"No, but—"

"And I won't, either. I never asked to be spared anything. And I don't regret refusing to marry Nathan. I didn't love him." She gathered up the material of her long apron, making a pouch out of it. "When are you leaving to go to the meeting?"

"This afternoon."

"I'll get started on the list right away. Tell Cassie to come back and finish the dishes."

Nearly six thousand attended the council meeting at Takatokah, called by the western Cherokees ostensibly to welcome the new arrivals. The first days were a reunion of sorts, with everyone getting acquainted and reacquainted with each other. Will tried to join in, but he found the reminiscences about the past painful. He was glad when John Brown, the chief of the western Cherokees, stepped up to address the gathering, signaling the beginning of the formal speeches of welcome.

"We joyfully welcome you to our country. The whole land is before you. You may freely go wherever you choose and select any places for settlement which may please you, with this restriction, that you do not interfere with the private rights of individuals. You are fully entitled to the elective franchise, are lawful voters in any of the districts in which you reside, and are eligible to any of the offices within the gift of the people. Next October, according to law, the term of service of the chiefs will expire and any of you are eligible to those seats. Next July will be an election in our districts for members of both houses of our legislature, for judges, sheriffs, et cetera. At those elections you will be voters and you are eligible to any of those offices. A government was, many years since, organized in this country, and a code of laws was established, suited to our condition and under which our people have lived in peace and prosperity. It is expected that you will all be subject to our government and laws until they shall be constitutionally altered or repealed and that in all this you will demean yourselves as good and peaceable citizens."

But John Ross objected to the loose form of government practiced by the western Cherokees and urged that the code of law be revised and extended, and a new constitution written. At approximately the same time as the proposals and counterproposals were going back and forth, Will noticed Shawano Stuart and The Blade arrive, along with the Ridges, Elias Boudinot, and several other members of the treaty party. They immediately became the cynosure of hostile glares.

"Why are those traitors here?" Kipp snarled. "John Ross should order them to leave."

"He seeks peace and a united Cherokee Nation. He has never once wavered from that goal," Will replied thoughtfully, aware that their leader had never stopped fighting despite the personal losses he had suffered.

"But he forgets our laws," Kipp stated and stalked away.

Gazing after him, Will realized for the first time how all-consuming his son's hatred had become. Kipp had always been angry about something, but this behavior went beyond anger and resentment to something much more volatile and violent. And the faces of the men now joining his son showed the same thirst for vengeance that was so evident in Kipp's.

⤇ 33 ⤆

*H*eavy with child, Phoebe waddled to the chair next to Temple's, then carefully eased herself into it and leaned back to enjoy the cool breeze that wafted through the dogtrot of the double log cabin. When she placed a hand on the large mound of her protruding stomach, Temple caught the movement and glanced sharply at her.

"Are you all right?" She continued rhythmically snapping beans into the pan on her lap while she studied her maid. The baby wasn't due for another two months yet, but babies didn't always come when they were due.

"I'm fine." Phoebe picked up the pail of beans and lodged it between her knees. "With as much kicking and carrying on as this baby's doing, it has to be a boy. Little Lije was like that, wasn't he?"

"He was very active." Temple smiled at her son, who was happily rocking back and forth on the wooden horse Shawano had made for him, complete with a set of leather reins.

From the dogtrot, Temple could watch the work being done on their new home. Already, wooden planks skirted the lower half of the skeletal frame of the two-story house. Nestled amidst a grove of trees with a hill rising behind it to break the north wind, the house was large, larger even than their previous home in what was now Georgia.

Within days after rejoining his father, The Blade had started working on plans for the house. A month later, he hired a master carpenter from Arkansas and construction on it had begun.

Often in the first few months, Temple had wondered at the change in him. Before, he had left most of the decisions to his father, but here he had taken charge almost from the moment they arrived. In nearly any direction she looked, she could see the results of his recent labors, from the enlarged Negro quarters to the orchard of young apple and peach trees; from the new fields of cotton and corn to the new storage sheds. She had never seen him work so long or so hard, but he had a son now. She was certain that was the cause.

Again she smiled at Lije as he rocked vigorously back and forth, exhorting his wooden steed to go faster. The gleaming black hair came from both of them, but the deep blue shade of his eyes came from The Blade. Lije wasn't three yet, but already he had a mind of his own.

Hearing a whisper of movement behind her, Temple started to turn. Phoebe screamed and struggled out of her chair, dumping the pail of beans onto the dirt floor of the dogtrot. Temple came quickly to her feet.

"Kipp." All the high alertness and tension drained from her in a rush of relief. "We never heard you ride up. Where is your horse?" She expected to see it tied to the rear post of the dogtrot, but it wasn't there.

"I left it back in the trees. Are you alone?" He stayed in the deep shadows of the cabin wall, his gaze darting suspiciously about.

When Lije ran over and hid behind her skirts, Temple grew irritated with her brother. "No, I am not alone. Phoebe and Lije are here."

"That isn't what I meant."

"No, they are not here," she snapped, well aware that he was referring to The Blade and Shawano. Forcing the anger from her voice, she bent down and gently pushed Lije toward a kneeling Phoebe. "Help Phoebe pick up the beans and put them in the pail." But she made no attempt to keep the anger from her expression when she faced Kipp. "Don't sneak up on us like that again."

"I never meant to frighten you."

"Well, you did. Now, what is it you want?"

"To see you." He shifted uncomfortably, but never left the shadows. "I was on my way home. The council meeting adjourned today." His eyes took on a mean look. "I noticed your husband didn't stay long."

"No, he didn't." The Blade attended only one day of the session. From what little he had told her, Temple surmised that he and the others hadn't been made to feel welcome.

"He was there long enough to cause trouble. He and the Ridges were seen talking to Brown. Everyone knows they convinced the western Cherokees to walk out of the meeting without voting on Ross's proposal to write a new constitution and code of laws."

"I know nothing about that." The pounding of a hammer echoed across the clearing.

"Your new house?"

"Yes." She nodded affirmatively.

"A new house, an orchard, new fields. And we live in a shanty that wouldn't have been considered fit for our Negroes at Gordon Glen."

"You can build something better."

"With what?" He sneered. "The government hasn't paid *us* yet for our home and property. And when they do, it won't be as much as they paid your husband and his father for theirs, even though ours was worth more."

"I don't know that and neither do you!" Temple flared.

"If you only came to hurl more of your accusations at my husband, then you can leave right now. I don't want to hear it."

"I—I came to ask you to come visit Eliza tomorrow. She has been alone lately. She could use some company. And I know Father would like to see you too."

Taken aback by his unexpected request, Temple didn't know what to say. Somehow this concern for Eliza and her father didn't sound like Kipp.

"Will you come tomorrow?" There was an edge to his voice that took the question and turned it into a demand.

"I am not certain I can. The Blade sent word he would be back tomorrow."

"Where is he?"

Temple hesitated, fighting the uneasiness she felt at Kipp's questions. "He went to Arkansas to buy more blacks."

"And he'll be back tomorrow. What time?"

"Early afternoon, I expect. Why?"

Kipp shrugged. "If he won't be back till then, you can still come visit in the morning, have dinner, and be back here in the afternoon."

"I suppose."

"Doesn't the old man spend his mornings at the sawmill?"

"Yes." She eyed him suspiciously. "How did you know?"

"That's the talk around. I heard you could set your clock by him, that he leaves every day exactly at eleven-thirty for dinner."

"He usually comes home for dinner if there aren't any problems at the mill," Temple admitted, then frowned. "Why are you asking me all these questions?"

"Because I want you to see that you have no reason for not coming tomorrow."

"Why does it have to be tomorrow?"

"Why not tomorrow? It has been nearly two months since your last visit."

"I know." What with the new house, spring work, and sudden rainstorms, something always seemed to prevent her from going.

"Temple, when have I ever asked you to do something for me? Please, I want you to come tomorrow. It's important. I wouldn't ask otherwise," Kipp insisted, the urgency in his voice as frightening as the look in his black eyes. "Will you come? Do I have to beg?"

"No. I'll be there." She hadn't realized how much tension had been in him until she saw the relief smooth it from his broad features.

"Good." He smiled.

Kipp stayed a few more minutes, then left. Temple moved to the back of the dogtrot and watched him cross the narrow clearing behind the log cabin. *Cunning, furtive.* Temple didn't want to associate those words with her brother, yet those were the impressions he had given her.

He was a man now, with wide, muscled shoulders like their father's but without his extreme height. She found it difficult to think of her brother as being handsome, but he was.

She had become used to his spiteful anger and his vicious prejudices. Sometimes she forgot how hard he had taken Xandra's death and, even harder for him, their mother's. His family and their well-being were important to him. He did care. As much as Kipp hated The Blade, and as upset as he was that she had gone back to him, he hadn't turned his back on her. He still came to see her. She shouldn't have been surprised by his concern over Eliza and their father or his insistence that she come to visit.

When he reached the spot where he had concealed his horse, Kipp untied the reins and swung quickly into the saddle. When the horse and rider emerged from the trees and entered a patch of bright sunlight, Temple saw the horse's lathered sides. Why had he ridden his horse into a sweat just to get here? Why the urgency? Temple became uneasy all over again, doubt and suspicion rushing back.

* * *

A black cloud moved stealthily across the moon, stealing its light and intensifying the darkness of the midnight hour. The flames from a half dozen torches dipped and swayed in the errant night breeze as if dancing to the rhythm of silent drums. Their wavering glow played across the faces of the men closest to them, many of which were hidden behind masks. Beyond the yellow light, the night seemed darker, making indistinct the shadowy shapes of more men, several hundred on foot and on horseback.

Kipp stood among them, his lips dry, his stomach muscles knotted with tension. Blood thudded through his veins. His breath came shallow and fast. A black kerchief was tied around his neck, ready to be raised to conceal the lower half of his face. Tiny beads of sweat formed on his upper lip, but he didn't wipe at them. He didn't want to draw attention to himself. Gripped by an icy-cold excitement that both chilled and stimulated, Kipp shook inside. He was afraid, yet eager, a potent combination that seemed to heighten all his senses and fill him with a wild kind of exhilaration and apprehension. He was certain the warriors of old must have felt this way on the eve of a raid on the enemy.

A man stepped into the center of the secret gathering, the flickering torchlight casting shadows over the planes of his face. He held a paper in his hand and began to read from it, a deadly flatness in his voice.

" 'Whereas a law has been in existence for many years, but not committed to writing, that if any citizen or citizens of this nation should treat and dispose of any lands belonging to this nation without special permission from the national authorities, he or they shall suffer death.' " It was the Blood Law of the Cherokees.

After it was read in full, the accused were named: Major Ridge, who had once been among the executioners of the chieftain Doublehead, who had violated the Blood Law thirty years ago; his son John Ridge, the author of the written law that had just been read; his cousin Elias Boudinot and Boudinot's brother Stand Watie; John A. Bell; George Adair; James Starr; Shawano Stuart; The Blade Stuart; and the others who had signed the false treaty.

There, in the black hour of midnight at the secret meeting grounds, court was convened, and judges heard the evidence against each of the accused. Their verdict was the same in every instance: guilty. The sentence was death.

Numbers corresponding to the number of men present were placed in a hat. Beside twelve of the numbers, there was an *X* mark. It was the duty of the twelve who drew the marked numbers to carry out the court's death sentence. Everyone came forward and drew a number from the hat—everyone except Allen Ross, the son of their chief. He was asked to return home and stay with his father and try to prevent him from learning of their plans.

Kipp stepped forward, dry-mouthed, and pulled a number from the hat. The *X* leapt out at him. The blood pounded in his ears like a thousand war drums. Once the initial shock passed, a calmness settled over him. He thought of the blood that had drenched Xandra's skirt, remembered the smell of it and the sticky wetness, and recalled the dark stain it had left on his own clothes. His mother, and the blood she coughed up. And his little brother. He would have his chance to avenge their deaths and he was glad of it. Glad.

Shortly after breakfast the next morning, one of the black cooks accidentally knocked over a kettle, spilling boiling water onto a young helper. The carriage had just pulled up in front of the house to transport Temple and Lije to her father's when Temple heard the earsplitting shriek. She ran to the kitchen and found the twelve-year-old colored girl screaming in agony. Both legs were burned from the upper part of her thighs down to her bare feet. Her skin already showed signs of blistering.

The next hour was a chaos of sobbing, frantic orders, and

endless advice. Temple sent someone to fetch her basket of medicine. She slathered a creamy salve on the girl's legs, then had a litter carry the writhing girl to her cabin in the black quarters. There Temple administered a heavy dose of laudanum to ease the girl's pain.

When she left the cabin, there was Lije, playing in a water puddle with two half-naked Negro children close to his own age. His clothes, his face, his hair were coated with mud. Temple marched him back to the log house, where she bathed him, washed his hair, and dressed him in clean clothes.

"Miss Temple." Phoebe paused in the doorway, one hand pressing at the small of her back. "Dulcie just told me that in all the confusion with the accident in the kitchen, she forgot to put the roast on to cook. She wants to know what she should fix Master Stuart for dinner now."

"How could she forget?" Impatiently, Temple raked the comb through Lije's wet hair, ignoring the face he made as the teeth dug into his scalp. "I don't know why it should surprise me," she muttered irritably. "Nothing else has gone right this morning. What time is it?"

"I heard the clock strike half past ten a few minutes ago."

"Is it that late?" Temple pushed to her feet. "Finish combing Lije's hair while I go to the kitchen and see about dinner."

"But aren't you—"

"There is no point in going to see Father and Eliza now. I would have to turn around and leave almost as soon as I got there. We'll go tomorrow. Kipp will have to understand that this morning has been one calamity after another!"

A little more than an hour later, substituting smoked ham for the beef roast, Temple had the noon meal ready to serve and the table set. She stepped outside to check on Lije. He was there, pretending to feed blades of grass to his rocking horse.

"He likes it, Mama. I get some more." He ran to the grassy area in front of the cabin. Stopping, he pointed excitedly toward the road. "Look, Mama! Here comes Papa Stuart. Please, can we go meet him? I want to ride in his buggy."

Unable to resist the eager appeal of those brilliant blue eyes, Temple smiled and nodded permission. "But you have to walk with me. I don't want you running in front of the horse."

"Hurry, Mama." He ran back and grabbed her hand.

Responding to the tug of his hand, she quickened her pace to a running walk. When they reached the dirt road in front of the cabin, Temple saw the oncoming buggy and lifted a hand to wave to Shawano Stuart.

A dozen masked men sprang from behind the trees on either side of the road. Three of them grabbed the horse's bridle and forced it to a halt. "No." Temple caught Lije by the shoulders and pulled him back to her side. There was a flash of Shawano's silver-handled cane as he tried to beat off his attackers. "Phoebe!" she cried, then pushed Lije toward the cabin. "Go find Phoebe and stay with her. Quickly."

Instinctively, Temple ran toward the buggy. "No! What are you doing?" she cried, fear and anger mixing together. "Stop it!"

The men paid no attention to her as they pulled Shawano from the buggy. He struggled valiantly and Temple had a glimpse of the fierce fighter he had once been. Then the first knife was plunged into his back.

"No!" she screamed.

A man turned to block her path. When she saw the pair of dark accusing eyes above the black kerchief, Temple stopped. She didn't have to see the rest of his face. She recognized those eyes.

"Kipp, no," she moaned softly.

Before he turned away, she saw the lust for revenge that burned so vividly in his eyes. When he joined the others, Temple suddenly understood what was happening. Shawano Stuart was now paying the price for his crime against the

Nation. And the price was death. Ice cold, she watched knife after bloody knife tear at the old man's body. Unable to stand any more, she looked away, shutting her eyes in horror and revulsion.

"Papa Stuart! Papa Stuart!" Lije's sobbing voice sounded behind her.

She turned as he came running toward her. Phoebe lumbered after him as fast as her child-heavy body would allow. Temple scooped him into her arms and turned him away from the sight, forcing his head against her shoulder so he wouldn't witness the execution of his grandfather. She wished she could cover his ears so he wouldn't hear the sounds of the knives plunging into the body or the gasping moans.

She hugged Lije tightly, oblivious to his frightened struggles and the tears streaming down her cheeks. It was here, the day she had long dreaded. The Blade—had they killed him already? Or was his death yet to come? She sank to the ground, clutching their son in her arms.

The Blade. With each stab of the knife, she silently screamed his name. She couldn't pray for his life to be spared. She had known, as The Blade had known, that when he signed that treaty, he had signed the warrant for his death. He had sacrificed his life with that one act.

The dull thudding sound ceased. Unwillingly, her eyes were drawn to the death scene as the twelve executioners marched single file over the body, ritualistically stamping on the lifeless form, then continuing into the trees. She could hear the noisy rustling of horses in the woods, their snorts followed by the rapid pounding of hooves.

She was vaguely conscious of others venturing toward her, but Phoebe was the only one she took any notice of. "Take Lije away." Temple gave her frightened and weeping son into Phoebe's arms, shielding his eyes from the sight of his slain grandfather. "Don't let him see," she whispered, her own gaze riveted to the body.

Phoebe scurried away carrying Lije. Temple tried to go to

Shawano, but her legs were slow to cooperate. Finally, she knelt beside him and stared at the spreading scarlet stains from the multiple wounds to his chest. She lifted her glance to his face and the sightless eyes that stared directly into the sun. Slowly, tentatively, Temple reached out and gently closed their lids with the tips of her fingers.

He was dead.

"Shawano." She spoke his name softly and slid an arm under his head and shoulders, then pulled the heavy weight of him onto her, cradling his head on her lap. "He didn't see, Shawano." She smoothed his mane of snow white hair. "Your grandson didn't see."

Someone led the horse and buggy away while the rest drifted closer. Temple was too numbed by the violent tragedy to be more than remotely aware of the small crowd that gathered around her. There were no more tears to blur her eyes, no more sobs to choke her throat, just the horrible emptiness of grief, shock, and fear.

She heard the thunder of hoofbeats and felt the ground vibrating beneath her. A horse slid to a halt near her, its stiffened front legs entering the outside range of her vision. She didn't look up. Help had arrived too late for Shawano.

"Father," a voice groaned.

The Blade's voice. When he sank to the ground beside the body, Temple lifted her head. She had almost convinced herself she would never see him alive again. But there he was. She drank in the sight of him.

"You are alive. You are still alive," she whispered brokenly. "I thought they had killed you too."

Rage like none she had ever seen twisted his face. "Who?" he demanded thickly. "Who did this?"

"They were waiting for him . . . in the woods . . . when he came home for dinner." She had to force the words out. With each one it became more difficult to keep from crying. She didn't want to tell The Blade what had happened, she didn't want to describe it to him. She didn't want to hurt him with all the painful details. "He is dead. What does it matter who, or how?"

"Damn them." His shoulders slumped as he hung his head, pressing a white-knuckled fist to his face. "Damn them to hell."

She felt his pain and his anger. It tortured her, especially when she remembered she wasn't supposed to have been there this morning to witness it. "Kipp warned me, but I—"

"You knew!" The Blade seized her arm in an iron grip. "You knew and you stood by and let them murder him!"

"No, I—" Roughly, he released her and rolled swiftly to his feet. When she reached up, Temple saw the blood on her hand—Shawano's blood. "I didn't know."

It was true. She hadn't realized why Kipp had been so anxious for her to visit her father's . . . she hadn't guessed this was his reason.

But if she had, what would she have done? Shawano had broken the law. His death was inevitable. Knowing that, would she have kept silent? Dear God, she truly didn't know. She didn't think she would have, but how could she be sure?

The Blade swung away from her and snatched up the horse's trailing reins. Temple watched in disbelief as he stepped a foot into the stirrup. "Where are you going?"

His eyes were like chips of blue ice. "I will not make it so easy for the assassins to find me. They will have to search."

He couldn't believe she would betray him, thought Temple. But he did. It was there in the accusing glare of his eyes. He swung into the saddle and rode off into the woods.

"*I* wish she would stop crying," Will muttered under his breath as a tearful Phoebe shuffled out of the parlor. She hadn't stopped weeping and blowing her nose since they had arrived at the Stuarts' the previous afternoon.

"She is worried about Deu." Eliza spoke softly to keep her voice from carrying to Temple. "He went with The Blade."

"I know." Will sighed. He didn't object to the pregnant woman's concern for her man, but her tears were a constant reminder to Temple of yesterday's violence.

A violence that hadn't been limited to the killing of his old friend Shawano Stuart. At dawn yesterday, John Ridge had been dragged from his bed and taken outside. There he had been held and stabbed repeatedly while his family looked on. Elias Boudinot had been lured from the site of the new house he was building by men requesting medicine for ailing members of their family. Halfway to the mission, he had been stabbed in the back and his skull cleaved by a tomahawk. The body of Major Ridge had been found with five bullet holes in it along Line Road a mile inside Arkansas.

The Blade, Stand Watie, and others of the treaty party had managed to escape traps that had been set for them. All had taken to the hills. Some threatened to avenge the deaths of their comrades and kin by taking the life of John Ross. John Ross himself had been appalled when he learned of the killings and disavowed any knowledge of the perpetrators.

News of the deaths had spread like a grass fire whipped by angry winds. Feelings were running high throughout the entire Nation. Will knew it wasn't over and he was certain his daughter knew it as well.

She stood at the parlor window, staring at the freshly turned sod of Shawano Stuart's grave. There was a ghostly pallor to her face, which was wiped clean of any expression, as if she were waiting . . . waiting to receive word of The Blade's death. Even while he understood her lack of emotion, it frightened him. Temple, his strong, fiery daughter, was but a pale shadow of her former self—her graceful body rigid with tension, and her dark, luminous eyes painfully dry.

Eliza lightly squeezed his hand and whispered, "Ask her to come stay with us. It isn't good for her to remain here."

He nodded briefly and walked over to her. If she was aware of his presence, she gave no sign of it. "Temple, Eliza and I want you and Lije to come home with us."

"No." There was no emotion in her answer, just a simple refusal.

"I wouldn't suggest it if I didn't think it was best for you to get away."

"No," Temple repeated more forcefully, the tone of her voice still level. "I am not leaving here. This is my son's home. It is my home. There is a house to be built, crops to be tended, and a sawmill to run. No matter what happens, we will not leave."

Although Will doubted her calmness, her determination was unmistakable. He felt a swell of pride for this proud, courageous woman who was his daughter. He had lost so much, but looking at Temple, he realized how much he still had.

"If that is what you want, Temple, then I will do everything

I can to help. But I don't like the idea of you staying here alone. Kipp can—"

"No!" Her sudden flare of anger took him by surprise. Will remembered now the depth of Kipp's hatred toward all who had signed the treaty. How could he have forgotten the glitter of satisfaction that had been in his son's eyes when he had ridden home to inform them of the deaths of the Ridges, Boudinot, and, yes, Shawano? Will privately acknowledged that his choice of company for Temple had been a poor one and didn't argue with her further.

During the ride home that evening, the hills were bathed in the blood-red glow of a setting sun. Red, the color was everywhere in the Nation . . . and in the hearts of too many men. Will quietly studied Kipp when he joined them to ride alongside the team of horses. A rifle was in his hand, the long muzzle resting in the crook of his left arm.

Youth, Will thought, why did it behave so rashly without considering the consequences? A climate of fear and hatred now prevailed. Still, he recognized that it wasn't fair to blame only the young men. The swirl of rumors that had followed in the wake of the assassinations had claimed that older, supposedly wiser men had been involved as well.

How actively had his son participated in them? How damning was Kipp's absence? Had he been a member of one of the execution squads or merely a supporter? The questions haunted Will, but he didn't want to know the answers. Kipp was his son.

From the day he learned of the treaty, Will had deplored the actions of those who had signed it, regardless of their motives. They had broken the law. Yet, like John Ross, he had recognized that to take action against them could rip their nation apart at a time when they needed to stand together. And it was even more true today. The council meeting had shown that the western Cherokees and the treaty party were allied. Instead of uniting the various factions as Ross had hoped, the killings had created a rift even greater than before and made the possibility of a civil war very real. And his family—his son and daughter—was caught in the middle of the conflict.

All was quiet when they arrived home. Will halted the team in front of the shack, wrapped the reins around the brake handle, and climbed down. When he walked around the wagon to help Eliza, he noticed that Kipp didn't dismount.

Reaching up, he gripped Eliza by the waist and lifted her to the ground. Just for an instant, Will was conscious of the slight thickening of her middle. Briefly, he met the upward glance of her hazel eyes. He suddenly wondered whether their child's eyes would be flecked with gold like hers. With some surprise, he realized this was the first time he had thought of the baby growing in her womb as a living entity, separate and distinct yet forever a part of them.

"I will start supper while you unhitch the team." Eliza moved away.

He watched her, wanting to call her back and tell her what he was thinking. It had been a long time since he had talked to her. But Kipp was there. Will turned. "Give me a hand with the team."

"Call Shadrach. He's about somewhere. He can help you." Kipp's horse shifted beneath him as if anticipating a command. "I'm leaving. I will be gone a few days."

"Where?" Will noticed the way Kipp refused to look directly at him.

"To John Ross's home at Park Hill. I heard Watie has gathered a small army of men around him. He thinks Ross is responsible for his brother's death and seeks to avenge it by taking his life."

"So you go there to protect him."

"Yes. There are already twenty or so men around the house, but we don't know Watie's strength. General Arbuckle refuses to send any troops from Fort Gibson to protect Ross. He wants Ross to come in, but he will only arrest him if he does."

"Ross never sanctioned these assassinations, did he?" It was the closest Will would come to asking his son about his knowledge of the events.

"No."

That one answer told Will that Kipp knew a great deal more. "I didn't think so." Will climbed back onto the wagon seat.

Kipp rode off into the rose-purple twilight. Clicking to the team, Will drove the wagon over to the small corral and lean-to.

Black Cassie scooped the last of the eggs and wild onions out of the heavy iron skillet. Eliza checked the table to make certain all was in readiness for the evening meal. A cloth covered the plate of hot corn pone. The jars of molasses and honey were set out. The new dishes and tableware were in place.

Satisfied, she stepped to the doorway to summon Will to the table. As she started to call out, she saw him sitting on the stoop, staring at an evening star that glittered faintly in the purpling sky.

Eliza suddenly wanted to cry. When he had returned from the council meeting, she had gotten the impression that he had emerged from the cocoon of grief and melancholy that had surrounded him all these months. She had dared to hope that the Will Gordon she loved was back. But there he was again, staring into space, Shawano's death and the other killings sending him back into that world of black despair.

"Will." She heard the ache in her voice and tried to rid herself of it. "Supper is ready."

When he stood, she started to turn away. "Is that all?" he asked. Puzzled by his strange question, Eliza frowned at him. "Are you not going to lecture me on idleness?"

In the half-light of eventide, she couldn't be sure if that was a smile she saw in his eyes. She took a step closer, moving out of the doorway and onto the stoop. It was a smile.

"Will." Dazed, she reached out to touch him, afraid she was dreaming this.

But he took her hand and gently pulled her toward him. "I had forgotten how very beautiful you are," he murmured, then claimed her lips in a kiss that was at once sweet in its gentleness and searing in its passion. It had been months since he had kissed her like that. She dissolved against him, happy and confused, her heart racing, her mind spinning.

"I don't understand," she whispered against his shirt.

"I am not certain that I do either." He lifted her head away from his chest and framed her face in his hands, absently stroking her hair. "Somewhere on the trail, I lost my faith in tomorrow. I found it again. I don't know where or how. Maybe it came from the baby you are carrying, or maybe Temple's determination to build a home for her son, or maybe seeing Kipp's destructive hate. Or maybe it was your impatience and love. Or maybe it was all of that. I don't claim that it makes sense. I only know that before I didn't care, and now I want tomorrow to come."

"So do I." Eliza smiled through her tears, loving him more than she had thought it possible to love a man.

His hands slid down her shoulders. He turned, slipping an arm around her and holding her close to his side while he gazed at the shadowy land of their new home. "It's too late to plant any crops this year. But we have plenty of grass. We can sell the wagon and buy some cattle, fatten them on it. I know how to build, even though our cabin is a poor example of my work. I designed and constructed half the buildings at Gordon Glen. A lot of homes, barns, mills, and schools need to be built. If Temple will hire out two of her skilled blacks to help me, I can get my share of the contracts. It won't be easy at first, but we will make it."

"We will make it just fine." Listening to him, Eliza could picture it all happening.

"See that knoll over there." Will pointed to a large, dark hump of ground west of the cabin. "When the government pays us our compensation for Gordon Glen, that is where we will build our new home."

"Oh, yes." She smiled widely.

"Miz 'Liza, these eggs be gettin' cold," Cassie warned.

Eliza started to laugh, and Will joined in. Cassie looked at them and shook her head.

ᙓ 35 ᙔ

*F*or Temple, those first days after Shawano's death were the worst. The horror of it remained with her, flashes of it returning at odd moments, making even the sight of a carving knife abhorrent to her. And there was the strain of not knowing where The Blade was. Someone said he had been seen with Watie's men, but Temple couldn't be sure of that. Her one consolation was knowing that bad news raced through the area faster than a cyclone. If he were dead, she would know it within hours. As a result, every time a rider approached the cabin her tension and dread mounted.

Lije's bewilderment over the tragic events was equally difficult to cope with. He kept wanting to know when his father was coming home and where his Papa Stuart had gone. His young mind couldn't grasp the permanence of death.

There was much confusion and there were many rumors afterward. It was said that Watie and his men scoured the countryside looking for the assassins to exact their own revenge. Supposedly, more armed bands were combing the area, intent on flushing other traitors from their hiding places and executing them for their crimes. Adding to the chaos, dragoons thundered out of Fort Gibson, chasing down every rumor and questioning all about the murders in an effort to apprehend the killers. Regardless of Ross's protestations that this was an internal matter to be settled by the Cherokees and not the military, Temple now wondered whether Kipp would be arrested.

On July 1, the special meeting of the National Council convened as scheduled, its original purpose to unite the various factions through compromise. But one of the first acts of the council was to declare an amnesty for crimes that had been committed after they had arrived this past winter. In effect, Kipp was pardoned for his role in the death of Shawano Stuart. The council further stated that the slain men were outlaws, as were all who signed the treaty.

Temple was now married to a man branded an outlaw. The council had offered to withdraw the condemnation from any who would publicly admit their wrong, but Temple knew The Blade would never consent to that. He still believed he had acted in the best interests of his people, and if there had been any wrong done, it had been by Ross with his stalling tactics.

The situation seemed more hopeless than before. To keep from thinking about it, Temple threw herself into the work to be done, letting it demand all her time and energy. There was a great deal to supervise in addition to her regular duties as mistress of a burgeoning plantation: the construction of the new house, the operation of the sawmill, and the field work of the blacks. Trying to assume the responsibilities that had previously been borne by two men kept her in a state of near exhaustion.

The second week of August, a wagon carrying a white family and all their possessions rolled to a stop in front of the double log cabin. Chained to the back of it were six Negroes, four males and two female, all of them adults. Temple looked them over. All six were young, strong, and relatively unmarked. She needed prime workers for the field and wondered if the man would consider selling any of them.

"I reckon you to be Mrs. Stuart," the man said.

"I am." Before she could say more, he reached in his pocket and handed her a letter.

"My name's Harve Jacobs, and this here's my wife, Maudie, and our three young'ns."

The handwriting was The Blade's. Hastily, Temple skimmed the contents of the letter, trying to still the excited trembling of her hands. But it merely introduced Harve Jacobs as the new overseer he had hired. There were no personal messages.

"My husband . . . is he all right? Do you know where he is?"

"No, ma'am, I don't. He hired me over in Arkansas and said for me to bring my family here. Then he gave me these niggers and a bill of sale for 'em. That's all I know."

"I see." She struggled to contain her disappointment. She had thought—she had hoped he might have sent some message for her. If not for her, then for Lije.

For nearly two months, she'd had no word from him. It was like living the agony of their previous separation all over again. Temple tried to be grateful that some of the workload was being taken from her shoulders, but it was hard. Very hard. She folded the letter of introduction and slipped it into the pocket of her dress.

The following week, on the hottest day in August, Phoebe went into labor. Temple sat beside her cot, gripping a brown hand and wiping the rivers of sweat from Phoebe's face. After eight hours of labor, Phoebe seemed no closer to giving birth than when she had first started. The black midwife sat in the rocking chair in the corner, knitting away at a pair of socks, seemingly unconcerned by the delay. Temple longed to scream at her to do something, but she was too tired and too hot. She dipped the rag in the basin of water, squeezed out the excess, and wiped Phoebe's face again.

Another contraction twisted through Phoebe and she groaned loudly, squeezing Temple's hand so tightly that Temple thought the bones in her fingers would snap in two. She crooned softly with no idea at all what she was saying. After an interminable amount of time, the contraction passed. Phoebe sagged back against the straw mattress, breathing hard and fast, gulping in air.

"Deu. I want Deu," she moaned. "Why isn't he here?"

"A birthing bed is no place for a man to be. You know that, Phoebe." Temple wished she hadn't mentioned him. It only made her think of The Blade and how much she missed him.

"I want him here," Phoebe sobbed. "I want my Deu."

"You know he can't come."

"Why? He did before when you and Master Blade were apart."

"That was different then. Deu can't come. He might be followed when he left here. He won't do that, Phoebe. You know he won't."

"But we're having a baby."

"*You are* having the baby," Temple snapped, then muttered to herself, "and I wish you would hurry up."

But it was another hour before the midwife put aside her knitting and came over to the cot. She checked the writhing girl and smiled. "It ain't gwine t' be long now, missy."

In less than twenty minutes, Temple was holding a squalling, slippery black baby in her arms. "It's a boy, Phoebe." She smiled, temporarily forgetting how tired she was. "A big, strapping boy."

Breathing long and slow, Phoebe smiled and briefly closed her eyes. "Deu'll be proud of him."

Temple bathed the infant, wrapped him in a soft swaddling cloth, then gave him to Phoebe to nurse. She watched them for a time, smiling at the greedy way the babe suckled at Phoebe's breast. "He is so big. I think we will call him Ike, after your father. He reminds me of him," Temple said, exercising the mistress's right to name the child of her servant.

"I like that, Miss Temple." Phoebe gazed at her baby son and lightly smoothed the downy wet hair on his head. "I like that just fine."

The sweltering August heat lingered, making sleep impossible. After four fitful nights, Temple ordered cots to be set up in the dogtrot for her and Lije. But it made little difference as she lay there drenched in sweat with not a breath of air stirring. Listlessly, she waved a hand to chase away a mosquito buzzing near her ear. She was tired, yet sleep continued to elude her. For a time, Temple stared at the heat lightning dancing across the sky, taunting her with its false promise of cooling rain. Sighing, she closed her eyes and listened enviously to the soft breathing of her sleeping son.

There was a whisper of movement, the light padding of bare feet on dirt. Instantly alert, Temple propped herself up on an elbow. A dark figure moved toward her through the shadows. "Who's there?"

"It's me, Miz Temple, Dulcie," came an answering whisper from the cook. "Phoebe sent me t' fetch you. She say you's t' come right 'way."

"The baby." Temple scrambled off the cot and grabbed her wrapper, tugging it on. "Is little Ike sick?"

"She don't say. She jus' say fer me t' fetch you."

"Stay here with Lije until I come back."

"Yes'm."

Moving as quietly and quickly as possible, Temple slipped inside the cabin and retrieved her basket of medicine from the locked cabinet, then set off for the Negro quarters, running most of the way. When she reached Phoebe's cabin, the door was shut, despite the night's suffocating heat.

Impatiently, Temple pushed it open and hurried inside. "What's wrong? Is Ike—" She stopped short, everything freezing inside when she saw the man who was standing beside Phoebe, the baby in his arms. She started to reach out to him, but her hand wouldn't raise. "The Blade," she whispered. "He's dead, isn't he?"

"No, Miss Temple." Deu smiled gently. "He's alive. I promise you that."

Temple shuddered violently in relief, then became conscious of the open door behind her. She hurriedly closed it. "You shouldn't have come, Deu. They could be watching the plantation."

"There's no one out there, Miss Temple. We checked that before I snuck in."

"*We.*" She spun around. "The Blade is here?"

"He's keeping watch from a safe place. He said for you not to go looking for him."

"Why can't he—" But Temple immediately retracted the question. "Never mind." He wasn't coming in because he didn't want to see her. He still believed she had known of the planned assassination and failed to warn his father.

"He wanted to know if the overseer was working out."

"He seems to be." Temple didn't want to talk about the plantation, the crops, or the new house. "He appears to be experienced and knowledgeable about crops, growing conditions, and the rest. He is strict, but I haven't heard any reports that he has been overly harsh with the workers. The house should be finished by September."

"He wanted me to ask if there was anything you and Lije needed."

Yes. Him. That was what she wanted to say, but she couldn't tell that to Deu. "No. We are both doing well. Tell him . . ." She paused, battling back her tears. "Tell him that his son misses him. And that . . . I miss him, too. Take care of him for me, Deu."

"I will."

There were too many tears in her eyes. She turned and bolted from the cabin, then forced herself to walk sedately, in case someone other than The Blade was watching.

Could The Blade see her? she wondered. He had to. Wherever he was hiding, he would have chosen a place that would allow him to keep an eye on Deu's cabin and observe the approaches to the Negro quarters. The wooded slope to her right; from that vantage point he could see not only the quarters but the house clearing as well. Temple scanned the hillside, but the shadowy shapes of trees and underbrush blurred together in a black mass.

For an instant, she looked directly at him. Instinctively, The Blade recoiled and placed a silencing hand over his horse's muzzle. It was a full second before he realized she couldn't see him. It was too dark and he had chosen his cover too well. But how had she known he was there? Dammit, he had told Deu not to tell her. He'd have his black hide for this.

Then the anger was gone from him as he stared at Temple, a wraithlike figure in the pale moonlight, the white of her nightdress making her appear to float over the ground, the ebony sheen of her long black hair falling all the way to her waist like a hooded cape. There was something lonely and forlorn about her. He almost stepped from behind the concealing brush. But he checked the impulse and resisted the urge to go to her.

It wasn't safe. It wasn't safe anywhere for him. And no matter how much he hated himself for thinking it, The Blade wasn't sure how much he could trust her. He knew she would not expose him or inform her brother of his presence, but if an attempt was made on his life, what would she do? He was an outlaw; anyone could kill him with impunity. How far would Temple go to protect him, considering that she believed he was guilty and that he was bound to die for his crime?

Had she let his father ride into that ambush? "Kipp warned me," she had said, then claimed she hadn't known of the plot. Which was the truth? Kipp had been one of the assassins. That much The Blade knew. But Temple's foreknowledge . . . every time he was on the verge of believing she hadn't known, he would recall his father's body, red with blood, and hear her voice saying "Kipp warned me," and the doubt would start all over again.

"Why, Temple?" he murmured thickly. "Why?"

⚛ 36 ⚛

Jed Parmelee walked over to the wagon and smiled reassuringly at his wife. The corners of Cecilia's mouth lifted briefly in response, making her lips look even thinner and her apprehension more pronounced. A velvet bonnet in the same forest green shade as her fur-trimmed pelisse mantle covered most of her blond hair, leaving only the long ringlets at the sides to show.

"The commander of my new dragoon company, Captain Collins, has invited us to have tea with him and his wife while our quarters are being readied. He'll be along soon to escort us to his quarters."

"Now? But I'm all dusty from the trip, and my dress is crushed," Cecilia protested. "If he wants us to join him for tea, why can't we go to our new home first so I can freshen up?"

"Because we have no quarters until the rooms are vacated by the second lieutenant currently occupying them."

"You mean we are turning someone out?"

"And he will turn out someone else. It's a common occurrence in the army. It's called ranking out," Jed explained patiently, recognizing that she wasn't familiar with many aspects of military life even after nine months as his wife. "Hopefully it won't happen to us for a while."

Her glance strayed to the roughly hewn timbers that supported the roofed walkway, then traveled to the chinked log walls of the buildings that lined the inner perimeter of the fort's palisades. "I didn't expect it to be like this." Cecilia tried without success to keep the disgust and dismay out of her voice as she eyed three soldiers sentenced to the stocks. She shuddered at the ghastly spectacle they made with their heads and hands thrust through the openings.

"This is the frontier, Cecilia. I warned you it might be crude." But Jed was aware his description was something of an understatement as the beat of a drum grew louder, signaling the approach of an infantry corporal. Behind him was yet another soldier. This one carried a keg and a sign on his back labeling him as a whiskey runner.

In the army, they called Fort Gibson the Charnel House—a place where bodies were deposited. But it was the frontier. Here, at least he had a better chance of promotion than in the East. Most of the men he had graduated with from West Point were still second lieutenants. He had managed to make first, but he didn't plan to wait another ten years before he achieved the rank of captain. And in the army, a lieutenant never made captain until either the captain ahead of him was promoted to lieutenant colonel, or his own valor in the field of battle was rewarded with a promotion. And Jed had every intention of rising higher in the ranks.

Which was why he was here. That, and eight months of utter boredom as a quartermaster, sitting behind a desk pushing papers. After fighting in the Seminole war and participating in the removal of the Cherokees, Jed couldn't stand the inaction, the complete lack of anything more challenging than accounting for every nail and horseshoe on the post. For eight months he had tried, for Cecilia's sake, then applied for a transfer to a western post of the frontier.

It had been either that or resign from the army and accept a job offer in the private sector. With all the railroads being built in the East, West Point graduates were in great demand.

Jed could have had his pick of positions and virtually named his own salary. It was what Cecilia had wanted him to do. What woman wouldn't want her husband to earn more than the twenty-five dollars a month the army paid a lieutenant, not to mention the prestige that went along with a high-paying job? But Jed wanted a military career. Cecilia had known that before she married him last April. Still, seeing her here in these primitive surroundings, knowing she was expecting their first child in two and a half months, Jed felt guilty.

"Do you feel all right? There's a doctor on the post. I—"

"I am fine." The quick tilt of her head rejected his concern almost defiantly, but a hint of fear lurked in her eyes.

Jed sighed. "I wish you had stayed in Boston with your parents until after the baby was born, as we originally planned."

"I'm your wife now," Cecilia asserted. "My place is at your side."

She was aware that both Jed and her parents had been strongly opposed to her making the trip with a baby on the way, but she had refused to listen to them or acknowledge the validity of their arguments. The very instant she had learned Jed was to be stationed in the Indian Territory, she had become determined to accompany him.

That woman was here. Cecilia trembled in anger at the memory of those days last summer when Jed had fallen ill with a malarial fever. She had sat up all night with him while the fever raged, a fever the doctor felt certain Jed had contracted during his long stint in the swamps of Florida three years previously. She had held his hand and bathed his sweating brow—and listened in jealous fury while he mumbled endlessly of his love for that woman.

Temple.

Cecilia despised the name, and the woman who had stolen her husband's love. If it meant she would die in this godforsaken wilderness giving birth to his child, then so be it. But no one and nothing would have induced her to let Jed come here alone, even for a few months. Cecilia was not about to risk losing him, and certainly not to an Indian. The mere thought was too degrading and humiliating to be endured. She prayed that Temple Stuart had turned into a fat and ugly squaw. She had been told Indian women deteriorated badly with age. Cecilia desperately hoped it was true.

"Are you warm enough?"

At first she didn't understand why Jed should ask that. The day was mild and the sun was warm. Then she saw him glance at her hand and realized that he had mistaken her faint tremors of anger for shivers. "I am quite comfortable," she assured him and slipped her hand inside the fur muff on her lap.

Seeking to avoid further questions, Cecilia looked away, pretending to be interested in the approach of a horse and buggy. A pair of small, gloved hands pulled back on the reins, slowing the horse to a stop next to the wagon. As the driver leaned forward, emerging from the shadows of the buggy's hood, Cecilia saw that it was a woman—*that* woman.

Raw with jealousy, Cecilia was stunned that she had remembered her so clearly after all this time. The sultry fullness of her lips, the devil-black of her hair and eyes, the hint of the exotic in those classically beautiful features. How had she known Jed was here? Had he written her he was coming?

"Excuse me. I was wondering if you could help me. I am—"

"Temple." Jed sounded surprised. Was it an act?

"Jed? Is that you?" Unassisted, the woman climbed out of the buggy, a look of amazement on her face as he walked swiftly around the wagon to greet her. "What are you doing here?"

He stopped in front of her, catching up both her hands, gazing at her with a look of undisguised adoration. "I've been assigned to the company of dragoons here at Fort Gibson. I have to report for duty tomorrow." Then his glance swung guiltily to her, and Cecilia knew this meeting was accidental. Somehow, it made it worse. "I would like you to meet my wife—"

"Mrs. Stuart and I are already acquainted, Jed," Cecilia inserted, painfully aware that her husband had yet to release the woman's hands. "We met several years ago at a rally in Boston, before you and I were married."

The woman frowned slightly, then smiled. "We did. I remember now. So much has happened since then." Her expression sobered briefly before brightening again—falsely, Cecilia thought. "But, please, let me offer you my best wishes, Mrs. Parmelee. And for you, too," she said, turning back to Jed.

"How have you been?"

"Very well."

But Cecilia noticed, with a degree of malicious satisfaction, that the woman wasn't dressed as well as she had been in Boston. Her cloak was made from coarse wool, and the cloth of her skirt appeared to be homespun.

"A year ago at this time, we had crossed the Mississippi and were heading out across Missouri," Jed recalled, then regret flickered in his expression. "I never had a chance to tell you good-bye before I left."

"I know." Temple self-consciously withdrew her hands from his grasp.

"You haven't explained what you're doing here at the fort."

"I was told . . . my husband had taken refuge here. We have had some . . . trouble. Perhaps you heard."

"About the murders of the Ridges and Boudinot? Yes, I heard." Jed nodded.

"Hopefully, all this trouble will soon be behind us." But would it? In her heart, Temple doubted it. The bitterness and desire for revenge on both sides went too deep for it ever to be buried completely. There would never be peace. Temple knew that. But she hoped a truce could be established, however uneasy it might be. "Our new house at Grand View has been completed. You and your wife must come for a visit sometime soon."

"I—we'd like that. However, I'm afraid we'll have to wait until early summer. You see, Cecilia is . . . in a family way."

"How wonderful for both of you." Temple turned to include Cecilia.

But Cecilia could care less what the woman thought. She was too upset and too angry. It took every ounce of her strength to hold her tongue and not start screaming at Jed. When Jed helped Temple back into the buggy, Cecilia could hardly wait for her to drive off.

The very instant the buggy was out of earshot, she hissed angrily at Jed, "You weren't serious about visiting her house next summer, were you? This may be the frontier, but I am not going to socialize with Indians, Jed Parmelee. Is that clear?"

His West Point shoulders stiffened. He opened his mouth as if to argue, then nodded. "Very clear."

Temple went to the sutler's store, the common gathering place for visitors to the fort. Outside it she found Deu and sent him to fetch The Blade. A half dozen men lounged under the store's wide overhang. She tried to ignore their curious stares, just as she tried to ignore the nervous flutterings in the pit of her stomach.

A moment later, The Blade stepped out of the store and paused beneath the wide overhang. Tall and lean, like a mountain cat in winter, he fixed a narrowed gaze on her yet remained alert to every movement around him. Three months ago, Temple had heard he had been knifed during a scuffle with one of Ross's men at a trading post near Webber's Falls. He had managed to escape out a back door. She had never learned whether or not the wound had been serious.

His gaze flickered to the buggy—his father's buggy—and her anger instantly vanished. "Deu said you wanted to see me."

"I think we should talk. Privately," she added, reminding him of the men outside the store.

He hesitated briefly. "We can walk down by the river."

But he made no move to help her. His arms remained at his sides when she climbed out of the buggy. His avoidance of any contact made Temple all the more aware of the rift between them. Once, they both would have eagerly sought any excuse to touch. Now there was an awkwardness, an unnatural reserve crackling like an invisible barrier between them. Could it be eliminated with mere words?

She started walking toward the river, conscious that he followed, lagging half a step behind. Where would she start? She had rehearsed it so many times, yet now her mind was blank.

"How is Lije?" he asked, shattering the silence that sounded louder than the wind.

She glanced at him gratefully. "He's fine. We moved into the new house in October."

"I heard."

"We still need furniture to fill all those empty rooms." And you, she thought, to fill the emptiness of the bed. "I gave my father a contract to build two more storage sheds for the plantation. Our crops were bountiful this year, and the price I obtained for them far exceeded even Mr. Jacobs's expectations."

"I heard."

"I have plans being drawn to expand the sawmill operation. With all the building going on, we already have more orders for lumber than we can currently fill. You have only to look at the accounts to see that the profits already made show the worth of expanding to accommodate the area growth." She was talking all around the things she truly wanted to say, but she couldn't seem to stop. "And I have a new half sister. Eliza had a baby girl in December. They have named her Susannah."

"I heard."

"I didn't come here to speak to you about any of this."
Temple stared at the winter-bleak landscape, so barren of life
... like their marriage. No, it was only dormant. She had to
believe that. "I wanted to talk to you about your father's
death. I ... I truly didn't know it was going to happen. I
know what I said about Kipp. He had come by the day before
and insisted that I go see my father the next morning. At the
time I thought it odd that he was so determined I visit them
on that particular day. He never said why it was so important.
But he was concerned about me. Kipp knew what was going
to happen and he didn't want me there to see it." Temple
paused, feeling again the misery of hindsight. "I planned to
go. The carriage was in front of the cabin, waiting to take us.
Then one of the kitchen girls was scalded by boiling water,
and Lije got all muddy while I was treating her burns, and I
didn't go. When they attacked the buggy, only then did I
realize ... everything."

"You just stood by."

"No!" When she turned on him, she saw the pain behind
the accusing look and quelled her temper. "No. Lije was
there. All I could think of ... I couldn't let him see his
grandfather die like that. I couldn't. It would have hurt your
father too much."

"You never attempted to warn him of the ambush."

"I didn't know of it until I saw the men," she insisted
again. "I called out to Shawano, but it was too late. They
were already on him."

But she didn't ask whether or not he believed her. Studying
the proud and faintly defiant tilt of her head, The Blade realized
she never would. She had told him her story and he either
accepted it as true or he didn't.

She looked pale and tense, waiting for some response from
him. He had been through hell these last months, thinking
about her, wondering, questioning her loyalty and her love.

There was satisfaction in knowing she had suffered, too. Dammit, he loved her, and it was like being possessed by a thousand furies constantly tormenting him.

"If you had known, if Kipp had told you, what would you have done, Temple? Would you have warned my father?"

Her shoulders sagged beneath the cloak. "I don't know," she admitted with a troubled shake of her head. "I have thought about it often. If Kipp had told me, I think I would have questioned him. I don't like the secrecy . . . the trial in the dark of the night. Shawano had a right to know why he was to die. He deserved that."

"Yes." For the first time, a measure of ease slowly filtered through him. Like him, Temple objected to the indignity of his father's death. That they would die for their actions, both had known. But The Blade would never forgive the murderers for the manner of his father's death.

"A council meeting was held at our new capital of Tahlequah a few days ago," Temple began, her gaze now on his face, neither pleading nor begging, yet earnest. "They rescinded the outlaw decree against the treaty signers. Come home . . . when you can."

She lowered her head and started to turn away. The control that had held him so still throughout their meeting broke. The agony of being apart these last months, of being close to her now, of watching those lips tell him the truth, he could endure no more.

"Temple." He caught her arm. The sensation of her firm flesh beneath his fingers rippled through him. He drew her back to him, seizing her other arm as well while he gazed at her upturned face, seeing the shimmer of tears in those deep black eyes. "I could not stay away if I tried." His voice vibrated huskily. "I am coming home."

The sunlight glinted off the waters of the Grand River as they embraced in a kiss that burned the doubts and bridged the differences that would always exist. They were together. And neither chose to question for how long.

**Please turn the page
for a special bonus chapter
from
Janet Dailey**

Legacies

*Coming soon
from
Little, Brown & Company*

Chapter One

Springfield, Massachusetts
May 1860

The carriage rolled up to the three-story brick home in the town's more fashionable residential district. With an agility that belied his advancing years, its driver assisted his passenger, a lovely young woman of nineteen gowned in a visiting dress in two shades of blue that flattered the honey-gold of her hair and accented her blue eyes. Accepting the hand he offered, she stepped from the carriage. A matching parasol shaded her face from the bright rays of the afternoon sun, but the driver noticed her flawless complexion and elegant bone structure nonetheless.

" 'Tis waiting right here I'll be when you're ready to leave, Miss Parmelee."

"Thank you." Diane Parmelee flashed him a quick and easy smile full of a potent charm that dazzled.

Within seconds of her knocking, the Fletchers' Irish

housekeeper, Bridget O'Shaughnessy, stood before her, a white dust cap blending with the silver of her hair.

"How are you, Bridie," Diane greeted her with a warm smile.

The housekeeper gaped at her in momentary astonishment. "Saints be praised, it's Miss Diane. And all grown up, too. What a day for visitors this is. Is the Captain with you?" She peered beyond Diane.

"No, my father is still at his post in St. Louis."

"Look at me, jabbering away and leaving you standing out there," the housekeeper declared in self-reproach and waved her inside. "Come in, come in." Diane closed her parasol and stepped into the oval entry hall. The housekeeper instantly relieved her of the parasol and wagged her hand in self-remonstration. "I know I should be asking after your mother, but it's mad I get just thinking about her. 'Tis not my place to be judging her, I know, but it's hard I'm finding it to forgive her for divorcing the Captain to marry up with that rich Thomas Austin. 'Twas an awful thing for the Captain, him being a gentleman and an officer."

Diane laughed in genuine affection. "Bridie, you haven't changed at all," she declared, unable to take offense at the housekeeper's criticism of her mother. As much as Diane regretted her parents' recent divorce, she was old enough to understand the differences that had finally pulled apart their marriage—her father loved Army life and the frontier while her mother longed for the more genteel existence and permanent home Tom Austin offered her.

"It's for certain and sure that you have," the woman countered. " 'Tis a full-grown vision of loveliness you've become. I know 'tis sorry Mrs. Fletcher is going to be that she isn't here this afternoon to see you, but this is the day the ladies of the Library Society have their tea."

Diane experienced a twinge of disappointment. She had always enjoyed the company of Mrs. Fletcher, who had advised her on so much since Diane's return east several years hence. "I had hoped to catch her at home. But I'm staying at the Wickhams. Let me leave my card—"

"You can't be going without seeing Mr. Fletcher," the housekeeper stated flatly. "It's my hide he'll be having if you do. Come with me. It's in his study he is." Bustling off, she ushered Diane down the hall to a set of wooden doors, knocked once and slid them open. "Begging your pardon, sir. It's another visitor that's come to see you." Without announcing Diane by name, the housekeeper stepped back to admit her.

Diane walked into the study and Payton Fletcher moved quickly to greet her. At sixty years of age, he was a portly man with round cheeks and white hair flowing from the edges of his bald crown.

"Diane, what a delightful surprise." Both hands reached out to clasp hers in welcome. "What are you doing here in Springfield?"

"I'm staying at Judge Wickham's this summer with their granddaughter Ann Elizabeth while Mother is making a grand tour of Europe. Naturally one of the first things I wanted to do after I arrived was to pay a call on my father's favorite godparents."

"We are his only godparents," Payton Fletcher asserted, a white eyebrow arching at her curious choice of words.

"So you are," Diane said with a teasing gleam in her eyes, then leaned forward to brush a kiss on his cheek.

"What? Oh, of course, you were making a joke, weren't you? You young people will have to forgive an old man for being a bit slow." He looked to a point beyond her left shoulder. At that instant, Diane realized someone else was in the room, and the housekeeper's phrase 'another visitor' echoed in her mind. Before she could turn to look, Payton Fletcher was saying with a slightly addled frown, "You two do know each other, don't you?"

"We do." The deep, masculine register of the answering voice sent a tremor of excitement through Diane.

Its pitch was lower than she remembered, but Diane recognized it just the same. Exercising the greatest control, she slowly turned to face him, conscious of her heart thudding against her ribs.

Lije Stuart stood near the study window. He was an inch over six feet, and his black hair lay ruffled along the edge of his forehead. He wore gray trousers and a dark cutaway coat tailored to fit smoothly across his wide shoulders and leanly muscled chest. His familiar face was more rugged and compelling than it had been the last time she saw him five years ago, but his skin still had a bronze cast to it that spoke of his Cherokee ancestry, a contrast to the startling blue of his eyes.

Born and raised at Fort Gibson in the Indian Territory, Diane had known Lije Stuart her whole life. She had been a girl of fourteen when the Army closed Fort Gibson and reassigned her father to a post in the East. In the intervening years, she had often wondered if she would ever see Lije again—and whether she would adore him as she once had.

Facing him, Diane at last had her answer as the sight of him made her catch her breath. With practiced poise, she crossed the room and extended a gloved hand in greeting.

"Lije, finding you here is the most wonderful surprise." She made no attempt to mask the delight in her voice or her smile despite the mockingly demure tilt of her head.

"It's good to see you again, too, Diane." Lije's response was reserved, a habit once dictated by the difference in their ages.

But the Diane Parmelee standing before him now was no longer the lovely and innocent young girl he had known. She had grown into a woman of stunning beauty. Her face was almost mystically perfect, the kind that could rule a man's fantasies. Her hair swept back from it in a glorious, golden cascade, like an angel's. And her eyes sparkled with a richness for life. They were focused on him with an intensity that had his blood heating.

Desire flared through him just as it always had when he was around her. And, as always, Lije banked it. He took her hand. Her gloved fingers closed on it in an unusual mingling of delicacy and strength.

She gracefully made a half-turn toward Payton Fletcher. "The last time I saw Lije was at the annual May celebration held at the Cherokee Female Seminary in Tahlequah. After the May Queen was crowned, the military band from the fort played on the lawn behind the building and everyone danced—except me. My mother forbade it. She said fourteen was too young. I was totally crushed. You see, Payton, Lije had previously promised he would dance with me, and I was excited at the prospect." Diane paused and slanted Lije a sideways glance that both teased and challenged. "Do you remember what you told me?"

"That we would dance together some day when you were older."

"I fully intend to hold you to that promise, Lije Stuart."

"I can't say that surprises me." Even as Lije smiled at her statement, he envisioned her in his arms, the two of them swirling around a dance floor, their eyes locked, nothing and no one else existing. He felt that twist of desire again, and again fought it back to direct his glance at Payton Fletcher. "Diane was always a very determined young lady. If she failed to get what she wanted one way, she searched until she found another."

"I confess I do tend to be single-minded about what I want." Her eyes were on him.

"A dance is a trivial request," Lije told her.

"Ah, but great things have come from less auspicious beginnings. Don't you agree, Payton?" She turned to the older man with a confident tilt of her head.

"I do, indeed," he replied with a decisive nod. "In fact, I was just telling Lije that his education at Harvard will prove to be a stepping stone toward a promising future."

"Susannah wrote me that you were studying law at Harvard," Diane said, referring to her childhood friend and Lije's nineteen-year-old aunt. "I had hoped you would pay a call on us after we moved to Boston this past spring."

"I suspect your mother would have given me a cold reception if I had." A wry smile curved his mouth, creating craggy dimples in his cheeks.

"You shouldn't have let that stop you," she chided, acknowledging indirectly that her mother's attitude was a problem. But it was an obstacle that was literally an ocean away, one that could be dealt with later.

"Perhaps I shouldn't have," Lije conceded with the smallest of shrugs. "Five years is a long time. People change."

Diane smiled. "I have to admit I have changed from that gawky fourteen-year-old girl with freckles you last saw."

"As I recall, you only had freckles because you went riding with your father without a hat. And you were never gawky," he stated. "Even as a child, you had a beauty and a radiance that captivated the heart of every male within miles."

"And now?" She waited for his answer, her breath catching.

"And now," his glance made a slow and thorough sweep of her before coming back to hold her gaze, "impossible as it seems, you are even more beautiful."

Diane saw the attraction in his eyes. At nineteen, she was sufficiently experienced in the ways of a man to know when one was interested in her. Lije was. She wanted to hug herself with the sheer joy of it.

"That, my dear, is a fact," Payton Fletcher declared. "One that I heartily echo. It was remiss of me not to tell you before how lovely you look. Lije's grandfather, Will Gordon, told me years ago that you can never give a woman too many compliments. I should have remem-

9

bered that. It's good to see his grandson did." He glanced at Lije. "You must be sure to give your grandfather my fondest regards when you see him."

"I will," Lije promised.

"Will Gordon and I went to school together," he told Diane.

"Yes, I know."

He paid no attention to the two young people before him who, through evasive glances and silent surveillance, were taking stock of all that had changed in the other. Instead, he was temporarily lost in those long ago days. "We had some grand times together. Many was the night Will had to carry me home." He chuckled at the memory and shook his head. "If it hadn't been for Will, I doubt if I ever would have graduated. He was the intelligent one. It's heartening to see that same intelligence in his grandson." He beamed in approval at Lije, then informed Diane, "Lije is too modest to tell you, but congratulations are in order. He has graduated from Harvard with honors."

"How wonderful! Congratulations."

"Thank you." He inclined his head.

"What are your plans now?"

"To return home and put my study of law to good use. I'll be leaving at the end of the week."

"So soon?" Diane protested. "Surely you can stay another week or two, can't you?"

"I've been gone for four years."

"What's another two weeks after four years?" She looked at him, her eyes aglow with challenge and . . . something else. "Judge Wickham is holding his annual summer party in two weeks. If you are a man of your word, you will be there to dance with me."

Payton Fletcher chuckled in approval. "Spoken like a true daughter of an Army officer who has learned, to her advantage, the value a man places on his honor. You will have no choice but to stay now, Lije."

"So it would seem," Lije agreed, his eyes on her, a sizzling undercurrent flowing between them. He had never been able to refuse her anything she wanted as a child. He found it equally impossible to refuse her as a woman. More than that, he didn't want to.

The afternoon socials, shopping expeditions, luncheons, lawn parties, and teas Diane arranged enabled her to spend a good part of every day with Lije. The first week passed in a rush that culminated with an invitation from Judge Wickham for the Fletchers and Lije to dine with them at the family estate.

Dinner was a formal affair, the meal itself lasting nearly two hours. Afterwards coffee was served on the terrace. Diane strolled with Lije to its far end to view the lawn's reflecting pool and steal a few moments alone. She paused to breathe in the warm night air, attuned to the night and its magic—and to the man beside her.

"This is a grand evening. Everything has turned out so well." She glanced back at the other members of their dinner party. "Judge Wickham was very impressed with you."

"Once he recovered from the shock of learning that

11

I was Cherokee," Lije replied dryly, a hint of censure in his tone. "You failed to inform him of that."

"Deliberately." Diane turned to face him, her eyes sparkling, her tone amused. "Not volunteering information is something I learned from my father. If they were to have any objections to my seeing you, I wanted them to voice them *after* they had become acquainted with you. I was confident that once they met you, they would recognize an intelligent and charming man who conducts himself as a proper gentleman. And tonight proves I was right. I think it would be more accurate to say the Wickhams were amazed rather than shocked to discover you are Cherokee. In fact, I think the Judge admires you even more because of it." She paused to examine his reaction. "You don't look properly impressed by that."

"Should I be?" Lije countered as the warm breeze carried the scent of her perfume to him, something soft and alluring and outrageously feminine.

"Judge Wickham is an extremely wealthy and influential man to have on your side. Do you remember when we were talking about your family's plantation at dinner and Mrs. Wickham asked how your mother managed to take care of such a large house? You have no idea how relieved I was when you explained that she had servants to look after it, the same as Mrs. Wickham. I forgot to warn you—the Wickhams are staunch abolitionists. They would have been appalled to learn your parents are slaveholders."

"Many people here in the North would be. It's a subject I've learned to avoid over the last four years."

"Spoken like a diplomat." She smiled in warm

approval, then paused, her look softening. "Every time I think about how fortunate I was to pay a call on Payton Fletcher on that particular day—if I had waited just a day or two more, you would have been gone and we would never have seen each other. I would have regretted that."

"Would you have?"

A tempting glow in her blue eyes was her only response.

Surrendering to the flirtation, Lije reached for her shoulders and gently pulled her toward him. Kissing her was something he had wanted for too long.

Diane had no time to think before the power of his lips whipped through her, igniting her emotions. It wasn't the mere touch of lips in a usual chaste kiss, but a hard, thorough demand that kept her wrapped in his arms. She reached up to take his face in her hands as she gave, unquestioningly, what he sought from her.

Diane knew this was not a gradual smoldering, but a passion so intense and quick it seemed they were already lovers. She felt the instant intimacy and instead of being frightened, she understood that her heart was already his. She couldn't deny him anything else.

Lije drew her closer and inhaled the warm, teasing fragrance that seemed to pulse from her skin. He reveled in the taste of her—alluring, giving and warm. The feel of her soft, slender body created a need in him as insistent as the buffeting wind off the Plains.

She made it impossible for him to think. Soon he would forget everything but her. Lije knew her power was the kind that could make a man hunger, make him ache. It could make him weak. Lije couldn't afford to lose his resolve. He had other priorities, other responsibilities.

He pulled back even as he wanted more and more of what she offered in abundance.

Diane's eyes opened slowly when her mouth was free. She looked directly at him and saw longings and caution and a glimpse of emotion that stirred her.

"I've wanted you to do that," she murmured, "for a long, long time."

Lije took a deep breath and exhaled it slowly. "I think we had better rejoin the others." At the moment, he didn't trust himself to be alone with her.

"Why?" But her teasing eyes told him she knew the answer.

"I should never have touched you."

"Why?"

"It leads to more, and I'll be leaving soon."

"Not for another week, at least. Not until you've danced with me, remember?" Without waiting for a response, she linked her arm with his and directed them both back to the others.

Strings of festive lanterns lit the terrace where couples whirled in an ever-moving circle to the lilting strains of a waltz. From the tented pavillion on the lawn came the sounds of laughter, tinkling crystal and chattering voices. But Lije was aware only of the woman in his arms, so beautiful in her white ball gown trimmed with blue forget-me-nots, her eyes aglow with happiness.

"Did you know my father taught your mother how to

waltz years ago?" There was a lightness in her voice that didn't match the heady tension that throbbed between them.

"I have heard the story before."

Her glance slid to his mouth, wreaking havoc with his control. "I remember the first time my father told me about it. He made it sound so magical. I think that's when I started wondering whether it would be like that if you and I danced together." Her eyes lifted their glance to once again lock with his. "It's more than magic, Lije. Much more." She threw a quick look at the other guests. "Everyone can see it. That's why they're staring at us."

Lije spared a glance at the guests on the sidelines, noting the number of feminine eyes that watched him over the top of fluttering fans, and the thinly disguised glares from many of the men. Their reaction was typical of others he had encountered during his four years in the East.

"They are staring because they are scandalized that you are dancing with a Cherokee when you could have your choice of a dozen other, more suitable partners," he told her.

Diane laughed easily. "I know them better than you do. Most of them are only pretending to be scandalized to cover their envy or their wounded egos. Especially the women. They look at you and secretly wish they could trade places with me, but they are too concerned with what other people would think."

"Aren't you?"

The curve of her lips deepened. "One of the advantages of being raised on the frontier is that polite society overlooks it when I indulge in what they would consider improper behavior in their own ranks. It's proven quite useful on occasions.''

"This being one of them.''

"Yes.'' Still smiling, Diane cast another glance over his arm at the onlooking guests as Lije guided her through a sweeping turn. ''Truthfully, I suspect half the women here are waiting to see if you scoop me up and carry me off somewhere to ravish me.'' She looked back to him, her smile fading as their eyes met. ''I have a feeling they'll be disppointed if you don't.''

"We can't have that, can we?'' His fingers tightened their grip on her gloved hand, a heat flowing between them, the ripe man-woman tension leaping between them to another level.

"No, we can't.'' Her voice turned husky with it.

The song ended in a flourish of notes. Lije stepped back and bowed to her, then took her hand, tucked it under his arm and escorted her from the floor to the shadowy edges of the terrace. A moment later they slipped from the gathering, unobserved, and sought the quiet of the side garden.

Once there, Lije pulled a laughing Diane into the shadows of a trellised arch laden with honeysuckle. Her laughter died as she looked into his eyes. His gaze was intense, a hot, hot blue that made her throat grow dry with anticipation. He bent his head to her, their lips met, brushed, his breath a warm caress against her skin.

With a half-smothered groan, he dragged her to him and claimed her lips in a driving kiss that was warm, hard, and demanding. Her mouth was like silk, smooth, slick and clinging. The desire that had simmered between them all evening rushed to the surface. Lije gave full rein to it, taking his fill of her lips, but it wasn't enough. He knew it even as he felt the tremble of longing that shuddered through her. In an attempt at control, he shifted his attention to her cheek, her jaw, the delicate lobe of her ear.

"Lije," she whispered his name, going soft and pliant in his embrace. "You have no idea how much I wanted this."

"No more than I." He rubbed his lips over the blue vein in her neck that throbbed so heavy and fast.

"You don't understand," she said with a small shake of her head, then pulled back to look at him, her eyes shimmering with a mixture of wonder and need. "I have adored you since I was a child. When the government closed Fort Gibson and we had to leave, I was heartbroken." She paused and smiled, raising a hand to run her fingers along the smooth line of his jaw. "It sounds silly, doesn't it? I was only a girl. What did I know about love? That's what I used to tell myself. But I never stopped hoping we would meet again someday. And I was always terrified that if we did, you would be married to someone else. I'm glad you're not." Her fingers slid into his hair, drawing him down. "Kiss me again, Lije."

He obliged her and lost himself in the softness of her lips, the heat of them, the bottomless pleasure of them. Just for the moment, he thought of nothing but her—not the past with its ghosts and not the future with its vague forebodings. He knew it was madness to forget his priorities and sink into her. But she was all softness and strength, all trembles and demands. The scent radiating from the skin of her neck made his head spin.

"I love you, Diane." He wanted her, in his arms and in his life.

"And I love you." Her voice trembled with deep feeling. She laughed a little shakily, then bent her head to rest the top of it against his shoulder. "Who would have guessed it would all turn out so glorious?"

Gripped by a feeling of urgency, he said, "Diane, I'll be leaving soon—"

"No." Her head came up, her eyes bright with confidence. "I won't let you go."

"I can't stay—" Regret riddled his voice.

"Of course you can. Just the other day I heard Judge Wickham mention that Senator Frederick was looking for a bright young man to fill a position he had open in his Boston office. Judge Wickham likes you. I know I could persuade him to recommend you. Don't you see how perfect it would be, with both of us in Boston?"

"Diane, no." He took her by the shoulders and held her gaze, needing to make it clear to her. "I'm going home."

She hesitated only fractionally. "Naturally you want to go home and visit your family, your parents. I understand that. Afterwards you can come back here and—"

"No."

"No?" She stiffened, then pulled away and turned from him in agitation. "Why? What on earth is there for you back there? There are so many more opportunities for you here, so much more you can do, so much more you can be."

"I have to go home. I *need* to go home." Lije didn't know how to put into words the unease he felt, the fears that never left him, the images of the past that haunted him and turned that need into a compulsion. "Come with me, Diane."

"Come with you?" She swung back around.

"I want you to be my wife."

"Just like that? You can't be serious."

"But I am." His eyes frosted over at her reaction to his proposal. He hadn't intended to take her home with him, but somehow the words slipped from his mouth.

"It's too soon to be talking about marriage. You know my mother would never give her consent if I were to go West so suddenly."

"Because I am Cherokee."

"Because you are a Stuart. She has never made a secret of her feelings toward your family."

"No, she hasn't."

"Then you see how impossible it is right now. In time—"

"I'm leaving in the morning."

"You're not being reasonable, Lije," she said angrily. "You won't listen to anything I say. It's all been so wonderful. Why do you have to ruin it like this?"

"Maybe you should have listened to your mother when she warned you a long time ago to stay away from me," he suggested in a cold, hard voice, his hurt concealed by his rising temper.

Diane retaliated in kind. "Perhaps I should have!"

Lije looked at her another long second, then turned and walked off into the night. Diane watched him for a moment, anger washing over her in waves even as tears stung her eyes. But her pride wouldn't let her run after him. He would return. She was sure of it.